MOONSHINE

MOONSHINE

A NOVEL

ALAYA JOHNSON

Thomas Dunne Books
St. Martin's Griffin
New York

This is a work of fiction. All of the characters, organizations, and events portrayed in this novel are either products of the author's imagination or are used fictitiously.

THOMAS DUNNE BOOKS.
An imprint of St. Martin's Press.

www.thomasdunnebooks.com
www.stmartins.com

Map by Kristine Dikeman

Library of Congress Cataloging-in-Publication Data

Johnson, Alaya Dawn, 1982–
    Moonshine / Alaya Johnson. — 1st ed.
        p. cm.
    ISBN 978-0-312-64806-0
    1. Vampires—Fiction.   2. Lower East Side (New York, N.Y.)—Fiction.   I. Title.
    PS3610.O315M66 2010
    813'.6—dc22

                                                                          2009039261

First Edition: May 2010

10 9 8 7 6 5 4 3 2 1

For the VLC, past and present. Here's hoping you like this almost as much as Mr. Darcy in the lake.

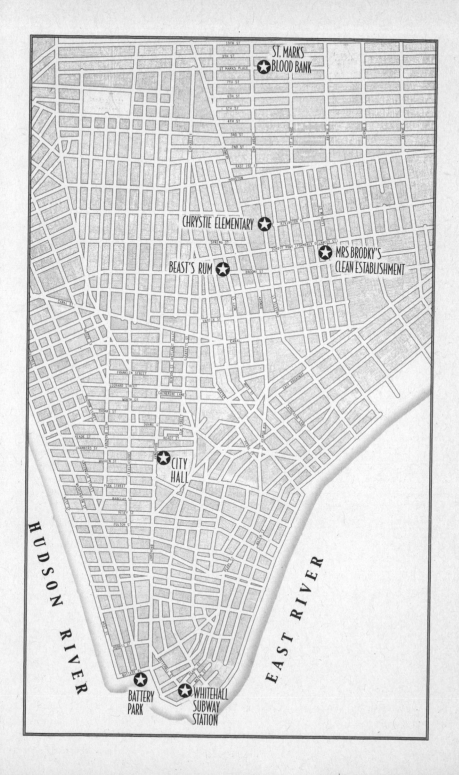

CHAPTER ONE

I skidded on a patch of ice as I rounded the corner onto Lafayette Street, only years of experience saving me as I tottered in the bare twelve inches between a shuttered horse-drawn hansom cab and a Model-T. The white-gloved matron behind the wheel had clearly come to regard her motor vehicle the way one might a pet cat that always vanished at the full moon, and the sight of my bicycle sliding gracefully past broke her remaining self-control. I can't imagine what she found so terrifying about me. Unless it was the grin I couldn't keep from my face as I dared the January ice. Daddy always did say I was too reckless in winter.

The matron shrieked and discovered the purpose of that curious little button in the middle of her steering wheel. Her car swerved—thankfully *away* from the horses, which were even now whinnying and snorting in agitation. I made it past the hansom and auto moments before one of the horses reared and whacked the Model-T's gleaming rear fender. I winced. Two more seconds and that would have been my stomach.

Damn Tammany Hall, I fumed. Like it would kill those bastards to do something useful like fixing roads between winning elections? To-night, of course, the criminally narrow streets were relatively clear. No one respectable wanted to be out after sundown on a new moon. I checked my watch—quarter 'til eight—and pedaled faster. It wouldn't do for the teacher to be tardy to her own class. Especially not this class. And especially not tonight.

That's when I saw it, of course. Just a huddled shadow on an un-speakably dirty street that hundreds of people had probably passed by today without comment. I sailed past it, too, before something made me dig my heels into the ground and turn around to ride back. It wasn't as though the back of my neck prickled, or I felt a telltale shiver crawl up my skin. I can't do anything like that, no matter what my students might whisper about me. But I do have a knack for noticing. It's a skill my daddy cultivated, since I can't shoot fish in a barrel and he needed his eldest to be good at something.

I had to kick the spokes to turn the handlebar hard right, then jig-ger them back out again so I could straighten the wheel. I crashed over the drainage ditch and slid on the worn soles of my boots over the sidewalk. I was deep in the shadow of a monolithic, grimy factory—the kind that put me in mind of hollow-eyed immigrant children locked in rooms by unscrupulous overseers so they won't escape. They hired vampire guards in those kinds of hellholes. I shuddered and looked, suddenly, back at the street. Deserted. I think the hair on the back of my neck would have risen then, if it weren't already smoth-ered by the respectable starch of my shirt collar.

I walked closer to the crawlspace—too small to even be an alley—between the tenement and a former munitions warehouse. A rat, startled by my approach, scrambled over a gray heap that was barely distinguishable from the other refuse and shot into the gutter by my bicycle. My eyes adjusted to the gloom. I could finally see the faint outline of the innocuous little hump that had so firmly caught my at-tention. It was covered in a child-sized peacoat that smelled of damp wool. Shaking—because by God there is no way to get used to this, no matter how long I've lived in this city—I pulled back the cloth. I saw a boy, with hair much redder than my own ochre-tinged brown. His skin was so pale beneath a shock of freckles that I knew what had happened even before I spotted the telltale punctures on his neck.

I sat back on my heels and clenched my teeth. His neck held seven separate wounds—shallow and rough, as if they'd been teasing him. I'd bet that if I pulled down the collared shirt and suit jacket—finely made, but worn—I'd see more along his back and arms. It looked like some sort of hazing ritual, and maybe a bit of revenge. It looked like the Turn Boys, and was just one more reason for me to despise them. The young vampire gang ran roughshod over their chosen kingdom of Little Italy and the greater Lower East Side. This poor kid was rather far down Lafayette for their activities, but I didn't doubt for a minute who had done this. I'd seen enough of their work to know.

A solitary car sped behind me on the road, sending a spray of icy mud over my bicycle and splashing onto my blue tweed skirt. I glanced at my watch. Ten minutes 'til eight. Damn. I had just enough time to speed down to the police station, report the body and get to class. But I also knew what the police would do when they got him. They didn't take any chances—especially not with the anonymous immigrant children. Too many kids went missing to waste the precious time hunting in one of the hundreds of lower Manhattan tenements for a distraught mother who probably didn't speak any English. So they took them to the morgues, turned up the electric lights, and staked them. Sometimes they cut off their heads for good measure, if turning looked likely.

This boy wouldn't keep his head.

He reminded me a bit of my little brother Harry, back in Montana. The same freckles and shock of red hair. He wore one forlorn blue mitten—the other must have fallen off in the struggle.

"Zephyr," I told myself sternly, attempting to speak some sense to my paralyzed brain, "Harry still laughs about putting a beehive in your knickers. It ain't him."

At which good, rousing inducement to sanity I discovered myself scooping the pathetically light body from the ground and toting it back to my bicycle. I always knew the situation was serious when I resorted to country grammar.

I didn't know what I was doing. I swear I almost never do—I operate on nothing but horrible instincts and a dash of self-preservation. I draped the boy around my shoulders, wrestled the handlebar straight, and started back down the street. I could leave him in the school building. It ought to be safe.

I huffed and pedaled faster, sweating now with the exertion. The boy wasn't heavy, but I've never been that strong and I'd just come back from a crisis across the bridge in Brooklyn. A Russian immigrant with a husband and kids, turned a week ago, had apparently missed the warning about alcohol. Or maybe she'd heard it, and dismissed it along with the rest of the Temperance Union's hand-wringing hogwash. I might have had little personal experience with Demon Alcohol, but there was no comparison between what it did to my little sister when she found her way into Daddy's stash, and what it did to Others unfortunate or reckless enough to imbibe. A fit of the giggles and a morning headache was nothing compared to . . . well, *that*.

The Russian vampire's skin had turned red, they told me. Not just flushed, like your average speakeasy drunk. Oh no, blood red. It started to bead on her skin, like sweat. It dribbled from her mouth. Her children were terrified, of course. No one had told them what had happened to their mother—only that she was sick. A week's legally acquired blood puddled onto the floor, burning through the wood with its foul-smelling venom. The oldest child and the father ran away. The youngest must have frozen—with shock, fear, disbelief, God-only-knows—because he stayed behind. The father didn't realize until it was too late. The mother—blood starved, drunk, newly turned and not a little crazed—turned upon her child and fed. She realized what she had done when she was sated. Too late.

Troy Kavanagh's pack of Defenders got to her first. He told me the woman begged them to stake her. They obliged, along with the boy. Kids are too dangerous to let turn. Or so Defenders like Troy claim. I know him from way back. Even before New York. He'd met my daddy for some big, legendary Yeti hunt up in north Montana, and when I came down here I worked with his group for a while. I may not be much of a shot, but you can't be the oldest daughter of the best demon hunter in Montana without learning a few tricks. I pulled my weight, but I had to leave. The Others might not be human, but they're still *people*, you know? Troy never seemed to get that.

He called me in during the cleanup to deal with the new widower and his son. Said it called for a "delicate hand." Troy thinks a strong jaw makes up for a lousy personality.

So I'd been on my bicycle all day and my tailbone felt like someone had been smashing it with a mallet and I had a dead boy—the kind you're *never* supposed to let turn, if you're an ignorant Other-phobe like Troy—who could double as a vampire pincushion draped across my neck, and damn if I wasn't getting some odd looks as I huffed my way through the busy Canal Street intersection. Why did things like this always happen to me?

I had to laugh, and saw my breath float away in the glare of the electric lamps. Because I'm certifiable.

Two minutes to eight, I shot past a snarl of traffic on Bowery and stopped at the corner of Rivington and Chrystie. Sweat dripped down my neck and made my shirt cling to my back. My buttocks were still quite wet. My toes seemed to have lost all feeling. I leaned, trembling, over the handlebars and panted. Behind me rose the ragged edifice of Chrystie Elementary, smog-crusted and sporadically heated. Only three of its classrooms are equipped with electric lighting, and even that is about as reliable as a succubus in heat. An immigrant school— with quite a few Others, no less—was not a high priority for our de- lightful city government.

The boy on my neck started to groan. Not a normal groan—you know, made of air and vocal cords and wholesome biology. A distinctly otherworldly one that should have been impossible for such a small child to make. It was too loud, for one thing, like a ship's foghorn in my ears. Aside from his mouth, his body lay perfectly still. No air entered and exited his chest. I shuddered.

"Vampires are people," I said quietly, to steady myself. I had not been present at many Awakenings, but I knew enough to realize that I had very little time to put the boy safely away. He looked barely eleven years old—he'd be wilder than most. I struggled off the bicycle just as the boy began to stir in earnest. The motion put me off balance and I found myself sprawling on the ice underneath the school's shadow, grappling with a weakly flopping vampire.

"Oh, bloody Christ," I muttered. Okay, one thing at a time. *Get up, Zephyr. You've got class in a minute.* Grimacing, I planted my right foot on a patch of sidewalk that looked miraculously ice-free and wobbled into a crouch. I started to hum a lullaby my mama liked to sing when I was growing up—maybe it worked on little vampires, too? But the boy was getting stronger, his groan turning into a kind of strangled roar. The few people left on the streets in this shaded, ill-lit area hurried past me, their eyes firmly fixed on the sidewalk.

"I could be dying, you know!" I shouted after them. Right. Bloody heartless city. Gripping the squirming boy with my left hand, I pulled my bicycle out of the gutter with my right and hauled them both to the school steps.

"Having some trouble, Miss Hollis?"

I froze momentarily, white-knuckled on the handlebars. I knew that voice. And I can't say I was entirely pleased to hear it. I turned to face him with a smile I suspected was more than a little harried.

He was leaning on the stone railing halfway up the steps, his arms crossed nonchalantly. Amir, he had called himself, when he first appeared in my class last week. No last name, or at least none he would give me.

He reminded me of Rudolph Valentino in *The Sheik*—foreign, handsome, dangerous—but darker, his features broader and a little more attractive. His English was impeccable, if oddly accented. Except after class, when I questioned what possible use he had for a course in Basic Literacy and Elocution. *Then* he'd given a pitch-perfect impression of a Russian immigrant, two months off the boat.

"That boy is freshly turned," he said, nodding at the child but not moving.

I grit my teeth. "I am aware of that, Amir."

"The situation is under control, then?"

At that precise, cosmically aligned moment, the boy gave a bone shuddering snarl and latched his prepubescent fangs into the (now quite wilted) collar of my shirt.

"You can't bleed a shirt, you idiotic—" I was forced to cut off my tirade, for the boy—with a speed I could hardly credit—had wrapped his legs around my torso and forced me to fall. Amir reached me a second later and attempted to remove the boy, who clung to me like an otherworldly leech.

"What time is it?" I shouted over the mewling growls the boy made as he fumbled for the location of my actual neck. Ah, the untold benefits of conservative shirts.

Amir paused. He looked quite nonplussed, which, despite the exacerbating circumstances, pleased me inordinately. "Are you serious?" he said.

I swatted the boy's mittened hand away when it wandered over my breasts and pressed my back up against the stone railing. "Perfectly."

He had managed to grip one of the boy's arms, and so had to reach awkwardly with his left hand to pull out a pocket watch I imagine would not have looked out of place on President Coolidge himself.

"A minute past eight," he said. "Shall we tell the blood-crazed vampire that you're late? Maybe he'll be polite enough to resume his mauling after you've finished."

I glowered at him, but was prevented from coming up with an appropriately dry retort by the sensation of gums and fast-sharpening teeth rasping across my suddenly exposed throat.

I cursed and struggled away from his mouth. Amir now had him gripped by the waist and was slowly prying him off of me.

"Did he bite you?" Amir gasped. To my distant amusement, he seemed quite concerned.

"Vampire gums are not known to be fatal."

"Oh, should I just let him go, then? Since you find this so easy."

"I am perfectly capable of dealing with this myself, Amir," I heard myself saying, despite the copious evidence to the contrary.

With an odd, dangerous smile, Amir lowered his brush-thick eye-lashes and let the boy go. With a noise like a cat strangling to death on a hairball, the boy launched himself at my neck. The fangs, dull as they were, were good enough to break my skin at a direct attack. I shrieked—still more out of annoyance than fear—and reached deep into my pocket for my switchblade. Pure blessed silver, that blade, a gift from Daddy before I left home. I'd never used it after I left Troy. I'd almost forgotten it was there.

With a practiced movement, I laid the dull edge of the blade against the exposed, pallid flesh of his collarbone. He flinched away from the burning touch of blessed metal. The hesitation was enough to allow Amir to yank him off of me fully. For a moment I had the absurdly funny view of a little vampire struggling like an upturned cockroach.

I stood up. Only a little blood had escaped the tiny puncture wounds on my neck, but I wiped it away carefully and adjusted my wilting collar.

"It bit you?" Amir asked, his voice quiet. The vampire's noises were gentler in Amir's grip. Apparently, it did not regard him as quite so tasty a meal.

I shrugged. "Barely a scratch," I said. Still, my heart was racing.

"Even less can turn a person."

My, how serious he sounded. It made me smile. "Oh, don't worry about me. What time is it?"

Warily, he reached for his watch, hanging freely from his waistcoat. "Three minutes past."

I cursed, and picked up my bicycle. "I must go. Would you . . .

please, there's a room in the basement I think will hold him. Could you take care of him for me? Just until I'm done. I wouldn't normally ask this, but . . ."

He smiled, but it didn't quite reach those dark eyes. "You're late. Go ahead. I'll just have to miss dear Mr. Hamilton tonight."

I barely registered his gently mocking tone, as I was already up the stairs and opening the door to the school. I knew *The Federalist Papers* wasn't the most popular choice as a learning text, but I've always felt recent immigrants to this country should at least be aware of the ideals of its founding—even when they did not live up to the reality.

"Thank you," I said to him, awkwardly, from where he still stood on the steps. The vampire seemed to hardly trouble him at all, now. Not for the fist time, I wondered *what* precisely Amir was. Surely not human.

"Zephyr," he said, just before I shut the door behind me. "How do you know you won't turn?"

His voice was so strange and devoid of mockery that I paused and, to my surprise, answered him.

"Why, because I can't turn, of course. I'm immune."

"Is that . . . normal, for humans?"

I shrugged. "I've never met anyone else with it." And I'd long ago given up asking my parents how it had happened.

"Oh," was all he said. Since moving to the city, I'd managed to keep that peculiarity of mine from everyone except my roommate. I would have wondered why I'd so blithely revealed it to Amir if I weren't already so late.

"Good evening, everyone," I said as I opened the door.

A few responded with a strained, "Good evening, Miss Hollis." I hardly counted it as rudeness. It was a new moon, after all.

"We'll continue with Alexander Hamilton's Federalist number ten today," I said, hoping that work would distract them from noticing that

I looked like a drowned mongoose. Papers rustled and the electric lamps above us flickered. Had he taken the boy to the basement? Could he manage alone? Class had never seemed so long, and nearly half my students wanted to talk to me after. I could hardly rein in my impatience when Sarra, a solidly human Russian who attended my night classes because of her late hours at the sewing factory, insisted on quizzing me about the proper interpretation of the eighteenth amendment.

"So it says only the *selling* of alcohol is illegal?" she repeated, with determined emphasis. Clearly, this issue had been weighing upon her ever since she discovered this nation's draconian stance on her home country's national beverage.

"Because," she continued, "Boris has cousin, Naum, maybe you heard of him? Came here two years ago, and has a . . . you know, *method* with potatoes in a bathtub . . ."

She paused here, as though she expected me to beg for the recipe. Internally, I shuddered, but made the appropriate noises of appreciation. My solitary experience with a professional liquor (scotch, and possibly the foulest potion I've had the displeasure of drinking) made me more than wary of bathtub *gin*, let alone potato vodka.

"But, Miss Hollis, Naum is *family* and it is just a little alcohol and—"

"It's a gift, right?" I said quickly. "You won't give him any money?"

She pursed her lips, but seemed happy enough to nod. "Gifts, maybe. Gifts okay, yes?"

I smiled slightly. "It's not illegal to drink alcohol, Sarra. Just to sell it." A curious loophole that provided the semilegal rationale behind a hundred gin joints. "You don't have anything to worry about."

She nodded, satisfied. "Good. I bring you some next time. Have a nice day, Miss Hollis."

She handed me back the tattered classroom copy of *The Federalist Papers*, and turned to leave. I put it back with the others on the shelf and mentally steeled myself to discover what had happened to Amir and the vampire boy. However, when I turned back around to leave, I saw Giuseppe Rossi, a vampire who lived in a basement tenement in

Little Italy and had been attending my classes for the past year, standing quietly by the door. I had never known him to linger after class—his family was large and his wife absent, which left him with little time. Curious, I put the last of my papers into my bag and slung it over my shoulder. Giuseppe spoke English very well, but he still had difficulty reading.

"Miss Hollis," he said, when I was halfway to the door. I paused. His skin was pallid under the yellow electric lights. Not a hint of blood tinged his lips or fingertips. It had clearly been a long time since his last feeding. Concerned, I stepped closer. Was there a polite way of asking where he got his supplies? I knew of a few who would help him, if he could no longer afford the street corner blood vendors.

"Yes, Giuseppe?" I said.

"I . . . have a problem. I would not have bothered you with it, only I'm afraid for my family and you're the only one I know who can help." He raised his eyes. "Or, perhaps, will help?"

I walked the rest of the way toward him and gripped his hand briefly. "Of course, Giuseppe. You must know that I'll do anything I can."

He smiled, relieved. "Yes, I had hoped . . . see, Miss Hollis, when I first came to this country, I was not like this. I had a wife. She had given me three children, and carried our fourth. It was hard, but we were happy. And then one night, when I left the factory late, they found me."

My throat felt dry. I had heard too many such tales, but each one hit me with the force of fresh tragedy. Daddy says I feel too much, but I don't. He's a demon hunter. He just feels too little.

"Who?" I asked.

"That little gang of young *vampiri*, the ones Rinaldo lets run wild."

Oh, God. That little boy, covered in bites and gone mad in the basement. "The Turn Boys," I said.

It wasn't a question, but he nodded. "They turned me. My wife, she tried, but in a year she ran away. That's what I get for not marrying a good Italiana, they said. I needed blood, and money. The tunnel work . . ." He shrugged.

I had forgotten he did work on the new tunnel that would soon run from Canal Street into New Jersey. A good job for a vampire, even one as young (and proportionately sun-resistant) as Giuseppe. But it wouldn't pay nearly enough for his four children.

"So, I went to Rinaldo," he continued. "I delivered for him. Just a few times a week. And he gave me blood and money. It worked, for a while. But last week . . . I was delivering a little outside his territory. Some boys from another gang jumped me. The Westies, I think, but cannot prove. They took everything. Rinaldo says he doesn't care, that I owe him the money."

How I hated these mob bosses, self-styled kings of the neighborhood, who could destroy one man's life so callously. As if it were his fault that some rival gang had stolen the delivery.

"How much?" I asked, dreading the answer.

"Two hundred dollars."

I sucked in air, sharply, between my clenched teeth. That was more than I made in three months of teaching.

"I have one hundred," he said, "but I need to borrow the rest. He says he will . . . my children . . ."

Giuseppe looked close to tears and I realized I had never seen a vampire cry. With hardly a thought, I put my hand over his again and looked firmly into his unnaturally clear, bloodless eyes.

"You'll get through this, I promise." I reached deep into my pocket and pulled out the small stash of folded bills I had received just that morning from the local Citizen's Council, which paid my meager teaching salary each month. "Here," I said, pressing it into his hand, "this is fifty dollars. If you need help in the future, I hope you'll ask me or the Citizen's Council . . . even Tammany Hall would be better than *Rinaldo*."

I couldn't imagine what would have possessed him to get involved with the notorious bootlegger, Other-exploiter and gangster. He let the Turn Boys run wild, after all, and the Turn Boys had destroyed Giuseppe's life.

Giuseppe pressed the bills briefly against his cheek and then turned away, as if to wipe his eyes.

"I have no words," he said, finally. "I swear, I will pay you back, Zephyr."

The sound of my first name brought my thoughts back, abruptly, to Amir. "Only what you can," I said. Suddenly I was desperate to leave. How long had I lingered here?

Thankfully, Giuseppe pressed my hand only briefly before leaving. I waited to hear him exit the front doors before I shut the lights, and then made my way by memory through the deserted school halls and into the basement.

As I did so, it slowly dawned on me that I had, in a moment of impulsive pity, given away my entire month's salary. My rent would be due at the boarding house in three days—a full twelve dollars, paid in cash and upfront. Mrs. Brodsky would hardly be sympathetic. Indeed, I could be assured of being soundly turned out in the middle of a New York winter with my belongings strewn about me on the sidewalk. I shuddered at the thought. Mrs. Brodsky was willing enough to serve me dinners without meat—who was she to complain if her boarders wanted cheaper food for the same price?—but she was decidedly lacking in basic human compassion.

"Well," I said to myself, as cheerfully as I could, "you have at least three more days of that lumpy bed."

"Do most do-gooders talk to themselves as frequently as you?"

Amir was below me on the basement steps, carrying an oil lamp and looking quite as good as he had two hours before, when he *hadn't* been wrestling with a freshly turned vampire in an abandoned school basement. This bothered me more than it should. I felt positively dowdy beside him.

"Do most wastrels accost innocent women on staircases?" I said. It was uncharitable of me, seeing as how he'd just risked life and limb for my sake. No matter that it didn't seem to show.

He laughed—it was rich and warm and made me blink in the weak light. "A wastrel, am I? What kind of a wastrel attends immigrant night school?"

I crossed my arms over my chest and forced myself to breathe. "I haven't figured that out, yet."

He laughed again. I had never heard anything quite like it before. "Are you coming down, or will we just argue on the steps all night?"

Feeling decidedly silly, I followed the wavering light of his lamp down the stairs.

"Are you all right?" I made myself ask, when the silence had lasted for half a minute. I was surprised by how keenly I meant the question.

He shrugged. "The boy can't hurt me. I'm surprised you lasted as long with him as you did."

I took this as a compliment. "How is he?"

He paused before a closed door a few feet away from the steps. "Sleeping. I brought him a few pints."

He had an odd look on his face, wistful and angry all at once. I almost touched the sleeve of his gray wool sweater, but some self-preserving instinct stopped me. I somehow knew that touching Amir would not be the innocent gesture of sympathy and friendship it had been with Giuseppe. He was feral and mysterious and Other, a combination I found too fascinating to be safe.

"Why such a small child?" he asked softly. "What possible purpose . . . ?"

His question seemed so strangely naive. "Sport," I said. "The Turn Boys play with humans like cats play with mice. And far more cruelly."

"What will you do with him?" he asked.

I glanced up at Amir, startled. "I . . . I suppose I hadn't thought of it. I just saw him, and I couldn't leave him there . . ."

The sudden realization of my dilemma cut off my words. What in hell *could* I do? I could hardly bring him back to my boarding house and risk him running wild amongst the other girls. I could leave him here, but what if he broke out during school hours? I would have given him to one of the charitable groups that deal with newly turned vampires, but they had a policy to stake anyone under sixteen. And if even *they* were afraid of the children, what good was I?

I sighed and leaned against the wall by the door. I felt a prodigious headache roaring into the space behind my temples. It had been a long day.

Amir looked at me. I mean *looked* at me, with his dangerously dark eyes and ridiculous eyelashes, just canvassing my face until I could feel the blush radiating from my cheeks. It felt impudent and entirely inappropriate, yet I could not say a word.

"I'll take him," he said, just when I thought I might melt from the intensity of his gaze. "I know a place where he'll be safe. He'll come back to himself. It might take the children longer, but they all do, eventually."

God, how I wished I knew what he was. Or even just who. He was all mysteries, and yet so very physical, a mere foot from me in this damp, freezing basement.

"But . . . *why?*" I was proud of myself for managing to get even that much out.

He smiled. "My own reasons. And I need to ask you a favor."

It's just a smile. "Like what?"

"I gather do-gooding does not always come with vast monetary rewards? Well, it's a simple request, and I can offer you a lot of money. It's what wastrels have, you see, to make up for their lack of sense and moral fortitude."

I couldn't tell if he was mocking himself or me. It was hardly a surprise to learn that he had money. No one who dressed as well and as carelessly as he could be lacking in funds.

"What do you need?" I asked. This, at least, was familiar territory.

"I need you to find me a vampire."

I blinked, slowly. He was still there. "And why do you think I'm a good person to ask?"

"Because you're immune, somehow. And no one would ever suspect you. Your perverse love of blood suckers is well-known in this town."

Just in time, I started to feel angry. "And why on earth would I help you hurt an innocent fellow-creature?"

His smile could have cut diamonds. "Somehow I don't think you'll mind. Do you want to know who it is?"

"I don't imagine I have a choice."

He cocked his head in acknowledgment. "True enough."

"So who?"

"*Rinaldo.*"

CHAPTER TWO

He spit it out like vampire venom and I could almost imagine that I saw the name burning a hole into the wall behind me. In the deep shadows cast by the lamplight, his naturally imposing features looked positively demonic—and I have hunted demons. I might have felt my own loathing for the mob boss mere minutes ago, but it paled in the face of Amir's hatred. Whatever grievance lay between them, I could only imagine it was dangerous.

"*Find* him?" I managed to say, into Amir's closed and expectant silence. "But everyone knows about Rinaldo."

He shifted slightly and the light from the lamp settled in a more reassuring pattern on his face: wide, generous lips, prominent cheekbones and almond eyes that made him look striking. "But has anyone ever seen him? Most of his officers don't even know he's a vampire."

"He is?"

For a moment, I could have sworn that his dark eyes glowed like coals. "Oh, yes."

Before I could check if it was just the reflection from the lamp, he turned away and unlatched the door. The room beyond was dark, but

I could just make out the boy lying on the rough brick floor. His eyes were closed, and his chest moved slightly—perhaps once every ten seconds. His skin was still very pale, but a rosy blush now stained his fingertips. I couldn't see his lips. I will not berate myself for a moment of primal panic. Vampires might be people, but they are certainly not human. They are like sentient lions in our midst, and we are their natural prey.

Amir's fingers brushed my neck briefly, where the tiny wounds caused by the boy's attack had already scabbed over. It could have been an accident, it could have been a moment of wordless reassurance, but I felt it like the tingling of laudanum syrup down my throat. I stood beside the door while he picked the boy up from the dusty floor and tossed him over his shoulder. The gesture was oddly tender, but I couldn't read his face. The boy stirred when Amir touched him, but while the movements were unnaturally quick, he did not seem likely to attack. Amir had even stuffed the lonely blue mitten in the pocket of the boy's coat. I did not know much about Awakenings, and even less those of children, but they generally involved a period of animallike feeding and general disorientation that could last for weeks.

"Are you sure?" I asked, nodding to the boy. Amir's simple solution to my problem raised so many questions. *Who are you? How can you be sure it's safe? Why do you seem to care as much as I do?* So many questions, and none I could ask.

"I don't normally involve myself in your kind's affairs, but I'm taking a personal interest."

My kind? I frowned. "How magnanimous."

"If you don't want my help, just say the word."

I looked away. I felt his eyes on me for a moment longer, and then he handed me the lamp and began walking. I followed him, inexplicably afraid of losing them both in the dark. We climbed the stairs in silence, and then walked through the halls, the click of my heels on the stone floors echoing unnervingly. In the entrance hall, I picked up my bicycle and adjusted my bag. Amir paused by the door; I waited.

"So, will you help?" he asked, not facing me.

The boy's red hair stuck out in all directions, stiff with grime. Rinaldo was hardly a simple (or safe) request, but I had no money and not many other options for finding some before Sunday. And there was the boy. Oh, I knew I owed Amir. So did he. Could that be why he had done it?

And really, did it matter? I had never in my life denied someone help when they asked for it. I could hardly start now, just because the person asking was stranger than anyone I'd ever met.

"I'll need to know more," I said.

He turned partly toward me, so the lamplight gilded the edge of his smile. "I'm afraid I don't know much more about Rinaldo, or I'd find him myself."

"But why—"

His expression turned suddenly regal and unforgiving. "My reasons are my business. Think on it. I'll talk to you tomorrow?"

I set the lamp on the ledge by the door and extinguished it. "Well, I promised the Third Street soup kitchen I'd help in the morning and at noon I have to join the fair wages for night workers picket at City Hall . . . I might be able to talk after that, but there's a local-chapter suffragette meeting at six and those always take a glacial *age* and . . ."

I stopped. I couldn't mention *that*. His eyebrows had risen far enough already.

"And here I imagined you writing genteel letters to Tammany Hall. Do you *sleep?*"

"I can't just ignore injustice." I knew I sounded strident and harsh, but I didn't care. How dare he look at me like that, as though he found me ridiculous?

"Apparently not. So even I'm worth do-gooding for?"

"I hardly know you."

He opened the door and I gasped at the sudden blast of freezing air. I fastened the remaining buttons on my coat and quickly reached for my gloves.

"Didn't your father ever teach you not to help strangers?"

He was mocking me again. I looked up at him and gave my best aloof smile. "Lucky for you I don't listen to my daddy."

He laughed—that uncommon, beautiful noise—and turned up the collar of my coat. "Why, Miss Hollis, I declare—is that an accent?"

And before I could respond, before I could *blush*, he was gone and the door was gently gliding shut. The air smelled like him, briefly. Like oranges and frankincense and firewood.

Like nothing human, and nothing I could name.

I bicycled home slowly, barely conscious of the flow of human, equine and motored traffic. Amir had intrigued me since I first encountered him in the back of my classroom, but now I felt as though he had pried apart my brain and tucked himself immovably inside. It was a strange sensation. I was supposed to help him track down a ruthless vampire mob boss who terrorized the immigrants in this city and supplied almost all of the gin joints below Fourteenth Street. A vampire who apparently wouldn't reveal his actual whereabouts to even his own officers. And Amir thought I could find him because I was immune to vampire bites and no one would suspect a local charity worker? But I had to admit the idea appealed to me. Rinaldo had terrorized our community for long enough. Given this opportunity, what moral option did I have but to stop him? A bluestocking, Daddy called me, and he didn't mean it as a compliment. And I must be, because otherwise I wouldn't have saved that boy. Amir ought to be able to hold him for now, but eventually . . . I knew that despite my best efforts, we might still have to stake him. The boy would have a family, though. At the least I ought to find them.

I might have been tempted to dismiss the entire affair as a dream if not for the mud stains on my skirt and the bite marks on my neck. I'd have to hide those from Mrs. Brodsky. Five minutes after I left the school, I turned the corner on Ludlow Street from Delancey and wobbled to a stop before Number Eighty-seven. I deposited my bicycle behind the grate under the stairs before nearly falling through the immaculately clean front door. Mrs. Brodsky might have a heart the size of a pea, but she atones for her sins with a scrub brush.

None of that modern urban marvel, electricity, had yet found its way into more than two rooms of our well-scrubbed corner of the universe, and so I made my way through the dark hallway by smell and habit until I reached the kitchen. Katya was by the stove, ladling the contents of a cast-iron pot into a large bowl. None of the other girls were downstairs at this hour, so I pulled up a stool to the small counter and collapsed onto it. It finally occurred to me that I was starving. When had I last eaten? Breakfast? I would have made a more conscious effort to eat food if I could afford it. Troy would sometimes invite me to dinner with him at the Algonquin or some other fabulously high-class restaurant because he knew I could never bear to refuse. I hated how he flaunted his money when so many had such desperate need of it. I attempted to confound him with embarrassing and odd requests for meatless food, but he always just smiled at me and gave an extra-large tip to the waiter. Zephyr Hollis, dining with a demon hunter at the Algonquin. I suppose hunger compromises everyone's principles.

Katya put the steaming bowl in front of me a few moments after I sat down, with a heavy pewter spoon and tall glass of water. She moved slowly now—eight months pregnant and almost bursting with it.

I thanked her and swallowed a few burning mouthfuls of matzo ball and carrot. The broth was thin and oversalted, but I hardly noticed it anymore. After two years of Mrs. Brodsky's meatless soup, I had stopped wishing it were better and generally felt grateful it existed at all. It was all too easy to starve in this anonymous human ocean of a city.

"Where is she?" I asked, when my stomach had stopped feeling as though it were eating itself.

Katya gave a lopsided smile and pointed upstairs.

"Oh, no, Mr. Brodsky, again?" Mr. Brodsky was our whispered term for the unmarried sailor our otherwise starched and respectable matron occasionally took up to her rooms for "tea." We wouldn't dream of confronting her with it, but it did give us something to gossip about when she gave any of us lectures for missing curfew.

Katya laughed and began to put away the remaining kitchen utensils. I didn't know if she could speak, but I had never heard her say a word in the seven months she had been with us. Her husband, a construction worker, had been killed when the subway tunnel he was excavating collapsed, suffocating him to death. She discovered she was pregnant a week later—no other circumstance would have induced Mrs. Brodsky to relax her notoriously strict standards of propriety and allow a pregnant girl to live in her boarding house. Katya lived off her husband's meager pension and helped Mrs. Brodsky with the chores.

I bid her good night after washing out my bowl and climbed up to my fourth-floor room. My legs felt like jelly fire by the time I made it there, red-faced and huffing. *Do you sleep?* Amir had asked. Lord, but I felt like I needed a week of it. Aileen was still awake, of course, when I entered our room. She was smoking on her bed and ashing out the window, a twopenny erotic novel with an anatomically impossible cover illustration gripped in her left hand.

She had wrapped a pair of rayon hose around her black curls. These were a substitute for an actual silk turban, which she could hardly afford. Add to this a teddy that looked two sizes too large, and yet still managed to seem perfectly in fashion. Aileen, despite an ineradicable Irish accent, was every inch a New York vamp, and she dedicated hours to maintaining the lifestyle, despite her pittance of a factory salary. She twisted the caps on bottles of holy water, which would have driven me to bloody suicide, but did not seem to bother her all that much. She had perfected, she informed me, the art of screwing tops while simultaneously reading about other people screwing.

She glanced up. "I told you not to teach on a new moon. Did they chase you out of the building? Or did you just roll around in the gutter for fun?"

"Definitely fun," I said, leaning against the door to catch my breath.

"Mother Mary!" she said, when I dropped my coat and she saw the mud now drying on my posterior. "Are you sure you wouldn't prefer the factory?"

I unbuttoned the skirt and kicked it off into the space between our beds. "After today, I'll think about it."

She smiled sympathetically. "Well, I know what will cheer you up. This auteur"—she paused and glanced again at the cover of her novel—"ah, Verity Lovelace, has quite a way with the risqué euphemism."

My shirt joined my skirt on the floor and I pulled out a robe from the top of my trunk.

"Better than 'dew-filled love chasm'?" I asked as I unfastened the hooks of my brassiere.

"Oh, you can't imagine. Here." She flipped to a page whose corner she had folded down. " 'Her anus was a perfection of unblemished beauty, its youthful folds ruddy as an apple, with a delicate budding cherry at its center.' "

I unfastened the last clip and took a deep, unconstricted breath. "Oh, my," I said, grinning at her. "Don't tell me he pops her cherry?"

Aileen giggled and rolled over on her stomach. "It's terribly shocking. And rather messy, if you trust Madame Lovelace."

"Aileen, if I didn't know any better, I'd say you were interested."

She waved her hand airily. "Oh, who's to say? With the right man, anything could interest me."

"If Mrs. Brodsky doesn't get to him first." Aileen groaned. "She's like your mother away from home," I teased.

"My mother, God rest her soul, wasn't a bloody parole officer."

Our landlady doted on Aileen and had taken a forceful interest in her affairs. She considered me the corrupting influence, of course. There were times when I was tempted to show her Aileen's novel collection. I tied my robe and picked up a terry cloth. "Any hot water left?"

"Not unless you want to heat it yourself. Mr. Brodsky is here, after all."

I grimaced. "Of course. Well, let me know if you come across any other gems."

Aileen gave me a wide-eyed look of conspiratorial understanding. I walked back through the dimly lit hall to the bathroom. The water ran into the claw-footed porcelain tub lukewarm at first, and then frigid. My schedule meant I was frequently forced to take cold baths, but I still scowled at the ceiling that separated me from Mr. Brodsky. I was sure *he* didn't have to struggle to wash his hair in water only slightly warmer than an icy puddle. Of course, he also had to satisfy the no-doubt terrifying appetite of *Mrs*. Brodsky. I bet she scrubbed him herself. With steel wool. After a precise two and a half minutes, I leapt out of the tub and quickly dried my prickling skin with the terry cloth. Wet, my hair brushed the tops of my shoulders, but it always dried to a frizzy halo of loose curls that I rarely had the time to tame. Mama's hair is a beautiful shade of strawberry blond, and hangs straight as a pin to the backs of her thighs. But I have hair like Daddy. Of course.

When I got back to the room, Aileen had turned down the lamp and was lying upside down on her bed, staring at the ceiling. The hose lay discarded on the floor beside her. I pulled on a cotton nightgown, a gift from Mama on my twelfth birthday, and sunk onto my bed. It might be a lumpy mattress, but it felt like a little corner of heaven after days like this.

"Anything good happen?" I asked.

"They are doing it in the dining car of the Oriental Express."

I thought about it. "Does that sound uncomfortable to you?"

"I think it sounds uncomfortable to Verity Lovelace. So," she said, still looking at the ceiling, "what happened?"

"Turn Boys. They got this little kid, and I swear he looked so much like Harry. And I . . ." I wasn't sure how to even describe the rest of it.

Aileen turned to face me. "The pols staked him?"

"Well, no, um . . . actually, I carried him to the school and then one of my students . . . well, I mean, he went to one class but he certainly doesn't need it. Anyway he's absolutely not human and he seemed to be able to handle the boy and he said he would take care of him for me if I did him a favor."

Aileen took nearly a minute to digest this incoherent torrent of information, and it was even more difficult than usual to read her expression.

"Are those bite marks on your neck?" she asked, finally.

My hand flew to the wounds, and I wished I'd had the presence of mind to hide them. Aileen greatly disapproved of some of my "risks," as she called them, and I hated to give her more ammunition. "It was just the boy," I said defensively. "He was blood-mad."

Aileen pursed her lips. "I can imagine. And what are you, charity-mad?"

"That's unfair."

"Is it? Back in Dublin, I saw a new-turned child sucker kill thirty factory workers and two pols before they managed to stake him. Bloody hell, Zephyr, you of all people ought to know how dangerous they are. You deal with them every day!"

Damn, but she was right. I knew it had been crazy when I took him to the school, but every other option had seemed—*still* seemed—untenable. It just didn't seem fair to me that the tragedy of children being turned had to be compounded by their being prematurely staked.

"And though I'm sure this will hardly matter to a crusader such as yourself, you and this student of yours broke the law. You know, one of those ones they actually care about enforcing."

"Amir . . . I don't know how, but I know he'll deal with it. No one will find out. Not unless you're planning to—"

"*Zephyr.*"

"Sorry."

She was silent for so long I wondered if she had fallen asleep. But she sat up abruptly and extinguished the lamp.

"So," she said, still backward on her bed, "do I want to know what this favor is?"

Finding a vampire mob boss so Amir could kill him? "Probably not."

She sighed. "Oh, Zephyr. Why can't you just go dancing like the rest of us?"

I thought about Amir and Rinaldo during my entire shift at the soup kitchen the next morning, ladling bowls of thick oat porridge and carefully rationing the brown sugar. I had never really considered myself a vindictive person, but after learning what Rinaldo had done to Giuseppe, and the dozens of other horrors I had heard over the years, I discovered that I was almost eager to deliver him to a just reward. The police sure as hell would never deal with him—they all probably took his bribes. And Defender groups like Troy's were far too happy staking twopenny vampires and Other nests for bigoted citizens' pay to bother with real evil. I understood the dangers, of course. I wouldn't agree to this blindly, but it seemed that if I had a chance, I should try. Amir was right—who would suspect me? And no one here knew of my immunity.

But first I needed to do some research. As soon as I could politely get away, I decided to take advantage of the forty minutes I had before the picket began. I pedaled like mad to Canal Street and then walked my bicycle over the dust and piles of rubble to the main construction site. The workers were just starting their lunch hour, but I could tell immediately that none of the men lounging on the winches or the ground on this bright afternoon were vampires. No, suckers would still be deep in the tunnel, separated by the sun from these normal, mortal men. The younger the vampire, the less susceptible they are to the burning effects of sunlight. Still, it isn't pleasant for any of them, and the unnatural contrasts between the pallor of their skin and the red of their feedings is all too apparent in the day. The workers fell silent as I passed them. Self-consciously, I pulled my cloche hat further down, so that it shaded my eyes. A construction site like this was not, as Mama would say, a place where any respectable young lady should find herself. I didn't fear for my safety, and certainly not for my mother's Victorian sense of propriety, but the silence and the stares made me wish I hadn't come down here on such a whim. Couldn't I have waited until night, when he would have been at home? The men didn't even catcall, which made me feel annoyed and grateful all at once. Tall and skinny and breasts like bumps on a board—it might be the fashion at F. Scott Fitzgerald's legendarily glamorous Long Island parties, but here I felt like a gawky teenager.

I grit my teeth and reminded myself of how little time I had for this errand.

"Is Giuseppe here today?" I asked the worker closest to my right—a swarthy man with day-old stubble and a bowler hat tilted on his head.

"What's a girl like you want with a sucker?" he asked. His accent was broad and faintly southern. "You're such a skinny little chit, he'll barely get a snack."

This joke seemed to strike him and his companions as hugely witty, because they practically laughed themselves off their seats. I was about to give up and ask someone else when he finally recovered himself.

"Hey, Giuseppe!" he yelled in the general direction of the scaffolded mouth of the tunnel. "Got a bleeder here to see ya."

Squinting into the shadows, I could just barely see a tall figure materialize in the entrance. I thanked the man and started to walk down the sharply sloping bank.

One of the men behind me said something that involved "dessert" and slang I didn't recognize. I felt his friends' laughter like a splash of ice water on my back as I hurried toward Giuseppe.

As soon as I walked beneath the ice-encrusted wooden scaffolds, I realized what a mistake I had made. Giuseppe hung back in the shadows so I could hardly see his face, but I could tell from the frightened and furious look in his inhumanly bright eyes that I wasn't precisely a welcome guest. He was wary, probably because he couldn't imagine why I would have sought him here. And when he found out? *Oh, bloody stakes. I am such an idiot.*

"Miss Hollis? Has something happened? If it's the money . . ." He looked around and lowered his voice. His right hand was worrying at something in his pocket, his left was pulling at the brim of his cap. I could feel his nervousness, and I'm as much an empath as my bicycle. "I will pay you back, I swear, but—"

I shook my head quickly, and forced myself not to back up. I would have felt so much safer in the light. "No, no, it's not about that. I told you yesterday, you only need to pay me back when you can. It's . . ." I hesitated, and then rushed on. "You see, I'd just wanted to ask you a few questions about Rinaldo."

The words, in their unadorned gall, made him freeze. I winced. My plans might have seemed sane in bed or the cocooning safety of a morning soup kitchen, but in the presence of one of the countless victims of Rinaldo's brutality I felt like a little girl, ignorantly courting death. I almost apologized and left, but Giuseppe roughly grabbed my elbow and forced me deeper into the tunnel. My eyes adjusted to the dim light provided by a few intermittently hung electric bulbs and more gas lamps. I grew aware of the hard, curious stares of the other workers. But I could only hear water, dripping somewhere behind me, and the low-pitched buzz of the electrical lights. Even my footsteps were muffled by the packed dirt and none of the men here put much store in breathing. Their eyes seemed to blaze out of the gloom—predatory, inhuman, watchful. The air smelled like damp earth and something barely recognizable—the curious antiseptic tang of a pack of vampires. I felt like a lamb lured into the lion's den. Immunity, as Aileen so often warned me, didn't mean "the buggers won't bleed you to death."

"Zephyr, you know you shouldn't be here," Giuseppe said, his voice so low I had to lean in to hear him. We were a few yards away from the nearest vampire, but I knew how good their hearing was. "Has he threatened you?" He looked so worried. But of course he would—how long had he been living with Rinaldo's terror?

My breathing was very shallow. I felt light-headed. "Not exactly . . ." I said. "But I wanted to know if you've ever met him. I mean, in person."

I met his incredulous stare, willfulness winning out over pragmatic fear by a hairsbreadth.

"Is this for one of your *societies?*"

I'd heard that emphasis on the last word before, but usually from my father or Troy. I had never expected to hear such derision from one of my students. Of course, I had provoked him. I shook my head slowly.

"I promised someone I'd help them. I just need some information."

"So why come to me? Why here?"

Breathe in, Zephyr. "I . . . It was thoughtless to ask you here. I apologize. I thought you might know because—"

"I don't know anything about Rinaldo, *Miss Hollis.* I don't know why you think I do. Now, if you pardon me, I have work."

His eyes grew brighter for a moment, and his irises turned black. Inhuman light pulsed behind them in a fluid, mesmerizing dance that would have put me entirely in his power had I not been immune. After a shocked moment, I pretended to relax and angle my neck toward him. I hadn't been the object of a vampire's Sway for so long I had almost forgotten they could do it. If only I'd thought to wear some garlic—then I could reasonably pretend to not be affected, since the root tended to impair younger vampires.

Surreptitiously, I reached into my pocket and gripped the silver switchblade. Was Giuseppe really planning to bleed me? But after a few seconds the light dimmed and his eyes returned to their normal light brown. A warning, then.

The harsh set of his mouth softened. "So maybe you remember how dangerous this is," he whispered. And then, louder, "Let her pass!"

He stalked away. The other men in the tunnel seemed to lose their rigid focus on me.

Well, there's nothing dishonorable about a retreat. Otherwise known as getting the hell out of here before I'm eaten alive. Quickly, I picked up my bicycle from where it had fallen earlier and hurried to the exit. I wanted to run, but it seemed undignified and anyway, I didn't want to do any more damage to my reputation than I had already. I could hear the whispers now: "That night-school teacher got ran out of the tunnel by a bunch of suckers. And she teaches 'em, too, the sap."

I was underneath the outer scaffolding and about to reemerge into daylight when a large icicle came loose from a wooden plank above me. Before I could duck, someone snatched it out of the air with inhuman speed. Sudden alarm burned away the fear and left me angry and battle-ready. I whirled on my rescuer, the switchblade in my palm before I was aware of even grabbing it. He stood half in the sunlight, perfectly still, as though flaunting his Otherness. And he was Other in more ways than just the obvious, for though his skin turned almost gray in the light, it was chocolate brown in the shadows. He held the icicle in his left hand. None of the ice melted around his fingers, and it looked like nothing so much as a stake. An incongruous picture. When it became obvious to even my slow brain that this man had no intention of attacking me, I relaxed and nervously pocketed the blade again.

"Th-thank you," I stammered. The man was older than most of the other workers here—well, at least his appearance was older. From his graying hair and beard, I judged him to be at least fifty when he turned.

"You're that teacher, right? The vampire suffragette? What do you want with Rinaldo?" he asked, after looking at me for an uncomfortably long moment.

I cursed to myself and attempted to come up with a plausible, innocent explanation. Like, "Oh no, I was asking about my *brother* named Rinaldo, not the infamous mob boss. How silly!" Also, *vampire suffragette*? Oh, my reputation.

"I . . ." I'm criminally stupid? "I don't really—"

He cut me off with a smile that was oddly reassuring. "No one's ever seen Rinaldo. Least not one of us. Sure as hell not Giuseppe, poor fool. Closest we ever get is his second, that Dore. A century old if he's a day." He twirled the icicle, blindingly fast, in his fingers for a moment and then let it fall and shatter on the ground. "You don't want to meet Dore, and you sure don't want to get noticed by Rinaldo. So whoever you're helping, do you both a favor and tell him to scat. You've had better ideas, you know?"

My mouth twisted in a derisive half-smile. Truer words had never been spoken. I started to respond, but he just nodded and walked back inside.

The prosaically human jeers of the men as I hopped back on my bicycle were almost reassuring. At least their eyes didn't glow. At least, however poorly restrained, they did not long for my blood.

My voice was unusually breathy during the chants at our "Night Hours, Equal Pay" City Hall demonstration. Our Honorable Mayor Jimmy Walker, who owed half his good fortune to his looks and the other half to Tammany Hall, was considering a veto on legislation that would help increase the wages of Others who worked night shifts on construction sites and factories. I hadn't helped organize this demonstration, but I was a member of both citizens groups that sponsored it—the Human Coalition for Others Rights and the Family Action Committee for Nonhuman Laborers. I attended their meetings only occasionally, as I was already so busy with my thirty-one other societies. Daddy says I'm a bit of an overachiever. Aileen says I'm a softhearted moron. I'm sure they'd have a great deal to discuss if the earth imploded and they managed to meet.

I was standing next to Iris Tomkins, a woman whose dedication to progressive causes was matched only by her girth. She was in the minority of local activists who could claim some social standing among New York's elite. On the bottom rung, to be sure, but Iris played her role as society dame to the hilt. I rather liked her, particularly because she shared my opinion of the frequently tendentious ramblings that passed for discussion at suffragette meetings. She described herself as an Anarcha-Feminist Socialite—Emma Goldman with just a dash of Oscar Wilde. Right now, her bellowing chants of "Fight for the night— Jimmy, do what's right" made my labored contributions perfectly unnecessary.

Eventually, I just gave up and mouthed the words. It would appear that my vampire confrontation skills were sorely rusted. Before, with Daddy or Troy, I had never been so unnerved after a fight. Of course, I had never been alone in a cave full of them. I had never been threatened by someone I had known for more than a year, and I had never seriously considered courting the danger of a master vampire.

Dear old Jimmy was obliged to walk past us on the way to his car about an hour after noon. The press had arrived in force by then, and were snapping photographs and scribbling notes throughout our crowd. I was standing in the front row, my right arm trapped in Iris's sturdy elbow and my left holding up one end of a sign that read:

JIMMY, WOULD *YOU* TAKE 50¢ A NIGHT?

Iris had decided to bolster my apparent lack of spirits with her own, which she correctly judged to be more than sufficient for two people. Her voice was so strident she was practically singing the chants. I leaned on her and was grateful for the support. It seemed to have slipped my mind to eat anything this morning, despite the fact that I had given breakfast to hundreds of indigents.

"Are you okay, dear?" Iris paused, midchant, to ask. I straightened immediately and then waited for the white haze to clear.

"Oh, sorry, I think I'm just a little hungry."

She nodded sympathetically and patted my hand. I was spared any remonstrances about my deplorable eating habits because "Beau James" Walker, the Night Mayor of New York himself, was standing less than two feet away from us.

I had to give him credit. He knew we hated him, and he saw the press as well as anyone, but he appeared as though the situation didn't perturb him at all. He took his time going down the steps, chatting with his aides and exchanging a smile and a word with those who came up to speak to him. He didn't ignore us, either. Just looked to both sides and waved, as though we were some welcoming party. As well he might, I supposed. He was a popular mayor. A handsome, clever dilettante in an age where the creative pursuit of leisure seemed to have become the national aesthetic. Never mind that the infant mortality rates in some Lower East Side tenements and Harlem were enough to make God weep, or that Others and Negroes were routinely treated as less than human. Some people had a great deal of money, and the press was happy enough to pretend that the rest of us had some too.

He had paused near the two of us, and for some reason when he turned to answer his aide's questions, his eyes locked on mine. Almost as if he recognized . . . Before I could really process what he was doing, he walked past his aide and stopped in front of me.

The gossip press had nicknamed him the Night Mayor due to his penchant for all-night parties, and he had the pallor of a man not much given to daylight. He wore a navy fedora and a cream silk suit, which I was forced to admit combined to a rather devastating effect. His smile was curious and very self-assured.

"I seem to recall seeing you before."

"I . . . you do?" It was the best I could manage, as my wits had taken a holiday. I needed some food, very badly.

"Last week, was it? Some demonstration about infant mortality? You must like coming here."

He remembered me? Thank God, *that* woke me up. "Well, you seem to have difficulty separating morality from financial interests. We thought we'd point you in the right direction."

He laughed, tipped his hat at me, and walked into the cab of his silver-trimmed Duesenberg.

Iris was positively jumping in excitement, and several protestors crowded around us as soon as he drove off.

"Ah, that was excellent, Zephyr. Excellent. They'll be sure to print that in the paper tomorrow. How clever! You're like our own Dorothy Parker!"

I looked at her and laughed. "The Algonquin has better food."

"So, how often would you say you demonstrate here?" I looked up. A female reporter, surprisingly enough, had managed to squeeze in beside Iris.

"Oh, maybe twice a month. Well, once a week, lately."

The reporter—devastatingly beautiful and impeccably attired, with a mauve silk cloche hat over her perfectly bobbed auburn hair and a low-hipped day dress that must have come straight from Chanel—scribbled in her notebook with a small smile.

"Aren't you busy," she said, looking back up.

Her lips were glossy and cherry red, her eyebrows plucked to delicate arches. I resisted the sudden urge to smooth out my own. Iris leaned over so she was directly in the reporter's line of sight—as though anyone could have missed her—and declared, "The injustices of our present mayor's administration are so numerous that we could hold a different demonstration each day of the week without exhausting them."

The reporter turned to Iris and then beamed. "My, Mrs. Tomkins, you're looking well. And as active as ever, I see. My mother always said you'd tire of these social causes someday."

Iris paused, and then gave the reporter a hard look. "Oh, Lily Harding, is that you? Goodness, how you've changed, I didn't even recognize you! How is that dear mother of yours? Still gardening?"

Iris gave Lily one of her patented hugs—the kind that would threaten to strangle an African rhinoceros—and they fell to renewing what appeared to be a lifelong acquaintance. Iris was the godmother of Lily's younger sister and she and their mother had attended the same boarding school. Lily was present in an official capacity as the Other beat reporter for the *Evening Herald*.

"And my young friend here," Iris said, after they had finished catching up with each other, "has already made quite a name for herself. She teaches a night school on the Lower East Side, if you would believe it, filled with all sorts of vampires and demons and skinwalkers. She is quite fearless."

Lily gave a bit of a wide-eyed glance at the poster we were carrying, and I shrugged my shoulders at Iris's unthinking hypocrisy. I understood how hard it was for even those who fought for their equal treatment to regard Others as anything besides dangerous animals.

"Zephyr Hollis, right?" Lily said. "They call you the vampire suffragette."

I could hardly contain my wince. "I'm late to the party, apparently. I heard that for the first time this morning."

She gave that small, knowing smile again. It was certainly smug, but held enough humor for me to warm to her slightly. "And?" she said.

"I shall strive to take it as a compliment."

She laughed at that, and it was such a beautiful, refined ladylike little thing that all my warm feelings vanished in a sudden freeze. God's blood, but I felt like a braying wildebeest next to this paragon. So, of course, Iris immediately suggested that she take us both out to lunch and refused to be gainsaid, even when I pointed out that I had taken my bicycle to the rally. Apparently, she knew of a method by which a bicycle could be affixed to the back of a car with some rope and little trouble. She hailed a taxicab while Lily and I stood on the street corner, forced to engage in mutually wary small talk.

"Where are you from, originally? Surely not New York? You have a bit of an accent."

I was reminded of Amir's comment the night before, and blushed. "Montana," I said, briefly. "The town of Yarrow. And you must be from Long Island."

She arched those perfect eyebrows. "My," she drawled, "however did you guess? Manhasset, to be precise."

I just looked at her, carefully taking in the patterned silk scarf, pearl ear bobs, and countless other testaments to generational wealth and privilege, and smiled. We locked gazes for a moment and then she looked away, which I counted as a victory. Over her shoulder, I caught a brief glimpse of a tall figure, standing still in the milling crowd. I could only see the back of his head and just a bit of his cheek, but for a moment I was convinced that it was Amir.

I gasped a little and wondered if I should call out to him or run over. My mother's voice chastised me that it would be unseemly to appear so eager—though, so eager for what? Someone momentarily blocked my view of him, and when I could see again, he had vanished. Which was odd, because Amir was quite tall enough to stand out in any crowd.

"See someone you know?" Lily asked.

"I . . . I thought so, but I was mistaken," I said, ignoring her hauteur. By this time Iris had found a cab, and I reluctantly followed Lily into it.

Lily engaged Iris in an exclusive conversation for the entire trip, on subjects she knew I could have nothing to contribute. Well, who was I to refuse a free meal because of social awkwardness? I couldn't say I minded being left out of the conversation. My thoughts had fastened onto Amir and refused to let go. Had he really been to the rally? And if so, why? If he contacted me today, surely I would have to give my final answer to his request for help. And even though I knew what the prudent response should be, I found I was still inclined to be reckless.

After an only minimally awkward meal where Lily and Iris dined on some outlandishly priced prime rib and I ate cucumber sandwiches with potato leek soup, Iris excused herself to go "freshen up" in the facilities. Left alone again with Lily, I was made exquisitely aware of how much our posh surroundings complemented her, and how out of place they made me. The boy might have ruined last night's conservative shirt collar, but I had more where that came from. I yearned for Lily's fashionably low V-neck blouse and knee-length jacket. Privately, of course. Outwardly, I was perfectly serene, I'm sure.

I was still thinking about Amir and how to even approach his request. It had occurred to me over lunch that if Lily was an Other beat reporter, and I needed information about Rinaldo, we might be ideally placed to make a deal with each other. Seeing as how horribly my great idea had turned out this morning, I attempted to consider all the angles. Then I gave up because I knew I was going to ask anyway.

"You know," I said, as soon as Iris left, "I have a great deal of contact with Others."

Lily gave me an appraising look and leaned toward me. "So I've heard. I've been meaning to find you."

"I need some information, and I think you might be able to help."

"Perhaps. What do I get out of this?"

"I feed you stories. I could make your career. Tenement abuse. Other police corruption. I could tell you the location of Defender raids before they happen."

I could tell that my offer excited her, because her eyes had gone quite innocently wide and her foot began tapping the floor incessantly. Very good, Zephyr. Now you've dangled the bait, you just need to reel in the fish.

"And what information do you need?"

I hoped I didn't look as nervous as I felt. Mentioning this vampire's name seemed to be the conversational equivalent of a stick of TNT. "Everything you know about Rinaldo. Any rumors, any sightings, any activity. I need it. I'm looking into . . . something. If it pans out, you'll get the exclusive. And believe me, it could be huge."

She frowned. "Rinaldo? You mean that gin runner out of Little Italy? But he's not even my beat. Crime is at least five promotions away." She rolled her eyes.

I smiled and lowered my voice to a whisper. It didn't look as though anyone was close enough to hear, but I wasn't stupid enough to trust that. "Oh, but it *is* your beat. Rinaldo is a vampire. He controls a gang of young vampires called the Turn Boys who terrorize the neighborhood. But no one's ever seen him. No one knows where he is. But, I figure, a sucker that powerful must come out to play. I want to track him down, but I need some help. I can move in certain circles." I looked at my clothes with a self-deprecating smile. "You can move in others."

She matched my whisper. "You think he might have infiltrated society?"

"He's rich enough. And older vampires are better at disguising what they are."

She leaned back in her chair and let out a very unladylike whistle. I liked her better for it. "Dear God. This is some goddamn story. Are you serious?"

"Perfectly."

She grinned and clapped her hands. For a moment, she looked like a delighted child, not a sophisticated young ingénue. "Well, for the record, you're crazy. Even the veterans at my paper hardly touch Rinaldo."

"But you'll help?"

"You're lucky, Zephyr Hollis. Because I'm pretty crazy, too."

We were still smiling at each other when Iris returned to the table.

"Well, look at the two of you!" she said, negotiating her way back into her chair. "Did something amusing happen while I was gone?"

"Oh, just that Zephyr is going to help me become the most famous female journalist in the country."

Iris looked at me, the laugh lines around her eyes crinkling. "Goodness, is that so? You should come to our suffragette meeting tonight, Lily. We're debating prophylactics."

Lily looked so genuinely horrified that I had to smother a laugh.

"Don't even think of it!" She shuddered. "A *suffragette* meeting. I'm already a journalist. Don't ask me to commit social suicide."

Iris and I attended the suffragette meeting together, and I sat back while she held forth on the "multiple, incontrovertible" benefits to the active promotion of prophylactic birth control. "It will help improve the lives of the lower classes by an immeasurable margin," she said, and then made heavy use of Margaret Sanger. There were a few men present, and I found myself peering around the crowded room to see if I spotted Amir. I didn't know why I thought I would see him, and the excitement I felt at each false alarm was enough to make me want to sink to the floor in embarrassment. It was just that he was so unfamiliar, so completely different in looks and manner and speech than anyone I'd ever encountered.

In the end, those assembled voted to investigate the matter further and reconvene at a later date.

"A fine waste of a meeting," Iris grumbled to me, as we left the back room in the Jewish Russian coffee shop that hosted our monthly gathering. "You'd think we were selling twopenny romances on the streets!"

I thought of Aileen and Verity Lovelace's popped cherry. "I imagine if we were, there'd be a great deal more demand for prophylactics," I said, valiantly suppressing a fit of the giggles. Iris, with a yawn, pulled back a chair from an empty table in the front shop, and sprawled into it. For a moment, I was afraid that the spindle legs might crack under her bulk, but it managed to hold her up.

"I believe I shall revivify with some coffee," Iris said. "Should I order two?"

I shook my head. "I'd love to, but I have to leave. I have . . ."

She nodded knowingly, which thankfully saved me from concocting some inadequate excuse. "The energies of youth, I see. Well, take care. I daresay I'll see you at some event, soon. And it seemed you and Lily got on swimmingly. Perhaps there's hope for the darling little closed-minded debutante yet, eh?"

Iris winked at me and I felt such an overwhelming burst of affection that I nearly hugged her. I managed to make do with pressing her hand and promising to see her at the Socialist Worker's Party meeting next week. Just as I turned to leave, I caught a glimpse of a tall figure walking out of the shop. His hair was dark and curled, his attire several degrees more refined than the average in this Lower East Side haunt. I ran from the shop and onto the sidewalk, where snow I hadn't even known was expected covered the ground two inches deep. Through the blanketing white, I attempted to catch a glimpse of the man I had just seen leave, but it appeared that the only people on the sidewalk beside myself were two respectable Hasidim in beaver hats and heavy black coats.

"You're losing your mind," I said. I hadn't even buttoned my coat or replaced my hat and gloves. I did so before the snow made me even colder and went to fetch my bicycle.

I pedaled home quickly, even though I had nearly two hours before I was expected at the club. I would need at least that much time to get ready. My encounter with the incomparable Lily had at least proven that. I didn't want to embarrass myself in this adventure any more than strictly necessary. And in any case, this might be the last chance I had to, well, go *dancing*, as Aileen would put it. Amir hadn't found me, and without him as the miraculous source of my financial reprieve, I would have to take other measures. And seeing as how those measures either involved telegraphing Daddy back in Montana to ask for a loan or selling my soul to the Citizen's Council . . . obviously, I would have to take the Citizen's Council. Oh, Daddy had the money. He stockpiled as if Yarrow was Fort Knox. But I would die before I asked him for help. It would just prove that he was right, that I couldn't make it on my own in this city as a useless "do-gooder."

They would probably make me teach hygiene and nutrition courses. I hated those. Marching into people's homes like some Bible-spouting missionary to tell them that the food their grandmothers' grandmothers made is scientifically inadequate. Fewer cheap vegetables, more meats. As though they could afford them. *Damn* Amir for getting my hopes up.

It was early, yet—just half past seven—but Aileen was waiting when I made it home.

"Thank God!" I said, shutting the door behind me.

She looked up from her book, a different one from last night. "You didn't think I'd make it?"

"I thought you might forget. It *is* Friday."

"How could I miss your big debut?" She held up a flapper dress of patterned rose silk with long fringes.

I tugged off my boots and ran to touch it. "I can't believe you got this! How could you even afford—"

She shrugged her shoulders languidly. "Oh, this girl I know. Spends all her money on clothes, and this is at least three years out of date. That whole flapper thing, just a touch passé. Still . . ." She held it up against me. "It will look *très* chic on you."

"I promise I'll pay you back tomorrow. Horace said he'd give me something for this."

Aileen rolled her eyes. "If that fat bootlegger actually gives you a dime, you had better buy some food. You look scrawnier than my grandmother during the potato famine."

"Aileen, how could you know what your grandmother looked like during the potato famine?"

She dropped the dress on her bed and held her arms akimbo. "I'll have you know the Sight hasn't skipped a generation of Dunne women since St. Patrick himself drove the snakes out of the Emerald Isle."

Her accent had grown so strong as to be nearly unintelligible by the end of the sentence. "Goodness," I said, "does your family keep a leprechaun too?"

Her mouth twitched dangerously. "We gave him to Bonnie Prince Charlie."

"And yet they didn't think to plant some rutabagas."

We both started laughing. "Oh, get ready," she said, gasping. "I sense dramatic changes for you tonight."

I shook my head. "I just hope I don't get jeered off the stage. Have you heard they actually use a *hook* up at the Apollo?"

"Take a bath! You can be nervous after I make you look ravishing."

I followed her orders, and when I returned to the room she had laid out what looked to be her entire cosmetic collection. It was extensive—being a true vamp in this city required rigorous maintenance. She sat me on our wobbly chair in front of the cracked mirror.

"Don't overdo it," I said, nervously, when she picked up a jar of flesh-colored cream.

"Ah, don't worry, chick," she said, in an uncanny impression of an old Irish fortune-teller, "I'll be gentle as a lamb."

I had to close my eyes.

"There!" she said, after half an hour. "Perfection. Well, open your eyes. You can always wipe it off if you truly hate it."

Thus fortified, I saw what Aileen had wrought. A strange, fey face stared at me from the mirror. Her eyes seemed impossibly large, and lined with just barely less kohl than your average vamp. High cheekbones delicately emphasized with a light flush. Glossy red lips with a distinct impression of a pout from the full bottom. I had never liked that tendency of my lower lip to protrude. Now, Aileen had somehow turned it into something almost . . . sexy.

"Oh," I said.

"I am a genius. When do you have to be there, again?"

"Eight thirty. The set starts at nine and I have to practice with the band." Just saying that out loud sent a colony of butterflies to my stomach. I could hardly believe that Horace had agreed to let me sing the opening set at his nightclub. Admittedly, almost no one showed up at such an early hour on a Friday. And he owed me a favor after I had saved his favorite trombone player from being staked by one of Troy's overzealous Defenders. Still, I had secretly dreamed of a chance like this for most of my life. I used to sing in our church choir until Daddy appropriated Sundays for my training (over Mama's objections). Afterward, my vocal exertions were mainly confined to the backyard during chores. If Harry was in a good mood, he'd sometimes sit and listen with the chickens, but mostly he and the others would make fun of me. Mama says I have a great voice, but then again, she's my mama and the competition isn't exactly fierce in Yarrow.

Aileen picked up an egg I hadn't noticed lying on the dresser and cracked it on a bowl.

"You don't want to cook that first?"

She grinned, and began separating the white from the yolk. "I read about this hairstyle in a glossy last year and I just had to try it out."

I turned to her, my mouth open in horror. "Putting *egg whites* on my *hair?*"

"Josephine Baker does it."

I closed my mouth and faced the mirror again. Josephine Baker was about as close as I came to worshipping a person, and Aileen knew it.

"Have you done this before?" I asked, when she started smearing the clear goop over my curls.

"It didn't sound very hard in the article."

I closed my eyes again.

As long as you didn't actually touch my head—which felt like nothing so much as a hair-textured helmet—the effect was unusual and striking. The egg whites had hardened my natural curls into tight, cherubic ringlets that clung close to my scalp. It also drew out the natural red of my color, so that in the lamplight my hair appeared fiery. It complemented the rose of the dress, which stopped a daring two inches above my knees. I wore Aileen's rayon hose and her best pair of heels, just slightly too small. I completed the outfit with a doubled rope of real rose pearls—a gift from Mama just before I left—matching ear bobs, and a simple lace bandeau.

I tossed my all-too-tattered and pedestrian coat on top of this splendor and enjoyed the ignominy of riding my bicycle in a flapper dress through the snow to reach the club a few minutes late. Aileen had promised to come by later to hear me sing.

I locked my bicycle to the fence outside a neighboring church and then walked down the steps at 201 East Twenty-fourth Street. They were no different from any other in this quiet, supposedly residential neighborhood, but anyone could tell you where to find Horace's. At the bottom was an equally featureless green door with a slide for the mailman.

I knocked. "Hey, it's me!" I called. "Let me in, it's freezing out here!"

From inside came the muffled sounds of someone shuffling to the door and shunting aside several bolts. It was Horace, dressed to the nines in tea-green tails with outrageously padded shoulders and matching hat. He looked mildly surprised to see me.

"Thought you turned chicken," he said in his rumbling southern drawl. I imagined it could be made to sound threatening, but Horace was like a personification of a swing jazz riff—far too concerned with beauty and aesthetics to reach beyond the mellow rhythm of his natural state. Of course, he was also famous for being one of the most tight-fisted bootleggers in Manhattan, but he never raised his voice while conducting business.

"And I hope you got some decent glad rags. Schoolmistress is cute, but not very smooth."

Horace poured himself a glass of something amber (and blazingly alcoholic, from the smell). I shook my head when he offered it to me and removed my coat and gloves while he sipped.

"This okay?" I asked, tossing my jacket over a chair.

Horace looked me up and down and smiled. "All right. Well, copacetic, honey. You sure clean up. Get on stage, why don't you? The boys are almost ready."

Horace's place wasn't very large—the stage was only twenty or so feet from the bar. "You're going to pay me for this, right?" I said, after I climbed the stage.

The piano player—a sub, I guessed, since I didn't recognize his graying widow's peak or blue eyes—laughed, and played a little riff. I had never seen a white musician at Horace's before.

Horace smiled and raised his glass. "Tips, doll. You'll get tips."

Great. A big load of help tips would be when Mrs. Brodsky came a-calling on Sunday.

The drummer sat down and beat a three-quarter rhythm on his snare. "You ready, Zephyr?" he asked. I looked at my little band: piano, drums, bass and trumpet. I might not be Josephine Baker, but they were good players. It would do.

People began to trickle in a few minutes after nine. Horace was presiding on his throne in front of the band, and waving to the regulars. The patrons at this honorable establishment tended to be the white upper class looking for a thrill (and, occasionally, good music) and middle-class blacks. Almost no one from my neighborhood could afford Horace. Rinaldo's gin joints were much less classy and far more convenient.

The band played light, upbeat versions of new songs like the "Gin House Blues" and "Muskrat Ramble." I tapped my foot absently to the music and scanned the crowd. Aileen showed up twenty minutes after nine and made her way like a magnet to a table of apparently unattached men. She was wearing enough makeup to make mine seem like a dab of powder, and her knee-length dress revealed an astonishing amount of skin. It seemed like half the back was out! I shook my head. Go dancing, indeed.

It was only when Horace waved his hand and announced me as the opening act that I realized why I was still listlessly scanning the crowd. For some reason, I still expected to see Amir. But I hadn't even told him I'd be singing here. The chances of him coming on his own were astonishingly slim. What was wrong with me?

"And now I give you the vampire suffragette herself, Zephyr Hollis."

Aileen cheered very loudly. I knew she was only being supportive, but the sound seemed to drown out the rest of the polite applause. A steady hum of chatter replaced the noise as I adjusted the microphone. Vampire suffragette. *Damn, damn, damn. I have a head full of egg whites. My dress is three years out of date. Oh, fucking bleeder, what possessed me to think this was a good idea?*

Panicked, I looked at the band. They took it as a cue and launched into the first number, Irving Berlin's "Remember."

The intro was just a few bars long. I took a breath and focused on the shiny floorboards of the small stage. Not exactly a crowd-winning technique, but I was afraid the other option might be just passing out.

"Remember the night, the night you said I love you . . ."

It wasn't great, but at least the notes were mostly in tune. By the time I made it through a few lines, I had found my confidence again.

"Remember we found a lonely spot," I sang, finally managing to lift my head and look at the audience. A lot more people seemed to have arrived since I began singing. And most of them were actually paying attention to me, instead of chatting with their neighbors. And no stage hooks! Encouraged, I managed to embellish a little as I reached the coda.

"You promised that you'd forget me not, but you forgot to remember."

I glanced at the band and finished my triumphant high note just as they cut out. Smiling (seductively and serenely, *not* like a giddy five-year-old), I turned back to the audience.

And there he was, lounging in the front row in a fashionably ostentatious tuxedo with knee-length tails, a patterned red handkerchief and patent-leather shoes, smiling up at me as though I hadn't last seen him with a blood-mad child vampire slung over his shoulder. And though I'd been looking for him all day, I realized that the sight of him lounging so casually made my latent stage fright roar like a cornered lion. He nodded at me.

Oh, bloody stakes.

The next few numbers had a bit more bite.

We ended at half past ten, when the main act was getting ready backstage. A few people besides Aileen actually stood up to applaud, which astonished me. I should have been happier, but the image of Amir reclining languidly, his eyes half-lidded, made me clench my teeth.

"You were good," Horace said, as soon as I walked back into the club. He sounded surprised. I didn't blame him. "You can do it again next week."

I looked up at him. Aileen hadn't really been unfair when she called him a fat bootlegger. "How much?"

He raised his eyebrows. "Four dollars."

"I bet I could get a few other joints interested in the singing vampire suffragette." I almost gagged on the name, but I could see that I had hit upon my major selling point. Horace actually put down his drink.

"I *made* you . . ."

"I've only sung here once! Ten dollars, plus two for encores."

"Five, and no encores."

"Six, and you had better pay two for encores."

He stuck out his hand. "All right, birdie. Deal. I give you three tonight." He held up his hand to forestall my objections. " 'Cause you're just starting out, you understand. In this business, you gotta learn to negotiate *before* the performance."

He pulled a wad of bills out of his pocket that almost made me salivate just looking at it. But then he fished out three silver dollars and pushed them across the table.

I shook my head ruefully. "Good advice."

I stood up and ordered a glass of water from the bar. Around me, the dense crowd of people chatted and drank Horace's bootleg gin. In places like this, you'd never know that alcohol had been illegal for the last six years. Even a pair of nearby vampires—a man and woman staggering a little as they passed me—seemed to have caught the drunken mood. I assumed they hadn't imbibed, as they both had that healthy fingertip flush that indicated a recent feeding. Alcohol would have made quick work of that. I drank another glass of water, hunting for Aileen in the sudden press of people. And Amir, of course, if he wasn't planning to vanish. Someone in front of me sat down, and the answer was immediately obvious. Aileen always did have a tendency to accost the most handsome man in the room. Maybe she was even now hinting that she wouldn't mind if he popped her cherry.

I stalked toward them, barely acknowledging the compliments a few people gave me as I swept past. I would absolutely *not* allow . . . well, I had no idea, but apparently I felt quite strongly about it.

"You're from Arabia, you say?" Aileen was corked, drinking something clear from a tumbler and swaying. Her face was very prettily flushed, but Amir's eyes were straying to the decadently large ostrich feather that she had fastened to the purple turban wrapped around her head. And well he might, for each time she swayed forward, the rather worse-for-wear fringe would tickle his nose.

"My father is a king in my homeland," he said, gently pushing aside the frond.

"A prince!" I exclaimed, walking up to them. I had never actually heard Dorothy Parker speak, but I imagined that at this moment I could probably match her for brittle sarcasm. "How lucky, Aileen. If his majesty overheats, you can fan him with your feather. Or would the ostrich like it back?"

Aileen stuck out her bottom lip and sighed. "You're being rude, Zephyr," she whispered, quite loudly.

I turned to Amir. "I'm terrified. What's the punishment for rudeness in Arabia? Something terribly barbaric?"

Aileen took another drink and giggled. "Yes, is it? Do you cut off their hands?"

Amir looked as though he wanted to laugh out loud, but said quite gravely, "Oh, noses, for certain."

My extremely drunk—and extremely gullible—roommate gasped and put a hand quite comically to her face. "No!"

Amir nodded sagely and took a drink from his own glass. "I'm quite serious."

"You lop them off with your own scimitar, I'm sure," I said.

Amir gave me a long, amused look and my heart began to pound. I supposed I would have flushed, had I not been red already from the excitement. "Forged of the finest steel—" he began.

"And quenched in the heart of a virgin?"

Amir laughed out loud at that. The sound was even more affecting than I remembered. Surreptitiously, Aileen squeezed my elbow. I couldn't even feel annoyed with her, because I knew precisely how she felt.

His grin was distinctly predatory. "No, Miss Hollis. We only quench our blades in the blood of vampires."

Aileen finished her drink in one long pull and set it firmly on the table. "That is probably a load of bollocks," she declared, loudly enough that a few nearby people turned to hear what lady would use such language. "But you tell it quite well."

Amir bowed slightly. "You're very kind."

I grabbed Aileen's elbow and turned her away from Amir. "Do me a favor and flirt with some other eligible chaps? I need a moment."

"Oh, you two know each other?" she whispered. "Don't tell me he's that weird one from your class—"

I nodded.

She whistled. "Lucky Zephyr. All right, I'll back off. I don't stand by poaching, and never have. Good luck to you."

She tipped her feather at me and tottered off between the tables, and had no trouble at all striking up a conversation with a young gentleman of average looks who was perhaps made more appealing by his diamond cuff links and hand-tooled leather shoes.

When I turned to face Amir again, he had reseated himself at the table and was looking up at me with an expression I couldn't decipher. He seemed almost sad, which was odd. I leaned against the edge of the stage, where a much larger band was setting up, and faced him. I felt a little more in control of the situation when I could look down at him.

"You were excellent," he said, surprising me.

"Scimitars?"

He smiled. "Singing."

I bit my lip and looked away. "Right. Of course. Um . . . thank you."

He shook his head and signaled to a nearby waitress. "A gin and tonic, please."

When she returned with the drink, Amir handed it to me.

"But I don't drink," I said.

This seemed to delight him. "The tireless efforts of the Temperance Union, vindicated. I thought we'd have a toast. To the singing vampire suffragette."

He raised his glass. Bemused, I clinked his with mine and tentatively sipped. The alcohol was as vile as I remembered it, but it made my throat tingle and heat in a not unpleasant manner. I took another.

"What a bloody stupid name. Did you know they called me that?"

"Darling, who doesn't? And now you sing! It's a coup."

I frowned at my glass—much safer than staring for too long at his face—and took another gulp. "Is that how you found me?"

"I heard a rumor. I was curious. You are a bit of a contradiction, aren't you? A wholesome Montanan girl comes to the city, dabbles in demon hunting and then reinvents herself as a martyr to the poor and disenfranchised?"

I looked down at him in immediate indignation. The alcohol seemed to have made all my other confusing reactions of far less consequence.

"I did not 'reinvent' myself. I'm not proud of working with the Defenders, but I never staked a vampire that didn't deserve it. I tried to restrain them."

Amir looked contemplative. "The lies we tell ourselves to sleep at night," he said softly. "Fine. If you believe that. Still, I'm glad you were good at your job."

"Why? So I can murder someone for you?" I was honestly furious, now, and the taste of the alcohol didn't seem to matter, compared to the way its warmth fed my fire.

He shook his head. "I'll be the one to commit murder, if it comes to that. But you know I need your help to find him."

"You're counting on that, right?" God, his eyes were so dark close up. They seemed to suck in the light around them, to almost glow themselves. A new drink appeared in my hand without my being aware of taking it.

"Have you ever refused help to someone who asked it?" he said.

An image flashed through my brain: Amir in a sweater and knickers, a boy cradled over his shoulder.

"How is he?" I asked, sitting down abruptly in the chair closest to him. Aileen's shoes were too small, my knees too weak. This close, I caught myself breathing deeply of his impossible scent. I wondered if he noticed.

"Safe," he said.

I understood why he wouldn't tell me more—what we had done was illegal enough to put us both in prison for decades if anyone found out. "Is he still . . ." I trailed off, unwilling to say "blood-mad."

He shrugged. "The same."

"I have to find his family. They should at least—"

"Yes. At least."

The reminder of my debt to him made my insides twist and my heart pound. Or maybe that was just the intent look he had fixed on me. As though we were alone in his bedroom instead of in the middle of a nightclub. "He couldn't have been older than eleven," I said. "We don't know if they ever . . . come back. The children. What if he's like that forever? What should we do?" I took another sip and saw that I was halfway through the glass. *Impressive for a chick who doesn't drink, Zephyr.*

He reached across the table and brushed the top of my hand with his fingertips. I took a moment to marvel over the relative darkness of his skin, a milky coffee to my own antique pearl.

"Zephyr. Whatever happens, I'll take care of him."

I heard the hard double entendre, but I was familiar with such choices. I nodded.

"So," I said, forcing myself to sound light, to look at him, "you want me to help you? I think you ought to give me a good reason, first."

The slow traverse his eyes made of my secondhand dress, rayon hose, scuffed shoes and tattered lace bandeau made me suddenly cringe. I had the impression that he'd made an exact calculation of my worth.

"Two hundred dollars," he said. I didn't know whether to be elated or offended. Or hurt.

I slammed my glass on the table, sloshing some of the drink on my hand. "Don't talk to me like I'm some high-class whore," I said. "I may be poor, but I won't do this just for the money."

His expression was bemused as he knocked back the rest of his drink. "I find that it suffices for most of you."

I stood and gave him an ironic curtsy. "We're humans, Amir, not a bloody monolith. Good luck finding someone else to buy."

I'd gone perhaps three steps when he roughly grabbed my wrist and swung me around to face him. He looked so furious that I flinched and tried to back away. His grip was uncomfortably warm.

"Rinaldo has taken something very precious from me," he said in a low whisper, and I realized that most of his anger wasn't meant for me at all. "And it behooves me to get it back. There are . . . consequences if I don't. Does that satisfy you?" he said.

He let go of my wrist and I stared at him. It was not, in fact, much of an apology or an explanation, but it did feel like a peace offering.

"I need your help," he said, when I didn't respond.

"Now you're just manipulating me."

That laugh again. And why was his body so warm? "Of course."

"I'll still need two hundred dollars."

He nodded with faux gravity. I couldn't help but giggle. To my surprise, he held out his hand. And quite a lovely hand, too, with long tapered fingers and perfectly manicured nails. "Will you dance?"

I frowned, and turned around. Behind me, Horace's crew had pushed back enough of the tables to make room for a small dance floor, and the main act was ready to play. The white piano player acted as band leader, so he was angled toward the musicians while they all faced us. They started with the Charleston—of course—and dozens of couples streamed into the center of the room. For fortification, I went back to the table and finished my drink before allowing Amir to lead me into the crowded space. The Charleston is like a full-contact sport in any joint smaller than the Cotton Club. I tend to spend most of my time dodging every one else's elbows and trying not to stomp on people's feet. With Amir, however, the area around us seemed miraculously clear. Maybe because he was a good dancer—on beat and relaxed, he moved like the Charleston was an actual dance and not some kind of race.

"Have you ever done a dance marathon?" I asked him. I might have yelled it, actually. The alcohol had rushed to my head and I had passed over corked and was well on my way to splifficated.

He laughed. "Do I hear an invitation?"

I shook my head in strenuous disapproval. "Flagrant waste of the public's time and energy," I said in my best schoolmarm voice.

"Ah. And singing in nightclubs?"

"Oh, just undercover work for the Temperance Union. A wilier bunch of criminals and deviants I have never seen."

I was quite shocked when Amir whirled me around for a partner dance. His hand rested with gentle pressure on the small of my back, and he held me a quite unseemly inch away from his torso.

I am very bad at partner dancing. Daddy might have shot me himself if he caught me doing it back in Montana, and practicing with Aileen hadn't been much help to either of us. So of course I stepped on Amir's shoes.

He gave a little wince and put a few judicious inches of extra distance between us, wearing a smile that was at once ironic and thoughtful.

"I imagine the Temperance Union doesn't give you much time to practice," he said. His voice had gotten very low. I wouldn't have thought I'd be able to hear it over the din of the band and other people's chatter, but every syllable hummed in my ears like bumblebees. As though we were dancing in our own bubble, separated from the vulgar world.

He isn't human, Zephyr. I looked up at him, unnerved by how intently he met my gaze and yet unable to look away. *How much of this is real?* For the first time since we met, I felt threatened. I didn't like to think about why.

Behind me, a dancer smashed his elbow into my shoulder, sending me sprawling into Amir. So much for the magical bubble. Angry, and not a little embarrassed, I whirled around and looked for the offender.

"God damn it," I muttered. There were at least fifty people dancing around us, and all of them seemed to have rather overenthusiastic elbows.

"Don't tell me you're upset there's someone here clumsier than you?"

His breath tickled my ear. A second before I turned to retort, a strange movement near the door caught my eye. It was Aileen's ratty ostrich feather, hanging from her turban at an odd angle. She was stumbling up the stairs, her limp hand gripped by a well-dressed man. After a moment I recognized him as the fellow with the diamond cuff links she had discovered after I kicked her off Amir. I felt a grudging admiration for her fast work.

Amir tried to pull me back toward him. "What, no reply?" he said, gently mocking.

I shook him off, distracted. The man opened the door and yanked on Aileen's arm. Slowly, she followed him.

"Zephyr?"

Something was wrong. Like I said, I don't have any special senses. But I notice things. Too bad the alcohol was delaying the translation of my vague unease into something concrete.

The man pulled Aileen through and shut the door.

I didn't hear the click, but it felt like a blast through my thoughts. Aileen's feather hadn't been knocked askew. It was broken. And what kind of gentleman who can afford diamond cuff links goes abroad on a night as frigid as this without a coat and hat?

One who can't feel the cold.

"Oh, God."

I broke away from Amir and sprinted to the door. How long? About ten seconds. They couldn't have gotten very far. But they didn't need to get very far, did they? Horace was a smart guy; he picked a quiet street for his illicit operations. All this flashed through my head on a detached, parallel track as I threw open the door and sprinted up the snow-covered steps.

Prints in the snow on the sidewalk—one large male, one stumbling female—headed to the right. But they were mixed with others—the two vampires I'd seen earlier were giggling and staggering in the opposite direction down the street. Could Aileen . . . but no, she wasn't with them. My breath rasped in my throat. But my hands were steady as I reached under my shockingly short skirt and pulled out the silver knife from my girdle. My thoughts focused, short and staccato. The gentle, shearing sound of the blade pulling free from its casing. The barely audible crunch of my shoes on the snow. The deserted street. The dim gas streetlights. Aileen's footsteps disappeared a few feet away from the club. The larger ones continued around to the small garbage alley two houses down from Horace's. I followed them, pressed my back against the cold, wet brick and peered into the darkened alley.

He had her against the fire escape. The broken feather had fallen to the snow. Her eyes and jaw were slack. She could have just been drunk, except for the way her neck angled so invitingly toward her partner. For a moment, I caught his silhouette, and there could be no doubt about what he was. His eyes glowed like inhuman searchlights. His lips, in anticipation of a feed, had turned bloodred, but the rest of his skin was pale and blue-veined as a corpse. I adjusted my grip on the knife, fury building up under my rigid focus. He wasn't blood-mad. For him to disguise himself so well in the club, he must be firmly in control. No, he was joyriding, and he was about to take my best friend.

"I told you it was a stupid feather," I said, walking into the alley.

He whirled on me, and moved a few steps from her body. She wobbled and dropped to her knees on the slushy bricks. Without his Sway focused on her, she should regain consciousness in a few minutes.

Of course, now that I had his full attention, it occurred to me that this murderous, experienced vampire was staring at me like a tasty treat. Any human blood nourishes vampires—which is why we have the Blood Banks—but fresh blood drained from live bodies is apparently pure pleasure. A few vampires renounce all claims to morality and indulge in it. And if I could, I would personally pour a gallon of holy water down each of these vampire's throats, because their reckless, immoral actions tainted and destroyed the lives of millions of decent Others.

Was I really thinking of politics as I stood shivering in a deserted alley, a vampire stalking toward me, armed with only a blessed silver blade and righteous indignation? Of course I was—they don't call me the vampire suffragette for nothing.

"Lucky chance," he said, his eyes pulsing like a lightning bug. His voice was achingly melodic, a sign of an old, powerful vampire. Even I wasn't immune to the force of a perfect vampire voice. Thankfully, I'd never had the misfortune to hear one.

Oh, the dance was so familiar. Something like pleasure thrummed through my veins as I let my muscles relax, my mouth drop open, my chin fall back. He saw the blade in my hand, but it didn't worry him. Why would it? I was just a girl, and under his Sway.

He was mere inches away from me now. He raised his arm, and diamonds refracted the glow of his eyes. He caressed my hair, and I could hear the stiffened locks crackle beneath his touch. He frowned.

"Vamp freaks," he muttered.

I slowly raised my right hand, so that the blade hovered behind his back. Piercing the heart from behind was a difficult move, and I was out of practice, but I never doubted that I could do it. I'm Zephyr Hollis, and there aren't many in Montana who don't know Daddy's name. I waited for the moment just before feeding when a vampire is at its most vulnerable, but instead of baring his fangs, he looked up.

"What are you doing?" he asked.

Killing you, I almost answered. But he wasn't speaking to me. Someone else had entered the alley. Every instinct screamed for me to turn around and confront this new threat, but I knew that to do so would ruin my ruse and probably kill Aileen. But damn it, what timing! A second later, and this playboy vampire would have exsanguinated right in the snow.

"I think you should leave."

I actually whimpered, the only evidence of the truly Herculean force of will that had prevented me from turning to Amir and screaming in impotent rage.

The vampire smiled and yanked me closer to him. "Do you? Well, after I've had a snack."

I had another chance! I prayed that Amir would repent of the world's dumbest, most completely unwelcome rescue attempt and stay back. *Dear God*, I thought with fervent desire, *please don't let him be an idiot.*

For the record, I do not believe in prayer.

Amir didn't make any noise, but one moment my vampire was a fingernail-length away from death and the next he was rolling around in the powdery snow with my would-be Galahad. It appeared they were both attempting to strangle each other. I took a moment to debate the merits of still pretending to be Swayed.

"You complete bloody, ignorant . . . misogynist!" I yelled. Ah, that was so much better.

I was pretty sure the snow-encrusted one on top, attempting to bang the other's head into the ground, was Amir. "You're quite welcome," he said, only a hint of gasp in his voice. With a roar, the vampire overwhelmed him and they began to roll around again.

"Oh yes, I can hardly thank you enough. If you had come just a little later, I might have killed him."

"That's funny," he said, grunting with the effort of keeping the vampire's hands from his throat. "I thought you didn't kill your fellow rational creatures."

Behind them, Aileen had struggled up from her knees and was looking around the alley like she had no idea where she was.

"What, they don't have self-defense in Arabia?"

Amir might have responded, but the vampire had turned him face-first into the snow and I gathered that arguing with me wasn't his first priority. I ran over to Aileen, whose face was pale with fright.

"Did I almost . . . was he about to . . . ?"

I gripped her hands, which were colder than even mine. "Did he bite you?" I said, softly. I dreaded the answer. There wasn't much you could do while you waited to see if a turn would take.

Aileen pressed her hands into her neck and then shook her head. I sighed in pure relief.

"Zephyr!"

The word was strangled, but I recognized a call for help when I heard one. I squeezed Aileen's shoulder. "I'll be right back."

The vampire had managed to pull Amir's head back like it was the top of a bow, and was using his elbow to slowly squeeze all the air from his lungs. Amir had scored at least one point—deep gouges marked the vampire's right cheek.

I moved steadily, calmly and swiftly. I'm just human, I can't move even a tenth as fast as an old vampire at top strength, but he never saw me coming. One minute he was strangling Amir, the next my knife had slid into that perfect spot just to the left of his shoulder blades and up, piercing his heart with pure blessed silver.

They never scream. Or turn to dust. Or turn to bats, or anything like the prosaic images in the movies. Oh, no, when you kill a vampire, they do only one thing: they pop. In one fluid motion I pulled my knife out of his all-too-permeable flesh (like an orange with firm skin but rotting pulp) and kicked him clear of Amir. Not a moment too soon, either: his entire body began to shake as rivulets of blood gushed from every orifice. This wasn't survivable, like when vampires were dumb enough to drink alcohol. This was lifeblood and food blood. This was the essence of their undead existence. When every ounce of blood in his body had soaked the snow around him, a clear sputum followed, and then something gelatinous and fatty. After two minutes, all that was left was a deflated balloon of gray skin.

Aileen fell on her knees again and vomited. Loudly. Amir recovered himself and moved behind me. We didn't touch, but I felt his warmth like an oven, like a bulwark against the cold.

"Does that always happen?" Amir asked, quietly.

"It's worse, the older the vampire." Something Daddy used to say came back to me. "It's . . . really the best way of telling how old they are."

"And how old was he?"

I thought of the yellow, rotting lumpy fat that had sunk into the bloody snow. "A little over two centuries."

I knelt to clean my blade in the snow and snapped it back home. My wrist ached a little from the impact. Unthinking, I hitched up my skirt to replace the knife.

"Zephyr . . ."

I was glad to have him so close to me, though I would never tell him so. There were cloves in that scent, too, and tea and something utterly indefinable. This close, I could barely smell the reek emanating from what was left of the vampire's body.

I rubbed my wrist. "I've only done that twice before. It's a hard thrust."

His hand hovered over my fingers, but he didn't hold them. "Listen, I'm—"

He stopped abruptly when I walked away from him and toward the body. The popped sucker's expensively tailored clothes were useless, but that didn't mean that everything should go to waste. With every appearance of calm, I squatted in snow that smelled like rotting meat and ammonia and carefully removed his cuff links. I stood up and stepped over the body to reach Aileen. She had huddled against the side of the building, breathing deep, shaky breaths like she was desperate to control herself. I considered giving her the cuff links, but decided that she might not be in the best frame of mind to appreciate her good fortune.

"You're safe," I said putting my arm around her shoulders. She leaned into me and let out a long stream of curses, not all of them in English. I led her around the body and toward Amir.

"I didn't see it coming," she said.

Amir surprised us both by responding. "Most of us never do."

We went back to Horace's. Aileen looked like . . . well, she'd almost been sucker dinner, but the lights inside were dim and the smoke was thick and almost no one looked at her ruined rayon hose or unraveling turban. Hell, in a certain light, it might have been a style. I wanted to go home, but Aileen insisted on a drink and under the circumstances I didn't think I could refuse her. The three of us just sat at the bar, quiet and brooding. For a few moments, there had been something so horribly *right* about the simple moral equations of kill and survive. Pure delight in my physical prowess, in the perfect execution of moves that had been remorselessly drilled into me since I could walk. But I couldn't be like Daddy. I couldn't demonize a whole race of creatures just to get my jollies by killing them. This was the first time I'd been in a true battle in more than two years and I was terrified that I had *missed* it. At some point, a man came up to the bar, looking nearly as disheveled as the three of us. He took a look at Amir's drying suit and thumped him on the back.

"Did that sucker get to you, too?" he said.

Amir raised his eyebrows. "I suppose?"

"Bowled me over right in the street. It's not a new moon, is it? Something's made them go crazy, I tell you."

"You probably just didn't look where you were going," I muttered to my drink. The man gave me a curious look, shrugged, and drifted onto the dance floor.

On Aileen's third gin and tonic, I ordered my second. Amir watched us silently, but he made no move to leave. I almost wondered why he stayed, except that it seemed quite natural. In the end, Aileen got well and truly ossified. I wasn't entirely steady myself. The alcohol made her giggly again, but it seemed to teeter on the edge of hysteria. I remembered the first time I had seen Daddy pop a vampire. I'd had nightmares for weeks, and it hadn't been trying to kill me. We would have to talk about it, but at the moment I was engaged in being drunk for the first time in my life, and it seemed like a bit of a full-time occupation to just keep the room in more or less the correct orientation.

Amir casually tossed some coins on the table to pay for the drinks and stood up.

"I think I should take you girls home."

Aileen seemed to be passed out on the counter, though she periodically giggled. I leaned forward and rested my head on Amir's quite excellent shoulder while I hunted for his pocket watch.

"Dear, perhaps we should save the groping for someplace more private?"

I nodded and then shook my head vigorously. "No, I mean, where is that darling horological device?"

He laughed a little and pulled his watch from his left pants pocket. "One in the morning," he said.

I groaned. "It's closed! Our home, I mean. Mrs. Brodsky closes it . . . quite punctually . . . at midnight."

"Ah." He put his hands firmly on my shoulders and set me upright again. He looked thoughtful, and a little worried. A line of stress seemed to have been gouged between his eyebrows. "Well, I suppose you'll have to come back with me, then."

Fireworks in my chest. I giggled. "What about our virtue?" I said, all wide-eyed innocence.

He snorted. "Quite safe, I assure you. You and your friend smell like a bathtub distillery."

Aileen had fallen asleep in the cab by the time we made it to his building—a large edifice of gray stone on East Twenty-sixth Street. I assumed it was an apartment building until he opened the heavy front doors with his key and we entered the darkened lobby of what was almost certainly a warehouse. Of all the places I had imagined Amir living . . . No wonder he had hesitated to take us here. It was a little awkward, as he had to carry Aileen, but he pulled back the grate of the elevator and then used his key to activate the controls. I eyed the elevator lever warily and just barely restrained myself from asking if he knew what he was doing.

After an initial lurch, the elevator went up smoothly enough. He stopped it at the top floor. Attempting to school my expression so that I wouldn't embarrass him with any overt dismay (and who was I to be such a snob, anyway?), I pulled back the grate and stepped inside.

I stared. A prince, he had said. Suddenly, I could believe it. The transformation from the dusty, barely lit warehouse down below could not be more complete. The floors were marble, with a few carpets of intricate Persian design. Decorations covered every wall—including many instruments I couldn't identify. It looked as though it sprawled across the entire top floor of the warehouse, but just the part that I could see was worth more than everything my father had owned in his lifetime.

Amir went to put Aileen in his spare bedroom, and when he returned discovered that I had managed to take just a few more steps inside.

"Nice, isn't it?" he said.

I lashed out instinctively at the complacent pride in his voice. "Oh, wealth by hereditary privilege. How impressive! There are families starving—"

I stopped, because my vehemence seemed to have made the world start wobbling again.

"Is the boy here?" I asked, when Amir put his arm around me and led me down a hall. Maybe the Temperance Union has a point, I thought.

He shook his head. "My brother has him. His place is safer."

In my current state, this seemed like a perfectly reasonable answer. I looked up and saw that we were in a room with a canopied bed and intricately embroidered pillows. I sat on the bed and unbuckled my shoes. Lord, but my feet hurt.

"Tomorrow I'll come up with a plan for Rinaldo," I said, looking up at him. His hair was damp, and curled around his ears.

He seemed almost as complacent and smug as he had back at Horace's, but something like curiosity or tenderness dusted his features. "And you'll expect payment in full?"

I shimmied out of my hose, completely ignoring Amir's delicately raised eyebrows. "I live in this town. I see what he does to all of us. I'm taking your money because it looks like you won't miss it. I'm helping you because . . ."

"I need it." He leaned on the bedpost and slid down beside me. "Even though I'm a complete bloody, ignorant misogynist?"

Oh, just give it up, Zephyr. Just kiss him.

So of course I said, "You're not human."

He shook his head. "Does that bother you, Miss Hollis?"

His nose touched mine, his hand caressed my neck. Without warning, the fireworks spread from my chest to my . . . I moaned, we fell sideways among the pillows. His heat, his smell, the overt signs of his Otherness had never bothered me. Now, they were doing a good deal more than that.

"Why didn't you use any of your powers against that vampire?"

He had been about to kiss me, but he pulled back. I wanted to kick myself. "I couldn't," he said.

How odd. My eyes fluttered shut and I felt his lips brush mine. He nibbled my pouty bottom lip. Gently, his hand rose from my neck to caress my hair.

He froze. "Zephyr . . . what on earth—?"

I laughed, but couldn't seem to open my eyes. Which was a shame, since his expression was sure to be priceless. "Josephine Baker," I said.

"Pardon?"

"Egg whites."

"Are you serious?"

"I think Aileen was."

He kissed me again, chastely, on the forehead. "Good night, chanteuse."

I fell asleep before he closed the door.

CHAPTER THREE

I awoke a few hours later, when the barest hint of sun was lightening the sky. I was in possession of a headache fit to fell civilizations, and so at first I imagined that the distant banging was occurring inside my skull. Then I heard the moans. I might have been moaning, but I was reasonably sure that my voice wasn't that deep. Unless Horace's bathtub gin was a hell of a lot stronger than even I had realized.

I heard it again—a thump, like someone falling against a wall, and a muffled grunt. Shaking off the last vestiges of sleep, I realized who that must be. He sounded like he was in trouble. Carefully, so as not to be blinded by the pain in my head, I stood up. The hallway was dark, but there was only one closed door at the end of it, and I could tell just from the ornate designs on the inlaid mahogany paneling that it would be Amir's.

Gently, I turned the knob and poked my head inside. At first I didn't see him amidst the ostentatious furnishings—more carpets, a massive canopied bed, and what looked like dozens of antique plates and vases, all lovingly displayed; even the discarded silk pajama top on the floor spoke of a profligate way with money. I clicked my tongue against my teeth and was about to launch into a familiar internal bromide about excessive personal wealth when another low-voiced groan reminded me of why I had come here. I opened the door fully. He was slumped against the wall beside an ottoman. His hair appeared to be standing straight up. His skin was rich as ever, but his color was ashen. He had squeezed his eyes shut and clenched his fists, as though he struggled to rein in his temper.

"Amir?" I whispered.

His whole body began to tremble like a taut harp string. With an impossible, terrifying quickness he smashed his shoulders and head into the wall behind him, hard enough to rattle a Chinese vase sitting in the corner of the room. I flinched, but didn't jump back.

"Are you—"

"Go away," he said. His voice was quiet, but in a way that promised violence.

I ignored it. He hadn't opened his eyes. "But . . . has something happened?"

"*Zephyr.*" Definitely a warning.

I knelt and brushed his knuckles with my fingertips. It was enough, apparently. He flinched away from me as though I had stabbed him. He let out a roar that sounded more lion than human, and I became aware of the intense heat radiating from his skin. In fact, if I looked closely, it seemed almost as though he was glowing . . .

Smoke began to billow from his ears—great puffs of sulphur and charred orange. He opened his eyes, and I now understood the good sense he had in closing them: they had transformed into two burning orbs of flame. Their ashes smudged his cheekbones. I scooted a few inches back. I was reasonably sanguine about strange Other abilities, but this was a first even for me.

"Changed your mind?" he said. His voice was unrecognizably low; sparks flew from his lips. And I must be insane, because the first thought I had was how fascinating a kiss with him would be right now. Before my all-too-human body burnt to a crisp, I suppose.

His hands were still clenched; his body still trembled. Something was very wrong.

"Ah, no," I said. His heat was beginning to sear my skin. I coughed. "I don't believe I have."

He shook his head and the fire dimmed. "Go away, Zephyr." His voice cracked at the end of my name. He groaned and smashed his head against the wall again.

I tried to grip his hand, but the heat was too intense. "Is there anything I can do?" I asked. "And don't tell me to go away," I said quickly, "because I won't."

"Bloody do-gooder."

"You expect me to just ignore you when you're . . ." I trailed off when I realized what I had been about to say. *In so much pain.* Of course. That's what I was looking at. I felt slightly embarrassed. The lion roars and fire eyeballs had distracted me from what ought to have been obvious from the first.

"Where does it hurt?" I asked.

His lips stretched into a brief smile. "Everywhere. And you can't do a thing about it, I promise, so just go away." His voice had lightened until it was close to normal again.

"Will it stop?" I asked, settling beside him against the wall.

He nodded slowly, like a drunk attempting to preserve his balance. "Always has before. I maintain optimism."

"How long?"

"Generally last six hours or so. I'm about three hours through."

"Oh."

He turned his head toward me. The flames in his eyes had receded to the point where I could faintly see his familiar, dark irises.

"You're an ifrit?" I hazarded.

He drew himself up a little. "Amir al-Natar ibn Kashkash, prince of the Djinni, at your service."

"No kidding?"

I looked around his room. The Chinese and Ottoman vases seemed, upon closer inspection, to be several centuries old. A prince? Yes, either that or his daddy was a Rockefeller. And I hadn't ever heard of a Rockefeller whose eyes could double as torches.

"It's an honor, your highness. Too bad you seem to waste your hereditary wealth on useless antiques—"

"There is nothing useless about my collection. You're looking at some of the finest examples of Ming and Ch'ing dynasty art in the world."

Really? Despite myself, I stood to take a closer look. "Who made them?"

He frowned at me. "Who?" he asked, as though the question had never occurred to him. "I usually don't bother with the artists. I just take what I like."

"Why does that not surprise me?"

I felt a sudden blast of heat from him, and he crushed his knuckles into his hands. "If you're going to stay," he said, "at least do something useful."

I considered it. "Would you like me to sing?" I asked. "Or I could tell you about the latest suffragette meeting—"

"Sing," he commanded, very prince-like. And, well, I obeyed.

I knew Aileen had woken up when I heard her violent vomiting down the hall. I could only hope she had made it to the toilet. Amir had collapsed into a profound sleep, his body so relaxed (and cool) that I knew his mysterious attack had finally ended. I helped him to his bed and left him there—I couldn't do anything more for him now and I had a feeling Aileen would not be her cheerily cynical self this morning. In any event, she had apparently located the commode, which was adjacent to the kitchen. I looked around this place curiously, for it occurred to me that I did not know much about djinn, and I couldn't quite imagine what they ate. Infidel babies?

"Not since the Crusades, surely," I muttered, and then laughed. I would have to tell that to Amir. The kitchen didn't look like any actual cooking had taken place in the last decade . . . at least, it didn't resemble any of the kitchens I was acquainted with. No stains on the cutting board, no patina of smoke and grease and steam coating the floors and ceiling above. The electric stove was spotless, the tiled floor unblemished as a catalog spread. It seemed unbelievable, but then again, I did not spend much time in the homes of the wealthy. For all I knew, such godly standards were de rigeur for the upper crust. Lily might find the state of Amir's kitchen deplorable. Or, more likely, she would find it extremely vulgar to ever set foot in a kitchen at all.

Aileen had been in there for a while. I walked back to the bathroom door and rapped lightly.

"Is death imminent?"

She coughed and spat. "Do you have a knife?" she said, shakily.

"Oh, dear," I said, mimicking her accent, "but your wrists are your best feature!"

She laughed. A little hollow, perhaps, but certainly an expression of humor. "But apparently my neck is the really hot ticket."

Oh, Aileen. "I'm going to find us some food," I said. "Wish me luck. It feels a bit like I'm raiding King Tut's tomb."

"Do mummies eat people?"

"Mostly they stay dead. But the reanimated ones like scarab beetles."

"Avoid the crawlies, then."

Just another type of zombie, Daddy had said during one of his lectures. "But the damn wogs wouldn't know how to bring back a cat if Mohammed bit one on the tail."

He has a way with words, does Daddy.

Aileen groaned and I left her to it. Back in the kitchen, I noticed a curious squat porcelain white box, nestled against the wall beside the regular cabinets. When I paid attention, I realized that it was the source of the steady hum that filled the room. I pulled it open. A rush of cold air hit my face and arms. Water condensed on the countertop nearby. I looked inside more closely. A self-cooling cabinet? Where on earth had Amir found such a marvel? I realized it must be akin to the mechanistic cooling systems used by the reformed meatpacking industry, but I had never heard of a unit for home use before. What a flagrant waste of money! He probably used this kitchen a handful of times a year. As usual, food trumped indignation and I was soon pulling out carafes of milk and a carton of fresh eggs. The rest of the cold-cabinet had been filled with six or seven unmarked cardboard boxes. Curious, I opened one.

Sausages. Well, no, upon closer inspection they had not even that dubious pedigree. Long, pink and one partially eaten . . .

"Hot dogs!"

I giggled until I could barely breathe. Hot dogs! A prince of the Djinni with a cabinet full of street-corner frankfurters! What a delightful discovery. I couldn't wait to tease him about it. I shook my head and closed the cabinet. A loaf of bread was in the pantry above the stove, and I set myself to making breakfast.

Aileen wandered back into the daylight as I was putting the first slab of French toast on the griddle. She looked so pale and fragile beneath the crumpled red of her evening gown that for a moment I wondered if she would pass out. But she settled herself against the wall and stared at me with baleful gray eyes.

"Where's that boy of yours?" she asked, her voice oddly flat.

I flipped over the slice. "He's hardly a boy."

"Of course not. Did you two exhaust yourselves last night?"

There was something hard beneath her words. I remembered the worst moments of the last few hours, when Amir had burned so hot he singed the carpet beneath him. "He's asleep," I said quietly. "We didn't do anything."

Aileen laughed. This time, it held no humor. "Whyever not? Isn't that why you warned me away from him? Why you sicced me on that delightfully rich vampire? What a wasted opportunity."

I dropped the second slice of bread into the pan so abruptly that drops of oil burned my skin. "I didn't know."

"You shouldn't let that get around. The vampire suffragette not recognizing a sucker? It'll ruin your reputation."

I flipped the slice; more oil splattered. *"I didn't know.* You think I'd have let you walk into that if I'd even suspected? He was old, he knew how to hide. Jesus, Aileen, I try to *help* vampires, not hunt them—"

"Funny how you're so good at it."

I whirled on her. "Aileen—"

She was crying. "I know."

I ran and hugged her. After a moment she returned the embrace, her entire body trembling. It was enough to make me wish I could kill that vampire again. After a while she pulled away and wiped her eyes with her sleeve.

"I think your breakfast is burning."

After I had stuffed myself full of slightly charred French toast and powdered sugar (surprisingly delicious), Aileen and I headed back home. I left a note on Amir's pillow telling him I had an idea of how I could infiltrate Rinaldo's gang and he should find me whenever he woke up. His face was beautiful in sleep—chiseled and cold, an Arabian prince. I thought it odd that seeing his eyes erupt into orbs of flame had done nothing to ease my attraction. His hair dipped over one eye. I pushed it back and then left.

After I retrieved my bicycle and shook the snow from the seat, we headed home. Aileen perched on the handlebars and I attempted to be slightly more cautious as we barreled through the melting snow. She even managed to keep her balance when I had to kick the wheel straight after sharp turns. We must have been a sight, really, to all the respectable ladies exiting their Deusenbergs at the shops on Madison Avenue. I felt a distinct urge to blow a raspberry at their fur-lined hats. A few blocks away from Ludlow Street, a roadblock forced me to plow to a halt. Emergency workers were lifting a gurney into an ambulance. Not in itself unusual, but the gurney was covered with a thick black shroud used only in rare cases of vampire burning.

Strange. The old ones are usually smart enough not to get caught in daylight. "I wonder if it was deliberate . . ." I mused aloud.

"Zeph, I hate to distract you from your favorite pastime, but do you think we could just go home?" Aileen sounded so weary that I silently detoured around the ambulance. I guess I could stand not knowing what had happened there. Aileen went up the stairs ahead of me when we finally made it home. I trudged after her slowly—my thighs burned and I was suddenly aware of how little sleep I had gotten last night. I opened the door and was immediately assaulted by the dulcet tones of Mrs. Brodsky's generous Russian accent.

"Aileen, do you always do what that wild girl asks of you? It's not safe to be out so late at night, and now look, something has happened, I know it . . ."

Of course, all her solicitousness vanished once the "wild girl" herself appeared.

"I do not keep whores in this house, do you hear me? This is a clean establishment, with a clean reputation."

I rolled my eyes. Well, we agreed on that much. "Good morning, Mrs. Brodsky," I said with patently false heartiness. Aileen was staring into the space just past Mrs. Brodsky's shoulder, her jaw slack. If I didn't know any better, I'd almost think she'd been Swayed.

"Yes, you! Do you not know the rules? Do you not understand the importance of my reputation?"

"Quite sorry, Mrs. Brodsky," I said, putting my arm around Aileen's shoulders. "We got a bit carried away last night and lost track of time. We kept ourselves perfectly clean, I promise. Shiny as ever. But Aileen is a bit sick, so if you wouldn't mind . . ."

I gave Aileen a little shove as I attempted to move past Mrs. Brodsky and up the stairs. Our way was blocked by Mrs. Brodsky's broom.

"Sick? What did you do to her. I swear, Miss Hollis, this time—"

"I think she might vomit, actually. She was doing it all night." I wrinkled my nose. "Green and slimy. I'm sure it's such a chore to clean."

Mrs. Brodsky removed the broom. "Aileen, you must tell me if it is very bad, yes?"

As my roommate appeared comatose, I just nodded and continued pushing her up the steps. By the time we reached the first landing, Aileen seemed to have revived again.

"Are you feeling okay?" I asked, opening the door to our room. "You seemed sort of . . ."

She fell onto her bed fully clothed. She turned to look at me. "I saw you . . . in my head. I don't know if I imagined it or not, but you were using the wrong blade," she said, her voice tight. "And don't ask me what it means, I'm the last one who could tell you."

She slammed her pillow on top of her head. I left her alone.

I wanted to sleep. Truly, I longed for it more than a gourmet dinner at the Ritz, but I had promised the St. Marks Blood Bank to make deliveries. I had decided it would be a perfect opportunity for me to set my ingenious gang-infiltrating plan in motion. I had toyed with disguising myself as a boy, but romantic as the idea was, I didn't relish the thought of the torture I would endure if they found me out. Far better to hide in plain sight: to approach Rinaldo's gang as the "vampire suffragette," a do-gooder too stupid to tell the criminals from the victims. And, hopefully, they would let enough information about their boss slip that I'd be able to find him for Amir.

I took a quick bath and then dressed myself in my least-rumpled conservative blouse and skirt (I would need to do the laundry soon). I said good-bye to Aileen, but the pillow was still over her head and I didn't know if she heard me. I listened at the top of the staircase and then descended as quietly as possible. The hallway looked clear when I reached the bottom of the stairs. I sprinted the rest of the way to the door.

Which, of course, was being conspicuously cleaned by my landlady.

"Zephyr Hollis," she said, enunciating each syllable like pickles caught between her teeth.

"Mrs. Brodsky." I made no effort to hide my annoyance. Did she really think I would tailor my life to her petty, old-fashioned rules of propriety?

She gave me a long stare and tossed her dirty rag in the bucket of soapy water at her feet. She wasn't really that old—no more than forty, but it was hard to remember that when she carried herself like a Victorian spinster of sixty-five.

"The rent is due tomorrow morning," she said. "You and that Aileen have been very gay recently. You think you can afford it? There's a hundred girls who would kill for the nice living you have here. Don't forget that."

And sadly, she was probably right. Insufferable as she was, when Mrs. Brodsky said "no gentlemen callers," she *included* the ones with money. Which was why I bit sharply on my tongue, forced myself to smile, and said as sweetly as possible, "Of course I'll have the money for you tomorrow. And I will take your warning to heart."

From her narrowed eyes, I knew she didn't quite know what to make of this, but she opened the door for me.

"Someone called asking for you. Said her name was Lily Harding. 'Tell Miss Hollis I request she meet me at the Roosevelt at one,' she said."

I let out an involuntary laugh. Aside from the Russian accent, Mrs. Brodsky gave an uncanny impersonation of the debutante journalist. She gave me a smile that was almost conspiratorial.

"Friends in high places, Zephyr? Well, you should not forget where you come from. You'll never be one of them."

Bemused, I nodded and trotted down the steps. My landlady had a sense of humor? Unfortunately, I doubted her vestige of humanity extended to compassionate understanding about late rent payments.

I was surprised Lily had gotten in touch with me so quickly, but if she wanted to meet, she must have some information. I pedaled with more verve than normal on my way to the Blood Bank. If I was to reach Lily by one, I barely had any time to make the deliveries.

A few human citizens were waiting in the cramped lobby when I walked inside the tiny storefront donation center on St. Marks Place. Despite the standing offer for a full twenty-five cents for every healthy pint, the lines at stations like these across the city were chronically empty. People had a superstitious fear of vampires. Even though they might know that such willing donations greatly curbed all incidences of blood-madness and rogue suckers, they shied away from giving their own blood. The tabloids regularly ran sordid features about vampires stalking donors after tasting their blood. Utter hogwash, of course, but it kept even the kindhearted ones away. I gave once a month and delivered when I could.

Ysabel, the Ukrainian Jewish grandmother who managed the center, beamed when I walked up to the desk.

"Zephyr, you made it! I had wondered when I heard about your little . . . engagement last night. Were you wonderful? I'm sure you were wonderful. I wish I could have gone, but Saul, you know, he loved to dance and he isn't quite up to it anymore. Shame." She lowered her voice, as though imparting some juicy secret. "And I don't think the wine is kosher."

I could only imagine Rinaldo hauling a Rebbi to his basement to bless the bathtubs. "I think you might be right," I said, just managing to keep a straight face. "Also, illegal."

Ysabel tapped the pen she had tucked behind her ear against her steel-gray chignon. "Right. I keep forgetting." She shook her head. "Don't know how I could, the way Saul goes on about it."

"So . . ."

"Oh, of course, the deliveries!" She reached under the desk and pulled out a small sheet of paper with a list of names and addresses, with a figure of their pint allotment alongside.

"There's ten bruxa there. Mostly regulars. If any crazy bruxa stops you, just give him what he wants, right? You're too valuable to lose, dear."

Ysabel gave me this warning every time I delivered. I didn't bother to protest my competence anymore. She didn't know I was immune, and last night proved it was perfectly valid to worry about my safety. After all, I was toting the equivalent of a full human body's worth of blood on the back of my bicycle. She opened the storage room door. The golem, about half her height, stood stoic guard over the blood. It looked like a vaguely man-shaped blob of red clay, except for the pair of glowing marbles it had for eyes and the deep slit of its mouth The Hebrew letters for "truth" had been inscribed on its forehead. Its blobby hand held a stick, but otherwise no other weapons. It looked up at Ysabel and then stepped aside for her. She barely paid it any attention, but I sidled carefully out of its range. That stick looked painful.

"Do you have any extras?" I asked, moving to help her with the box.

She looked up, curious. A few stray hairs floated around her face, making her look curiously young and guileless. "We could spare three more pints, perhaps. Do you know of someone else?"

"A widowed vampire with three children who takes my night classes," I lied blithely as I picked up the crate and settled it on the desk. Human blood sloshed inside. "He's run afoul of Rinaldo and come on hard times . . . I think he could use the help."

Ysabel grimaced sympathetically and gave me three extra bags.

I felt far more pleased with myself than guilty when I left the room of potential donors with their long, curious stares, and strapped the crate on the back platform of my bicycle. I rationalized that even if I wasn't actually planning to give the extra blood to Giuseppe, my planned use for it could only help him. I labored through the cramped streets and hauled the crate up each flight of tenement stairs for my deliveries. The street price of clean human blood was higher than thirty-proof whiskey. I could deal with trouble, but I didn't want to hand it roses. By the time I finished, my blouse sported damp patches under each arm and the biting cold air felt positively refreshing. I put the three remaining pints in my own bag and dropped off the crate at the Blood Bank.

My pace slowed considerably as I neared Little Italy. I knew that this wasn't a very good idea. It seemed, however, like a very smart idea, and the one most likely to succeed at infiltrating Rinaldo's gang. The real question was why I was suddenly so eager for it. I'd escaped from Troy and the Defender life and thanked the good Lord for my luck. I hated everything they stood for, so why was I now so eager to begin the ultimate vampire hunt?

Because Rinaldo was worth hunting. He was the evil scourge the

Defenders pretended to be fighting. But I couldn't discount the primal rush that had gripped me as I played with that vampire last night. It had been sweeter than I remembered to plunge that blade into his heart. I shied from the thought. What was wrong with me? *You aren't your daddy.*

The Beast's Rum was technically a speakeasy—in the sense that its primary purpose was the sale of illegal spirits—but it operated with far more of the sensibility of a pre-Prohibition pub. For one, the door opened right onto the Mott Street sidewalk, and old men sat outside, puffing on smelly cigars and drinking fragrant pints of unpasteurized beer. No se-cret knocks, no changing addresses; to go to the Rum, all you needed was an unhealthy lack of self-preservation and a tolerance for strange smells.

Inside, the bar was so dark that I had to wait several moments for my eyes to adjust. When they did, I noticed that most of the chatter had fallen silent and more than a dozen pairs of eyes—mostly glowing—had turned to stare at me like I was a tasty worm that had wandered its unfortunate way into the chicken coop. The vampires in the room were all male and disturbingly young—the oldest among them couldn't have been turned any older than sixteen. One straddling a stool near-est to the bar looked about thirteen, despite his slicked-back brown hair. Just a little older than the innocent child he and the other boys had punctured to death. Oh, I had no doubt which lion's den I had entered. I was standing in the middle of the infamous Turn Boys gang, and I wasn't even that scared. Carefully, I opened my messenger bag and pulled out a thick, transparent bag of blood. The room suddenly fell silent enough to hear the faint rumble from a subway train passing below. Not a breath stirred the air but mine.

Okay, I revise that bit about not being scared.

The child at the bar leaned forward slightly. His eyes were a little brighter than the others' and his threatening smile wavered oddly. I wondered how long it had taken him to recover his mind—whatever he had left of it. I wondered if the little boy I had plucked from the gutter ever would. It occurred to me that this child might be their leader.

"Bank grade?" he said. His accent was a curious mixture of Italian and broad-voweled New York, and weirdly beautiful.

I nodded. "Fresh, O-negative."

"You a dealer?"

The bartender—not a vampire, but not human either, judging from the scales on his jaw—laughed and poured himself a shot of some liquor. "Not unless charity's got a street price."

The boy gave him an amused glance. "You reckon I should know her. Should I?" he asked, turning toward me again.

I sighed. Two days and I already hated this newly discovered reputation of mine. "I teach night school at Chrystie Elementary."

Light dawned in his eyes. Literally—I don't recommend long conversations with vampires for suggestible stomachs. "The vampire suffragette! Boys, we got a live social activist. How about making her welcome." He and the others laughed, their voices eerily high and in sync. I took a deep breath.

"You afraid of us?" he asked, cutting abruptly into the laughter.

I tossed him the first bag of blood and pulled out a second. "AB, for those of you who like it crunchy."

He turned the bag curiously in his tiny, graceful, vicious hands. In an impossibly swift move, he put the bag to his lips, broke the seal and drank half the blood. He tossed the remaining half to a vampire behind him and smiled. No blood stained him, but his cherubic ruby lips and flushed cheeks evoked a primal fear. Lord, I wanted to run away, but I knew they'd never let me out now.

"Good," he said, voice cracking as it dipped to a lower register. "So, we're your little charity, or you want something."

"Think of it as a peace offering," I said, tossing him the second bag.

"You afraid of us?"

"A little."

"*Very* good. Why don't you tell the boys and me what Charity Do-good wants with a bunch of no-good criminals."

Good question. But I didn't think "I want to help kill your boss" would go over very well.

"Well . . ." I said, looking around the room. Did those watching eyes look just a little less predatory? Maybe wishful thinking, but I pulled out the last bag of blood and held it to my chest like a protective talisman. "I've been in need of some cash recently."

"Terrible pity."

"So . . . I was wondering if any of you fine boys needed a tutor."

Sweaty and covered in the spray of muddy water from a taxicab careening through a pothole, I staggered into the cocktail lounge of the Roosevelt Hotel ten minutes after one. I saw Lily almost immediately—she had taken a table in full view of the rest of the room and was busy laughing and entertaining some broad-shouldered blond male. Something about those shoulders struck me as familiar, but I was so exhausted and exhilarated that I ignored the tease of memory and walked toward her. I noticed a few of the older ladies looking at me surreptitiously behind their cups of tea with shocked and disapproving expressions. Well, they never liked me anyway; the extra mud just made it easier to reach conclusions. Lily was drinking coffee and nibbling on a plate of cucumber sandwiches. She stood up when she saw me and clapped her hands, unguardedly pleased for a moment.

"I was growing afraid you wouldn't make it."

"I almost didn't. You are now speaking to the official tutor of the notorious Turn Boys. Turns out their leader has seen the virtues of literacy."

Lily gasped, but I could tell she was suppressing more exuberant expressions of joy. "No! Did they toss you in the gutter first?"

Trust Lily to not have missed my stained clothes.

"She hasn't gotten rid of that damned bicycle, of course."

Oh, how I wished I didn't recognize that voice.

He of the familiar broad shoulders and blond hair rose from his chair and turned to face us.

"Troy," I said. I suspect I might have sounded sullen.

"Zephyr, dear." He bowed gallantly and plucked my fingers for a kiss before I could snatch them back. "I know you hate putting on airs, but maybe you'll consider changing your clothes the next time before you come to the Roosevelt? The maitre d' is eyeing you like a blood-mad sucker."

From his rigidly parted and pomaded hair to the shine given his shoes by an underpaid Negro laborer each morning, Troy had escaped his humble roots and was punctiliously determined that no point of decorum should give them away. I knew I couldn't be the only person who saw through this, but he was a handsome Defender, and high society tended to be forgiving on such grounds.

Lily laughed nervously. "Then perhaps we should all sit down."

Troy pulled out the extra chair and I seated myself reluctantly between them. Lily was wearing a charming sea-green day frock of patterned silk with a ragged fringe and a knitted camisole. Even last night, in my best clothes, she would have outshone me. I twisted my mouth.

"So, how do you know each other?" she asked, pushing the plate of tiny sandwiches toward me.

"Oh, my daddy knows him—"

Troy rushed to interrupt my gleefully revealing explanation. "Her father and I had some business dealings in the past."

Well, that's one word for it. I would have supplied a sarcastic rejoinder, but it didn't seem like Lily was very hungry and her sandwiches tasted better than they looked.

"You're one of Lily's sources?" I asked, around a mouthful of cucumber.

He nodded. "Among other things."

I turned to Lily. She was staring at his cornflower blue eyes. Well, I wished her happy of him.

"What do you know about djinn?" I asked, taking another sandwich. If he had to be here, he could at least be useful.

As usual, professional interests elicited actual emotion. "Genies?" he said, and I smiled to myself at how the careless slang revealed more about his background than a thousand shoe polishes. "There aren't many of them, I know that much. I've never met one. Your dad never has, far as I know. They're not one of the Others that hunters care about, anyway. They're sort of . . . princes among the succubi and demons. They have awesome powers in their own dimension, but here they have to let a human bind them. They can only use power when the human makes wishes."

"Like *Arabian Nights*," said Lily, who had retrieved a pen and note-pad from somewhere. I thought it a shame that Amir couldn't have turned out to live in an oil lamp.

"Not very accurate, but sure. There's all sorts of arcane rules governing the relationship between the genie and their vessel. Anyway, you don't find many genies around here because they don't like to bind themselves to humans. They're immortal, but I guess they don't much enjoy waiting around for one of us to die."

Lily tittered. "How grisly!"

Troy leaned forward and patted her hand. In lieu of vomiting, I picked up Lily's glass of ice water and took a long drink. Watching an independent woman pander to a man like that set my teeth on edge.

"I've heard *Ladies' Home Journal* has an opening in their textiles department," I said, looking at her over the rim of the glass. She blushed faintly and leaned back in her chair.

"Textiles, Zephyr? How shocking! And one would think you'd only ever heard of burlap and rayon."

"Well, burlap is *excellent* for keeping off the blood from an exsanguinated vampire. The blood burns, you know. And the gobbets . . . well, I'm sure Troy's told you. And I suppose rayon does make a decent pair of hose, which are useful for suffocating skinwalkers back into their native form. But really," I said, putting the glass down on the table with an audible thump. Lily jerked back. "I'm an old-fashioned girl. I prefer silk."

Lily and I stared at each other; our horns locked, unwilling to back down.

"Would you like to see my sword?"

Lily and I turned to him in unison. I imagine her expression of incredulity mirrored my own. Unperturbed, Troy held out a three-foot short sword in a nondescript black scabbard with a silver pommel.

"Off to the Crusades?" Lily asked, one eyebrow delicately arched.

"I think they killed off Saladin last millennium."

Troy eyed the two of us like an approaching army. "It was blessed in Mont Saint-Michel," he said.

I smiled indulgently at him. "And the Hudson is filled with holy water. So," I said, turning to Lily while Troy blushed, "cucumber sandwiches are surprisingly delicious, but you must have had some other reason to ask me here."

Lily promptly forgot her demeanor of affected girlishness. "I've had a bit of luck. I can't believe it, but you were right about Rinaldo—"

"You mean it isn't blessed?" Troy said, apparently in such a sulk that he wasn't even aware of having interrupted us.

I turned to him impatiently. "It's as blessed as my bathtub, Troy."

"How do you know?"

"That woman behind you?" I gestured to a painfully skinny woman with cobweb-pale skin sitting with an older man. "She's at least half fairie."

Troy frowned and not very surreptitiously moved his sword behind him so it was less than two feet away from the other table. She didn't stop talking, let alone react to the presence of such a large blessed blade.

"Oh, Jesus Bloody Christ," he spat. "I'll stake him." He stood up abruptly and stalked out of the room, with only the stiffest of nods to the two of us.

"Dear," Lily said, a smile playing on her lips. "He seems terribly upset. Do you think he'll do something rash?"

"Don't worry. Humans are the only creatures Troy *doesn't* murder. Vampire mob bosses, on the other hand . . ."

"Yes, how did you know that? It took me ages to get my source to confirm it."

I shrugged. "Someone I know."

"Getting cagey, Zephyr? I thought this was a mutually beneficial relationship."

"Of course. Why don't you tell me what you have, first. And I'll tell you all about the Turn Boys."

She bit the inside of her cheek, like a child trying to contain excitement, and flipped through some scribbled-over pages in her notebook.

"So, Rinaldo is a vampire. Not an old one, apparently, but rumor has it he never goes out in sunlight. Better at passing than most young vampires, though. Probably has some old ones around helping. My source seemed pretty sure he wasn't a vampire when he first got in the business. Way before Prohibition. By the time he set up the current bootleg racketeering thing, he'd vanished from all the runners and soldiers. Only gives orders now through Dore, the second-in-command . . ." She looked at me speculatively. "And the Turn Boys. My source says he uses them like . . . 'shock troops,' somehow."

"Terrorizing the neighborhood, apparently."

"And you're going to *tutor* them?"

I grimaced. "I know. But they know who I am, and they didn't kill me. Their leader is the youngest vampire I've ever seen—he wasn't turned a day older than thirteen."

Lily looked shocked. "And the police don't stake him on sight?"

"He's a Turn Boy. They call him Nicholas. He doesn't seem like an old vampire, but . . ."

"And this Nicholas wants you to tutor him? In what, efficient body disposal?"

"He wants me to teach him to read." I was still incredulous. Nicholas had been very determined about it.

Lily laughed and clapped her hands in delight. "Well done! Improving literacy among the Turn Boys . . . talk about adding to your reputation. If you get yourself killed, though, you had better make sure I get the scoop."

"If I get myself killed, try to make sure no one stakes me."

She cocked her head. "Deal."

"So," I said, curiously unaffected by discussion of my demise, "did you find out what Rinaldo is doing now? Anything different?"

Lily flipped through her notebook again. "Oh, this is big. My source—he's a human runner with a knack for eavesdropping charms—says there's a lot of talk about diversifying. You know, Demon Alcohol is big business, but a fifth of the city can't drink it without weeping blood. There's rumors some dealer approached Rinaldo about a German biologist who's developed some kind of drink made from pig's blood and . . . this fungus called ergot."

"Pig's blood? Sounds expensive."

"Well, that's the strange thing. My source thinks that the German has found some way to brew it. I've looked this up a bit, and I suspect he might have discovered how to make red blood cells replicate. You would only need a few starter pigs, and . . ."

"Cheap, intoxicating blood for our forgotten fifth." I recalled the two vampires at Horace's last night who had seemed inexplicably inebriated. Could this have already hit the streets? "My God, he's going to control the city. What are they calling it?"

"The German gave it some ludicrous little title . . . yes, 'Circe's Tears.' But the dealer just uses his name instead." She smiled. "Faust. This is a killer story, Zephyr. It goes all over the city already, and I've barely started. I think this could be it. My big scoop."

I looked at her doubtfully. "If you're right, every journalist in town will be all over this in a few days."

She waved her hand lazily. "Oh, sure, Bill Oliver might write about 'mysterious disturbances,' and maybe even ask Beau Jimmy a few questions, but no one's going to do a whole investigative report. No one will trace the funding and the distribution and the supply line." Her eyes narrowed in very pointed pleasure. "No one has my sources."

Her gaze shifted to just past my shoulder and her smile disappeared. An odd silence had descended in the lounge and I could faintly hear the sound of two voices raised in barely civil argument.

Lily sucked in her lips, furious. "That stupid maitre d'. Let him in!"

Confused, I turned around. My body jolted so badly my chair shook when I saw Amir. He wore an impeccably tailored day suit, which suited him far more than it ever would Troy. He looked every inch the prince he claimed to be, but the maitre d' stood implacably in his path. That professional bigot, who had so narrowly allowed me entry into his sanctum, had apparently decided that Amir was beyond the pale.

"I'm afraid we don't allow *Negroes*," said the maitre d' with careful enunciation.

I turned to Lily. She was gnawing on her bottom lip. I could do nothing to help Amir, but . . .

"Oh, Lily, rescue him!"

To my surprise, she obeyed. With determined grace she ran forward and kissed him on both cheeks like a long-lost friend. She gave a withering look to the baffled maitre d' before leading Amir back to our table. I could tell that Lily amused him, but his posture was stiff with fury. An embarrassed blush rose, nonsensically, to my cheeks.

"Amir—" I said, standing up and rushing into some incoherent apology.

He shook his head. "Never mind. I take it you know my savior?"

Lily looked between the two of us. "For someone who leaves the ghetto only on her bicycle, you sure know a lot of people, Zephyr."

I smiled. "The curious life of the vampire suffragette. Lily, Amir. Amir, Lily."

Lily's gaze was rapt as she allowed him to take her hand. I could almost watch her internal struggle as she weighed his handsome looks and apparent wealth against his cultural defects.

Beauty won. "Would you like to sit with us? Zephyr seems to have eaten all the food, but . . ."

Amir shook his head. He had brushed his hair back, but a glossy lock had fallen above his temple. "Much as I'd love to, I'm afraid I can't. I've only stopped by to deliver a message to Miss Hollis."

"A message?" I said.

His full, nonfiery gaze rested upon me and I wished I could be sitting down. "It's the boy."

Lily paid the bill and walked with us into the lobby, practically radiating curiosity.

"Is he human?" she whispered when we fell behind, but I knew Amir could hear her.

"What do you think?"

She put the tip of her pen to her red lips and sucked thoughtfully. "Those eyes . . . a demon?"

"You can't be interested. He's a lot more scandalous than a suffragette meeting."

She gave a dramatic sigh. "But what a scandal!"

We reached the revolving doors. Amir paused and looked at me impatiently.

I took the hint. "Lily," I said, "don't you have somewhere to . . ."

"Right. Your mysterious message. You'd better not let *The Sun* scoop me, whatever it is." She collected her fur coat from the concierge and jammed a shallow-brimmed cloche over her daringly bobbed hair. "But I'll see you soon, I hope?"

I nodded. "As soon as I learn anything."

She and Amir exchanged a loaded (annoying) farewell and then she kissed me firmly on the cheeks, as though she had forgotten I looked like a stray the maid brought in. I waved back as she dashed outside.

"She doesn't have any taste," I said.

The subtle tension still hadn't left Amir, and I wondered if it had more to do with whatever he had been through last night than the scuffle in the restaurant. He didn't look tired, but I sensed it anyway.

"No doubt. I am, as you pointed out, not a safe social decision."

I looked up at him, abruptly embarrassed by the ironic cast of his smile. "I didn't mean it like that. I mean, she's a silly girl. Smart, but silly."

"And beautiful."

Demon eyes, Lily had called them. Even their amusement was too powerful to ignore. "Are you trying to make me jealous?"

He shrugged. "Very crudely. Will you come with me? I think you'll want to see him."

I accepted the change in subject gratefully. "He's recovered?"

"He's . . . strange, but not mad. He doesn't remember much."

He went ahead of me through the revolving doors. I buttoned my jacket, replaced my hat and followed him. Outside, it had begun to snow again, an earnest dusting that was rapidly building on the inches left last night. I sighed. Bicycling in the snow could be fun, but I was tired of coming home covered in mud puddles. We were halfway down the stairs when Troy—caked with snow and without even a hat to cover him—called out to me.

"Oh, you're back?" I said. He glared at me. Amir moved a few steps closer, as though to protect me, but I rolled my eyes and waved him away. Honestly, Troy was a giant blond baby with a love of violent projectiles. I'd had a huge crush on him when I was sixteen. He had been my first kiss. I'd had some crazy notion of him asking Daddy for permission, but instead he made me promise not to tell. In retrospect, I could only be grateful that he'd been mature enough to realize neither of us wanted anything approaching "till death do us part." Daddy loves him.

"Did you get your money back?" I asked, when he didn't say anything.

He laughed humorlessly. "Funny you should ask that, Zephyr. The fellow that sold the sword to me swore it was blessed."

I squinted against a frigid gust of wind. "Well, I'm sure he did."

"Oh, he proved it. He keeps a pet ghoul. The damn beast *sizzled*, Zeph. Like a fried egg."

I grimaced. "To call you a Neanderthal, Troy, is an insult to hairy protohumans."

"Do you have it?" Amir asked, surprising both of us.

Troy looked at him for a moment and then shrugged. He removed the short sword from the holster under his jacket. Amir held it gingerly, as though it were some fragile object . . . or it burned him.

"It's blessed," he said shortly, handing it to me. I unsheathed it and stared at the slightly curved blade.

"But, he held it less than a foot away from a fairie!"

Troy looked smug enough to burst. "I guess she wasn't a fairie, Zeph."

"She was," I said, emphasizing the words with a few experimental swipes. The air whistled past the dangerously sharp blade. "I'm a hundred times better at recognizing Others than you are."

"It wouldn't affect a fairie," Amir said. "It's strongly blessed, but not Christian."

"Not Christian?" Troy repeated, stupidly, as though the thought of other religions had never once crossed his tiny Defender mind. "What good is it, then?"

Amir glanced at me for a moment, his mouth quirking with delicious, shared mockery. "Not much, in this country," he said.

Troy stamped his foot, leaving an angry print on the snow. "Oh, bloody Christ."

"Could I buy it off of you?"

"Why the hell not. Who are you, anyway? Nice of you to introduce us, Zephyr."

I resisted the urge to stick my tongue out at him. "Amir, meet Troy; he knows my daddy. Troy, meet Amir, he's . . . a temporary employer."

Troy looked surprised. "Employer? You're not getting into the business again, are you?"

I shook my head vehemently, as this was a little uncomfortably close to the truth.

Amir handed Troy fifty dollars. "I think that should satisfy?" he said.

Troy pouted. "I paid eighty for the damn thing."

"I imagine that's more than anyone else will give you for a pagan blade," Amir said, allowing a measure of his disdain to show.

Troy considered for a moment and then pocketed the money. "Right. Jesus, it's cold out here. I'll see you around, Zephyr. If you're looking for more work, you know where to find me."

"Under a damn rock, I hope," I muttered as he ran up the steps.

Amir laughed. "Old friend?"

"Slim pickings in Montana."

We were in a palace. I hadn't had time to notice our surroundings—just some vague impressions of marble arches and trickling water. As far as I could tell, Amir had taken us here by closing his eyes and snapping his fingers. After a mercifully brief instant of pure, stomach-inverting vertigo, I staggered against Amir and realized that we were certainly not in Manhattan anymore. We stood in an arcaded courtyard, facing a pillar of smoke that was apparently Amir's brother Kardal.

The smoke resolved itself into something vaguely human after Amir frowned at him with literal fire in his eyes. "You are that human my brother has made so much of?"

If molten rock had a voice, I imagine it would sound much like Kardal—deeper than a tuba and rough and warm. And at the moment, the earth disapproved. I felt myself shaking and tried to stop.

"Yes, the very same, Kardal," Amir said impatiently. "Could you stop that?"

"Stop what?" Kardal asked, all too innocently. Ah, definitely siblings. I had too many of my own not to recognize the signs.

"You're older, right?" I said to the smoky djinn.

He smiled and grew a little more solid. "Of course."

Amir rolled his eyes. "It's just three centuries, Kardal. You'd think you're as old as Kashkash, the way you go on."

"Three *centuries?*"

Both brothers stared at me, as though they only now remembered my human lifespan.

"You'll find that Amir tends to behave like a human one-tenth his age," Kardal said, almost apologetically. "It's because he's still young and reckless."

I had to smile. "Well, that at least explains the hot dogs."

Amir gave me a startled glance, both guilty and pleased. "I'm taking her to the boy."

Kardal's figure billowed, and what I could make of his expression seemed quizzical. "Strange. Now you even collect humans," he said. "You ought to spend more time with your own kind."

Amir said something in that other language—the annoyance, if not the meaning, came through—and dragged me by the hand like a child's pulltoy through a series of arcaded corridors.

"So," I said, doing my best to sound unfazed, "where are we?"

On the far side of an enclosed garden redolent with honeysuckle and a hundred tiny blooming roses, a door led to a spiral staircase. Amir went up ahead of me.

"My brother's home," he said.

I couldn't see his face so it was hard to tell if he was being deliberately evasive. "Of course. Where would I address a letter? Thirteen and a half Mad Hatter Lane, Wonderland? That dusty lamp in the corner of the pawn shop?"

Amir didn't pause his ascent, but he did laugh. I stumbled. "Shadukiam, the fabled city of roses."

I had heard the name before—or at least read it years ago, when Daddy had brought home an abridged version of *Arabian Nights* as an apology present to Mama.

"Do all the djinn live here?" I asked, panting.

"I don't." His tone was icy. I wished I hadn't asked. Still, I thought of his palatial, isolated apartment and wondered why he would live there when *this* was an option. Troy had given me a clue as to why he hadn't used his powers with the vampire last night, but that didn't explain much else. His bouts of horrible pain, his mysterious vendetta against Rinaldo . . . his interest in me. Did it all fit into one picture? Amir had taken off his suit jacket and loosened his tie, which combined to emphasize an unaffected, casual beauty. I would have sighed, but I was already taking large gulps of air just to stagger up the never-ending staircase.

How much was he hiding from me? I already knew he was danger-ous, but did I have anything to fear? His eyes said no, but Daddy says you don't trust Other eyes. Not if you want to stay alive . . . or human.

We reached the top of the stairs. Amir drew out a key and unlocked the door while I leaned against the wall with my head between my knees.

"Your brother . . ." I gasped, between breaths, "should really . . . look into some elevators!"

Amir put his hand on my shoulder and offered me a glass of water with his other. I had not the slightest clue where it came from, but I guzzled it gratefully.

"Elevators," Amir said, when I straightened up, "are not very useful to a creature made of smoke."

"And the stairs are what, decoration?"

"Of course."

Amir opened the door. We emerged onto a large, shaded verandah that overlooked vast olive and fig groves bounded by a river perhaps two miles away. The air was thick and redolent with earth and fruit. And to imagine in New York it was a snowy twenty degrees! Kardal's palace felt like Eden. I pulled off my hat and my jacket and set my water on the balcony.

"Where's the boy?" I asked.

Feet shuffled behind me. "Say hello to Miss Hollis, Judah."

I whirled around.

"Hello, Miss Hollis," the boy said, quietly but unmistakably.

He'd come back. I wiped—surreptitiously, I hoped—my eyes with the back of my hand and knelt before him in the shadows of a screened room just off of the balcony. "Why, hello, Judah. Do you remember me?"

His wide brown eyes glowed dangerously, brighter than any vam-pire I had seen apart from Nicholas of the Turn Boys. He shook his head slowly. The puncture wounds had healed without a scar. His skin was pallid, but his cheeks blushed telltale rose and I wondered where Amir had been getting the blood to feed him. Could he conjure it here like a glass of water?

"Do you remember your full name, Judah? Your parents? Do you remember where you live?" He shook his head silently to each of my questions.

I looked up at Amir. His eyebrows were furrowed and his lips compressed to a thin, pale line.

"Do you think he'll remember anything else?" I asked, hesitantly.

I felt a sudden blast of heat from him and the boy dashed behind the screen door to the inner chamber. Ten feet in less than a second. I shivered.

"Judah," I called in a singsong voice, like trying to coax a frightened cat from up a tree. I followed his path through the screen door. "It's okay. We won't—"

"Mama?" he said. He spun on his heel to face me in the center of a room strewn with cushions. Suddenly, his eyes rolled back and he collapsed to the floor. Amir and I ran forward. Judah's eyes were still open, though I could only see the glowing whites. He trembled slightly, but not like a human having a seizure. He was speaking with a distant calm that disturbed me far more than his most feral growling.

"Mama, Mama, can we see the boats again? I promise not to be scared this time. I know it's just a horn, I promise."

"Judah . . . Judah, what do you mean? Who's your mama? What boats?"

"There's little ones, too," Judah said, his voice growing weaker. "But don't leave me there alone . . ." His eyes drifted shut and his body relaxed into boneless sleep. Amir was giving me a look I could interpret only as panic, so I picked up Judah myself and rested him as comfortably as I could on the pillows littering the floor of the screened chamber. When I came back out, Amir was standing beside the balcony, his hands bent behind his neck.

"What do you think that was?" I asked, keeping a safe distance away. Amir really did have heat-control problems when stressed.

"Bloody hell, Zephyr, how should I know? Do *you* have the Baedeker guidebook for rehabilitating eleven-year-old vampires? Because I seem to have lost it."

"Amir," I said, "kindly stop blasting me like a furnace."

The shimmer of heat surrounding his body subsided. And yet I didn't feel entirely cool. His irises glowed like banked embers; the shadows emphasized his powerful jaw line; his gray waistcoat and shirt looked like nothing more than barriers to my sudden desire. A most extremely, flagrantly, humiliatingly *not appropriate* desire.

"Sorry," he said, in blessed distraction. He ran his hand through his hair, loosening more tendrils to fall in his eyes. "As my brothers would be happy to tell you, I'm not precisely experienced at this responsibility business. And it's overrated, let me tell you."

I smiled. "You're the youngest?"

"Is it so obvious? No, don't answer that." He glanced at the room where Judah slept. "Do you think he remembered something? Maybe when he wakes up he can tell us who he is and solve our troubles."

I nodded, but I wondered. He had seemed to be in a trance. "If not, it's at least a place to start looking," I said.

He raised his eyebrows. "Boats. With horns."

"I await better ideas, oh fiery one."

"None forthcoming." He sighed. "What will we do with him?"

I considered. Reckless, his brother had called him. "I wonder why you care? Somehow, you don't seem like the sort of person who'd normally bother."

He frowned. "Bother with what?"

"Caring."

"I care!" he said indignantly. "In fact, I've always been especially fond of your world."

I thought about his apartment, filled with priceless artifacts from dozens of different cultures. "About other *people*," I said.

His lips twisted. "People," he said, "tend to be too much trouble. Oh, I know you'd be violating some secret do-gooder code to admit it, but . . ."

Touché. In some ways I did understand his misanthropy. "So why help Judah?" I asked.

He held my gaze for a beat, and then another. "Maybe I just . . . sympathize a little, Miss Hollis. Surely that's not a crime."

My heart and head and everything else began to pound as if I was about to get shot out of a cannon. Three beats and I looked away.

"I'll search for his family," I said quietly. "I'll start in the tenements near where I found him. People should have heard of a missing eleven-year-old boy. Did he remember anything else?"

"Just his name. And something about the rosebushes reminded him of his mother."

Rosebushes? "And I'm going to need at least some of the money now for . . . initial expenses."

"You mean rent money?"

"What would you know of it, oh prince?" I shot back, annoyed with a number of things too vague or embarrassing to bear consideration.

He broke into a full, appreciative grin that made my face flush in one magnificent burst. With mocking slowness, he took his wallet from his waistcoat. He pulled out ten twenties and handed them to me.

"In full, upfront. Now, who says I don't keep up my side of business transactions?"

I took a discreet sniff of the bills. "It's not the business transaction that really worries me about you, Amir." I realized as soon as I said it that this time I'd cut him.

"Right, how could I forget? Your continued incredulity that I possess a caring soul."

"I just wonder about your motives."

"So the charity girl is the only one with motives pure enough? I seem to recall you having something to do with a great deal of contracted killings of Others not so long ago. With that Troy character? You thought I didn't recognize him? And yet all your famous deeds of charity to the Other community come purely from the spirit of giving, of course. They have nothing at all to do with wanting to erase the guilt of all those innocent Other deaths on your conscience?"

Bloody stakes, when Amir fought he went for the damn jugular. "They weren't innocent."

"Of course not. Defenders never act on insufficient evidence."

I closed my eyes. It was hard to forget some of those kills. The utter shock on their faces . . . the discoveries, later, of children and families and business feuds between the mark and the contractor.

"Zephyr—"

"Fine," I said, forcing all of that shut. "I have blood on my hands. Are you pure, then?"

He shook his head. "I . . . had strong sympathies for his plight. I've been there."

I could tell that he meant this admission to somehow equate with mine, but the difference between helping someone because you sympathize with them and helping because of a lifelong quest to expiate your own and your father's sins was stark as a silver bullet.

I let out a shaky laugh and walked to the balcony. God, I was tired.

"I found a way into the Turn Boys today." My voice was perfectly steady.

He jumped and sat lightly on the railing. "I shouldn't have said that."

"Why not?" I said. "It's true."

He reached out and tugged on one of my frizzy curls. I sucked in a sharp breath. "I'm much too good at hurting you, aren't I? I wonder why . . . Of course it isn't true, Zephyr. Guilt is a reason to donate to the Blood Bank once a month. It isn't a reason to never sleep and stop eating meat and go around the whole city on that damn rickety bicycle of yours from meeting to protest to class with barely a thought for your own survival."

In the sunlight, his dark skin and hair seemed to beg for me to touch them, to make certain that their beauty was real. Daddy always said there were certain Other charms to which I would never be immune.

His hand strayed from my hair to my temple. "I admire you more than I can say."

"How do I know you're not seducing me?" I said, since desire had apparently washed away all barriers between my thoughts and my words.

His eyes crinkled with laughter. "Am I? I wouldn't appear to be doing a very good job of it."

Well, Jesus Bloody Christ.

I kissed him.

It was a marvelous kiss. Sweet and playfully hungry at first, and then deepening to hard desperation when he picked me up. And tell me I didn't feel like a chorus of angels was singing Handel's *Messiah* behind us as I finally gave in to the desire that had been simmering since I first met him. Hallelujah! I pressed myself against him with a small groan.

"I take it back," Amir said, laughing between kisses. "I'm an excellent seducer."

"I'm an excellent seductress. I kissed you, remember?"

He laughed again. I loved his laugh. "I couldn't forget. How does 'excellent seducee' sound?"

"That," I said, "is most assuredly not proper English."

"*Samehni*, Miss Hollis," he murmured into my neck. "I'm shocked, I must say, that such a proper country girl would be so . . . forward in her attentions."

His attempt at "chiding schoolmarm" was ruined by the almost-purr in his voice and his hands even now straying beneath my blouse. "This is," I said, my own delivery hampered by a sudden urge to unbutton his waistcoat, "the modern era, and I am a modern girl who wants . . . some modern . . . affection."

So perhaps I could not claim as much experience as Lily or Aileen, but I'd kissed boys other than Troy and done more than that besides. I was a long way from Yarrow, and if Daddy objected he could write a letter to the Butte *Daily Post* about his wayward daughter for all I cared.

"If you're so very fast . . ." Amir said, kissing my collarbone. I gasped. ". . . then why are you shivering?"

"I am not," I said, shivering.

He buried his face in my egg-free hair. "You're not," he agreed. And then, without the slightest hesitation at all, he tipped us over the balcony. The rush of air flowing past us merged with the vertigo of the transition between worlds, and we landed in a mess of laughter and pillows back in his New York bedroom. Momentum tumbled us from the edge of his bed onto the floor.

"I usually do that much better," Amir said. He started to unbutton my blouse and then paused, looking at me with that disconcerting intensity. My breathing, already none too steady, seemed to stop entirely. I felt torn between scrambling on top of him and backing away carefully, as though from an angry bull. I most emphatically did not subscribe to my parents' backward, Victorian morals. On the other hand, Amir was a djinn, and the ferocity of my desire had become a tad disconcerting.

"You're turning blue," he said.

I coughed, and sucked in a much needed gulp of air. He smiled at me—cool, ironic, inviting—and suddenly I was yanking apart his dress shirt, buttons flying onto the Persian rug, while heat seemed to blossom like flowers along both of our bodies. He laughed.

"Now that," he said, "is modern affection."

He'd begun to do this curious thing with his teeth and my earlobe when we both froze at the sound of the elevator door opening inside. There were people in the apartment.

And they seemed to be calling my name. In a sort of daze, I fumbled for the buttons of my blouse. Amir stood up angrily, and threw open the door.

"Zephyr, dear!" said my mama's voice. "I hope you don't mind us stopping by so suddenly, but your daddy had some business and the local Fairie Transport owed us a trip. We tried your place, but that colleen you live with said you were here. Something about some sort of vision . . . she seems a bit odd, honestly."

Amir uttered a string of what sounded like foreign curses and met my panicked gaze. For my part, I was cursing Aileen seven ways to

Sunday. A vision, indeed! I'd had no idea she was capable of this sort of petty revenge.

My mother's voice drew closer: "What a curious sort of place this is! We had to try all the floors. And someone should call the cleaners, I think a rat must have died on the fifth floor . . ." She trailed off, staring first at Amir, half naked in the doorway, and me flushed, blouse tragically askew.

"Oh dear," she said. "I do hope you used a prophylactic."

CHAPTER FOUR

"Winnie, what nonsense are you spouting at the girl now?" said my daddy.

"John, dear, maybe we had better come back lat—"

"Not again, Winnie! Where's my crazy girl? Think this fancy place is hers? Maybe she's doing a lot better with that do-gooder nonsense than I thought . . ."

He had finally made it to the bedroom door. He froze, the tableau hardly better for my having stood up in my dishabille.

Daddy's gaze seemed to flay me where I stood and then moved to Amir. I could see the tiny little cogs in his brain working—the horrible bigotry triggered at the sight of Amir's dark skin and curly hair combined with his even worse status as Other. Daddy was halfway to his holsters when I realized I'd need something a little more emphatic than a yell to make him stop. So I reached for the closest object at hand and threw it at him. It shattered with a particularly satisfying crash.

"Zeph!" Dad said, pistols thankfully forgotten.

"That was a fourteenth-century Ming!" Amir said, dropping to his knees and cradling the pottery shards. He started to see if they fit back together, but I could tell just by looking it was a lost cause.

Daddy's hand was bleeding, but he didn't seem to notice. He frowned at me, a cloud of rage building behind his eyes that I knew would find its expression in thunderous denunciations, bullets, or both.

"Perhaps we could discuss this elsewhere, Daddy?" I said. I tried to physically move them out of the room, but Daddy was peering at Amir the way a scientist might observe a deformed cockroach.

"What," said my daddy, in a clipped sort of tone that sounded like cutting knives, "have you done to my daughter?"

Amir, apparently having come to the same conclusion about the broken vase, stood up. When he glared at my daddy, the flames in his eyes had ceased to be figurative.

His smile was tight-lipped and feral. "Nothing she didn't want, Mr. Hollis."

I groaned.

"My daughter and this . . . wog, this misbegotten hell creature?"

This proved too much for my mama. "John! We don't even know him! He might be a perfectly nice—"

Amir barked a laugh, but the temperature in the room went down at least ten degrees. "Misbegotten hell creature, at your service."

I felt the blush travel from my neck to my forehead. Lord, but I'd forgotten how embarrassing Daddy could be sometimes. I couldn't even bear to glance at Amir.

"Mama," I said, "could you please take your bellicose husband back to your hotel?"

Mama gave me a wry, self-deprecating smile that made me suddenly, unexpectedly long for our days together back in Yarrow.

Daddy started to look rebellious but I gripped his hands and said, "Please?" in my best Daddy's-little-girl voice.

It worked. "Bellicose. Where in seven hells did she learn words like that, Winnie? Devil knows I didn't teach her. Can't shoot fish in barrel, but Lord, if she could talk a demon to death . . ."

I glanced down at his holsters and fingered the mother-of-pearl inlay of the one on the right. "Daddy," I said, "how sure are you I still can't shoot?"

Daddy paused and stared at me. For a moment he just seemed surprised. Then, a smile started to wrinkle the stubble on his jaw. His laugh was small at first, then booming and good-hearted and infectious, just like I remembered it. I tried to stay angry, but it was always difficult in the face of that.

"Zephyr," Daddy said, and hugged me. I pressed my face into his chest. He smelled like a Montanan forest and sweet pipe tobacco and gunpowder. For a moment, it was home again. "Zephyr, it's good to see you. Still can't shoot, though."

I laughed. "You caught me."

"I know my little girl."

Mama tugged on his sleeve. "I think we'd better go, dear. Troy expected us a half hour ago."

"I'll . . . ah, show them out, Amir," I said. But when I turned around I could see that something was wrong. His eyes still hadn't returned to normal and he was standing rigid as a statue. I hoped to God I was mistaken, but it seemed as though he was about to have another attack. He just nodded curtly at me and I hustled my parents out of his bedroom.

My mother waved. "Nice meeting you . . . um . . ."

"Amir," I said.

"If you do anything else to my little girl—"

I stepped on Daddy's foot and slammed the bedroom door shut before he could utter anything else.

"We're at the Gramercy Park," Mama said, just before Daddy started the elevator. "Promise you'll stop by? We should be there for a few days at least before Troy's job."

"And no more funny business with that damn—"

"Bye, Daddy!" I shut the outer door.

For a moment, I closed my eyes and enjoyed the blissful silence. It was always helpful to remember why I had left home in the first place. But after a few moments, an odd smell intruded, a whiff of something rotten in the elevator shaft. Perhaps he did need to call in the cleaners.

I smelled him a moment before his fingers caressed my chin. That musk was unmistakable. Nothing human could smell like that, as though either he or I were about to combust. I looked up at him. His eyes were back to normal, but he seemed pale and exhausted. He acted nonchalant, with his hand behind me on the wall, but perhaps he leaned as much for support as effect.

"Sorry about the pot," I said, preemptively.

"Do you know how much that was worth?"

"Would you rather he shot you?"

Amir stared at me.

"He's from Montana."

"And a demon hunter. Perhaps you could have mentioned that your father's profession and my existence are historically unfriendly?"

He was much too close. I had a hard time catching my breath. I ducked underneath his arm and walked to the chaise lounge by the window.

"I didn't see how it could possibly be relevant."

"Oh, you were just waiting until he started firing silver bullets at me?"

He was still leaning against the wall, and even from several feet away didn't look very healthy. I didn't care. "I had nothing to do with that!"

"He's *your* father."

"Well, he's crazy."

"Throwing stones, Zephyr? Your father builds a lovely glass house."

Furious, I stalked into his bedroom to retrieve my hat and coat. "Oh, now you think I'm crazy?" I shouted over my shoulder. "Why are you begging for my help, then?"

I jammed the cloche over my curls and attempted to properly align the buttons on my shirt. Damn genie.

"Maybe I wouldn't have if I'd known what a raging hillbilly you had for a father."

Amir was still beside the elevator, but his back was pressed against the wall.

"Raging hillbilly?" I said, my voice shaking. I walked up to him and raised my hand, but he caught my wrist before I could slap him.

"I'm being charitable. Unless you think I'm a—how did he put it?—misbegotten wog as well."

I winced. "Amir, of course I don't. It's just . . . he's my daddy."

His grip on my wrist relaxed. There was something warm in his eyes that I couldn't quite place. "And what am I to you, my crazy vampire suffragette?"

Breathe. Please breathe. "I don't know," I whispered.

He bent down and brushed my lips very gently with his. "Almost always honest," he said. "Are you still going to storm out?"

He released me and I was immediately regretful of the loss. "I . . . I have a meeting. Nicholas. The head Turn Boy. I'm going to tutor him."

His eyes widened. "Are you? Sporting a death wish?"

Half of me wanted to touch him, but I took a deliberate step back and pressed the button for the elevator.

"Just fulfilling a contract," I said.

He winced and rested his head against the wall. Suddenly, I could see the muscles in his arms and naked torso spasm and contract. He groaned and sank to the floor.

"Amir, are you—"

"I think I made a mistake," he said. His voice was rough and deep. "You shouldn't do this."

The elevator slammed to a stop. Should I leave? But whatever was wrong with Amir, there wasn't much I could do to help him here.

"These attacks of yours, do they have something to do with Rinaldo and the Turn Boys?"

His eyes glowed like embers. "No," he said. His voice was clouded with pain. I wished I didn't suspect that Daddy's visit had a great deal to do with it.

I opened the door and slid back the elevator grate. "You're lying."

He gave a hiccupping laugh. "You have no way to know that."

"You're right," I said, stepping into the elevator, "I don't."

Nicholas had not greeted my initial offer with enthusiasm. In fact, he'd told me to "get out of here before we bleed you." But before I'd gone three blocks, the boy himself had stopped me and said I could teach him his letters, if I agreed to meet him back in the Beast's Rum that evening by seven. I guessed he changed his mind. He had "a bit of work" to do before that, he said, and I refrained from asking for specifics. I imagined that I would find this job easier if I let as little moral squeamishness intrude as possible. It wasn't as though tutoring the head of the Turn Boys, while odious on paper, would do anything to enable their criminal activities. If anything, I told myself as I bicycled through the icy streets, expanding his mental horizons might help him understand the evil of his own behavior.

I snorted, despite myself. Yes, Zephyr, that's why well-educated men like President Wilson sent a hundred thousand boys off to die in a war that protected the financial interests of American robber barons like J. P. Morgan. Because of his superior moral compass.

And what of mine? At least teaching Nicholas would do no additional harm to his victims. I had a sudden flash of Amir leaning against the wall of his apartment, pain obvious in his every movement. I had to help him.

I skidded to a halt in front of the Beast's Rum around two minutes past seven. Nicholas was waiting for me, leaning against the open door with lidded eyes and a smile that made my heart pound like a cornered deer's. He could tell, of course. It's not much use trying to hide your fear from a vampire.

"You're late," he said, quite mildly. I could tell that he meant for his disconcertingly young, musical voice to scare me, but instead I felt suddenly exasperated. It was like every damn man I'd spoken to for the last three days had been trying to scare me into doing something. I was sick of it. I roughly unwrapped the bike lock from the handlebars and secured it against a nearby lamppost.

"So," I said, when the lock clicked into place. "You want to learn the alphabet in the snow, or are we going inside?"

He grinned at me. I was reminded of chimpanzees, which are said to smile in anger instead of happiness. "Still want to do this, Florence Nightingale?"

I just nodded brusquely and swept past him into the dank interior of the Beast's Rum. He was in front of me a moment later, laughing in his jittery pubescent voice and calling out insults to the other members of the Turn Boys inside.

"Bruno," he said, addressing the scaled bartender I had seen the other day. "Any more of that new stuff?"

Bruno gave me a wary glance and then shrugged his shoulders. "Not yet, Nick. Should be getting a shipment later tonight. I'll have . one of your boys check the Pell Street drop."

Nicholas cocked his head to one side and collared a nearby Turn Boy. He gripped him hard around the back of his neck in a gesture that mimicked friendliness, but looked punishing.

"Charlie," Nicholas said, his right arm draped so tightly around Charlie's neck that the boy gasped for air. "I reckon it's your turn to check the drop, right? Seeing as how you screwed up the last shipment, right, *testa di minchia*?" Charlie looked at least a few years older, but Nicholas's dominance was unmistakable.

Charlie tried to get away, but Nicholas jerked around, tightening his arm on Charlie's windpipe. I winced, but stayed where I was. I'd known what I was getting into when I signed up for this, after all.

"Nick, Nicky," Charlie croaked, "I told you, it wasn't my fault. The damn Westies set us up. I couldn't do nothing."

"And what if the Westies set you up tonight, eh? You taking a cut from them, giving away all our goods?"

Charlie shook his head furiously. "Course not. You know I'd never do that to you, Nicholas. You're all I got. Turn Boys are my family. Nothing else."

"Not the Westies?"

"No!"

Nicholas bit his knuckles, reopening a scabbed-over cut. With the other hand, he forced open Charlie's mouth. "Swear it!" Nicholas shouted. He sounded like a kid demanding a pinky promise, but I didn't laugh.

"I swear," Charlie said. He whimpered. Softly, but the whole room had gone silent, and it was easy to hear him.

Nicholas balled his wounded hand into a fist and let the thick, almost-black blood drip into Charlie's mouth. Charlie gagged and even I wanted to back away. The smell of fetid vampire blood is no more pleasant in a living vampire than an exsanguinated one. At least I was used to it.

"Swallow, *idiota.* Maybe I'll let you have some good stuff to wash the taste from your mouth tonight."

He waited until Charlie gulped and then released him. The vampire staggered a few steps away, but no farther. He regarded Nicholas with an expression sickeningly close to worship. Perhaps he meant what he had said about the Turn Boys being his only family. What a harrowing thought.

Nicholas laughed, and slapped Charlie on the back. I tensed, expecting another round of violence, but Nicholas's mood seemed to have shifted as easily as the wind.

"All right, then. Sooner you get the drop, the happier we'll all be—am I right, boys?"

And damn if every other person in the bar didn't laugh and shout their agreement like they hadn't just watched the same boy vampire shove his poisonous, fetid blood down the throat of one of their fellows. Charlie gave a quick nod and ran with that unnatural vampire speed out the door. I thought I saw his shoulders shaking slightly—he, at least, wouldn't be so quick to forget what had happened this evening.

I was still staring at the empty door when Nicholas appeared by my elbow.

"Unavoidable delay," he said, like an upper-class gentleman delayed by a game of croquet. "You'll teach me back here." He opened a door tucked beside the far end of the bar. His arm could barely reach the pull cord for the single electrical light. The room was small—less than even the space I shared with Aileen back at Mrs. Brodsky's. It seemed like a storage closet that someone had haphazardly cleaned out. One half was still filled with dusty crates and broken instruments, and the other half held a simple pine table and two chairs. A battered player piano rested against the far wall.

"Do you play?" I asked.

Nicholas slammed the door shut behind him. "I hate music."

My heart started to race. I didn't want to trigger anything like the violent episode I'd just witnessed in the bar. I didn't have the throat of a vampire. If he tried to make me swallow his blood, I'd just die slowly and painfully.

"I—I'm sorry," I said. "I just saw all the instruments and wondered . . ."

Of course, it took me until now to notice they'd all been smashed, torn or shattered. Nicholas's work, I guessed.

"My father's," he said. "He loves to play."

Well, I'm certainly not the only person in the world with daddy issues.

"So," I said, rubbing my hands together in what I hoped was a professional and specter-dismissing fashion, "let's get started. Do you know the alphabet?"

Nicholas stared at me, and then sat down. "I can write my name," he said.

I stifled a sigh. "It's a start."

We'd struggled our way to L by the time Charlie returned with several unmarked casks from what I assumed was the Pell Street drop. The door to the main room was closed, but everyone inside was cheering his return, and the noise easily pierced the thin walls. Nicholas looked up, his eyes bright with blood fever, and I knew there was no chance of convincing him to pay attention to the rest of the alphabet. I felt exhausted and frustrated, anyway—I wasn't any closer to finding Rinaldo, and the tutoring had been tough going. Nicholas had a difficult time understanding how letters were formed, and kept drawing them backward and upside down. Rather similar to the mistakes a young child will make while learning to write, but Nicholas had to be a few years older than I. Perhaps turning so young had irrevocably locked some parts of his brain into a childish state. He certainly had the attention span of a boy. Perhaps once I had earned more of his trust, that trait would aid me in my efforts to trick some hint about Rinaldo from him.

Nicholas took a quick step to the door, then paused and tossed a few dollar coins on the table. "For tonight. You might not want to stay here any longer. The boys can get a little rowdy with this stuff."

Chivalry, coming from a thirteen-year-old vampire known for his cruel and senseless murders and iron grip on the streets, might seem hard to credit. And yet Nicholas was perfectly serious. It occurred to me for the first time that Nicholas didn't see himself as evil. But did anyone?

So I said, "Of course," and followed him back into the bar.

The room was packed now, the air filled with smoke from a hundred cigars and cigarettes. Most of the haze hovered over the bar where vampires clearly half-mad for blood were holding up silver dollars and fives and practically tossing them at Bruno. The bartender poured shots of a ruby-red drink from a black bottle. Nothing else. Charlie pushed his way through the crowd, angling toward Nicholas and me.

"Did you hear?" he yelled, barely audible over the din.

Nicholas frowned. "Not the Westies again?" I wondered if there was some kind of gang war brewing between Rinaldo and the Westies. This was the second time I'd heard of a shipment raid, counting Giuseppe's troubles.

Charlie took a quick step back, bumping into the crowd behind him. "No, no, drop went fine. Not a whiff of the micks. It's Dore!"

"I told you, Charlie, I don't give a fuck what that—"

"That's just it, Nick! He's dead! The runner told me. Popped in an alley. Sounds like it was a mess out there the other night—he said the crews scraped up at least four poppers this morning. The Boss doesn't know how it happened."

Nicholas let off a long, giddy laugh. He lifted Charlie off the floor in a bear hug that looked strong enough to crack human ribs and then yelled, "A round on the house!"

Charlie beat a retreat and I edged away from the roaring crowd. Against the walls, a few lucky vampires nursed their precious shots. Blood? But it seemed too bright and liquid. And certainly not alcohol. Even reckless vampires wouldn't risk exsanguinating with such gusto. Yet they seemed to be getting . . . splifficated.

"What did you call this stuff?" I asked Nicholas as he led me to the door.

He grinned. "I didn't, but I reckon a do-gooder like you will hear about it. Faust. And it's going to make us Turn Boys the kings of this whole damn town, just you wait."

Faust. The blood clone mixed with an intoxicating fungus that Lily had told me about. It had hit the streets even sooner than she thought— probably outside Horace's, given the similarities between these inebriated vampires and the two I'd seen last night. Cleanup crews had dealt with no less than four exsanguinated vampires this morning. I looked around the frenzy inside the Beast's Rum. The atmosphere was charged, just an inebriated incident away from violence. Kings of the whole damn town? I had no doubt in my mind that Nicholas spoke the clear, awful truth.

I wanted another encounter with Daddy like I wanted to fight a horde of zombies with an iron spoon, but I was afraid of what he might do if I didn't preemptively discuss a few parameters with him. And, of course, I was rather curious about what kind of commission Troy had snagged that would necessitate dragging my famous daddy all the way from Montana to help. It must be a big hunt. The Gramercy Park Hotel was more than a mile away from the Beast's Rum, but at least the ride gave me time to think. I wasn't sure what unnerved me more about Faust:

the sudden, unheralded appearance of a legal drug for vampires or the fact that it would make Rinaldo and the Turn Boys the undisputed kings of Manhattan's organized crime. And where power grew, violence was never far behind.

Too soon I saw the familiar wrought-iron gates and perfectly manicured topiary of Gramercy Park. Like Madison Avenue, this part of town alternately intimidated and infuriated me, but I had to admit that Troy knew how to treat a partner. I left my bicycle with the astonished concierge and then entered the elevator. This new hotel was at the pinnacle of New York chic. If Troy could afford to put my parents up here, he must be doing even better with his Defenders than I'd thought. The elevator operator wore a red velvet jacket with gold epaulets and embossed buttons. He seemed a little disdainful of my presence; his elevator was apparently used to more elegant personages.

"Penthouse?" he said, incredulously, when I named the floor.

"I'd ride up with the freight, but I don't think my daddy would appreciate it," I said sweetly.

"Your daddy . . ." He cleared his throat. "Mr. Hollis?"

I nodded.

He turned back to the controls, but I enjoyed the chagrined blush on the nape of his neck the entire ride up. To be perfectly honest, though, even I was shocked that Daddy had managed to score himself some of the priciest rooms available in this golden city. He might get the royal treatment in Yarrow and Butte, but New York was an altogether larger pond.

There was only one set of doors on this floor, so I knocked. Mama answered the door in a blue and burgundy kimono that made her look shockingly in fashion.

"Zephyr!" she said, hugging me like we hadn't just seen each other that afternoon. Then again, perhaps we were all better off pretending that had never happened. "Come in, your father's just taking care of his collection."

"Collection" was my mother's euphemism for Daddy's weapons.

Silver bullets were a convenient, but blunt-force instrument against many Others—especially vampires. So Daddy and his type of Defenders preferred old-fashioned blessed blades. At this moment, he was engaged in honing his knives to a razor-thin edge. He usually sang while he did this—disturbing, bloody lyrics he tacked on to traditional mining songs. And why not? All he had to do was change the manner of violent death. He and Troy used to get ossified after successful hunts in Yarrow and roar these songs late into the night. It looked to me like Daddy was expecting to have some old-time fun.

"Hello, Daddy," I said, when he didn't look up at me.

"Zephyr," he said. He almost never used my full name. My goodness, he was sulking!

"Daddy, what did you think I was doing in New York, anyway? Bible study and soup kitchens?"

He didn't look up. "I thought," he said, sliding the blade down the wetstone with a shudder-inducing flare, "that you were still my little girl. I guess I was wrong. Cause my little girl doesn't go giving herself away to damn pagan wog demons!"

He stabbed the knife in the table and took out the next from his carrying case.

"He is a djinn, Daddy. A prince of the Djinni, in fact, so you can take your—"

Mama winced. "Honey . . ."

"Doesn't matter what he is—"

"For once we agree, Daddy! It doesn't matter, because I'm a modern woman, in the modern era, in a modern city, and I can damn well give myself away to whoever I please!"

"Whomever, dear."

Daddy and I stared at my mother.

"Winnie," he said, his voice pained, "do you always have to do that?"

"Well, if she's going to teach those unfortunate illiterate immigrants how to read, she ought to at least speak properly."

Daddy and I looked at each other. He rolled his eyes and Mama pretended not to notice. "Sit down, little girl. I'm tired of looking up at you."

And thus the storm passed. Daddy still wasn't happy about Amir, but I could tell that he'd resigned himself to the situation. You might think Daddy is the kind to disown a disobedient daughter, but that's only if you buy his act. Daddy might hate a lot of things, but he loves me and Mama and the rest of us a lot more than that. I don't think there's a thing I could do to push him away. Not really. He'll always be there for me, and I'll always feel like I might want to kill him.

"So," I said, when I had properly admired his knives and tested their balance, "what's this fancy mission Troy's brought you in for? It must be big, if he's putting you up in a posh place like this."

Daddy put the last blade back in his case and folded it up carefully. "Huge, Zeph. A whole sucker nest. Real nasty buggers—all turned too young, they say, and cruel like you wouldn't believe. Torture, you know. Slow deaths. Bleeding, burning. Anyway, some guy has put up the cash to get rid of 'em, but Troy can't do this one on his own. So he asked me to come down."

My hands were shaking. I could hardly believe what I was hearing. "This nest, Daddy . . . they have a name?"

"Yeah. You must've heard of them, with all your do-gooder stuff. Turn Boys."

Bloody stakes. "And when do you think you're going to . . . ah . . . wipe them out?"

He shrugged. "Next few days. Troy says the client will give us the word when they're all in one place. Then we strike. Why, honey? You want in? I promise Troy will give you a good cut. At least six percent of the take. What this guy's paying us, that's good money."

Six percent? That must mean Daddy was getting at least thirty. He hadn't become the most famous demon hunter in Montana without a knack for deal-making. "Actually, Daddy, I have a problem. See, that nest you want to exterminate? I kind of need them alive for the next few days. I have another . . . uh, contract, and I need to use the Turn Boys to get some information. And if you kill them, no information."

Daddy looked at me like I'd sprouted horns, but Mama just narrowed her eyes.

"It's that Amir, isn't it?" she said.

I swallowed. "Well, yes. He's . . . well, something happened to him, I'm not sure what, but I think it's making him sick and he asked me to help."

Daddy sat up. "And that's it? He asks, you help? Sweetie, your heart's too big for your damn chest."

"Well, he's paying me. He's got a lot of money, you know. And anyway, it's a job and you can see how yours might cause mine some trouble."

Daddy gnawed on the inside of his lip—what he always did when Mama didn't allow him to smoke his pipe indoors. "I can see that, honey . . ."

"So you'll hold off?"

He shook his head slowly. "I can't really promise that. This is a bad bunch of suckers. If we get the chance, we gotta strike."

"And what about Amir?"

"Well, he's a man, ain't he? Maybe he should solve his own damn problems instead of paying my little girl like she's for sale!"

Oh lordy, not again. "Fine, fine. Could you at least tell me who's paying Troy? Or is that too much effort?"

Daddy looked like he was about to yell, but Mama put her hand on his shoulder. "We can't, sweetie. Troy hasn't told us. I'm not even sure he knows. Apparently the whole affair is very secretive."

I stood up. "This," I said, glaring between the two of them, "has been a lovely day. Thank you so much for your help."

Mama stopped me on the way to the door and handed me a cardboard box covered in gold foil.

"Hotel gave them to us, but I don't like chocolate and you know your daddy's allergic to strawberries. No animals, I promise. You look like you could stand some more food, Zephyr."

I hugged her. "Thanks, Mama. I'll talk to you tomorrow." I pitched my voice so Daddy could hear. "And don't you dare go hunting vampires without telling me first."

It was nearly eleven, and Mrs. Brodsky wouldn't hesitate to lock me out at midnight, but I still had to see Amir. Daddy's news about his mission couldn't wait. The snow that had restricted itself to flurries all night was now falling in wet, lacy curtains. I hunched over my handlebars and pedaled into the shrieking wind, which plastered the heavy, wet flakes against my exposed skin. I looked longingly at the few cabs that trundled past me, but didn't think any of them would willingly take my bike on board without Iris to force the issue. And in any case, I needed to save my money—I could count on Mrs. Brodsky to demand her share tomorrow. After struggling against the wind, I finally slid to a stop twenty minutes later, nearly frozen solid in my slush-filled boots and wet jacket. I walked to the warehouse door.

I stared at the massive, industrial padlock for nearly half a minute. Of course. The warehouse was locked after hours.

"Trust me to bike over half the city in a blizzard and forget I don't have a damn key," I muttered. I looked around, vainly hoping for some kind of doorbell, but of course even if this place had one, Amir wouldn't hear it all the way at the top of the building. Should I just go back home? The thought of riding another half hour in the snow made me want to curl in a ball and cry. Which would hardly befit the image of a hardy, tough-as-nails social activist, but there you go. It had been a long day.

"Oh, fuck me," I muttered, swinging a waterlogged leg back over my bike.

"I would, if I didn't think your father would use me for target practice."

I spun around so fast my jacket got tangled in the handlebars, causing me to stumble backward and sprawl in the snow. Amir's smiling, imperturbable face loomed above me.

"What are you doing here?" I yanked too hard at my jacket and heard something rip.

"Enjoying the show, I think."

"Goddamn smug fire-breathing djinn," I said, finally tearing myself clear of the bicycle. I stood up. "Are we going to go inside? Or would you rather watch me freeze to death?"

He blinked, as though it hadn't occurred to him that I might be cold. Of course, he was wearing nothing but trousers and a silk shirt, but he radiated heat like a potbelly stove. He wiped away a few damp curls plastered to my forehead, and at the instant of his touch I felt the world lurch around me.

We stood in his foyer. I dripped a puddle onto the marble floor while he lounged on the couch, as though he hadn't been standing on the sidewalk in a New York blizzard three seconds ago.

"I assume you must have some news," Amir said. I shrugged out of my jacket. I was tempted to take off my shirt as well, but the thought made me feel unexpectedly wary and shy. The events of this afternoon already felt like they'd happened to a different person. It couldn't possibly have been Zephyr Hollis who kissed the handsome djinn, tumbled into his bed, and was summarily tossed out of it by her gun-toting father? I hadn't imagined the mutual attraction, but it seemed likely that Daddy dearest had changed the equation. And I had no way of knowing how serious he'd been—even before the destroyed Ming vase. Did I really want to get involved with some cavalier, womanizing, materialistic, spendthrift djinn who had apparently not heard of a social movement since the schoolmarms took away his legal alcohol?

"You do have news, don't you? Unless you'd like to finish what we—"

"Just business," I said quickly, and sat down beside him. I wondered if he radiated a little extra heat for my benefit, because I suddenly felt warmer than I had for the last several hours.

"Ah," I said, leaning back against his rich brocade cushions, "sorry about your couch. I'm all wet."

"You destroy priceless antiques, yet apologize for water damage. Are you stalling?"

I sighed. Maybe I was. Daddy's news wasn't pleasant, but Amir needed to know. He seemed remarkably calm while I explained everything, but by the time I finished I could tell his mood had turned bleak. For the first time, I wondered how long his attack had lasted that morning.

"Amir," I said, tentatively, "how are you doing? Are the attacks—"

"As unpleasant as you remember," he said. His voice was sharp, final. He obviously didn't want to discuss it. "Your tutoring scheme . . . I see you made it back alive. Did you learn anything? Do you think you'll be able to find out where Rinaldo is before your father plugs them all full of silver bullets?"

I winced. "Well . . . Dore, you know, Rinaldo's fabled second-in-command, the only one who's seen his face in the last ten years? He died last night along with four others. They just found the body, but no one knows who did it."

"Maybe another gang? Or an internal hit, and they want it to look that way. It should throw Rinaldo off balance, though. He'll have to use someone else to speak to the officers. You think this Nicholas is close to him?"

"I don't know, I just get that feeling. I was going to take it slow, see if I could gain his trust, but Daddy and Troy's contract changes things. I'll have to see what I can do in the next few days. He has some kind of close connection to Rinaldo. I just have to figure out what."

Amir shook his head. "And then he'll kill you outright, or bleed you to death because he can't turn you. This is a bad idea."

I groaned. "And you have a better one? Spare me the chivalry, Amir, I've been getting it from everyone today. I need the money, you need the help. Let's leave it at that. Unless you think my gender obviates my right to risk my safety."

Amir stared at me for several long, uncomfortable seconds. Then he broke into a sudden grin. "Obviates my right to risk my safety." His mimicry was a little uncanny, right down to the hint of Montana drawl that always infects my speech when I'm angry. "Zephyr, *habibti*, I'm fully behind your right to risk your safety. It would just make me happier if you didn't end up on a slab in the basement of the Tombs."

Impulsively, I put my hand on his elbow. "I'm in no hurry to get there, either. I'll be careful."

Amir leaned forward until our noses touched and my eyes crossed. I could hardly breathe. But then he backed away with a sigh.

"I went through a lot of trouble to get that vase," he said wistfully.

My stomach twisted. "Yes, well . . . sorry about that." I looked up at his bemused expression and relaxed. "How did you get it, anyway? Rob an auction at Christie's?"

He snorted. "Just a well-timed temple fire. They guarded the antiques like dragons at that place, and refused to sell it to me."

"You set fire to a temple so you could get a *vase*? Was anyone killed?"

He looked caught out, like he'd expected me to chuckle over his youthful hijinks. "I . . . I mean, I doubt it. I pretended to be a demon and made a lot of noise."

"Pretended."

He ran his hand through his hair. "Right. Ming vases are a tool of the ruling class to suppress the proletariat. Apologies."

I rolled my eyes. "You are almost insufferable, Amir."

"Almost?"

I could forgive a great deal coupled with that smile. He cupped the back of my head in his hand, saying something low under his breath in that language of his I didn't understand. I loved the sound of it, though—liquid, like a stream, but peppered with rocks. I couldn't trust a voice like that. Too beautiful, and too unknowable. Other. I started to shiver again.

"I have to get home," I whispered. "Mrs. Brodsky will lock me out again."

His lips brushed mine, gentle as the silk of his shirt. "Would that be so bad? You could stay here."

Yes. No. Yes. "I . . ."

I squeezed my eyes shut, grabbed a fistful of his unruly black hair, and attacked. My tongue slid across his, rough and sweet, and traced the contours of his perfect teeth. He nibbled my lip while his skin blossomed like a hothouse against mine. Yes. Yes. Yes. No.

"I have to get back," I said, backing away so quickly I nearly fell off the couch.

Amir rubbed his mouth ruefully. "I clearly have to work on technique." He stood up. "Get your things. I'll take you there. No way you'll get back in time, otherwise. If you're going to die, at least make it respectable, like at the hands of murderous vampire thugs. Freezing to death would be beneath your dignity."

I opened the door to the boarding house in a daze, my nostrils still filled with his crackling scent, my body still radiating his warmth. I leaned against the hallway wall for a minute, elation warring with bone-jarring exhaustion. I needed to sleep. I wanted to sleep with Amir. I was well and truly screwed.

The hall was dark, but drafty, as though someone had left the front door open for a long time. To my surprise, a low light was still on in the kitchen, and I heard the scuffling of someone inside.

"Katya?" I whispered. "You shouldn't have waited up—"

I stopped abruptly on the threshold. The person sitting on a stool by the stove wasn't Katya, but Mrs. Brodsky. The resident dragon looked even worse than I felt—her eyes were the kind of bloodshot red-gray that I usually noted only in the single mothers I visited for the Citizen's Council. She was smoking a clumsily hand-rolled cigarette, and blowing in jittery puffs toward the drafty window.

"What do you do all night, Miss Zephyr? What could be so important, anyway?"

Given the disaster with Amir this afternoon, the remark felt like vinegar on a fresh wound. I shrugged my shoulders. "Good night, Mrs. Brodsky."

"Zephyr, wait."

"Yes?

"Aileen . . . is she quite well? She stayed in her room all day, she won't answer when I call. Is it a boy? I know what you modern girls do with boys these days, it would make a sailor blush."

I grimaced. If only. "She just . . . had a rough night. She'll be fine."

Mrs. Brodsky glared at me. "I know you, Miss Zephyr. I know the sorts of things you get into. You should not drag poor Aileen into your mischief. Your vampires and demons and fairie godmothers."

I valiantly suppressed the urge to roll my eyes and said, as pleasantly as possible, "I will attempt to be an influence to the good. Is that all?"

"You are forgetting something?"

She gave me a hard look, but I was too tired to attempt to decipher her preferred language of nonverbal shame and intimidation.

She shook her head. "It is past midnight. Sunday, Zephyr."

Ah, of course. I gave her a tight-lipped smile and fished Amir's wad of cash from my pocket. I counted out twenty-five dollars in slightly damp bills and tossed them on the stovetop.

"For the next two months. Good night, Mrs. Brodsky."

The lamp that usually rested at the top of the stairs had vanished. It was probably Lizzy, our across-the-hall neighbor, who was terrified of rats and refused to travel even three feet in the dark. She tended to hoard the communal lamp in the winter, when the rodents liked to huddle indoors.

"Do you think she's afraid of turning into a were-rat?" I asked Aileen once. Aileen had just stared at me.

"There's such a thing as a were-rat?" she said.

"Oh, don't worry," I'd said blithely. "They're not common."

Of course, now, creeping down the hall in my damp, Amir-scented clothing, I suddenly found myself jumping at every creak and shuffle in the dark. I almost drew my knife, but the thought of a former demon hunter trying to stake a cockroach was just a little too embarrassing. I eased alongside our door and then relaxed. See, nothing there.

My hand was on the doorknob when something shrieked and clawed me across my forearm. I whirled, back against the wall and silver blade in my hand nearly as fast. The thing—just a blue-black blur against a light wood floor—launched itself at my head. I dropped the knife and caught the creature as it sailed past. Before it could struggle much—I'd pegged this as a revenant *something* and knew its strength would surprise me—I grabbed the back of its tiny head and twisted until I heard a familiar crunch. No Other can survive a severed spinal cord. It's the cleanest kill you can make, but also the most difficult.

I was panting with exertion, but otherwise felt bizarrely calm. My hands didn't even shake as I held the furry creature up to the dim light filtering in through the window. Not a rat, but a small cat. From its unkempt fur and scarred tail, I guessed it must have been a stray. Some-one had branded the marks of a revenant on its back, and the wounds were raw enough to be recent.

And meant for me. A piece of paper had been tied around its neck with a bit of red ribbon. When had this been left here? This revenant might be small, but revenant *crabs* have been known to kill people who weren't prepared. What if Aileen had needed to use the bathroom? For the first time since the attack, I started to feel scared. I'd never forgive myself if something happened to her because of my own mess (and neither would Mrs. Brodsky). But who would do this? I put down the dead cat and read the note.

A PRESENT FOR TUTORING MY BOYS.

Dear God. Rinaldo. He knew something. I forced myself to breathe past the sudden constriction in my chest. Calm, Zephyr. He couldn't have learned everything. But how much? Could he have guessed my connection to Amir? Or was there some other reason he didn't want me around Nicholas? I stuffed the note hastily into my pocket and sheathed my knife. Whatever its import, I had to get rid of the revenant. I climbed the ladder to the roof, and tossed the cat into the alley. The rats would take far better care of it than I could. My arm was throbbing by the time I came back inside, so I washed the scratches—not very deep, thank-fully—in the sink before finally entering our room.

The lamp was out, but Aileen sat up as soon as I opened the door. "Is it safe to go out?" she asked. Her eyes were very wide and her face was ghostly pale. Had she heard my fight outside? But how would she have known what it was?

"Yes," I said.

Aileen nodded. She released the sheets and lowered herself with painful care onto her bed. "Good." She looked over at me. "Are you okay?"

I turned so my torso hid my scratched arm. "I'm fine. It was just a stray cat."

"Oh, was that it?" She sounded mildly surprised. "I just saw it was some kind of Other. Small, but dangerous. I thought it might be one of Lizzy's were-rats."

I pulled my nightgown over my head. "You saw it?"

"Oh no, not that kind of seeing. The other kind. My grandmother's kind."

I suddenly realized that Aileen was wearing the exact same clothes she had this morning. Her hair was matted as though she hadn't combed it all day. She looked terrible.

"Aileen, what's going on?"

"I saw you with Amir again. He's strange, Zephyr. You should be careful. I can't see it clearly, but I know you'll hurt yourself if you do what he wants."

Oh, no. Aileen sounded just like an old Irish soothsayer, but this time I knew she wasn't joking. I took the lamp from beside her bed and lit it hastily. In its glow she looked even more haggard than before.

"You think that you have the Sight?"

She buried her face in her pillow. "It's been hitting me all day. Every time I try to get up another one comes. Your parents came and I suddenly knew exactly where you were."

"Yeah, about that . . ."

Her smile was thin, but genuine. "Sorry. I realized later you probably wouldn't appreciate a parental visit."

"You could say so."

"Lord Jesus, I'm so tired I want to pass out. I think I might die."

This had been some goddamn day. How to phrase this as delicately as possible? "Do you think you might just be . . . upset?"

She narrowed her eyes, but I could tell she was interested. "About the other night, you mean."

"My first time on a vampire hit . . . well, it gets to you, right? It's not pretty. I could barely eat for a week. Have you eaten today?"

She shook her head.

"Maybe you should eat, and try to sleep and ignore the . . . visions, if you get them again. Maybe you did get the Sight this late, but it's pretty rare, right? Chances are you're just scared."

Aileen stuck out her jaw. "But how do you explain how I knew where you were?"

"You already know that Amir and I . . . well, we're working together, at least, so it wasn't that hard a guess."

"What about the were-rat?"

"Well, it *wasn't* a were-rat. It was a stray cat, and you probably heard it scratching the door."

"Bloody hell." Aileen put her hand on her forehead and sat up in bed. "Oh, bloody hell. If I am ever so fucking stupid again, I give you permission to bean me. Just keep going until I start making sense again. I'm going to get some food."

I smiled. "Wait, I have something that should make you feel better." I went to my trunk, where I'd stashed my finery from the night before and took out the two tiny objects secreted at the bottom.

"I think these are rightfully yours," I said, handing her two diamond cuff links.

She stared at them for a blank moment. Her hand shook when she remembered. "Are these . . . ?"

"He couldn't use them anymore."

She wiped her eyes hastily. "Go to sleep, Zeph. You look like hell."

I yawned. "Love you, too."

CHAPTER FIVE

My dreams were filled with fire, pillars of flame so great I could only admire them as a wonder of nature. Ash drifted onto my hair and streaked my cheeks. Sparks burned my skin, but the conflagration was oddly familiar and comforting. In the distance I could hear wailing sirens, but I knew firefighters could do nothing but wait this blaze out. Lucky that no other houses were nearby. The warehouse was a lonely monolith on this street. And didn't that, too, look familiar?

"Is she quite alight?"

It was a firefighter, but I'd never seen a female in the uniform before, and her girth strained against her suspenders.

"Is Amir okay? Have you seen him?"

"Amir," said the firefighter. "Isn't that a Mohammedan name?"

"Oh," said Aileen—who had appeared in the street beside me, clad in just her nightgown, "he's her boyfriend. A bit of a swell, actually. You should see his kitchen."

Aileen kicked me in the shins and I opened my eyes. Iris—dressed in a blue cardigan and tweed skirt, not oversized firefighter suspenders—was sitting on Aileen's bed. Aileen yanked me upright by my elbow and plopped down beside me.

"What time is it?" My voice was a hoarse croak. I felt like I could sleep for at least another day.

"Eight," Aileen said, yawning. "Which apparently makes us sluga-beds."

I closed my eyes and put my head on Aileen's shoulder. "Wake me up in five hours."

"Oh, come on, girls, at your age I'd have already taken a turn around the yard and read the morning paper."

"Was this before or after you made the orphans corner-tuck their sheets?" Aileen asked.

I giggled.

"No need to be smart," Iris said, but I could tell she was holding back a smile. "Well, I would leave you to your youthful slumbers, but something has come up. You've heard those sirens for the last two hours? There's some kind of new vampire drug on the streets. Hundreds of vampires nearly burned to death this morning when they were caught out in the sunlight."

"Burned to death?" I said slowly. "But that doesn't make sense. There aren't a hundred vampires old enough to burn to death in the whole city. New Orleans, maybe."

Iris nodded so vigorously that the bed shivered. "Yes, that's precisely the thing. This drug doesn't just make them blood-mad, it makes even the youngest vampires burn like they just turned six hundred."

I suddenly remembered the ambulance Aileen and I had seen just two days ago; I'd wondered why the gurney was draped in a sun-resistant shroud. Had that vampire burned by accident because of Faust? Horrified, I imagined the carnage that must have greeted the dawn this morning.

Well, that was one way to wake up. Did I smell charred, exsangui-nated vampire flesh coming through our drafty window?

"And it makes them blood-mad, too? Like when they Awaken?"

Iris shook her head. "It's not as bad as that, thank the Lord for small blessings. But I've heard of at least six bites being treated at St. Vincent's. I don't know how many others can't afford a doctor."

"But . . . I've seen this drug. They call it Faust. It's a pig's blood clone mixed with some kind of intoxicant. Why would they get blood-mad from drinking blood?"

Even Iris didn't have an answer for that. We sat in silence for a moment.

"Well," Aileen said suddenly, "it's like one of those new grapefruit diets, isn't it?"

"Torture?"

"Unnatural. See, they're glutting themselves on all this stuff that tastes like blood, but doesn't actually, well, nourish them the way real blood does. It's a clone of pigs' blood, right, which isn't nearly as good as human anyway. So they drink and they drink, but they still need more. So it's like when you eat nothing but grapefruits and crackers for three days and just give up and spend all your money on macaroni and cheese at Horn and Hardart."

I stared at Aileen incredulously. "So you're saying Faust makes vampires want to gorge at the Automat?"

"If it had human blood."

"Details, details."

Iris looked between the two of us and shook her head. "Why it causes blood-madness concerns me much less than it being out on the street at all. Would you believe that when I went to complain to the precinct captain this morning, he told me that this new drug was perfectly legal? I believe that our fine mayor might have fast-tracked this dangerous substance through the city council without any debate! Six people in the hospital in danger of turning, at least two dozen burned vampires languishing in the basement of the Tombs—"

"Not to mention the poppers," said Aileen. She seemed giddy with a weird, manic energy. But she'd gotten just as little sleep as I had.

Iris winced. "Of course. Full exsanguination is always a chore. Well, I came to you because I've called in some favors and the Temperance

Union has agreed to an emergency meeting tonight to discuss this new situation. I wanted to make sure I could count on you to be there to testify."

This is why she found me at eight in the morning? Only Iris. "Of course," I said. "But, Iris . . . the vampires have already had a taste. It might be too late to stop it."

Iris shrugged and gave a lopsided smile. "Well, we wouldn't be proper activists without lost causes, now, would we?" She stood up and grabbed her ivory-tipped umbrella. "I'm off to rally the rest of the troops. We're meeting in the basement of Second Avenue Presbyterian at seven."

After she had swept out of the room, Aileen and I looked at each other in mock horror.

"Take a good look at your future, Zeph."

"Iris is just a little . . . forceful," I said, yawning.

"She's a strident Victorian busybody, that's what."

"Anyway, we're just trying to help people. This Faust stuff is dangerous."

"And making it illegal will be just as effective and clever as Prohibition, I'm sure."

I sighed. "Well, we have to do something."

"That's my Zephyr."

I longed to go back to sleep, but my mind had already filled with the thousand things I needed to do today. And my first order of business was to help Judah find his family. I could only imagine how they'd react to finding their son turned into a vampire, but it had to be better than staked and beheaded. And then I'd renew my efforts to find Rinaldo. If we couldn't make Mayor Jimmy Walker listen (which I very much doubted), then perhaps this Faust problem was best traced to the source. I raised my arms above my head and stretched.

"Bloody hell, what happened to your arm?"

The sleeve of my nightgown had fallen down. I quickly tried to cover it up again, but Aileen already looked horrified. I recalled her terror the night before and cursed myself silently.

"It's nothing. The cat scratched me a little last night, that's all."

"Was it rabid? Those look deep, Zeph."

I shook my head. "Don't worry, it happened when I was carrying it outside."

"I didn't hear you go down the stairs."

"I can be quiet when I want to." Aileen just stared at me, as if she knew I was lying. "Anyway, I've got to go," I said hastily. I practically ran out to take a bath, and when I returned Aileen was lying down on her bed. Her eyes were open, but she didn't say anything to me when I said good-bye. Which was strange—Aileen usually didn't ignore me, even when she was annoyed.

As I bolted down the last of the congealed soup left on the stovetop (along with all six chocolate-covered strawberries Mama had given me), I wondered if she might actually be right about the Sight. It wasn't impossible to come on in your twenties, after all. Maybe being Swayed by an old vampire had triggered it. And she'd been right about the cat, hadn't she? She'd known *some* kind of Other was outside the door. I shuddered. I didn't want to think about how difficult Aileen's life would be from now on if she really were a seer. There was a reason that the street fortune-tellers cultivated that air of frenzied abstraction: real seers were always tormented, and sometimes driven insane, by their visions.

No wonder Aileen was terrified. I'd have to help her. But *after* this mess with Amir and Rinaldo died down.

I'd decided to start my search for Judah's parents at Lafayette, in the hopes that at least someone in the nearby tenements had seen something. If that didn't work out, I'd make my way down to South Ferry. It seemed the most likely nearby location for a boy to blow a ship's horn with his mother.

The tenement closest to the spot where I'd first discovered Judah was on Leonard Street, right by Benson Street. It looked like your average immigrant affair—an eight-story walk up of crumbling red brick and

sooty limestone. The landlord had apparently started to install fire es-
capes, but lost interest around the fifth floor, where rusting steel bars
hung forlornly over the impossibly steep drop to the street.

I pulled my jacket tight and headed for the door covered in several
garlands of garlic. Strange how the street was nearly deserted, except
for passersby determinedly hunched against the wind. Where were the
children? With the streets so white and icy on a Sunday morning, I
should have been tripping over them. I put my gloved hand on the
doorknob to see if it was open.

"What's your business?"

The voice was female, and heavily accented. I jumped backward,
nearly slipping on the ice. A woman rested quietly beside the door,
deep within the shadows of its granite overhang. My eyes had grown so
used to the early-morning snow glare that I had to squint to just make
out her figure: surprisingly tiny for such a large voice, and old, though
I knew that age could be hard to judge among immigrant women.

"I'm looking for someone," I said. A sudden gust of wind sprayed
snow against my exposed cheeks.

"I don't think today is a good day for moral instruction. Or is it
proper hygiene? Or dietary advice? Or are you a Lutheran?"

It was strange for someone to read me so clearly, and with such con-
tempt. I generally imagined that the immigrant families were grateful
for the Citizen's Council's efforts on their behalf, but clearly this wasn't
universally the case. I shrugged. "I'm Zephyr Hollis," I said, holding out
my hand. "There's a boy who went missing around here, and I'm hoping someone can help me find his parents."

The woman—who looked Jewish and sounded Eastern European—
kept her arms firmly crossed against her chest. She considered me for
several uncomfortable seconds, until I gave up and stuffed my hand
back in my pocket.

"Who is the boy?"

"His name is Judah. He's about eleven, with red hair and freckles."

"Immigrant?"

"I don't know. He doesn't have much of an accent."

She considered. "His clothes, then?"

I had a momentary flash of the small boy in Kardal's opulent palace, in his brightly colored pantaloons and pointy shoes. But I needed to go back further. "Corduroy knickers and a brown wool suit jacket. Gray peacoat and one knitted blue mitten."

The woman shook her head. "Not one of ours. Clothes too fine. When did you find him?"

"Thursday."

The door opened and another, younger woman stepped out into the cold. "Esther," she said, "go back inside. I'll take over for now."

Esther didn't take her eyes from me as she pulled the rifle she'd kept concealed in her coat and handed it to the other woman.

"Chavie, this lady is looking for the mother of a boy gone missing this Thursday. Did you hear anything?"

Chavie hefted the rifle and sighted down the empty street. "Thursday? The boys told me something about some commotion on Catherine Lane. I didn't hear about a kid, though."

"Th-thanks," I said, hoping they'd attribute my stutter to the cold and knowing they wouldn't. "If you don't mind my asking, what—"

Esther frowned, as though she dared me to finish the sentence. I swallowed, and said, "It's Faust, isn't it?"

Chavie tightened her grip on the rifle. "That's what they're calling it? Pig's blood. As if being a sucker wasn't enough of an abomination." She looked back out at the street. "There's still a few out there. Hiding in the shadows."

Esther put a hand on her elbow. "One of the girls on the fifth floor was bit this morning," she told me.

Well, that explained the lack of children. "Be careful," I said. I looked back at the rifle. I'm sure it made them feel safer, but still, I hated to see these things done improperly.

"Those bullets . . ." I said, and paused. If they used silver bullets, what would happen to the vampires they hit? But then, what would happen to them when their mundane lead caused a sucker no more trouble than an insect bite? I held my peace and left quickly.

Catherine Lane was a street of precisely one block, sandwiched between Leonard and Worth like a slice of pastrami. The solitary tenement was otherwise surrounded by warehouses and empty lots, so at
least my search was quickly narrowed. I approached the door with a
certain amount of trepidation, given my reception on Leonard Street.
I didn't want to get riddled with silver bullets for too closely resembling
a twitchy vampire. But the doorway was deserted and the battered red
oak doors were locked from the inside. I rattled them for a moment
and then knocked loudly, but no one came. I couldn't hear anything
but the sound of my own breath against the cold. The snow muffled
the sounds of traffic on Lafayette, so it seemed, for a moment, that I'd
been transported out of the city entirely. I'd gotten used to the con-
stant hum of noise in New York. This sort of deep, fearful silence
seemed more appropriate to the haunted edges of Yarrow than one of
the most populous urban centers on earth. Faust did this in *one night*?

I cupped my hands over my mouth and called up. "Hey, is anyone
there?"

Silence. It felt a little silly to be yelling at a building, but if whatever
had happened here last Thursday had anything to do with Judah, then
I had to find out about it.

I scuffled my feet in the snow and then began bouncing up and
down to generate some warmth. Okay, try again. "I'm fully human, I
promise. Zephyr Hollis. Maybe you've heard of me? I'm looking for information about a little boy."

I looked expectantly at the door. Well, damn, all I needed were
some tumbleweeds blowing down the street. "This is really embarrassing," I muttered. Maybe I could just wait on the block until someone
left. They couldn't stay in there forever.

"Hey, you!"

The door was still locked. I looked up and located the source of the
voice: a second-floor window with crude graffiti above it. An old woman

with iron curlers in her hair had pushed up her window and was leaning out into the street.

"You're that girl, right, the singing vampire suffragette?"

Well, at least now my face was warm. I just nodded. "I'm looking for the mother of a little boy. He was attacked around here on Thursday evening. Maybe the Turn Boys. Did you hear anything?"

The woman waved her hand in the air. "It's been a mess around here the past week, I don't mind telling you. Everyone's afraid to go out. Yeah, those damned kids of Rinaldo's were here last Thursday. Don't know what in hell they were up to, but it sure sounded nasty. All sorts of growling and screaming and laughing. Gave my granddaughter nightmares. I didn't know it was a little boy they got, though. Damn shame. You need someone to take the body, I guess?"

I hesitated. Suddenly, Amir's warning about what a dangerous and stupid thing I had done to save Judah came back to me. An eleven-year-old child. My God, even this old woman didn't imagine that he'd survived.

"That's right," I said. "Do you know anyone missing a child?"

She shook her head. "We were lucky none of our own got caught by those blood-mad suckers last night. Anyway, it sounded like Rinaldo's boys had been playing with him for a while." She clucked her tongue. "Heard them laughing and singing all the way down Lafayette. A little boy! It's too much, I tell you. No mother should have to deal with this. Her little boy staked and beheaded. I hope you find her. And if she needs some help, tell her to come to Catherine Lane."

She gave me a smart, almost soldierly nod, and I returned it. I recognized a kindred spirit when I saw one. "I will. Thanks for your help."

She closed her window and I turned to leave. It was clear Nicholas and the Turn Boys had stolen Judah someplace else and dumped him here. Well, that made South Ferry even more likely. I fetched my bicycle and slowly pedaled down Lafayette, looking in vain for any other clues. The Turn Boys were out of their territory here. I'd never heard of them attacking so far away from Little Italy. I'd almost think that they'd targeted Judah in particular, if I could think of any reason that a hardened gang would care about the fate of an eleven-year-old boy. That woman, Esther, on Leonard Street had thought Judah was a little too well-dressed for their part of town. She was probably right, now that I thought of it. Maybe the Turn Boys *had* targeted Judah—not because of a personal vendetta, but to let the more affluent residents of Lafayette and Park Row know that they were vulnerable. But in that case, why take the trouble to hide his body in an alley farther uptown?

I shook my head—and looked up just in time to see a firmly packed snowball sailing at my head. Ice crystals stung my cheek and eyelids, gritty snow filled my mouth. I spat and whirled around, but the children who'd pelted me were already screeching and running down the block. One of them looked back and waved.

"Damn kids," I said, and waved back. Just a few blocks away from the Leonard Street tenement, the atmosphere was noticeably less grim. I saw the reason immediately: the police were patrolling the streets around Elm and Park Row in unusual force this Sunday morning. I could hardly expect less for City Hall, of course. The precinct station was less than a block away, and the police tended to be quite good at protecting those who could afford to sweeten their salaries.

Like Judah's mother?

The precinct station was so crowded that the line of people waiting to get in had spilled into the street. Most of them had a familiar look: exhausted, harried, their clothes several years away from new and never stylish. I recognized shouted German and Yiddish and Russian and Italian mixed among the English. It seemed that the tenement residents farther uptown had decided to take their complaints about last night's disturbances directly to the source. As I pushed through the crowd I passed a man with a pale, almost jaundiced face, and a dirty handkerchief pressed to his neck. A woman stood beside him, fingering rosary beads and mumbling indecipherable prayers. I forced myself to look away—no one knew why some people were more susceptible to turning than others. But I'd been witness to that agonizing wait many times and had no wish to relive it.

At the front of the lobby, four police officers attempted to take statements. But the crowd up here had grown vocal with their impatience, and their angry shouts drowned out anything else.

"I told you, one of the suckers is still on our block! We're afraid to let the kids out, you've gotta—"

"Our daughter, she missing. You promise to—"

"But the Blood Bank is all out! How are we—"

Great. How the hell was I supposed to ask about Judah in this mess? At least I wouldn't have to worry about being discreet. In this press of people, the police officers would never remember me. I had maneuvered my way nearly to the front when I saw a familiar silhouette. She stood out against the lower-class crowd, if only because no thrift shops would ever sell a dress in such a bright shade of teal. And upon closer inspection, her whole ensemble—from suede heels to pert cloche hat— made her seem as at home among the tenement crowd as a fish in the Serengeti. She was taking notes while interviewing a young police officer who was markedly ill at ease. He eyed the mass of people in the station as though they might riot at any minute, or just crush him underfoot. His left hand rested firmly on the handle of his pistol.

Lily, of course, seemed entirely unaware of any of this.

"So how many people did you say have been attacked so far?" she asked, tapping her fountain pen against the edge of her reporter's notebook.

The police officer cleared his throat. "At least thirty reported here. More threats and sightings. It's been pretty bad."

"And, in your professional opinion, this is all attributable to that new vampire street-drug, Faust?"

He looked at Lily like she might have lost her mind. "Well, what the hell else could it be? Something has to be making the suckers burn like fried chicken."

I winced at the analogy. Lily just scribbled furiously. She seemed bizarrely . . . well, if not happy, then *energized*. She might not fit the scenery, but she clearly thrived on this type of disaster.

"I've heard rumors that Faust is being funneled through the notorious Italian mob boss, Rinaldo. Can you confirm that?"

The room seemed to grow immediately quieter, as though someone had muffled the roar with a giant wad of gauze.

The officer cleared his throat again. "I, ah, can't confirm that, no. There have been lots of rumors, right, and we can't say now where this stuff is coming from—"

But Lily wouldn't let up. "Isn't it true that most reports are coming from Little Italy and the immediate vicinity, which is, as I'm sure you know, controlled by Rinaldo and his gang?"

The people near me might be eavesdropping on Lily's interview, but behind us I could hear inarticulate shouting. The police officer craned his neck to look over the crowd.

"Listen, we don't know where this stuff is coming from. We're following leads."

Someone to my right shouted, "You're just afraid of that scum Rinaldo and his Turn Boys!" The officer flushed with embarrassment and gripped the handle of his gun. Even Lily seemed to notice this, but instead of getting nervous, she smiled. Goddamn, and I thought *I* lacked a sense of self-preservation.

The disturbance at the front of the station was getting louder now, and impossible to ignore. A man somewhere behind me was shouting loud enough to be heard over the din. "You're letting them in here? After what they did to us?"

A woman shrieked and a child started wailing. "She touched me, Jesus Christ, don't bite me, please I lost my husband—"

The rest of her plea was lost in a roar of inarticulate mob rage. The hapless police officer, lately the victim of an interrogation by Lily, crack reporter, tried to shout over the noise.

"Please, everyone, calm down. You're safe from Others in this—"
He looked around, shook his head, and motioned to a nearby officer.

"Christ. Galt, go get that damn sucker out of here. Don't know what the hell she's thinking."

Probably that she needed some help, just like everyone else. If this was a glimpse of what Faust would do to future human-Other relations, it made me furious. The officer fired his pistol into the ceiling, cracking off a bit of plaster. He plunged into the crowd a moment later. Lily made as if to chase after him, but I grabbed her by the elbow and dragged her behind the officer's desk. I could tell this was going to get ugly. Lily was too eager for her own damn good.

"Zephyr! I was hoping you'd come. I need a quote for my article."

I sighed. Better that than my inside source getting crushed to death by a mob. "Lily, you should be more careful. Angry crowd, terrified and armed police . . . it's not a stable combination."

Lily gave me what I suppose she thought was a contemptuous smile. "I know what I'm doing."

I just rolled my eyes and looked around for a back exit. We needed to get out of here; so much for my plan to find information about Judah. The crowd had surged to the left side of the station. They were yelling and spitting and shoving the few police officers to reach a huddled figure I could barely make out through the press of bodies. I wondered if we could edge along the wall until we reached the exit, but even the less crowded areas were too dense to make our way through.

"So, Zephyr Hollis, you're a well-known community figure. Who do you think is responsible for unleashing this horrifying drug?"

I looked back at her, incredulous. Didn't she see what was happening in here? "Who the hell do you *think* is responsible, Lily? The archduke of Prussia?"

A door on the opposite side of the room opened, letting in three more police officers. They each had a gun in one hand and a billy club in the other—clearly they weren't taking any chances with the situation. And neither was I.

"Ladies and gentlemen, please move to the back exit. We are clearing the station."

At first, no one listened, but a few intemperate smacks from billy clubs got their attention. Much as I abhor violence, I was grateful for the distraction. As the mob moved sluggishly toward the doorway, I saw just enough room for Lily and me to edge along the back wall to the side door.

"I'm not leaving," Lily said. "This is a scoop—"

"Fine, then scoop it from the doorway."

I stood up, grabbed her notebook and dragged her along behind me. Two shots, loud enough to make my ears ring, cracked the air. A shower of plaster fell onto my hair and shoulders. Lily shrieked, but she wasn't the only one.

"I said get back!"

"Take the bruxa!" The voice was male, but I couldn't see who owned it. I could, however, finally see the unfortunate vampire who had started this latest mess. She was pressed against a deputy's desk on the far left wall, frantically hitting anyone who came too close. Her skin was ash-gray and pulled so tight over her swollen joints I imagined I could hear them creaking. And yet I doubted she had been more than twenty when she turned. She needed blood, that much was obvious. The police officers surrounding part of the crowd looked at each other. One of them shrugged.

"Please leave the building. No humans or Others are permitted at this time."

A man dressed in dust-caked dungarees lunged forward to grab the vampire's arm. She cursed and jumped away with inhuman speed. He was left with a torn bit of her sleeve; she now stood on the desk. I stared at the police officers, waiting for them to take the vampire and shoo the crowd away. But when someone else lunged at her, they stayed back.

"What are they doing?" I asked, unable to believe what I was seeing.

Lily put a hand on my shoulder. "Letting them take her, I think."

To do what? Rip her limb from limb before feeding her pitiful ex-sanguinated corpse to the stray dogs? "Oh, fuck." I handed Lily back her notebook.

"Go through that door," I said, pointing to the one a few feet away.

"Don't you dare follow me. If you wait, you'll get your damn scoop." One way or another. VAMPIRE SUFFRAGETTE DEFIES LYNCH MOB or MORON SQUASHED LIKE BUG IN POLICE HEADQUARTERS? I gave Lily a shove in the right direction and then launched myself at the crowd. They let me pass fairly easily, I'm not sure why. Maybe the grim expression on my face, or the silver blade I'd taken from beneath my skirt. I came upon a police officer a few seconds later.

"Don't you dare let this mob take that woman!" I yelled, loudly enough that few people paused to listen.

The man winced and wiped his forehead as though I'd spit on him. "She's no woman. And you try reasoning with these folks. Now get back."

He shoved me behind him and I stumbled to one knee. Several pairs of feet kicked me in the shins and ribs before I managed to stagger upright again. More gunshots cracked the air, but this time I couldn't even tell if they came from the police. Several people were lunging for the vampire, who just barely eluded them. This couldn't go on for much longer. She might be faster, but no vampire that weak and desperate could evade a mob of bloodthirsty humans for long.

Well, just how stupid are you, Zephyr?

"Bastards!" the woman yelled. "Bastard police! You'll let them do this!" Someone rocked the desk.

Very, very stupid.

I let out a roar and shoved my way forward, pushing and stomping on anyone in my path. I didn't hesitate; I jumped onto the desk with the vampire and prayed that she wouldn't choose this moment to retaliate against her attackers. She didn't. She just stared at me. "Help?" she said.

I nodded and waved the knife at the crowd.

"Look at her! She's just like you. She has nothing to do with Faust and what happened last night. If you kill her, it's simple murder. But since some of you seem to have left your moral compasses at home, I'll make it simple. It's definitely murder to kill me. I'm still human."

"Give her up! We don't want to hurt you."

I laughed. "Well, I think that's the point. You're going to have to."

My gamble seemed to be working. The almost palpable anger of the crowd was slowly turning to confusion. People murmured among themselves. Even the police lowered their pistols with looks of obvious relief.

"Hey," said a woman close to the front of the crowd, "that's that girl. The one who teaches night school."

One of the police officers laughed. "Hey, vampire suffragette, sing us a song, why don't you?"

"A duet!"

The *police* knew about my singing debut? I guess Horace made sure to pay off everyone. "I don't give out songs for free, boys."

A few people laughed, but most were letting themselves be pushed through the double doors, back onto the street. After a few moments I jumped off the desk and held my hand up to the vampire to help her down. Out of danger, she'd begun to shake so badly I thought she might crack her brittle bones.

"Th-thank you," she said. Her accent was faintly Italian.

"How long has it been since you fed?"

She shook her head. "Tuesday. But, you see . . ." She looked carefully at me, and then drew the scarf from around her shoulders. When she pushed back the fabric, the problem was evident: a silver bullet, lodged beside her shoulder blades. Not enough to exsanguinate immediately, but enough to weaken her to death. Unless she got proper treatment, which certainly wasn't going to happen at an Other-phobic police station or hospital.

"Who did that?"

"Someone in my neighborhood. I didn't see who. They saw me walking and shot . . . I didn't know what to do."

There's vigilante justice for you. Lily, having decided that the situation was safe enough to ignore my warnings, approached the two of us.

"Well, never a boring moment with you around, is there?" She grinned and then ostentatiously kissed her reporter's notebook. "Gold, I tell you. Zephyr, you and I make a peachy team."

I returned the smile. "And I'm sure your paper loves human interest stories."

"What, sucker bites man? I already have plenty of that, thanks."

"Oh no, how about man shoots sucker with silver bullet? A few tenements have organized themselves into armed militias. Silver bullets and itchy trigger fingers, Lily. Along with some definitive information about where Faust is coming from."

Lily's mouth twisted. "Why do I think I won't be getting the better end of this bargain? What do you want for it, Zephyr?"

"Just take this woman down to the Blood Bank on St. Marks Place. Ask for Ysabel. If she can't help her, she'll know someone who can."

"Wait, why can't you do that? *I'm* not the do-gooder in this relationship."

I took a step away and pulled Lily closer to me, so hopefully the vampire wouldn't be able to hear us. "One of these tenement vigilante groups shot her a few hours ago with a silver bullet. Which can kill vampires in less than a day. I don't have time, dearest Lily. I promised Nicholas—you know, the Turn Boy—that I'd meet him at noon."

Lily sighed. "Fine. Deal. But you definitely have something solid about Faust and Rinaldo?"

"You know, I'm not sure it's sound journalistic practice to plant information in your sources and then quote the sources for corroborating evidence."

Lily let the corners of her mouth curve up into a cool, supercilious smile. "What you don't know about journalistic ethics could fill President Taft's belly, Zephyr. And anyway, so long as you have fresh evidence . . ."

"I do. Just take care of her."

Lily nodded. "I'll see you later tonight. Iris has finally convinced me to attend one of those ghastly meetings."

She set off at a brisk pace, forcing the vampire to struggle to keep up with her. I shook my head. For a reporter, Lily had certain remarkable blind spots on her observational skills.

"Miss, sorry, we need to clear the station." It was the police officer

Lily had been interviewing. I looked around the station and realized I was the only civilian left.

"Wait, could you just help me with one thing?" *Since I just saved your collective posteriors a few minutes ago.* I didn't say that part, but I raised my eyebrows high enough for him catch my meaning.

"Ah, right. What can I do for you?"

"I . . . um . . . I think I saw a little boy I heard went missing last Thursday. I'm wondering if anyone reported him missing."

"On Thursday?" He shook his head slowly. "None that I know of. Now last night and this morning? About seven." He shrugged.

I let out a slow breath, a little surprised at the depth of my disappointment. If no one had reported a missing child, then he could be one of hundreds of faceless immigrant children. Hell, he could even be indigent, for all I knew. I started to wonder if I'd ever find Judah's family.

The air outside was shocking cold after the heated mash of bodies inside the station, but I kept myself warm by bicycling furiously the rest of the way to South Ferry. There were a few ships docked when I arrived, and the piers were loaded with goods and milling people. I elbowed my way toward a likely-looking police boat. An officer lounging on the dock looked up when I approached. He listened sympathetically enough when I explained that I was looking for a missing little boy, but offered me no more help than the officers back in the precinct office.

"Sorry, miss, but there's a lot of parents and kids come to Battery Park. We don't even know all the ones that work on the ships, let alone anyone else."

Brilliant. "Would you say any of the ships here have particularly frightening horns?" I knew I was flailing, but I wouldn't compound it by looking embarrassed.

He laughed, as well he might. "Frightening, miss? For a little tyke, maybe. But I wouldn't know what. And none of the big ships dock here. You might try Chelsea."

"I . . . I don't suppose you'd mind . . . demonstrating? Your horn, I mean?"

He looked a tad uncomfortable, as though he were belatedly questioning my sanity. I gave him my brightest smile and he shrugged. "Eh, why not? Bill," he called, to one of the men on the boat. "Give the whistle a pull, will you? Lady down here wants to know how it sounds."

Bill obliged and I gave an involuntary start. Goodness, was that volume truly necessary? Still, it by no means seemed harsh or deep enough to frighten even a susceptible eleven-year-old at all used to the water. Besides, a series of docks like notches on a key went all around Manhattan. None of these seemed very child friendly, and all of them served thousands of ships. Maybe I could try Chelsea, but my shoulders slumped and I barely remembered to thank the officers before leaving. This felt like a dead end. I could only hope Judah remembered something else.

I had only twenty minutes left before my tutoring session with Nicholas. There were too many things I needed to know that only the leader of the Turn Boys could tell me: where they'd kidnapped Judah, how they planned to run Faust into the city, where Rinaldo's lair was located.

Nicholas, of course, would kill me before telling me any of it. Which meant I had to trick him.

The inside of the Beast's Rum was dark as a tomb, and nearly as quiet as one. Blackout blinds had been pulled over all of the windows, and I had to knock for nearly a minute before a shuffling, hooded vampire let me inside. The only sounds came from a few suckers quietly nursing bags of clean blood, and one muttering to himself in the corner. They looked miserable. I spared them my sympathy.

"Is Nicholas here?" I whispered to the one who had opened the door. He looked up and I realized, with a shock, that it was Charlie. He looked like he'd lost twenty pounds in the last twelve hours.

"In back," he said, his voice a rough whisper.

"You look like shit," I said.

He coughed. "Well. Faust is a kick in the balls."

"Hope it was worth it."

His beatific smile surprised me. "Oh, yes."

I started to walk away, but he reached out to grab my shoulder. I bit my lip against a shudder.

"Be careful. He's a bit . . . the Faust, you know."

He seemed worried, insistent that I understand. But I wasn't sure what I needed to know. That Nicholas was crazy? I'd gathered that already. Dangerous? I could handle it.

"Don't worry," I said, shrugging off his hand. "I'll be fine."

I bumped into a few tables before I found the door to the back room. A faint gas lamp illuminated the gloom inside. Nicholas sat on the floor, his back against the pile of ruined instruments. His skin was flushed with blood, but oddly pale beneath the blush. Faust with a chaser of Homo sapiens? I hoped the blood had been willingly donated, but I doubted it. His head lolled against his chest. I would have thought him asleep, if not for his glowing, open eyes.

"I won't let you," he whispered.

"Nicholas?"

"Please, not the cage, I don't need it anymore . . ." He didn't look at me, and something about his distant expression reminded me of Judah, hallucinating in Kardal's palace. "There's something in there with me. It roars, Papa."

My heart pounded. But before I could ask him what he meant, he raised his head. The fit had passed, whatever it was. He looked tired, but lucid.

His fingers beat an irregular tattoo on the dusty floor. "I didn't think you'd come."

He had never seemed more childlike, or more alien. "I told you, I need the money."

I waited, but he didn't seem inclined to move. After a moment, I shrugged and pulled up a chair from the table.

"Think you can get through the rest of the alphabet?"

"You know *La Bohème*? Musetta's waltz? *'Quando m'en vo' soletta la via.'*"

I was shocked. Imagine being made to feel like a rube by an illiterate vampire gangster. "I'm not really sure . . ."

He started to sing. If I'd been startled by his question, his voice nearly made my heart stop. I'd heard that the Italians would sometimes geld particularly talented boys right before puberty, and that the monstrous operation produced voices that were perfectly and eerily balanced between the falsetto of a boy and the tenor of a man. Nicholas's voice was high as a boy's, but somehow broader and richer. I had never heard a castrato—not even on a phonograph. A castrato voice, of course, had time to mature to adulthood whereas Nicholas's had been frozen, but I imagined that the two sounds could not be dissimilar. He moved his hands, as though in time to an unseen orchestra. His eyes splashed light in the darkened room when he hit that soaring high note. Of course I recognized the song then. My musical tastes might run more toward Negro jazz than Italian operas, but it was hard to avoid such a popular, heartbreaking melody. He cut himself off abruptly toward the end of the song, a gentle vibrato morphing effortlessly into a harsh laugh.

He stood, cracked the neck off a smashed guitar and hurled it at the far wall. The strings whistled by my face, but I didn't think he'd been aiming for me. Cold comfort.

"Papa loved that one," he said. His breathing was labored for no reason I could discern. "But he never made me sing it."

Back to troubled parental relationships, were we? Tread lightly, Zephyr. "Your papa . . . encouraged you to sing?"

He let off that harsh bark of a laugh again. I winced, expecting another projectile, but he held himself still. "*Encouraged*. That's a do-gooder word for you. You'd like some others? How's about *forced*? *Threatened*? Oh, here's a good one, *tortured*."

Tortured? How do you torture someone to sing? But given Nicholas's twisted expression and bright eyes, I was inclined to believe him. "No wonder you hate music," I said.

"You only hate what you love."

I sighed. Like Daddy yelling at me one minute and hugging me the next. "Parents," I said, for a moment forgetting that I was talking to Nicholas, and not just a troubled boy, "are a great trial to us all."

Nicholas took a few quick strides toward me and sat down on the other chair. "So, show me some letters, Charity."

I reached up to turn on the ceiling light. He made a great show of groaning and shielding his eyes from the light, but he didn't object. I wondered, as I wrote down the second half of the alphabet, why I felt so safe around him, compared to just yesterday. Did I really think he was less likely to snap and kill me? Or maybe it was as simple as knowing thine enemy. If I could predict his rages, there was less to fear. He had an even more difficult time concentrating today than he had yesterday, though I knew he was trying. I wanted to take pity on us both and give up, but I still had to implement my plan. I'd decided to represent the letters with the names of streets that he would be familiar with. And, conveniently, I planned to include as many streets in the vicinity of Judah's attack as possible. It was a long shot, but perhaps with enough prodding he would say enough to give me a clue as to where he'd found Judah.

"So, L is for Lafayette or Leonard," I said, writing the words down in large, round letters. Nicholas mouthed the word while following my pen with his finger. "Followed by M, which stands for . . ."

I let the ellipsis hang hopefully in the air for a few seconds. Nicholas looked up at me. "Morris?"

I allowed myself a small grin. "Yes, perfect." Morris was a tiny street even farther downtown than Leonard or Catherine. Of course, his dredging it up proved absolutely nothing. But why would he pick a street so much farther from his normal area? Because something had happened there recently? I felt vindicated when he picked "Pearl" for P, "Rector" for R. But when we finally reached S, Nicholas balked.

"This is stupid," he said, shoving the paper away from him so violently that the sheet ripped. "I already know the damn streets. Teach me something else."

"Well," I said, attempting to speak calmly around the sudden appearance of my heart in my throat, "I think this will be easier for you if we use examples of words you're already familiar with. This is . . . well, especially with Faust around, it's your part of town, isn't it."

He spat on the floor. I tried not to notice the gentle sizzle of his saliva when it hit the concrete. "My part of town. Ha. Don't let my papa hear you say that. This is his fucking oyster. I just get the scraps."

I restrained myself from commenting on his mixed metaphor. There was something more important there. His papa owned this part of town? That either meant his papa was the borough president or . . .

"Rinaldo? He's your father?"

Nicholas leaned over the table and grabbed my head with his left hand. He pulled me close to his face, as though he were leaning in for a kiss, but romance had nothing to do with his fierce, half-mad face.

"Just so we understand each other, Charity Do-good. Rinaldo ain't just my father. And what he did to me? Let's just say I don't want to hear nothing else about fucking Water Street, all right?"

The second most dangerous vampire in Lower Manhattan had his fangs less than an inch from my neck, and I could have danced for joy. *Water Street.* I'd bet my rent money that he turned Judah there.

But there were implications that I hadn't thought through. If Nicholas was Rinaldo's son, then he almost certainly knew the location of his father's secret lair. On the other hand, getting it out of him would be that much harder. For all he seemed to hate his father, I didn't want to be the one to detonate that complex welter of emotions I'd seen lurking so close to the surface. Bloody stakes, and I thought I'd had it tough. His own daddy *turned* him at thirteen. I'd had plenty of reasons to want to take out Rinaldo before. This was just more fuel for the fire.

I was so tired by the time I turned onto Ludlow Street that I almost fell off my bicycle. My God, I needed to sleep. I calculated that I had three hours before Iris's ad hoc Temperance Union meeting. Any little bit would help. But I'd only stored my bicycle under the staircase when a sudden scent overpowered me. Oranges, frankincense and myrrh.

"You smell like the three goddamn kings," I said.

"I think they were ifrits, actually."

His voice was warm with banked humor. For the first time since Daddy so rudely interrupted us, he actually sounded okay. I turned around. "How are you doing?" I asked. I wanted to touch him, but kept my hands firmly by my sides.

His lips twisted. "Making do," he said. "If you hadn't come back soon, I was going to check the Tombs."

"Haven't we already been through this? Give me some credit."

"It sounded like there was a war on this morning. I thought it more than likely you'd be in it."

I shook my head. "Stuck in my room, actually. This Faust stuff is a mess . . . I saw some things that first night at the club, but I didn't realize just how bad it was going to be. We have to find Rinaldo. We have to stop him."

Amir gave me a curious look, almost chagrined. "Stop? I'm afraid stopping him wasn't really part of my plan."

"Oh, that. After you get back whatever it is he took from you, then."

"Well . . . ah, I suppose I'd have no objections. But silly me, imagining you didn't approve of extrajudicial assassination."

That stopped me short. He was right—the plan smacked a little too much of my Defender past for me to do more than squirm uncomfortably. "What other options are there? If we have the chance . . . you know the police won't stop this."

He regarded me silently for a few moments. "I think, somehow, you are oversimplifying things, Zephyr."

I didn't respond and he shrugged. "And who am I to lecture you on morality? I prefer a more simple calculus. For example, is your inestimable father anywhere in the vicinity, and if not, would you like to come back with me?" He cupped one hand around the back of my head. Who needed central heating when you had a djinn nearby?

I laughed. "Tell me again, why exactly are you taking Basic Literacy and Elocution?"

"I heard a rumor about a teacher."

"That she was charming? Beautiful? Brilliant?"

He brushed his lips over my frozen nose and then lingered for a moment on my lips. "That she was *good*."

I sighed. I'd take what I could get. "Well, the good teacher has to check one thing before she can avoid her daddy's wrath in your apartment." I took his hand and started walking down the block.

"Walking? How . . . quaint. Won't you be cold?"

I scanned the block behind us, but we were alone except for a few children. "You can, uh, zap us there. Just wait until we're away from the street."

I didn't think it would be a good idea to tell him about the present Rinaldo left for me last night. I didn't want to awaken his latent chivalrous instincts any more than necessary. On the other hand, if someone was following me, I wanted them to learn as little about my involvement with Amir as possible.

Amir gave me a curious look. "Something did happen this morning, didn't it?"

We walked around the corner. "Just being cautious. Or did you forget that I'm attempting to infiltrate a gang of vicious mobsters so you can kill their leader?"

He grimaced. "Now you sound like Kardal. "

A seven-hundred-year-old talking column of smoke? "I do?"

To my surprise, instead of grabbing my shoulders and winking out of existence, Amir walked to the street corner and hailed a hansom cab.

"He thinks that I'm insane for getting you involved in this," Amir said as he opened the door and helped me inside.

"And you think?"

"That I'm desperate." He shut the door. "Where to?"

"Ah . . . the Saint Marks Blood Bank," I yelled to the driver through the hatch in back.

"Blood Bank?" he said. I couldn't see his face very clearly, but he sounded disapproving. "'S gonna be mobbed today, miss. Not too safe up there."

Amir rapped the ceiling with his fist. "We pay you to drive, not dispense advice. You heard what she said."

The carriage started to move a second later, though I thought I heard a string of muttered curses about "flighty flapper girls," and "unprincipled foreign gentlemen."

Amir settled back in his seat opposite me and stared out the window. I doubted he was looking at the scenery, because his expression was so intense I started to worry that he might accidentally start smoking.

"So, why the mundane transportation?"

He looked back at me. "I can't teleport anywhere I haven't been before. Unlike you, I don't spend much time in Blood Banks."

Something had soured his mood. The reminder of Kardal? I decided to tell him what I'd learned from Nicholas as a distraction.

"I'm not sure if it has anything to do with Judah, but something is upsetting him on Water Street. And I'm betting that something is Rinaldo."

Some of the strain left his eyes. "Good. We're getting closer. Of course, it's all moot if your father massacres the Turn Boys first, but still. What about Judah?"

I sighed. "Manhattan has a lot of boats. No luck on South Ferry; all the big boats dock elsewhere. Chelsea?"

"That's miles away from the Turn Boys. Didn't you say the neighbors heard them coming from farther south?"

I bit my lip. "You're right. It doesn't make any sense. He must be from the neighborhood. Maybe Nicholas attacked him after an incident with his father? I never thought I'd feel sorry for a vicious murderer like that, but . . ."

"Zephyr," he said, "you'd feel sorry for Jack the Ripper."

He kissed me. I wasn't prepared for it, and the shock bubbled from my chest to my toes like a bottle of exploded soda pop. My fingers felt around the rough edges of his ears before lacing themselves in his hair. I might have moaned. I think I moaned.

The hansom jerked to a stop and the cabbie rapped on the ceiling. "I won't have none of that, you hear?"

I giggled. "You run a clean establishment," I muttered in my best Mrs. Brodsky impersonation. Amir paid the cabbie and we alighted onto St. Marks Place in a fashion significantly higher-class than I was accustomed to.

Amir brushed back my hair and whispered in my ear, "You should hurry, don't you think?"

The room was so crowded that at first I couldn't find Ysabel. I saw only a few humans—the rest were vampires, the signs of Faust withdrawal clear on most of their faces. After a night of Faust, they were desperate for real nutrition. But I doubted the Blood Bank had enough for all of them. Ysabel and a younger assistant were hauling a crate of blood bags from the storage room. The golem was patrolling the area between the desk and the far wall. I'd never seen it do more than shuffle aside before, and the sight of it in full motion was almost unnerving.

When she saw me, Ysabel hollered my name and leapt over the golem to hug me. "I'm so glad to see you!" She looked around the room and shook her head. "Some day, eh? These times, I tell you. Saul says we're living like the Canaanites, and now the Faust has come to smite us. I just think it's a shame, and I don't mind saying so."

Behind us, Amir coughed. Ysabel yanked on my shoulder until I was low enough for her to whisper in my ear. "Is that a Mohammedan, Zephyr?"

I straightened abruptly. Amir wouldn't have even needed Other hearing for that. "Ysabel, meet Amir. I'm helping him with something."

Amir gave a small bow, which I could have hit him for. He really did think he was the prince of Arabia, didn't he?

"But I'm curious as to your opinion about Faust. Don't you agree that it can only benefit the city if its vampires have an outlet for personal enjoyment?"

Ysabel's lip curled. "Oy vey, don't you have eyes? Look at these bruxa! They look like they're having fun, do they? Burning in the sun and then about to starve to death. Zephyr, where'd you find this meshuggener?"

I glared at Amir. "He found me," I said. "And he'll wait outside." Apparently the full force of my fury was enough to convince him to beat a hasty retreat. What the hell was he thinking? Defending Faust because it was *fun*? In the middle of a Blood Bank mobbed with desperate vampires? Before Ysabel could ask me more questions about Amir, I asked her about Lily and the vampire from this morning.

Ysabel's angry demeanor vanished immediately. "Oh, of course, the poor bruxa. She was weak, you know, but you saved her life. We got that bullet out just in time." She clucked her tongue. "Silver bullets on an innocent bruxa. What's the city coming to? But that girl who was with her? You'd have thought she was in a garbage pit the way she held her nose. And then she insisted on asking everyone all these questions. You have some strange friends, *bubbala*."

I restrained a smile. I could only imagine Lily's distaste at having to come to such a low-class slum. But she was a good reporter: she'd never let anything get in the way of a story. I thanked Ysabel and promised to come by tomorrow morning to do what I could to help. The feeling of a hundred hungry vampire eyes resting on my neck was enough to make even my skin crawl. I left as soon as I could.

Amir was leaning against a lamppost, his hands in the pockets of his tweed sports jacket. He was watching the street boys cleaning horse manure and hawking a dozen different broadsheets. I could tell immediately that his buoyant mood had vanished. It made me feel guilty. He didn't look up when I stepped beside him.

"Why aren't they in school?" he asked. "Isn't that what boys do, now?"

"Not if their families can't afford it. Or if they don't have any families." I thought about the tenements filled with orphaned or stolen children, with the landlords who forced them into virtual slavery. But something stopped me from mentioning it to Amir.

"It's not so different from before, is it? I thought . . ." He shook his head. "I practically live in your world. Kardal's always complaining that I'm more human than Djinni. And Kashkash knows I often can't stand Shadukiam. But sometimes, I swear, it's like I don't know humans at all."

I considered how hard it was for some of the immigrants I taught to acclimatize to life in this country. A djinn with the same troubles?

"Why did you say that back there? About Faust. Can't you see what it's done already to these people?"

Amir didn't respond. He seemed very tense—he radiated enough heat now that I'd begun to sweat beneath my coat. Then he gripped my hand very tightly. What was wrong with him? Was he having another attack? But no, it didn't look quite like that.

"Will you come back with me, *habibti*? Forget about all this for a while?"

Something I'd said bothered him. It didn't take much to deduce that. But I didn't care, at least for now. He was staring in my eyes, his skin was touching mine, and I was melting like the puddle of snow at his feet. I nodded. We flew through nothing at all, and when we arrived I was the first to open my eyes, the first to see the macabre present waiting for him in his front hall.

A revenant tomcat—larger and mangier than the one that greeted me the day before—stood in a lake of blood. Not its own—several gallons of blood had been liberally splattered all over the room, but where it had come from was unclear. The cat launched itself toward us as soon as we arrived, screeching like its voice box was broken. The smell made me gag as I fumbled for my knife. Amir was faster. He grabbed the cat while shoving me aside, and then snapped its neck with such force that he nearly decapitated it. He tossed the still creature back on the floor, his lip curled in disgust. A horrible aftertaste of rot and hot tar almost overpowered the normally salty, metallic musk of blood.

"Goodness," I said, trying to control my breathing. "No need to be so overenthusiastic."

Amir whirled on me. "Bloody hell, Zephyr. Go home."

I walked into the emergency meeting of the Manhattan Temperance Union fifteen minutes late, my hands scrubbed so clean my skin cracked. My hair was damp and dripping down the nape of my neck. I was attempting not to think about the red stains on the sleeves of my blouse. Really, I was attempting not to think about much at all. Iris was holding forth in the front of the room, detailing the horrors she'd witnessed walking through the streets that morning. Lily leaned against the wall by the door in back, scribbling furiously. She nodded to me and then cocked her head toward the front of the room. I followed her gaze and saw an older man in the second row calmly writing in a reporter's notebook. A photographer stood nearby, and snapped a few blinding shots of the crowd and Iris. I sidled up to Lily.

"Competition?" I whispered.

"*The Sun*, those bastards. My story about the riot at the precinct made the front page of the evening edition, and now everyone wants to cover the Faustian Nightmare. They trotted out Bill Oliver for these old bags, if you'd believe it. Don't you dare talk to him, Zephyr! This is *my* story."

"Don't tell me he's tracking your big Faust exposé?"

She closed her eyes and crossed herself. "Good Lord, I hope not. He'll make a hash of it *and* take the credit."

A woman in the back row turned to us angrily and put her finger over her lips. "Shh!"

Lily rolled her eyes and lowered her voice. "Anyway, I think my dear god-aunt's going to call you up in a second."

I caught a sob in my throat and massaged my aching temples. I was sure they hurt a good deal less than Amir's, but that wasn't much comfort. I hadn't wanted to leave him there, alone. He hadn't let me stay.

"Zeph . . . are you okay? Are those *bloodstains*—"

I caught her eye and shook my head. "It's been a long day," I said. "We'll talk later."

"And now I'd like to introduce someone I think you all know," said Iris, utterly oblivious and in her element. "Zephyr Hollis. Though perhaps you'd know her better as the vampire—"

"Thank you, Iris!" I shouted from the back of the room. I wasn't sure if I could stop myself from screaming if I heard that moniker one more time. But once I made it to the Sunday-school podium and the eyes of every woman in that room focused their curious, severe stares upon me, I wondered what on earth I was doing. I mean, I hated the Temperance Union. I'd certainly never been shy with my opinion of their activities. I was half the age of their average member. I'd been able to vote since I turned twenty-one. To me, they were dinosaurs. To them, I was a know-nothing communist upstart, trying to take over their movement. And I expected them to listen to me about Faust? Iris thought my notoriety would give me more credibility. She didn't seem to understand that most of these women hated me for it.

"For every life alcohol destroys," I said, "Faust will destroy a dozen. I saw it today. Unless we act now, Faust could tear apart this city." I tried to be persuasive, but my mind felt numb from the grisly scene at Amir's—all that blood, the dead stray cat, the secret I kept about Rinaldo's "gift" the night before. I discussed all the immediate effects of Faust: blood-madness, severe burns, street vigilantes, public panic. Perhaps Prohibition was the wrong tactic, I said, but we needed to organize immediate public health measures in order to curtail the disasters already rippling through the community. "I've worked my whole life to improve human-Other relations. This threatens to destroy all of our progress in just a few weeks."

It wasn't much of an ending, but it was all I had to say. I left the podium to a few scattered, halfhearted claps. The local chapter president then opened up the floor for comment. A woman in the front row stood up so quickly she rocked her chair backward. She wore a tight cap pinned to her graying bun and a dress so hopelessly Victorian it actually featured a hint of a bustle.

"While I concede the potential dangers of Faust," she began, turning to look pointedly at Iris, "I don't understand the need for immediate action. After all, we had hundreds of years of evidence of alcohol's great societal harm. Evidence which some of you still don't feel is sufficient, despite our successes." And the gimlet stare turned toward me, of course. I leaned against the wall and gave a small shrug of indifference. She turned back toward the president. "Frankly, Grace, I'm shocked you called this meeting at all. If anything, we should be helping the women protect themselves from the monsters in their midst. I know I never feel safe walking the streets alone at night."

The murmurs of approval and applause (significantly more enthusiastic than for my presentation) told me all I needed to know about this evening's work. They would bicker and discuss the issue for the next several hours, at which point the vote would be called and, in due course, the issue of Faust would be neatly swept under their Progressive rug. I started to walk wearily for the door, but the lady had not quite finished.

"This might cause some harm now, but the comparison to alcohol is . . . well, misguided at best, Miss Hollis. I know you have some peculiar affection for their plight, but they're just vampires, after all."

My head snapped up. "And you're just past your time," I said, quite loudly. I left, then, and slammed the door shut on the shocked murmurs behind me. God smite me if I ever set foot among that gaggle of complacent puritans again in my life. The hallway outside the meeting room smelled like wet mold and rotting wood, but it was warmer here than outside. I sat down on the staircase leading out of the basement and wrapped my arms around my shoulders. I was exhausted unto death, but I still had a class to teach in an hour. Did that leave me time to check on Amir? Of course not, and I doubted he would want to see me anyway.

I closed my eyes and a dozen images flashed in painful staccato across my mind: Giuseppe's eyes as he begged me for help; the vampire woman nearly torn to pieces by a desperate mob; a revenant cat, its bones so easily snapped beneath my calm hands; vampire blood fouling an alley; the revenant marks branded into the skin of two stray cats.

I had refused to go home when he asked me to. And good thing, because one of his attacks found him minutes later, and someone had to clean up the mess. I wanted to throw out the cat, but Amir insisted I leave it.

"I'll take it to Kardal. Might be able to trace it. Rinaldo," he explained through gritted teeth, from the floor beside his sofa.

So I attempted to avoid looking at it. The ragged edges of broken skin, tendon and bones—all denuded of blood—would have made me feel queasy, even without the hot tar and rot smell of the blood.

"What do you think this is?" I asked. "That smell . . ."

"How should I know?" he snapped. "Maybe the Blood Bank kept a few bags past the expiration date." I refrained from pointing out the flaws in his suggestion, as he seemed to be in danger of setting his furniture on fire.

"I don't suppose you still insist upon your right to risk your safety?" he said, when I'd mopped up the last of the foul-smelling blood. "Perhaps I could buy it off you?"

I smiled, though I knew he couldn't see. "Yes and no, respectively."

When he sighed, the light on his side of the room grew momentarily brighter. "I had to try."

I stood up and walked over to him. "Tell me," I said, running my fingers along his jaw and nearly burning them, "what will happen to you if you don't find Rinaldo?"

Quick as a snap, flames darted from deep inside his eyes. He blinked, then groaned. "Nothing, Zephyr. Just some emotional distress."

But he was lying. I had no reason to think that, but I knew. If Amir didn't find Rinaldo, whatever was happening to him would get much, much worse. I hated that he didn't trust me enough to tell me the truth.

I hated that he had something to hide, because it made me start to question what, precisely, that might be.

"Zephyr?"

The hand on my knee was much cooler than his ever were. I opened my eyes and stared into Lily's worried face.

"Sorry," I said. "I must have dozed off."

"You're getting massacred in there," she said. "Don't you want to—"

I shook my head. "I don't fight *every* hopeless battle. Anyway, I have to get to class."

Lily nodded and then, after a moment's hesitation, sat down beside me. "Is it Nicholas?" she whispered. "Did he hurt you?"

"Concern! Goodness, Lily, don't move too fast, you might pull a muscle."

She rolled her eyes and elbowed me congenially in the ribs. "Fine, suit yourself. Just so long as you aren't withholding my proprietary source information."

I smiled and told her what I'd learned about the Faust shipments and Nicholas's plans for them. She clapped her hands in delight, and then looked around as though she might have summoned another reporter from the rotting plaster. "Another scoop!" she whispered. "Zephyr, you are the bat's pajamas!"

"So let's have some reciprocation, hmm? I don't suppose Scott and Zelda are having another bash in Long Island anytime soon?"

Lily's eyebrows were a fair way to her hairline. "*If* I managed to snag an invitation, do you really imagine I'd destroy my social standing by bringing a dowdy, bluenose, singing vampire suffragette?"

"You never know, I might charm them with my wit. In any case, you don't have a choice. I need to find Rinaldo, you need more juicy scoops."

Lily pursed her lips and gave me a hard stare. "Then you wear what I give you, and let me do the talking." She paused. "There's a party tomorrow night."

"Monday?"

"Oh, everyone's doing it. Friday night has gone passé. Anyway, it's some German viceroy or whatever, but I hear he's flown in a band and the booze. If you think Rinaldo is putting on the ritz, then it's a good place to look."

"There, was that so hard?"

Lily just narrowed her eyes. "*Whatever* I tell you to wear, you understand? None of these schoolmarm blouses and sad carpet skirts. I'm going to make you fashionable if it kills me."

"Whatever you say, Pygmalion."

With my bicycle at the boarding house, it took nearly forty minutes to walk from the church to Chrystie Elementary. Sunday was my favorite—and least popular—class: Immigration and Labor Law. It was my idea, and the Citizen's Council had let me do it out of pity, I suspect. After the barbarous Johnson-Reed Act had passed two years ago, with its harsh immigration quotas, their lives here had grown far more complicated. An immigrant's greatest armor would be knowledge of the law and of their rights, and I was determined to give it to them.

I longed for my bicycle, but Amir hadn't been in any condition to teleport by the time we had finished clearing up the worst of the mess. He wanted to try, but as I was unfamiliar with the finer points of teleportation safety (I'd never met a djinn before and fairies don't share their business secrets), I told him to bugger off. We did not exactly part on cordial terms. In fact, just thinking about it was enough to make my headache strain against my temples. I suspected that he was getting cold feet about my help. Chivalrous feet, to be precise. And a fine time for it, too.

"Well, fuck him," I said aloud, to the evident surprise of a hobbled drafthorse shivering on a street corner. "I'm going to find Rinaldo, no matter what he says."

The draft horse coughed and shook its head. "Oh, shut up," I snapped. "He's rich and Manhattan's indigent need funds."

The owner of the horse and the vegetable cart it was attached to spat in the general direction of the gutter and squinted at me. "Need a ride, ma'am?"

He looked trustworthy enough beneath his frayed corduroy cap, and Lord, but I was tired of walking.

I smiled. "Why, if you wouldn't mind."

He climbed in to the front cab, and gave me his hand to help me up. We trundled through the streets silently. He didn't seem inclined to conversation, for which I was grateful. He dropped me off at the corner of Chrystie and Rivington a full ten minutes before class was due to start. I hopped down, but when I turned to thank him he had removed his cap and I could tell that he was struggling to say something to me.

"You're that teacher, aren't you? The one they're always talking about?"

That's it, I thought, I'm moving to the Yukon, marrying a wholesome logger and dying in happy obscurity. What I said was, "I suppose so."

He nodded and rubbed his thumb along the brim of his cap. "See, my little girl, last month, she came down with this terrible fever. We thought it was polio, you know. Nearly died of worry. So anyways, then the fever breaks and she's fine, 'cept now she has wings on her back. They're tiny, they don't do nothing. But we're afraid to send her back to school, 'cause what if the teachers notice and report her? We don't want her to live with that . . ."

I sighed. In a city so overrun with vampires, it was easy sometimes to forget the persecution endured by other kinds of Others. Especially those, like this man's daughter, who suddenly discover within themselves some long-forgotten bit of Other power. If she was put on the registers as a fairie, our current laws denied her a vote, appeals in trials, fair wages and a host of other inalienables the full humans took for granted. And thus a bustling cottage industry of ad hoc surgeons had developed to rid these poor people of the obvious outward signs of their Otherness.

Well, the Citizen's Council wouldn't approve, but I knew how to help him. "You'll need fifty dollars," I said. "On the corner of Pell and

Mott is a Chinese herb shop run by a Mr. Chang. Ask to see him in private. As clean and safe as anything in the city."

He tried to give me money, which, given the sorry state of his horse, I couldn't very well accept. I smiled and extricated myself as quickly as possible, as it appeared he was about to declare my sainthood on the spot. But the encounter had set off my headache again. Others already had such trouble in our society. Women had won the vote five years ago, but when would Others gain equal rights? Now that Faust was overrunning the streets, maybe never. It was enough to make me want to run straight back to that interminable Temperance Union meeting and scream at the bigoted old biddies until my voice went hoarse. Which would, of course, accomplish precisely nothing. I sighed, straightened my spine, and went into the classroom.

There were seven people at the desks inside, to my surprise. In addition to the six regular students, Giuseppe sat in the back row, tapping his foot and looking out the window. He never attended this class. Had Rinaldo threatened him again? But I'd have to wait until after class to ask. I was explaining the nuances of police search procedures when Giuseppe raised his hand.

"But sometimes the police should arrest the Others and they don't. They're just corrupt. They exploit us when they can, and let the real criminals run free on the streets."

Everyone seemed to sit up a little bit straighter. They all knew to whom he referred.

"Well, police corruption—from both sides—is an unfortunate reality of our society, Giuseppe. The best thing is to leave those sorts of Others alone. There are no fair trials with unprincipled thugs. At least our government might give you a fighting chance."

I turned to the blackboard, but he refused to let it go. "And if you have no choice? If the police won't do a thing?"

I bit my lip. The fact of the matter was that sometimes there was nothing to do. One lone vampire like Giuseppe couldn't do anything to hurt Rinaldo's powerful gang.

"Pay them off and weather the storm, I suppose. And I'm sorry for it."

He didn't seem satisfied, but at least he let me continue the class. I wasn't surprised, however, when he stayed behind as the others filed out. I knew he had fallen on hard times, but after our meeting at the tunnel construction site, I didn't quite know what to say. I felt sorry for him, but very wary. He had tried to Sway me, after all. Of course, my attempt to discuss Rinaldo with him in the clear view of all those other vampires had been ill-advised, but the encounter still made me wonder how deep his violent tendencies lay.

"I heard about you and those boys," he said as soon as we were alone. His voice was deep, almost a growl. I couldn't help but notice that he looked several days away from his last feeding. His lips were a thin pink line against the pallor of his face. His fingernails were dark as fresh bruises. He shook his head. "What are you doing, Miss Hollis? Rinaldo is dangerous. You should not play with him." He had leaned in very close and I smelled a hint of something fetid and familiar on his unnaturally cool breath. Like blood and something else . . . alcohol? But he didn't seem like a vampire about to exsanguinate.

"Have you been drinking?" I asked.

He shrugged. "Faust is not a crime. But it is dangerous. You should stay away from the Turn Boys."

"How did you hear about that?"

"Word gets around. Everyone knows who you are."

Definitely the Yukon, I thought. "Listen, Giuseppe, I appreciate your concern, but I do know what I'm doing and I promise to be very careful. I'd like it, however, if you would refrain from talking about my . . . activities with the Turn Boys with other people. It won't be safe if I get too famous, will it?"

He closed his eyes for a moment and his hands began to shake. "Don't be a fool," he said, his voice tight with anger. "He will hurt you, Miss Hollis. You shouldn't be involved." And with that, he left the room with unconscious, unnatural speed.

I had to take a few deep breaths before I could turn off the lights and leave the classroom. I had no right to be angry with Giuseppe. He was only telling me what I already knew, and what Amir had finally realized this afternoon. This new investigation of mine had become flagrantly, recklessly dangerous. I was a moron to continue it. I should take Amir's money and keep as far away as I could.

But I knew I wouldn't. And that terrified me more than a hundred dead cats and a river of blood.

Amir was sitting on my stoop when I made it home, playing jacks in the lamplight with a few local kids. And losing badly, judging by the pile of jacks in front of his foes. He'd changed into a vest and breeches that wouldn't have been out of place on a longshoreman, but he made the faded black corduroy look elegant. The kids were giggling and giving him sidelong glances, like they expected him to vanish or burst into flames at any moment. Which he very well might.

I watched him lose that round, and then smile amiably when one of the boys shook up the jacks and tossed them on the concrete.

"'Kay, your turn to bounce," he said, handing Amir the ball.

Amir took it in two fingers and squinted at it like it might be a poisonous insect. Then he shrugged and bounced it.

He managed to scoop up half the jacks, but the ball soared high and off-kilter. It came down on the step below them and ricocheted toward the sidewalk. I caught it, smiling despite myself at Amir's curious, bemused expression.

"Well, there you are," he said. I threw him the ball. He caught it smoothly and turned back to the kids. "Sorry, boys, I'm afraid you'll have to finish trouncing me another time."

"You a sucker?" one of them asked. "You sure don't look like one."

Amir raised his eyebrows. I could tell just from the set of his lips that he was holding back a laugh. "No, a . . . genie, actually. Why do you ask?"

He and the other boy looked at each other and giggled. "My momma says Zephyr's a sucker licker, that's why. But I bet she likes genies, too."

Sucker licker? Good God, it just gets worse and worse. Amir took one look at me and then laughed out loud.

"I think you made her mad," he said.

I glared at all of them. "Benny, David, go home. Now."

They took one look at me, grabbed their jacks and sprinted across the street. Amir looked after them for a moment and then walked toward me.

"What a reputation you have," he said softly, tracing the bones of my neck with his index finger.

"How would you feel about the Yukon, Amir? Pristine wilderness, quaint cabin, no people."

"I'm not sure I'd be a great addition to a log cabin, dear. I might burn everyone down."

"Wonderful. Even fewer people."

He gave a soft laugh and leaned down for a gentle, teasing peck on my lips.

"What are you doing here? Shouldn't you be resting?"

"I'm not an invalid."

He obviously couldn't see himself at the height of his attacks. "And what about Kardal? Could he trace the tomcat?"

Amir rolled his eyes and leaned back against the balustrade of the staircase. "My brother," he said, "is a singularly useless individual. He couldn't get a trace, but he was certainly full of unwanted advice."

He looked so annoyed that I had to laugh. "You sound like I felt after the Temperance Union this afternoon. What a bunch of moldering, pious hypocrites."

"They just need something to loosen them up . . . a flask of rum in their punch, for example?"

In a moment of reckless abandon, I kissed him briefly. "See," I said, "we're perfect allies. Now what did you want?"

"I thought we should try to find Judah's mother. Kardal and I . . ."

Well, yes, I could see how two djinns might not be the best guardians of a confused, freshly-turned eleven-year-old vampire.

"Has he remembered anything else?"

Amir shook his head. "He doesn't even remember what he said about the boats. It's very odd."

"Well, maybe we just need something to jog Judah's memory. We could try South Ferry again. He might recognize something if we bring him along."

"Determined to earn your salary, aren't you? Shall we go?" he asked, smiling that slow, lazy smile that had gotten me into all this trouble in the first place.

"You know me, never happy unless I'm saving someone."

"And I'd hate to disappoint you."

We had not walked three steps before my stomach let out a painfully audible growl. Now that I thought about it, I hadn't eaten all day.

"Sounds like your stomach is auditioning for Wagner."

"Just a minor role. You want to wait here while I grab some food inside? I'd invite you in, but Mrs. Brodsky might attack me with a scrub brush."

I turned away, but Amir's voice caught me like a fishing line. "Don't be silly, Zephyr. I know just the place. If we hurry, we can make it before closing."

"You do know I don't eat wieners and sauerkraut, right?"

He pressed his lips together, forcefully reining in a smile. "If wieners were caviar, they'd serve it at the Plaza."

"And if the Plaza served hot dogs, I still couldn't afford it."

So we walked to Chinatown. It wasn't very far, but it had been a long day and I looked longingly at the few passing taxis.

He squeezed my hand, apparently happier than he had been for the last few days. Not that I couldn't still discern the signs of pain and stress around his eyes and mouth, but he held my hand and hummed under his breath and generally acted like a schoolboy given a surprise half-day due to inclement weather.

"What's gotten into you?" I finally demanded, when he stopped in his tracks and lifted me up for a kiss. "Did you find Rinaldo or something?"

He laughed. He didn't seem particularly in pain, but his hands were fire-hot even through my coat. "I have a few leads, as Sherlock Holmes might say." He set me down and stared for a moment. His eyes shone like banked fire through crystal. "This is curious, but I think I'm happy to see you."

I had to look away. I couldn't decipher the expression on his face—it seemed wistful and sad and resigned and giddy all at once, depending on how I squinted in the dark. And though I hated to admit it, his mood frightened me. Something had happened to him over the last few days. His attacks were coming closer and closer together. Rinaldo—whatever the source of their conflict—clearly knew Amir was planning something. No sense in threatening him otherwise. So why, given all the horrible events that had occurred over the past few days, was Amir so unfazed?

I shook my head and started walking. Amir stood still on the sidewalk for a moment and then jogged to catch up.

"I can be sad if you like," he said, still wearing a tentative smile. "Or is it just the thought of you in particular making me happy that makes you look as though you've just swallowed coal?"

I grimaced. "Feed me and I'll sing you an aria."

Lucky for me, the restaurant was just a block farther. He opened a door so nondescript (sandwiched between a tailor and a traditional Chinese herbalist) that I could have walked past it a hundred times without noticing. But as soon as we started up the painfully steep, creaking wooden stairs, the unmistakable smell of delicious food assaulted us. Garlic and duck fat and cloves and ginger and a hundred other scents I couldn't recognize made me stumble on the top step.

Amir's hands held my waist before I could so much as stub my toe. "Just a few more," he said, laughing. I couldn't help but smile up at him. My stomach suddenly felt so warm and taffy-stretched I thought it might float away. He opened another door at the top of the steps, and we walked through. The room held three long tables, with four or five Chinese men seated at each while they devoured an astonishing wealth of food with wooden chopsticks. I'd eaten Chinese food from street vendors before, but never in an actual restaurant. A hazard of depending on the charity of others willing to buy you dinner is that you have to eat what they like. An older man wearing an apron came from inside the open kitchen as soon as he saw us and greeted Amir in a string of rapid, incomprehensible Chinese. Amir responded in kind.

My eyebrows felt like they were about to wander into my hairline by the time we sat down at the table closest to the kitchen. "Basic literacy and elocution," I muttered. "How many languages do you know, anyway?"

Amir leaned back in his chair. "About eighty. Kardal speaks over a thousand, counting dialects. But we're djinn. I can learn any language in a week."

"Less obvious than flaming eyeballs, but . . ."

"Guess that's why you call us Others."

The food arrived ten minutes later: eggplant with hot pepper, garlic, heaps of chives and other greens I didn't recognize, vegetable dumplings, and two plates of strange springy blocks Amir called "doufu." It was enough food for at least four people. The waiter dropped a salad bowl full of white rice in front of me, smiled encouragingly, and made noises that I presumed meant something along the lines of "get on with it!"

I stared at Amir. "Is someone joining us?"

"Eat, Zephyr. You look like you're about to fade away."

I looked back at the food. The aroma was about to make my eyes water. Well, damn, if he wanted to give me this much food, who was I to say no? I lifted the chopsticks and clumsily grabbed a piece of eggplant. It seared the inside of my mouth, made my tongue burn with spice and cleared my nose. I cursed.

"Too spicy?"

I ate another piece. "Delicious," I said.

Amir only picked at the food, but my appetite sustained me through nearly all of the dishes. The doufu tasted a little strange at first, but by the end of the meal I'd cleared one of the plates. I was so full it hurt to stand. It felt wonderful.

"Thank you for that," I said, sincerely, when we went back into the blustery cold outside. He ran his fingers along the back of my neck in silent contentedness. I sighed, not entirely with pleasure. I was full, Amir was beautiful and engaging and happy beside me, Nicholas had finally given me a clue as to where he'd turned Judah . . . and yet I couldn't shake this uneasy feeling. Why did Amir need Rinaldo? What had happened to make him so nonchalant about his dire circumstances? I thought about Aileen and her strange warning: *I know you'll hurt yourself if you do what he wants.* But no, he'd paid me, and I wouldn't let Aileen's trauma-induced hysteria make me distrust him for no reason.

Amir vanished when we reached Water Street, mid-kiss. I could still feel his laughter on my lips, but I was suddenly alone. I shivered and waited for a few minutes until he returned with Judah. But they weren't alone. I didn't recognize the third person until I heard his unmistakable bass rumble: Kardal had taken a form that looked almost human, if you didn't stare for too long. Of course, he looked like a true Arabian, with his smoky skin, jeweled turban and long brocaded tunic. Quite a contrast with Amir's impeccably modern attire. The two brothers were engaged in a heated argument—apparently having forgotten all about Judah. I walked closer to the child. He looked up at me, but didn't touch.

"You've always been an irresponsible, callous, selfish ingrate, Amir, but now you've gone too far. This is your mess, brother! You can't expect some innocent human less than a tenth your age to get you out of it!"

"I don't expect her to get—"

"Oh, yes, you do. I know you. You're using her like you used that one in Osman's court, and that Bedouin girl and the French maid . . ."

"They had names, Kardal," Amir said, with such quiet anger that it shocked me.

"And I'm sure you don't remember them! Leave her out of it, Amir. She doesn't deserve you."

Amir was silent for a long moment, opening and flexing his hands. "Are you quite done?" he said finally.

"She doesn't deserve you," Kardal repeated, rather cruelly.

Amir looked up, as though he would supplicate the heavens. "Of course not. I promise to get her out of my mess. Does that satisfy you?"

Kardal shook his head, and began to fade. "We all thought Father was crazy, to breathe you into life so late."

Amir stared at the spot where his brother had been and put his hands to his temples. Then he turned to me, a pained, rueful smile on his face.

"Sorry you had to see that," he said.

"It sounds as though Kardal has given you a bad case of chivalry."

"I hope not. I value my skin far too much." He flashed a conspiratorial smile. "As you well know. Kardal can be so fourteenth century, sometimes. I, on the other hand, am fully on board with feminist ideals. You'll still help me?"

"You have to ask?" I said. I looked back down at Judah, who hadn't moved. The boy looked better, I supposed, though far less childlike than before. Not quite as befuddled and scared, more feral. Amir hadn't bothered dressing him for the winter chill, I noticed, but at least he didn't look like he'd stepped straight out of a sultan's palace. I wasn't afraid of him, but I suddenly wondered what kind of mother would thank me for returning this child to her.

"Judah," I said, bending so I could see him better, "we're going to walk around. You need to tell me if you recognize anything, okay? If anything seems familiar, you let me know. We're going to try to find your mother for you."

Judah seemed to consider my words for an overlong moment and then nodded. "My mother is very beautiful. She loves me. I remember that."

"And your papa?"

"My papa's gone," he said, very sure.

God, his voice was so high and innocent. But the notes beneath it were too seductive, pure vampire. If he lived a long time, I suspected that his would be a voice capable of controlling me. But for now, I was safe enough. He didn't know what he was capable of.

It didn't take us long to circle the neighborhood around Water Street and reach Battery Park, with its clear nighttime view of the South Ferry docks. But Judah responded to the place with the polite interest of a tourist. We were careful to walk near any landmarks he might recognize, but he just shook his head when we asked him if he remembered anything. We'd covered most of the park—and I was wondering if I'd ever feel my fingertips again—when a trash barge pulled into view from the East River. Judah stared at it, mesmerized, as the barge turned to go up the Hudson. Suddenly, it let out a deep bellow, utterly uncanny in the January stillness. I could see how a child might be frightened of that. And, indeed, Judah had turned away from the shoreline and regarded Amir with an expression of incipient panic.

"Do you recognize that?" Amir asked, and I glared at him. He couldn't even attempt to comfort the boy?

"It's very loud," Judah said, softly. "It's like a roar."

I would have comforted him myself then, only I was recalling the strange thing Nicholas had said this afternoon. Something about his papa putting him in a cage with a roaring beast. But it now occurred to me that the deep horn blast of a trash barge could sound very much like an animal with the right acoustics.

I ran until I reached the edge of the docks and looked down. Sure enough, storm drains here emptied into the water. Could *this* be Nicholas's cage?

"Amir," I said, when he and Judah came up behind me, "can you go down there and check for anything suspicious?"

"Those are storm drains," he said, as though I'd asked him to take a quick trip to the moon.

"Those storm drains might be where Rinaldo turned Nicholas."

"I think you might have taken the term 'lair' a little too literally, *habibti*. He's a vampire, not a mole rat."

"I didn't say he lived down there. But you must admit sewers would be a safe place to hide your mad child sucker."

I realized after I said this that Judah was still listening to our exchange. Amir glanced at him. "I'll take you back soon, I promise," he said, with a surprising touch of tenderness.

This shock only increased when Amir flashed me an indulgent smile and turned into a cloud of vapor. I shrieked. Judah grabbed my hand. The cloud that had been Amir hovered for a moment and then flowed over the side. A moment later, I heard something solid echoing off the concrete.

I cupped my hands over my mouth. "Are you . . . ah . . ."

"Dirty? Climbing through sewage? Wasting my time?"

"Corporeal?"

I trembled a little at his echoing laugh. "How charming. The vampire suffragette, overcome by a bit of smoke. There's nothing down here, you know. Unless you are interested in rat carcasses. Which I am decidedly not."

"Does it lead anywhere?"

"Not unless you can turn to smoke. There used to be a tunnel, but it looks like someone smashed it in. Please tell me—ah." He paused for a moment. "Well, look at that."

"What? What happened?"

"I've found something."

I managed to keep a semblance of calm when the smoke flew back up to the surface and reassembled into a fully clothed Amir. A fully clothed, *dirty* Amir. He held a wet and brown rag distastefully between two fingers.

"You brought the sewer sludge with you?"

"Oh, how quickly she turns critical. That isn't as easy as it looks, my dear."

"That trick could have saved you some trouble with that vampire I popped."

"*That trick* is one I find almost impossible in extremity. Unfortunately for my pride."

This made me smile, for some reason, and we looked at each other for a moment that might have turned to something else entirely if not for Judah standing quietly by.

"What is that thing, anyway?"

"You don't recognize it? Imagine it with a less liberal coating of muck."

I took a step closer and then gasped. He held a knitted blue mitten—the match for the one Judah had been wearing when I discovered him.

"They turned him here," I said. "In the storm drain."

Amir tucked the mitten gently in his pocket. "Looks like it."

A night guard approached us and so we hurried back onto the streets. "You two should go back," I said. "We can't do anything more tonight."

Amir agreed with me, but Judah was moving ahead of us, toward Whitehall Street. He turned the corner and stopped in the middle of the deserted road. He was staring at the wrought-iron electric lamps that flanked the Whitehall subway station.

"Yes," he said in a quiet, steady voice, "I know those."

Subway lights? Amir and I looked at each other. "Do . . . do you think you lived nearby?" I asked.

"I don't know," he said. It occurred to me that his voice was strangely cultivated, like that of a well-educated child. But what well-educated child would ride the subway enough to recognize its lights in the absence of any other memories? We walked closer to the entrance. On one side there was a small municipal garden. The flower beds and bushes were bare of anything but frozen snow, but something made me pause and walk closer to them. I wasn't much of a botanist, but even I could recognize the thorny, tangled brambles of a rosebush. And I could imagine how, in the height of their spring bloom, the scent would be redolent enough to stay in the memory of even an amnesiac vampire.

"Zephyr?"

I turned to Amir. "These are rosebushes. We must be near Judah's mother."

The feeling of success was a better bracer than a strong cup of coffee. I hopped and dashed down the steep steps to the subway station. The teller's booth was closed at this time of night, but the station wasn't quite empty: a poor indigent had made himself comfortable at the foot of the staircase. He had the distinctive smell of a man forced to wear the same winter clothes for months on end without recourse to a bath, with an undertone of something sharp and rotten. I thought I'd grown accustomed to strong smells from my time in the soup kitchen, but this went a step beyond even that. I thought he was sleeping, but he opened his eyes as soon as we approached.

I fumbled in my pockets for some coins, but Amir rolled his eyes and put a hand on my shoulder. "Do you recognize this boy?" he asked. The indigent apparently recognized a danger when he saw one, because he attempted to sit up. He seemed drunk, actually, which was strange because alcohol was the one smell that didn't waft to my nose. As soon as he saw Judah, he crossed himself and pressed his back into the wall behind him.

"Christ almighty, what'd you do to him? My blood's no good, I swear, I've spoiled it."

Amir raised his eyebrows. "Spoiled it? What, you forgot to put it in the ice box?"

"Alcohol, ashamed to say, sir. Distilled brandy, straight to the vein. Get the shots from one of Rinaldo's fellas."

He helpfully rolled up his odiferous sleeve in order to give us a better view of the yellowing injection sites all along the major vein in his arm. I held my breath and struggled not to gag. I'd seen a lot in my time in this city, but there were always further depths. This man probably wouldn't survive the winter.

"Okay, we understand," I said, voice nasal from breathing through my mouth. "But you recognize this boy?"

"Boy?" His laugh caught in his throat and turned into a sickly hack. "If that's a boy, you're Jimmy Walker. Someone's gone and turned him."

"But who was he before? Did you know his mother?"

His eyes softened a little. "Oh, of course. Lovely lady. Haven't seen her but once this past week. Eyes red like she'd been crying. Gave me two dollars for no reason at all. Shame this had to happen to her boy."

Amir and I looked at each other with guarded excitement.

"Do you know her name?" he asked. "Can you tell us what she looked like?"

The indigent narrowed his watery eyes. "Why? So you can give her that . . . thing? You should stake him and leave her in peace. Beautiful woman."

Brilliant. I'd really had enough of this. I fished two silver dollars from my pocket and dangled them in front of his nose. "This is yours if you help us. Clear enough?"

He looked between me and Amir. "You know, it just wouldn't be right . . ."

Amir, with delightful casualness, allowed a delicate stream of sulfur smoke to flow from his ears. The indigent's eyes widened.

"Now," said Amir, "why don't you tell us what you know."

"Never heard her name, I swear. Just saw her and the boy. They'd ride some mornings. She always looked a little posh for the subway, but you know what they say about traffic in the city nowadays." He laughed nervously, and wiped beads of greasy sweat from his forehead. "Brown hair. Long and proper, you know. Thirty, maybe thirty-five. Light brown eyes."

Now we were getting somewhere. "Does she live around here?" I asked.

He frowned. "Now, that's the thing. I don't really know. I never saw her leave the station. They were just here, and then . . . gone."

"You mean they disappeared?"

"No, no. They'd go over there." He pointed to where the platform continued for a few yards into the dark subway tunnel. He tried to snatch the coins from my hand. "I swear, that's all I know. Leave a poor fella alone, won't you? I need some sleep."

Amir shrugged, and I let the coins drop. "If you see her again, tell her to visit the Lower East Side Citizen's Council and leave a message for Zephyr Hollis about her son."

I almost winced to give my name, but to my eternal pleasure, he didn't recognize me. Perhaps I didn't need to move to the Yukon after all.

The man watched us warily until we reached the staircase. "You should stake that boy," he called, after we were out of range of his smell. "That sort of thing's illegal and you know it."

To our surprise, Judah paused and turned toward the man. "I wouldn't want your blood, anyway," he said, in a clear, carrying voice. "You smell, and I'm a good vampire."

A good vampire?

"Did you tell him that?" I whispered to Amir, when we left the station.

He shrugged and shook his head. "Maybe Kardal's been at him. Wouldn't surprise me, moral bastard."

In the distance I heard the sound of snickering and a sudden tinkle of broken glass. There must be a few speakeasies around here, and I wondered how many of them already were serving the new vampire wonder-drug. My jaw cracked with a yawn and Amir turned to me, as though shocked to remember that I was human. He held my hand and Judah's shoulder, and teleported us to the front of my building. The sensation felt like no more than an unpleasant jolt, now. And certainly easier than bicycling or taking the subway. The street was dead silent, but I was oppressively aware of glints in open windows up and down the block. It seemed the vigilante spirit had spread from Catherine Lane. And what if they recognized what Judah was? I shuddered.

"Take him back, Amir. Everyone's too keyed-up about Faust— there's no telling what they'll do if they see . . ."

He understood. "Careful," he said. "I'll find you tomorrow." He embraced me and planted a quick, fiery kiss on my forehead. He and Judah walked down the block until they were hidden in a puddle of shadow, and disappeared.

I pushed open the door to the bedroom quietly, but Aileen was still awake. She perched on the windowsill, chain-smoking in her oversized teddy and nylon-hose turban. Her hands were shaking.

"You're going to kill yourself, you keep up like this," she said. "Amir must know how dangerous what you're doing is. I don't trust him, Zephyr."

"Is that a . . ."

She shook her head and stubbed out a cigarette. "No, not a vision. Just run-of-the-mill concern." She cracked open the window and tipped out the bowl of butts and ashes. "So you believe me, then?"

I was so exhausted I thought I might faint where I stood. Aileen looked nearly as bad. The shadows under her eyes were almost black in the moonlight. "They haven't stopped?" I asked.

Aileen shrugged. "I feel like a radio for the other side. Smoking seems to stop them."

"Poor Aileen," I whispered. I hugged her tightly and waited until she could let go and cry. I couldn't have imagined a more horrible thing to happen to her. "We'll figure this out," I said. "There have to be ways to control the visions."

"But you thought I was just hungry, this morning. What happened?"

I sighed. "The thing outside the door last night? It wasn't just a stray cat. It was a revenant. You shouldn't have known it was an Other. I didn't want to believe it, but . . ."

Aileen pulled herself away from my shoulder. "Zeph, what was a revenant cat doing outside our door?"

I bit my lip, but I didn't have the energy to lie. "A threat," I said, "from our favorite gangster."

Aileen hiccupped and then laughed as she blew her nose into a handkerchief. "And I thought *I* had problems!"

CHAPTER SIX

Aileen and I woke up an hour before dawn to the sounds of shotguns echoing down the street. Aileen fell off her bed. I struggled up on one elbow and squinted at the window.

The next round of gunshots sounded like cannon fire from beneath our beds. Aileen moaned.

"This is getting ridiculous," I muttered. I stalked to the window and pushed it open. The icy wind blew in immediately, cutting through my flannel nightgown.

"Zeph, what are you—"

I grit my teeth and leaned out of the window. "Will you stop it?" I hollered, cupping my hands around my mouth. "This is not the bleeding O.K. Corral! It's Ludlow Street, and I'd like to go to work without getting shot!"

Aileen yanked me back inside by the arm and shut our window. "Are you barmy, Zeph? Don't answer that. Ugh, it's freezing."

We both tried to get an extra twenty minutes of sleep, but as soon as the sun rose the noise of gunshots was replaced by the incessant wail of sirens streaming all over the city. Aileen claimed use of the bathroom first, and I followed her, bleary-eyed and feeling more exhausted than I had when I went to sleep.

I said good-bye to Aileen and fetched my bicycle from beneath the staircase. Not a few street corners I passed had wary-looking sentinels awkwardly toting rifles. It was enough to make even the most sanguine pedestrian feel like she was taking her life in her hands just by going to work. The tensions were even higher around St. Marks, which held more than its fair share of gin joints. The streets were surprisingly empty, and the few people who had dared to go outside huddled under their hats and scarves and refused to acknowledge anyone as they hurried past.

I heard the commotion outside the Blood Bank before I saw it. It sounded like a prize fight in the tenth round—boisterous, dangerous and full of illicit, disturbing fun. More than a dozen vampires, already blistering red in the weak dawn sun, had smashed the front windows of the Bank with some loose bricks, and appeared to be raiding the stores. They huddled in the shadow of the westward-facing building, laughing drunkenly and guzzling the plastic bags of hard-won blood as carelessly as bottles of pop at a carnival. I looked for the golem and saw it lying among the broken glass. They had torn its squat torso in two, but the animated halves still flailed weakly against the pavement. A small crowd of onlookers stood on the edge of the block—some watching, some pleading with them to stop. The vampires weren't paying them the slightest attention. I let my bicycle drop to the sidewalk and sprinted forward.

"Ysabel?" I shouted.

She didn't respond, but I saw her a moment later. She was at the front, being restrained by her husband and a young man I recognized as one of her collection agents. She let forth a string of Yiddish I didn't understand but gathered wasn't entirely suitable for polite company. I pushed my way through the crowd and put my hand on her shoulder. She turned to me, a wild grimace on her face, and I flinched. She was weeping in her rage.

"Oh, Zephyr, *bubbala*, look at them! All our supplies . . ."

"Fellas!" One of the raiding vampires hurled a crate of blood out of the broken window. It smashed apart on the sidewalk, spilling blood bags. "Found the good stuff. It's all M."

They all rushed toward it, discarding what were, in some cases, nearly full bags of blood. I wanted to cry when I saw the precious red liquid seeping uselessly into the cobblestones.

"You demons!" Ysabel shrieked. "How can you do this? How can you waste so much! It's *not for you!*"

One of the raiding vampires, an older woman, finally deigned to notice her. "Hey, Grandma, you want some?" She squeezed a bag between her hands, splattering our faces and clothes with the dark-red preserved blood. Ysabel sank to her knees.

"That's it," I muttered. I headed toward them at a brisk walk, unsheathing my knife from beneath my skirt. They didn't pay me much attention. Not until I launched myself at the wide-eyed vampire who had taunted Ysabel. She crumpled beneath me—Faust evidently made vampires clumsy, in addition to reckless. I held the silver knife to her throat, smelled the distinctive scent of charring vampire flesh, and smiled.

"Let go of the damn blood," I said.

I thought I sounded eminently calm and reasonable, but apparently her fellows finally saw someone worth noticing. Their laughter died in their throats, and they stared at me in drunken shock. Suddenly the only sounds to break the silence were the strangled gurgles of the unfortunate woman beneath my blessed blade.

"You want her to die?" I said, when it appeared that they didn't quite grasp the point.

"Hey," said the one who had fallen on the pile of precious rare blood, "don't be like that. Just a bit of fun."

"Pardon me if I don't see theft and murder as a bit of fun."

"Murder? No one's murdered anyone!"

I stood up, hauling my vampire to her feet. "Yet," I said. "So, what is it? Stay here, and let her die? Or leave and save all your sorry asses?"

"Come on," croaked my prone vampire, "let's just go. Not worth it, right?"

I was still too angry to feel afraid, and it looked as though my insane scheme might just be working. The vampires looked warily at each other and then, one by one, began dropping their bags of blood. A few had even walked off when something slammed into my right side, smashing me against the cobblestones with bone-jarring force. My knife fell from my hand.

"She's just a bleeder," someone above me said with a contemptuous laugh.

"Zephyr!" That must be Ysabel.

And bloody stakes, suddenly I realized just how stupid I had been. No help for it now. One vampire grabbed my left arm, as though to hold me against the pavement.

"Always better fresh . . ." I looked up—it was the vampire I'd pinned down, looking flushed and filled with wild, reckless strength.

Behind her, another vampire crouched, after a piece of the action. Fuck. As Aileen said, being immune didn't mean they couldn't bleed me to death. And where the hell were the police when you needed them?

I bucked, dragging my arm in a painful jerk across the abrasive cobblestones while simultaneously contorting my body so I could aim a precise kick at the vampire's rib cage. She groaned and relaxed her grip just enough for me to wrench free and stand up. There were three other suckers within striking distance, but the most worrying was one to my immediate right. He rushed toward me, laughing at what he still clearly thought would be an easy mark. I let him come, filled with the familiar, eerie joy. He groped inexpertly for my throat. I dodged him, gripped his shoulders and used his momentum to knock him to the ground beside me. I slammed my boot on his neck. Scanned the ground for my blade, and knelt to pick it up. The remaining suckers paused, looking at me warily.

"Sun's getting stronger," I pointed out, blinking the sweat from my eyes.

Suddenly, they started running, bumping into each other in their haste to get away. "The sun isn't that bright," I muttered, looking around the suddenly deserted street. I saw the real reason for their rapid dispersal a moment later: the police had finally arrived. I'd been so involved in the fight that I hadn't even heard the sirens. A police officer hauled the vampire beneath my boot from the ground, and slapped special Other-grade handcuffs around his wrists.

"Are you all right, ma'am?" It was a young officer, looking at me in obvious concern. He was attractive in a wholesome, fresh-faced way. I smiled, but this seemed to worry him even more. I looked briefly down at myself: well, I suppose I'd be worried too. I was covered in so much blood—almost none of it my own—that I must have resembled Lizzie Borden.

"They didn't bite me," I said. "I'm fine. And you fellas sure took your own sweet time, huh?"

He shrugged awkwardly. "There are disturbances all over the city, unfortunately, ma'am. We've got a shortage."

I looked back at the ruined Blood Bank. "And now so do we," I said quietly. Ysabel came up behind me and enveloped me in a fierce hug.

"I never saw something so brave," she said, burying her face in my shirt. "I thought for sure you were dead. And they didn't bite you?"

I reassured her I was fine, though at this point I'd begun to wonder myself. What had I been thinking? My left arm ached—not broken, but I'd have lovely purpling bruises there by this evening. I'd left significant portions of my shoulder skin on the cobblestones. And all because I'd thought I could single-handedly fend off a marauding posse of more than a dozen suckers? The sensation of the knife beneath my skirts— and even worse, the knife in my hands—had begun to feel almost comforting in its familiarity. I had smiled when I felt that poor, Faust-addled sucker squirming beneath my blessed blade. *Smiled.* I was suddenly grateful that I'd skipped breakfast. At least now I didn't have anything to throw up.

I stayed with Ysabel for another half hour, while she surveyed the damage and collected what remained of the blood collection. Saul released the poor golem from its torment—erasing one of the Hebrew letters of "truth" inscribed on its forehead to read "dead." All told, the vampires had drunk or destroyed seventy percent of all the supplies, including most of the rare forms of blood. The shortage would cripple the Bank for at least the next week and a half, until the regulars could come back and donate. I described what suckers I remembered to one of the officers, though from his expression I doubted that they would look very hard for them.

"They won't do anything, will they?" Ysabel said, after the police had left.

I grimaced. "Well, between Rinaldo and Jimmy Walker, the wheels are so greased it's a wonder they don't spin off."

"Rinaldo's a schlemiel. But you mark my words, things keep up like this, it'll get too big for even old Mayor Herod to ignore."

It took me twice as long to bicycle home as normal, I ached so badly. My hip had taken a beating in the fall, too, it seemed. But Ysabel's words had given me an idea, and I didn't have much time to implement it. Jimmy Walker, corrupt and ineffectual though he may be, still had a nominal public mandate. Enough public pressure, and he'd have to change his policy. And if I was going to get recognized everywhere in this damn town anyway, I could at least use my notoriety for good. But first, I had to clean myself up. A brief glance in the mirror made me wince: I looked like I'd been on the losing end of a bar fight. And not far from the truth, at that. I took a sponge bath with tepid water, doing my best to clean the grit from the graze on my shoulder. It was only when I hobbled back to my room that the sobering truth dawned on me: I had run out of clothes. Three sensible skirts and five blouses served me quite well under normal circumstances. But now they were all either covered in mud or blood or both. I still had Aileen's flapper dress, but I couldn't very well wear it in the middle of the day.

I wrapped my kimono more tightly around my waist and went back down the stairs, gripping the banister like an arthritic pensioner. Mrs. Brodsky was in the parlor when I padded in. She seemed appalled at my state of undress, and I braced myself for her tirade, but something made her snap her mouth shut.

"Vampire?" she asked.

Oh, yes. I had forgotten that I looked nearly as terrible as I felt. "About twelve."

She clucked her tongue. "The other girls, they all have sensible jobs. But you, Zephyr . . ."

I rubbed my temples. "It's been a bad week. And I need to use the phone."

I called the offices of the *Evening Herald*, and could have cried when Lily came to the phone. I didn't know what I would have done if she was out on assignment. She, however, was decidedly less thrilled.

"I just got a visit from my friend at the *Daily News*. Want to know what their cover story is? 'Vampire Suffragette Fights Back: Our Girl Faces Down Sucker Pack.' And they have a money shot, Zephyr. You look like a fucking Valkyrie."

"Bloody stakes."

"You're supposed to be *my* source! You do something, I get to hear about it first!"

"It's not like I planned this, Lily!"

She sighed. "I figured. Aren't you supposed to *help* vampires?"

"It's been a bad week. Listen, if you want another scoop, I need your help."

Lily sounded immediately wary. "What kind of help? You know I can't violate my journalistic—"

"Oh, get off it, Lily. I just need some clothes."

"I'd say so."

"Ha ha. Everything I own is a bloody mess. I want to catch Jimmy Walker at recess and make a scene about the Faust disturbances. Given all my damn press lately, I'm sure you can parley that into a solid three inches. What do you say?"

It didn't take Lily long to decide. "I'll be there in half an hour."

Lily arrived twenty-eight minutes later, carrying what looked to me like half her wardrobe, but was apparently just the ten or so items she could bear to part with.

I looked enviously at her latest ensemble. A bias-cut dress of green chiffon velvet, with four dramatic blue stripes cutting diagonally down to the dropped hemline and then wrapping around back. I didn't know how I could pull anything like that off. In this neighborhood, it had seemed safer (and cheaper) to go with sensible. But being around Lily made me long for stylish.

I shrugged. "Well, have at it."

In the end, we settled on a green fitted vest with a double row of buttons, a wide-collared coat with black trim and matching skirt, with a daring little slit up the side. She produced a black velvet cloche trimmed with a green silk floret to finish everything off, and then stood back appraisingly.

"Not bad," she said, breaking into a sudden grin. "The shoes are a shame, but we've mostly hidden the bruises."

We took a taxi to City Hall, since I couldn't bear the thought of managing my bicycle, and Lily couldn't bear the thought of her precious garments splashing through slushy puddles. Well, so long as she paid, I was happy enough to travel in style.

As far as I knew, no organization had planned an anti-Faust demonstration that day, but a bit of a homegrown one had developed outside the marble steps anyway. I wasn't the only person furious about this situation, I realized. It made me more confident about confronting Jimmy Walker.

I looked at my pocket watch: here with five minutes to spare. The Night Mayor was nothing if not punctual about his lunch dates. No one paid me much attention as I jostled my way to the front of the crowd.

"Hey, move aside!" Lily shouted. "Vampire suffragette coming through!"

I could feel the dozens of eyes suddenly homing in on me like the sightlines of a rifle.

"Hey, is that her?" a girl close to me asked her companion. "The one who staked that whole pack of suckers this morning?"

"Guess you changed your mind about how good they are, eh, Zephyr?"

"Maybe Beau Jimmy will give you a medal for doing his job for him!"

I turned around and glared at Lily—and I apparently looked fierce enough to make her flinch. Good. Next time she might reconsider making a fool out of me to get color for her newspaper column.

"I don't judge all of humanity because of some damn fool drunks who get themselves in trouble," I said, loudly enough for the crowd to hear me.

"But you killed—" It was that girl again.

"I didn't *kill* anyone. I was defending myself, and I regret whatever harm I had to cause."

But I remembered the sensation of raw power when I held that vampire in my grip, delicately burning her flesh with my silver blade.

"So is *that* who you are?" said a drawling voice to my right. "Not just any overeager bluenose."

His pale visage barely flickered in my peripheral vision, but I suppose I could have identified him blindfolded. I turned to him leisurely, as though I was merely curious to see who would address me in so impertinent a fashion.

"Good afternoon, Mayor," I said.

"Likewise. You're making quite a name for yourself, Miss . . ."

"Hollis."

"Charming picture, by the way. I wish I could get press like that." He tipped his hat to Lily, gaping behind me.

"Well, perhaps if you hadn't let your mob connections dictate legislation, I wouldn't have had to fight off a pack of Faust-addled vampires this morning."

He gave me a hard, contemptuous smile that thinned his already bloodless lips. "Talk to me when you have a real scandal."

I was furious enough to spit, but I reined myself in. "Twenty new turnings in just the last two days. Dozens of vampires burned half to death in the Tombs. A dozen more poppers. And you think this isn't a fucking scandal?"

He laughed. "Watch your language, Miss Hollis. You're in the presence of a lady." He doffed his hat to Lily again, and stepped off the curb. "Good day, Miss Harding," he said, while his chauffeur opened the door to his Deusenberg. "Valiant attempt, by the by," he said, nodding in my direction, but as though I wasn't present at all. "The intent is chic, but you know what they say about silk purses and sow's ears."

I could hear my blood rushing past my ears. My breath wheezed in my chest, my neck felt rigid enough to crack. Part of me would have wept with joy to kill him.

"People are dead because of what you did," I yelled. So much for cool cultivation. I'd come here to make a scene and damn me if I didn't. "Good, loved, upstanding members of the community are dead because of Faust. Their blood is on your hands!"

"Good grief, they're not *people*, Miss Hollis. Just Others."

"Well, that was . . ."

"Don't talk to me. I can't handle you talking to me right now."

I was marching away from City Hall, rudely ignoring the few people who had come up afterward to speak to me. I knew I was behaving like the worst sort of disdainful, imperious Long Islander (maybe Lily put a spell on the clothes), but I didn't think I could handle human interaction at the moment. We were living in boom times, the war was over. But we lived in our own little cesspool of the Lower East Side, and they made money off of our suffering. To hear it said so explicitly, when the tragic toll of his actions was so abundantly, painfully clear . . .

"He's inhuman. I don't know why he calls us Others, I really don't."

Lily looked surprised. "But Zephyr, you're not—"

"Of course I am! To people like you and him? What's the real difference between a vampire suffragette and a vampire? Novelty, maybe."

Lily was silent for several minutes, though she kept pace with me as

I walked. "I don't agree with everything he does, you know," she said, finally. "Don't lump me with him just because we go to the same parties. I like women's suffrage. I might not want to go to a meeting, but I use prophylactics."

I slowed. "When families are living ten to a room, without heat or electricity, and meanwhile you and Beau Jimmy are bingeing for three days on illegally imported Cointreau at some glamorous Long Island party?"

It was odd, I thought, how angry this seemed to make her. "Jesus, Zephyr, what do you want from us? Blood?"

I had to smile. "It'd be a start."

After a beat, Lily laughed and shook her head. "Touché. Are you going somewhere? I can pay for the cab."

And with that, I felt the last of my anger dissipate. Lily couldn't help the world she was born into any more than I could. Getting angry with her or Jimmy Walker was only a proximate target of a much larger, systemic problem.

I graciously accepted Lily's offer of a cab fare and then left her for Gramercy Park. She would come by Mrs. Brodsky's later tonight to take me to the fancy party, but for now I had a few errands to run, of a sadly familial nature.

I found Daddy sitting with Troy and two other well-muscled Defenders in the parlor of his suite. A brace of arms worthy of a large militia covered the dining table. Knives, swords, bows, shotguns and dozens of rifles glittered dangerously. Caught unawares, the Turn Boys wouldn't stand a chance.

Troy saw me first. "Zephyr! So you changed your mind after all." He strode toward me and punctiliously helped me remove my coat before I could do so myself. "Loved the story in the paper," he said. "I knew you couldn't keep up with this Other-rights nonsense forever."

I wrenched my arms out of the coat and whirled on him. "Troy, you are quite—"

"Oh, leave her be," said Daddy, who had not so much as raised his head from the gun he was loading. "Zeph's gone soft. She thinks it's best to help monsters, not kill them."

Troy's blond brows came together and his lips pouted in a way that, five years ago, I had fancied I loved.

"But didn't you see the papers, Mr. Hollis?" Troy asked. "Derek, show him."

The bigger of the two Defenders shrugged and reached under his chair to pull out the morning paper. It was the first time I had seen it, and so despite myself I walked closer to get a good view.

Bloody Christ. Well, Lily had called it a money shot. My hat had fallen off, and my hair was flying as I apparently tossed a vampire over my shoulder. His mouth was open comically wide and mine held an expression that would not be out of place on an avenging goddess. Daddy looked impressed despite himself.

"When did that happen, sweetie?" he asked.

"This morning," I mumbled.

"But you didn't pop none of them, I bet."

"Daddy!"

Daddy turned to Troy. His smile was strange, disdainful with an edge of fondness.

Troy looked bizarrely disappointed. "Is that true, Zephyr?" It was almost flattering to think that he'd wanted me back in his Defenders so badly.

"I just need you fellas to . . . delay for a while. Give me a week."

"What for?" That was Derek, looking suspicious.

"I have a . . . side job I'm doing for someone. It sort of requires the Turn Boys to be alive for the next few days, right?"

"Is this some kind of trick?" Derek said. "I heard you were working for them. Some buddies of mine have seen you around that gin joint of theirs the past few days."

Oh, great. Now Daddy and Troy looked at me like they'd found out I was selling babies. "I'm not working for them. Exactly. Well, Nicholas thinks I'm teaching him his letters, but really I'm spying on him for this job I was telling you about, see?"

Troy crossed his arms over his chest and leaned against the table. "Well, it appears we're on opposite sides of this, then, Zephyr. I'm afraid there's no way the client will permit us to delay the strike."

Daddy frowned at me. "These Boys are nasty, Zephyr. I know you think suckers are just like us, but these guys are different. This damn wog of yours needs to learn to take care of himself."

"Daddy, you sound like an ignorant yokel. I'm perfectly capable of making my own—"

He stood up and tossed the gun to the floor. I winced, but the safety held. "Oh, I can see that! Rolling around in the hay with genies, teaching gangsters to read . . . vampire suffragette, they call you. Is that it, Zephyr? You just want the monsters to take over all of us and destroy our country?"

Daddy finished this with a very effective shake of his head and deep, bone-weary sigh. It made me furious. "You are the most self-absorbed, ignorant—"

Troy apparently decided this was too much. "Now, now, Zephyr, this is your father—"

"—pigheaded," I continued, even more loudly, "bigoted, small-minded little man I've ever known. It is none of your damn business why I do what I do, but I'll have you know it has piss-all to do with destroying the country!"

"Well, you're giving a damn good impression of it, sweetie," said Daddy, with such mildness that I wanted to stomp my foot like a little girl.

"There are ways to help people that don't involve rolling in with your own little private army and blowing your problem to ribbons. Ever heard of diplomacy, Daddy? But maybe not—you did vote for Wilson, after all."

"So you think that Wilson should have *tutored* the Germans? That would've helped! Shown them the error of their ways, would it?" He turned to the others. "My little girl sure has some strange notions."

"I am not," I said, emphasizing the negative with a pounded fist on the weapons table, "your little girl. And I'm not tutoring Nicholas to show him the error of his ways. I'm tutoring him to *help* someone. But what would you know about that? You boys strap on your weapons and call yourselves Defenders, but who are you really defending? Your pocketbooks, maybe. And your shrivelingly small self-conceptions."

"Little girl," said Daddy, quite deliberately, "you read too damn many books. Whatever this job of yours is, it's not worth it."

I took a deep breath and closed my eyes against his smug expression. "Daddy, Troy," I said, when I had calmed myself, "I can only tell you that this is important to me. If you could just—"

"Great bleeding Jesus, Zephyr, can't you see we got better things to do than play around with you? Now, your mother told you she'd let you know when we go out. That's got to be enough."

Mama caught up with me while I waited for the elevator. I smelled her before I felt the gentle tug on my sleeve. Pressed lavender, the same homemade perfume she'd worn all my life. I smiled despite myself as I turned around.

"Dear," she said, "your father didn't mean all that. He's been under a lot of stress lately. And seeing you with that genie . . ." Something in my expression made her hurry on. "You know how he always gets before a hit."

"But, Mama, this time the one he's hitting is Amir. I might be his little girl, but he couldn't care less about that."

At least Mama looked upset. She took my hand and squeezed it. "Maybe you're getting a little too involved, dear. Amir seemed very concerned about you. He seemed to think you were getting in over your head. Are you, Zephyr?"

It took me a long moment to process what she was saying. "Amir . . . you've seen Amir? Did you go back to his apartment?"

She laughed. "No, no, he came to see your father this morning, but John was out so I spoke to him. He has lovely manners. And he obviously cares about you, dear. He gave this to me."

She held out a scabbarded short-sword that took me a moment to recognize: the foreign-blessed blade that Troy had sold to Amir at discount.

"I could tell it was unusual. Amir said I should keep it. As a gesture of his good faith, he said."

Well, that sounded like Amir. Give my mother a blade blessed in the tradition most likely to kill him. "That was nice of him," I managed.

"I don't want anything bad to happen to him, either, Zephyr. I promise, as soon as I know when your daddy's moving out, I'll tell you. I think you still have a few days." Her mouth twisted a little. "I don't think Troy's mysterious client has paid his last installment."

I had to laugh. "Well, that would hold things up, now, wouldn't it?" The elevator arrived and I signaled for the operator to hold the doors. "Thanks, Mama," I said, kissing her cheek. "I guess I'll keep trying."

I needed to ditch the subtle approach with Nicholas and the Turn Boys. I didn't have time to waste trying to prize clues out with memory games. I was jittery with nerves by the time I sat down in the dimly lit back room. Nicholas looked better than he had yesterday, but I wondered if it was because he'd indulged in less Faust the night before, or just more fresh blood this morning. His cheeks were as rosy as the Nutcracker's.

A general lack of good ideas coupled with panic made me an utterly useless spy for the first half of our lesson. On the other hand, I was a tolerably good tutor, and Nicholas applied himself. We went through the rest of the alphabet almost painlessly, and he wrote his letters backward only about a quarter of the time. I took a primer from my bag that I had borrowed from Chrystie Elementary and helped him struggle through his first words, then his first sentence.

"Blessed are the . . . pure at . . . heart," he said triumphantly, after a battle of perhaps five minutes. But the smile fell from his face like an ill-handled soufflé when the meaning caught up with his reading. "That's a dumb sentence," he said. "Who needs the Bible, anyway, Charity? What good's it gonna do me?" I couldn't help feeling sorry for him. Turning so young had obviously damaged his mind, and I had a feeling that Rinaldo had left even more wreckage there before that.

Nicholas had started rocking gently back and forth. His gaze was fixed at some point past my shoulder.

"Too dark in here," he muttered. "A flat. The trains all got a flat."

"Where are you?" I whispered.

But he blinked and then stared at me, as though startled to find me so close. "What, you wanna kiss me, Charity?"

The contrast between his childish voice and leering eyes made me rock back in my chair. Nicholas probably would have continued in that vein, but at that exact moment Charlie poked his head into the room. He was so pale that in the dim light his head seemed to float disembodied. His hands shook a little, like an old man's.

"Nick," Charlie said, his voice rasping. "Kathryn's here. Won't leave unless she talks to you."

Nicholas frowned. "I'm fucking busy, Charlie. Tell her to blow off."

Kathryn had apparently heard this response, because her voice now pierced our inner sanctum. "You come out here now, you scum, you dirty ungrateful piece of slime!" Her voice—high-pitched, but melodious—broke. I could hear her sobs. "Come here!" she cried again.

Nicholas strode through the door and closed it firmly shut behind him. I was at the doorknob a second later. I turned it carefully, hoping to peek through the crack to the scene in the bar, but instead I had a view of Charlie's corduroy pants. I could just barely make out a swath of feminine blue fabric if I peered between his legs. Fashionably cut, I surmised, from the simple fact that the hem appeared to be more than five inches from the floor. Kathryn, whoever she was, whispered furiously to Nicholas, but emotion made few of her words audible.

". . . you must tell me . . ." I heard.

I strained to hear more clearly, but the conversation remained largely unintelligble. After a moment I stepped away from the door. So much for discovering his secrets that way.

I paused. Maybe he stored important Turn Boys paraphernalia in this room, in addition to broken instruments. I scrambled off the floor and scanned the walls.

I could still hear the stream of disjointed whispers as I located a set of wooden boxes shoved underneath the broken player piano. I pulled one out and lifted the top. Dust scattered and I held the edge of my green jacket over my nose to stop the sneeze. Lily was going to kill me. I quickly thumbed through the haphazard stacks of papers inside.

Music. Modern jazz, strangely enough, given that Nicholas seemed to have his grounding in a classical repertoire. Maybe these belonged to someone else? Joplin, Gershwin, Goodman, Armstrong . . . well, I'd like to visit whatever gin joint would play all this, but it didn't tell me anything at all about Rinaldo. I replaced the top and pulled out the second box.

"Get out of here!" Nicholas was yelling. "You're just a whore. Get out, you *puttana*."

Kathryn let out a wail that made me shudder. My God, what had happened to her? Why was Nicholas being so cruel? Could it be a lovers' quarrel? "Please, please," she begged, her voice so abject that I had to tune it out. I didn't have much time left, and couldn't afford to pay attention to the scene inside.

This second box held even stranger papers. Old maps of Manhattan, some dating back to the 1890s, with certain streets and buildings marked with indecipherable symbols. As I flipped through I started to notice a pattern: the areas with the most markings seemed to represent an area of Rinaldo's current activity. I even saw one mark that represented the Beast's Rum. These must be some of Rinaldo's old plans for his crime operations. Maybe even schedules and drop-off points and smuggling routes. Maybe, if I was lucky, a secret palace fit for a vampire.

A door slammed. Kathryn must have left.

"Bruno!" Nicholas called, his voice closer, "fetch me a pint. Rinaldo has some taste in women, eh?"

Rinaldo's taste! Fuck. He was about to come back. What to do? Frantically, I grabbed a handful of the pages—enough to glean some clues, but not so much that he would be able to notice with a casual glance—and raced back to the table. I'd just shoved them in my bag and seated myself when Nicholas burst into the room. He was furious, I could tell. But the anger had an edge to it. I knew better than to ask. So, Rinaldo had a mistress. That was something. And if she had anything to do with the horror that Rinaldo had perpetrated on Nicholas when he was thirteen, I could understand his hostility.

"Come on," he snapped, as though I was the one who had delayed the lesson. "I'm gonna learn this. He'll see."

He kept me there past dusk, and called it off only when I began to yawn in exhaustion. I didn't know what had happened to drive him like this. And given my other glimpses into Nicholas's tortured soul, I wasn't sure I wanted to.

Monday was my busiest teaching night. I had three in a row, including Modern Etiquette, my least favorite and most popular. If I didn't want to faint while demonstrating how to sip tea and write condolence letters, I needed food. There was a cheap coffee shop on Baxter I thought I could manage. My cab money from Lily was long gone, but Amir's payment could certainly cover some of that deliciously reviving Italian sludge and a pastry.

There were fewer people on the street than normal, and they all walked as though they could hardly bear to put one foot in front of the other. We were in the epicenter of the Faust epidemic, and after three days it seemed the fear had morphed into despair. A sharp wind blew a spray of icy snow from the awning of a bakery into my face. I winced and stumbled forward. I was still blinking the snow from my eyes when something pushed me hard from behind up against the bakery's display window. I grunted in pain as every bruise from this morning flared to aching life.

"What the hell?" I said, too tired and disoriented to even think of getting my knife. Glancing behind me, I saw a tall figure, made anonymous by a long coat and deep hood. He laughed and pushed me again. His breath stank of blood and a gentle hint of rot and tar. A vampire, then. Was that smell Faust, or just the result of a particularly unsavory feeding? I didn't much like either possibility.

"Please let me by," I said, biting off my words deliberately. To let him know he didn't scare me.

His laugh was high-pitched. "Rinaldo knows you, *puttana*," he said, his voice muffled and curiously gruff. "You the mouse, he the cat."

He leaned forward and laid his head on the back of my neck. Despite myself, I shivered. It was too late to bend down for my knife. Maybe I'd have to start putting slits in my skirts for easier access. Lord, but I hoped it didn't come to that. Nearby, a can rattled, as though kicked down the street. My strange assailant suddenly backed away and then ran with that unnatural speed of which only a sober vampire is capable.

I took a deep breath and looked up. I wasn't alone. A lone figure leaned against the brown bricks of the building opposite me, hands deep in his pockets. His eyes seemed to burn mine, and I had no doubt who had kicked the can that startled my mysterious assailant.

How much had he seen? I walked toward him, now far more disconcerted than I had been when the vampire first attacked.

"Are you okay?" we asked at the same time. He smiled slightly and offered me his arm. I took it, grateful for the warmth.

"So you were wrong, Zephyr," Amir said, after a moment.

This statement could have applied to many of my decisions in the last few days. "How, exactly?" I said.

"Rinaldo knows what you're doing. Or didn't you hear that fellow back there?"

I sighed. What marvelous luck.

All the tables in the café were taken except for a small one right by the kitchens. After we sat down, I ordered some much-needed coffee and then went back and forth with the waitress until she finally grasped that I honestly desired a sandwich consisting entirely of tomatoes and cheese.

Amir seemed amused. "That must get frustrating," he said. "Why do you persist, anyway? Surely a little slice of prosciutto never hurt anyone."

I shrugged. "I've visited a few slaughterhouses. And Mama would sometimes make me or Harry kill the chickens for supper. I just . . . lost my taste for it."

"You're really not worried?"

"About prosciutto?"

"*Rinaldo*."

I shrugged. Amir looked like he wanted to shake me, but settled for banging his hands on the table. "How did that vampire find you? What *else* could Rinaldo know?"

And wasn't that a good question? "But . . . but it really doesn't seem like Nicholas suspects a thing. I don't think he knows I'm spying on him."

"Maybe he's a good actor."

I shook my head. "But it doesn't make any sense. Why pretend around me, and then send all these threatening messages? If he wants to string me along, he should make me feel safe, not terrified."

Amir leaned back in his chair, thoughtful. The waitress delivered my sandwich with a contemptuous toss and my coffee with a little more reverence.

"You said Nicholas hates Rinaldo, right? Well, maybe Rinaldo knows something he's not saying. He's threatening you to stay away, but Nicholas is still in the dark."

I took a sip of the coffee, winced, and spooned three heaps of sugar inside. "Well, if the Turn Boys don't know, then I shouldn't worry."

"Unless Rinaldo decides to tell them," Amir said, with infuriating practicality, "or he tires of your interminably hard head and takes care of you himself."

I sighed. "Maybe this whole argument is moot. Look what I found today."

I reached into my bag, pulled out the stack of yellowing papers and pushed them across the table. "Go ahead," I said. "Look through them."

He was silent for a while, but I could tell that he was encouraged just by the way his foot began to tap against the table. "They're old, but . . ."

"He must have marked those when he started expanding the business. Which was around the time he became a vampire, according to Lily. Around the time he disappeared."

Amir looked up at me and grinned. "And maybe these will mark a mysterious location? Very clever." Suddenly, his face fell. "But what if they notice it's missing?"

"Not a chance. I found them buried in a dusty box under a player piano."

"Can I take them?" he asked. "Maybe you won't have to bother with the Turn Boys again, after all."

"Of course." I took a bite of my sandwich. "You might want to look for markings near the subway line. Maybe even Battery Park. Nicholas had some kind of spell—like Judah. He said something about a train having a flat."

"A flat? But train wheels don't have tires."

"Oh." I looked at him, nonplussed. "Well, I don't know what he meant then. I'm afraid to ask too many questions. Maybe he meant a car?"

"Maybe." He looked at the papers, but abstractly, as though he wasn't really considering them, and then back up at me. "That outfit . . . it looks nice on you," he said. "In between defeating a vampire pack bare-handed and causing scenes with the mayor, I wouldn't have thought you'd have time to dash into Saks."

I blushed. "So you heard about that?"

His smile was surprisingly gentle. "Dear, who hasn't?" He reached across the table, traced my jawline with a warm finger and followed the curve of my neck. He hit a bruise, hidden by the edge of my wide jacket collar, and I winced. Did his eyes always glow like that? Just an edge of something warm beneath the caramel brown, a hint of the embers I knew lurked there.

"Zephyr," he breathed, "I'm so sorry. I've been so thoughtless . . ."

I was gripped with an inexplicable panic, a conviction that I did not want his apology, despite the fact that I had no idea what on earth he was apologizing for. "It's actually on loan from Lily," I babbled. "I ran out of clothes. Rough week. She thinks of herself as Pygmalion to my Galatea. I suppose there are worse things than being the pet project of a socialite. Better than Professor Higgins, anyway—"

"Zephyr."

I closed my mouth.

"This ends now. Rinaldo, Faust, all of it. I can still count on your help with Judah?" I nodded, mechanically. "Good. Then I have some errands I need to run." He stood and tossed a crumpled wad of bills onto the table. "I have to go," he said, his face such a mask of determination I hardly recognized him. He put his hand on my shoulder, the same one that had crashed onto the cobblestones this morning. It hurt, but I barely registered the pain. "If you need help, if you can't find me . . . cast a summoning spell and call Kardal."

I was shivering. "Amir, I can't even warm a cup of coffee. A summoning spell? Wouldn't that bind him to me?"

He flashed a tight, ironic smile. "Get a corner-charmer to do it for you, then. And don't worry about Kardal. A subway rat would have as much chance of binding him. It's just the easiest way for him to notice you need help."

What was going on? I stood up, the better to implore him, but to my surprise he lifted my hat and kissed me. The kiss itself was more than a little inappropriate, but he took his time about it, parting my lips and touching my tongue as though he could eat me from the inside. I pulled myself closer to him, until each button from his vest imprinted itself on my chest. As though from far away, someone hooted. Amir abruptly disengaged. I gripped the back of my chair to keep from falling.

"Be safe, Zephyr," he said, his voice rough.

And then he was gone. The conventional way, though the door. The blast of cold air awakened me to the throbbing of my bruises.

"You want anything else, miss?" asked the waitress, halfway between titillated and appalled.

I shook my head and wiped my suddenly wet eyes. "No," I said. *Nothing you can give me.*

Three hours later I left Chrystie Elementary, aching and wondering how I was going to get through a high society party with Lily. I had a sudden flash of Eliza at the Duchess's ball: "How kind of you to let me come." Well, apparently the first order of business would be to keep my Montanan mouth well shut. Or filled with food.

"Miss Hollis?" I recognized the voice, but my exhausted brain took a moment to connect it with a name and a face. When it did, I was surprised. Giuseppe had been forceful, almost menacing, the last few times I'd run into him. Now he looked parchment-pale and contrite, under the flickering light from an electric street lamp.

"What is it?" I said, warily. He really did look terrible, but I was mindful of his strange appearance in my class yesterday. Perhaps he'd just been concerned for my safety, but I wondered.

"I wanted to apologize for my behavior the other day. It was . . . inexcusable. Mea culpa. You have been so generous to me and I . . ." He shook his head, and looked away, as though he were close to tears.

His lips were so pale as to be nearly indistinguishable from his pallid skin. If Nicholas, this afternoon, was a vampire in the pink (or red) of health, then Giuseppe was the picture of one at death's door. Aware of Giuseppe's sad history with Nicholas and Rinaldo, I could only grit my teeth at the unfairness of it. A vampire who starves to death doesn't exsanguinate. He merely falls, like a deflated balloon, and sinks to the earth.

"Giuseppe, I understand the strain you're under, but . . . please, if you need help, go to the Blood Bank on St. Marks, tell Ysabel I sent you."

He shook his head again, but I could tell that my offer had offended him. "Thank you, Miss Hollis, but I am fine. I have my own sources. It's just . . ." He trailed off, looked down, as though he was struggling to find words. "My son. My youngest. He fell ill, terribly ill last week. The doctors aren't sure . . ."

"What happened?"

Giuseppe swallowed. "Polio. He needs a hospital, but . . ."

Before he had finished the sentence, I was reaching into my bag and pulling out what remained of my funds from Amir. I handed it to him. "Please. Take it. That should at least see your son to a hospital. If there's anything else I can do . . ."

"Miss Hollis, I couldn't possibly."

He looked at the bills, torn.

I put my hand on his elbow. "Please. You can pay me back when this trouble blows over."

"You are an angel, Miss Hollis," he said. He pressed my hand and then headed off in the opposite direction. I stared after him when he left, frowning. That man seemed to be walking under his own personal storm cloud.

My pockets were empty as I walked home. A situation all too familiar.

The party was as swanky as Lily promised, and if my appearance was not quite so stunning as that of the city's most promising Other reporter, I didn't embarrass myself either. She had outfitted me this time in organza a shade of burgundy that complemented my hair. It had long sleeves and a high collar—in order to cover my bruises—but made its concession to fashion in the dropped waist and intricate silver beading along the raised hem. Lily had gone through the trouble of buying me a pair of slippers to match the dress, as she had nothing in her closet that could fit my "monstrous feet." My bandeau was made of black jet beads, accented by a large stencil of blue sequins in the shape of a lily. I wondered if this meant everyone in the room knew who had given me my clothes, but then realized it didn't matter. I was as obviously out of place here as Lily would be at a suffragette meeting. We were here to look for Rinaldo, and my clothes would have to do.

Lily was nearly engulfed by a ring of elegantly dressed men as soon as we stepped into the penthouse suite of the Lombardy Hotel. The imported band played discreetly in the corner, but it didn't look as if anyone was yet drunk enough to dance. A server passed me standing alone and lost outside of Lily's ring of admiring males, and placed a champagne flute discreetly in my hand. I took a sip. Funny, I'd always imagined that champagne must be sweeter, given how much everyone rhapsodizes over it. But it certainly tasted leagues better than Horace's bathtub swill, and I knocked the contents back for courage.

"So," I muttered, suddenly feeling much improved, "where's the food?"

I drifted away from Lily, admiring the exclusive and freakishly expensive gowns of the attending ladies. It angered me, in an abstract way, that these people could waste the equivalent of Giuseppe's yearly salary on one evening gown, but the intense desire the clothes provoked in me were either evidence of my most primitive sensibilities, or my most elevated ones. A few men gave me admiring glances and looked rather dapper in their evening suits. I caught myself forgetting the food table entirely and looking for Amir.

But of course Amir would never be welcome at a party like this, or in a hotel like the Lombardy. Lily had been my formal invitation inside, but my skin color was just as important. A guilty thought—wasn't I now a party to it? I continued wandering and finally caught sight of my personal Valhalla. The food table had been stocked with decadent mounds of caviar and foie gras, in addition to dozens of different cheeses and tiny tea sandwiches. I could hear the band quite clearly now—food and music, apparently, the two necessary items that could be reliably packed into the corner of a party. They were playing a number I recognized, though I was so busy downing gourmet cheese it took me a moment to recall the name. "Basin Street Blues." Curious, I popped a few olives in my mouth and examined the band. A fairly standard six-piece, with drums, bass, piano, two clarinets and a saxophone. They were quite good, filling the performance with deft jazz trills and unexpected syncopation.

"You enjoy the new Negro music, I take it?"

I turned to see that one of the dapper gentlemen I had been admiring earlier had joined me at my refreshment table refuge.

"You know, I'd always called it Jazz," I said.

His blond hair had been carefully parted down the middle, giving him a German look, which was only exacerbated by a chin with a cleft so firm it could have served as a handhold to a mountain climber. I think he fancied he looked quite handsome.

"Yes, of course," he said. His accent was New England, but of the variety jealous it had been forced to cross the Atlantic. "But it has the meanest roots. I told Arnold he should hire a string quartet instead, but he wouldn't hear of it. 'People want to dance,' he said." He looked at me and I found myself staring at the cleft in his chin. Did he ever lose things in there? Change, perhaps? "Do you like to dance, Miss . . ."

"H-Hollis," I said, suddenly flustered.

He smiled, and I was now overwhelmed at the depth of his dimples. "Bernard Simpson," he said, extending his hand. "Pleased to make your acquaintance."

Bernard Simpson? I remembered reading that name before. And come to think of it, that penny-romance face of his seemed familiar, too. *The Prisoner of Arabia?*" I said, recalling the name of the latest in a sad line of *Sheik* copycats.

He bowed. "At your service," he said. "I'm surprised you recognized me. They do wonders with makeup these days."

I had to gulp champagne to keep from laughing. The only reason I remembered the billboard was how much he'd resembled a wealthy New England prep schooler dressed up for a costume party. One could practically see the shoe-black running out of his hair.

Luckily, Lily came to my rescue as I was fumbling for a method of complimenting his travesty of a film. "Pardon, Bernie, but I have to take Zephyr away from you for a moment."

He nodded and then Lily was off, dragging me through the crowd until we could manage a bit of privacy near the glass windows that overlooked the city.

"What a world-class bore," she said, rolling her eyes in Bernard's direction. "And that ghastly movie of his! His daddy's a financier in Hollywood. Bernie thinks he's handsome enough, but seems to have overlooked the fact that he can't act."

I giggled. Was this my second glass of champagne? "Well, your rescue was well-timed. I think we can both be sure he is not a secret vampire mob boss."

"None of that gaggle of boys over there, either."

"And here I thought you were flirting shamelessly."

Lily smiled. "That, too."

"Well, where does that leave us?"

She leaned against the wall, and adjusted the spaghetti-thin straps of her blue gown. "If he's here, Rinaldo should be older. With the respectable, cultural-attaché, port and cigars crowd. So we talk, we flatter, we move on."

"Are you sure you'll recognize the signs?"

"If I see anyone at all suspicious, I'll make sure you meet them."

"Right," I said, eyeing my glass and seeing it was empty. "Let's get to it."

"Wait, there's something else. I met with a contact I've been cultivating for the past few days. Part of *le grand exposé*. Dore's regular shoe-shine boy." Lily looked like she'd just eaten a canary.

"What kind of a vampire has a shoe-shine boy?" I asked.

"This one, apparently. Before his untimely end, he was known for enjoying a certain standard of living. And it turns out that while this kid shined our sucker's shoes, he overheard a few fascinating things."

I rested my head against the wall, as it was throbbing with excitement. "Does he know where Rinaldo—"

She shook her head, cutting me off. "Sadly, the boy didn't know anything about that. But he did hear Dore discussing some new 'opportunity,' a few weeks ago. Something he called a new 'line of business' opened up by some mysterious contact in Germany. Well, where have we heard that recently? Faust, of course. But Rinaldo didn't discover Faust himself. It looks like someone, some very rich someone, bought the recipe and the means of production from the German, contacted Rinaldo—out of all the bootleggers and gin-runners in this city, might I add—and suggested they make a deal."

This just got deeper and deeper. "Well, who was it?" I whispered. "Who made the deal?"

She shook her head. "The kid didn't know. I don't think Dore knew. But maybe the seller picked Rinaldo because he felt some kind of solidarity with him. Because he's a sucker? Which might mean our seller is Other, too, but Dore never actually saw him."

"So it could mean anything."

"Welcome to journalism."

I sighed and Lily extended her elbow. "Well, time to be fabulous. Which entails not sitting by the refreshment table as though it's your personal trough."

I glared, took her elbow and glided back into the thick of the party. The crowd had grown since we began our tête-à-tête, and I began to detect the social waves that always come over a party when someone important enters. It's a certain quality of forced nonchalance, rapt attention masquerading as indifference. For a moment I wondered if the new arrival could be someone interesting—a musician like Benny Goodman or Josephine Baker—but I saw his utterly disappointing face soon enough: Jimmy Walker, living up to his name as the Night Mayor of New York, with his latest vaudeville floozy dangling off his arm.

"Oh, damn," Lily said. She tugged on my elbow. "Come on, we've got to hide you. Hopefully he's on his way to a better party."

But I stayed stubbornly where I was. "How dare he?" I muttered, nearly overcome. Lily groaned and put her hand to her forehead.

"Well, he dares. Mayors do that, you know."

"Bad ones, maybe. I bet you voted for him."

"Well . . . I . . ."

Suddenly, Lily grew rigid. Beau Jimmy had spotted us. He gave a little wave and inclined his head. From this close, I could see that his bearcat was a favorite of the recent tabloids, a particularly voluptuous and vivacious member of the Ziegfeld girls. He left her in apparently breathless conversation with two other men and sauntered over to us.

"I'm going to murder you," Lily muttered under her breath, while keeping a perfect smile plastered on her face. "I'm going to murder you and dance on your corpse and not a jury in the world will convict me."

"Oh, why even go to trial? Just give Beau Jimmy a kiss."

"Torture," she whispered, "*then* murder."

"Miss Harding, Miss Hollis. Politics must be jading me, because I have a hard time believing this meeting is a coincidence." I was sure his charming smile was just as insincere as Lily's, but it was at least more convincing. He had the rosy flush of the freshly inebriated, though he'd just arrived. Knowing our mayor, it was probably his third party of the night.

"Oh, no," Lily said, laughing, her voice at least an octave higher than normal. "It's such a surprise—"

"I can't quite believe it, myself," I interrupted, loudly. Lily gave my ankle a vicious thwack. "I expect you think your attentions are flattering?" In fact, I was starting to wonder. Why, after a dozen meetings on the steps of City Hall, had our estimable mayor chosen now to acknowledge my existence?

I don't know how I could tell, since I doubt a single muscle had moved in his practiced, insouciant smile, but I got the sudden impression that he was now genuinely interested. I had engaged the game. "How fascinating," he said, his deep voice not precisely loud, but deliberately carrying. "What do you think attracted me first, Miss Hollis? Your witty chants at the sucker rallies? Are the shrill voices of your suffragettes like an aria to mine ears?"

I sensed, not so much as heard, Lily's silent wail beside me as she imagined her imminent social demise. I didn't worry—I somehow doubted her place in society was as fragile as she liked to imagine.

I smiled sweetly. "Oh, I see the trouble now. Of course. You'd never have passed those horrible laws if we'd just asked more politely. Perhaps we should have sung, is that it? You hear a little Gershwin and Faust's approval goes to committee?"

Around us, muffled laughter. Jimmy Walker narrowed his eyes, but his smile was broad and genuine. "You battle-axes? Hardly a Wagnerian chorus. Care to prove me wrong, Miss Hollis? I think someone told me you sang."

This suggestion was greeted with such enthusiasm by the crowd that I had only to clear my throat in sudden terror for all to construe it as agreement.

"Arnold!" shouted our odious mayor. "Tell the band they've got an addition."

"Lily," I whispered, frantic. "Wait, I don't want to sing. Tell them to stop—"

She just pursed her lips and took two glasses of champagne from a passing waiter. "Knock 'em dead, Zeph," she said, pressing a flute into my hand.

I only had time to glare at her before a laughing crowd carried me forward to the band. I gulped down the champagne.

"Don't worry," said the piano player, near my elbow. "You'll do fine." I took a deep breath and he took the empty glass. "You remember me, right?" he said, looking hopeful. I took in his short stature and receding hairline for a blank moment. Then it came to me, then: the white piano player from Horace's! I was overcome with relief.

"Thanks," I said. "I'm not sure how this happened."

"Price of fame, I guess. You want to try 'Tea for Two'? I'd say this party needs a little kick."

He was so clearly doing his best to put me at ease that I had to smile. At least he'd played with me before. Maybe this wouldn't be a complete disaster.

The drummer counted out the beat and suddenly I was facing the expectant party crowd, tipsy and nervous and determined to not make a complete ass of myself. I think I succeeded. At least, people clapped and the piano player nodded at me and Lily managed to say, "Not bad," instead of the furious diatribe I'd expected. As for Beau Jimmy, he tipped his wineglass in my direction and then acceded to the demands of his Ziegfeld girl, who seemed to want to attend another party.

After my run-in with the mayor, I stuck to the refreshment table. Lily combed the crowd for likely prospects in our Rinaldo hunt. She quickly homed in on an older gentleman—balding, liver spots on his pate and puffing away on a monstrous Cuban cigar. Aside from an occasional cough, she seemed undeterred by the smoke. I could only admire her fortitude. And now that I headed over, I saw some faint hint of Other about him. Probably not vampire, but perhaps worth a shot.

"Why, Lily," I said, laughing like I was precariously inebriated, "you've been hogging his attentions all to yourself without so much as introducing me. How gauche!"

As I expected, Mr. Cuban Cigar was delighted to make the acquaintance of another young, flatteringly curious girl. Lily gave me just one dirty look before turning the charm back on. I supposed she realized that I must have had a reason to barge in on her reconnaissance work. Mr. Cuban Cigar's real name was Earl something-or-other, and he played around with stock options down on Wall Street. The sort of stultifyingly boring activity made electric to some people by the addition of very large Federal Reserve notes. His evening suit might as well have been made of sewn-together hundred-dollar bills: he'd made every other effort to broadcast his wealth. Even diamond cuff links, twice as large as those holding together the sleeves of the sucker I popped in the alley three nights ago. I looked him over very carefully and attempted to sniff while Lily spoke. Not a vampire. But something else . . . I noticed it, finally, when I pretended to lose my balance. He caught me and held me against him for a few moments longer than appropriate. Certainly long enough for me to see that the markings on his scalp weren't liver spots, but stretch marks. And if I glanced down his starched, high collar, I could see that they covered the rest of his body, as well. A skinwalker. Do it long enough and the physical effects are just as obvious as chronic drinking.

And occasionally just as debilitating. In the modern era, skinwalkers could either be born with their abilities or acquire them through highly immoral means. And in the latter case, they tended to be as sensitive to sunlight and alcohol as any vampire. Was it possible that everyone had mistaken Rinaldo for a vampire, when really he was just something Other?

"Oh, Lily, look!" I cried, stumbling forward. "It's dear Arnold! We really must say hello. Pleasure to meet you," I shouted over my shoulder. He looked bemused, so I blew him a kiss. There, that ought to do it. Now, the only problem with faking drunk loudly is that you can't suddenly turn sober again. And rich men, apparently, adore drunk women. It took us almost an hour to get out of the party and back on the streets, where we could finally speak.

"So that man with the stinky cigar really was a vampire?" Lily asked in a low voice. There was no need on the silent streets, but I understood her caution.

I shook my head and explained my theory about the similarities between the physical effects of long-term vampirism and skinwalking. "But it's possible our informants just don't know enough to tell the difference."

She looked thoughtful. "And Rinaldo doesn't bother to disabuse them? I suppose it could be useful, being able to turn into any other person you like."

"Not *any* other person. Even the old Indian shamans can only change into a few different shapes. Mostly animals. But you're right, if you don't know your boss can change shapes, he has a lot more power over you."

"If this is true, he could be anyone! That shape at the party could be fake, too. How would we know?"

I shivered. "Slow down, I don't know if he was Rinaldo, just that he's an Other. We'll just keep the skinwalker angle in mind. You research Earl what's-his-name, I'll pump my contact for more information, and we'll meet tomorrow. Deal?"

Lily nodded. "You know, it's strange. I've been wondering why no one wants the Other beat, lately. I'm the one getting all the scoops. It's like . . . like Others are the connective tissue of the entire city, really. More than politics and crime and certainly more than celebrity gossip. And they just hand it to me, like it's nothing at all."

We kept walking, though a cab occasionally drove past. "No one wants to deal with it," I said. "Newspapers are elite institutions. Well, yours is, anyway. Doing real reporting on Others exposes their failures like nothing else. There's so much corruption and neglect . . ." I looked at her, my breath fogging the air between us. She seemed oddly pensive, as though she were taking my words seriously for the first time. "Faust is their kind of story. But the other side? The suicides and staked children and crowded tenements? They won't want those. I'm giving you Faust and Rinaldo, Lily. But give me something for it, too. Write some stories you folks don't like to read."

Lily gripped her elbows and leaned back suddenly against the corner of a building. "That woman, that vampire with the silver bullet . . . my God, how does she live like that? That endless threat. I went to Exeter, you know. And they taught us that suckers were evil people who had given their immortal souls for eternal life on earth. They chose depravity and it was therefore our Christian duty to persecute them for it. But she didn't choose anything, did she?"

I didn't respond. For all her faults, Lily was an excellent reporter. She observed, instead of just grafting her own expectations onto events. She dug beneath the surface. Enough of that, and no matter what sort of drivel she'd been raised with, she would understand the living nightmare that gripped so many people in this city. It was happening already. In some ways, I felt sorry for her. It was hard knowledge to live with, and even harder to experience every day.

"Zeph . . . what do you know about Amir?"

I stumbled a little. "What, still interested?"

She shook her head slowly, for once not rising to my bait. "Oh, he's hit on all sixes, I won't argue that. It's just . . . we never really *know* Others, do we?"

"Lily, that sounds remarkably close to the prejudice you just got through telling me might be wrong."

She glared at me, which was an odd sort of relief. "Listen, I never said I thought he shouldn't be allowed in the Roosevelt tea room. And maybe you're right, and that Vampire woman should get a vote and decent wages. That still doesn't mean they aren't different, that you can understand them like we understand each other."

"Oh, so now *we* understand each other?"

She pushed herself off the wall. "Fine," she said. "Fine. Never mind. I knew you wouldn't listen."

I stared after her for a moment and then staggered to catch up.

CHAPTER SEVEN

Aileen and I ate breakfast in the parlor with a few other girls who were all hurrying out. I hardly tasted Mrs. Brodsky's infamously weak coffee and Katya's thick oat porridge. Mrs. Brodsky hovered like the proverbial hen, yelling with extra vigor at the latecomers running down the stairs.

"Go! Hurry! You think you keep your job if you don't show up! I expect my girls to pay. This is not a charitable establishment!"

Aileen widened her eyes. "I'm glad she cleared that one up."

"Oh, but don't forget Mr. Brodsky. She's the soul of giving to that man. I should know, since she gives it right above us."

We burst into laughter, earning me a sharp look from our proprietress. After we'd subsided back to our food and morning exhaustion, I wondered about the changes in Aileen. She looked so harried and tense. The night before she'd awoken in the middle of the night, screaming. A nightmare, she'd told me, but I wondered.

"How was work yesterday?" I asked to fill the silence. "Read any interesting tidbits in your novels?"

She put down her empty coffee cup and picked up the porridge. "I quit, actually."

"You . . ."

"Quit. I had a vision in the middle of the floor. Fell off my chair and started yelling and screaming. Thought I saw a whole army of suckers marching through the factory. Boss told me to go home and rest, but I just quit. No sense in working there anymore. Not after this."

"What are you going to do? Mrs. Brodsky might kick you out, Aileen, and I barely scrape up the rent each month myself."

She shook her head. "Oh, Zeph, of course I'd never ask you to put me up. Don't worry. I already made a bit of lettuce." She reached into her pocket and dumped a pile of change onto the table. "Four dollars," she said quietly. "Just from four hours telling fortunes on Skid Row. If I'd known penny bangles and gypsy earrings would get me so much, I'd've quit ages ago."

I held her hand impulsively. "Fortunes? Did you tell real ones?"

"You know, that's the funny thing. I didn't mean to, but when I started I found that I would sometimes get real glimpses. I saw a woman die, but I didn't tell her. I didn't tell most of them. But now the visions feel more . . . controlled. Like if I focus the power, there's less chance of it sneaking up on me. That's something, isn't it?"

I'll help you, I wanted to say, I'll make this better somehow, I'll give you back your old ersatz vamp life, your twopenny romances, your casual flings, I won't let this ruin everything. But instead, what came out was, "Why can't you just go dancing like the rest of us?"

Charlie found me in the cramped back offices of the Citizen's Council, where I was poring over the financial records in anticipation of our tax filing. Since they kept me on retainer, I had to do any odd jobs they asked of me. I was not precisely a genius with figures, but apparently a significant improvement over anyone else available on such a small salary.

"Heya, Zephyr," he said, almost shyly. I hadn't heard him come in, and had to cover my shriek with a cough. The presence of such a young vampire, with such an ugly reputation, in such a small room was less than reassuring.

"Charlie! What . . ."

"It's Nick," he said, scraping his shoe listlessly in a pocket of cracked marble. "Said he wants you early."

Well, damn. I'd been planning to see Amir before tutoring Nicholas, in the hope that he'd found any clues in those maps, or learned anymore from Judah. Daddy and Troy weren't going to give me much more time, and I needed to be armed with information before I spied on Nicholas again.

"I'm busy, Charlie," I said. "I agreed to tutor Nicholas, not be his servant."

Charlie frowned. He looked genuinely worried for me, and so boyishly cute I tried not to wonder if the flush along his fingertips and ears had been legally gained. "I think you gotta come. Nick's in one of his moods. Didn't even drink Faust last night, and it's like he's going nuts." He froze and looked up at me. "Don't tell him I said that. Hates it when we use that word."

I could imagine. "Of course not, Charlie," I said. "Can he wait a few minutes?"

"Oh, sure," he said, relieved. "Just don't come down to the Rum. It's a mess, you know. The Faust dried up around midnight 'cause the new shipment we was supposed to get never showed. Word is the Boss is pissed to hell 'cause this nigger or whoever he's buying from just vanished, and the German guy ain't takin' his telegrams." He snapped his fingers. "Town's gone as dry as a desert. Just between you and me, it's not so bad. Faust . . . never thought I'd say it, but you can have too much of a good thing. Still, I got a name to make for myself, Zephyr. Nick was pissed when I lost that booze to the Westies, but I'm going to do one better. I'm going to find Dore's killer. The Boss has put a bounty on the head of whoever popped him."

I kept my face carefully neutral, attempting to digest this torrent of information that had improbably fallen out of Charlie's lips. Perhaps I'd been pumping the wrong Turn Boy all this time. A bounty on the head of Dore's killer, the "nigger" supplier suddenly cutting off all business (I'd have to tell Lily), and something I'd forgotten: the escalating rivalry between Rinaldo's gang and the Westies.

"Nicholas can't get too mad," I said, carefully. "The Westies have stolen a few shipments in the last few weeks, haven't they?"

Charlie frowned and shook his head. "I don't think so. If they'd done it more'n once, I think Nick might have declared war! Nick doesn't like poaching."

"But . . . I'd heard it was one of Rinaldo's runners, not Nick's," I said. This was strange.

He shrugged. "Hey, maybe. We don't got much contact with the Boss. Specially not now that Dore's been popped. I didn't hear nothing about it, though."

I didn't think it would be safe for Giuseppe if I pressed further, so I shrugged and put the tax papers into a more or less orderly pile.

"I'm ready then. Where does Nicholas expect me to tutor him, if not the Rum?" And despite my curiosity at this new turn of events, I wished I'd explored that back room more when I had the chance.

"Broad Street station," he said.

"But it's still under construction."

"That's all right. Nick's got a place. He'll see you when you go, but . . ." He scuffled his feet in the marble again and looked up at me. "Mind if I take you there, Zephyr?"

I stared at Charlie, my mouth open. "How old are you, Charlie?"

"Got turned last year, up in Boston." And he couldn't have been a day older than fifteen when he turned. Sixteen. Well, goodness me, the boy had a crush. I smiled and let him take my arm.

Nick's "place" was little more than a large man-made cave filled with piles of rocks and discarded construction equipment from the work

site. He led me into it from the main entrance while the workers conspicuously ignored us. He'd brought a few gas lamps to light the room,
but otherwise it was entirely devoid of signs of habitation. I wondered
why he'd chosen to take me here. Maybe it reminded him of the
strange, dark place with water rushing past and roaring boat horns and
some sort of flat? But why would he want to remember the site of his
horrific turning? I could tell immediately that Charlie had been right
about Nicholas's "mood." The head Turn Boy was pale, like he'd forgotten to feed, or deliberately denied himself. He'd managed to lead me
here without speaking at all, limiting himself to grunts and gestures.
I'd worry for my safety, if not for the fact that he seemed so internally
focused, as though he only noticed me as a physical object in the
room. Admittedly, I wasn't an expert on mob hits, but this didn't seem
like the proper attitude for a murder, even from someone as strange
and depraved as Nicholas.

"Charlie told me it was urgent," I said, finally, when he'd been pacing the length of the cave silently for a full minute. My voice echoed
like a disobliging guest.

"Charlie's a pest," he said. He kept pacing.

Brilliant. I run away from my paid job and now Nicholas won't even
talk to me. "Hey," I said, just to get his attention. "I heard your Negro
supplier cut off your line to Faust."

As I hoped, he looked at me. "You have your ears in strange places,
Charity. But I can tell you that thief ain't quite a nigger. The Boss
wouldn't stand for it."

And is "the Boss" a skinwalker, in addition to a bigot, I wanted to
ask? Nicholas had led me to believe that his father had turned Nicholas himself, but wasn't it possible that Rinaldo had enlisted someone
else to do the job? Dore, perhaps? Which would explain Nicholas's
obvious antipathy to his father's late second-in-command. On the
other hand, maybe Amir had a particularly good reason for thinking
that Rinaldo was a vampire. I needed to talk to him.

Thankfully, Nicholas stopped his pacing and pulled some sort of
letter from his pocket.

"Want you to read this," he muttered, handing it to me. The creases were worn and the edges frayed from worrying hands. And yet the paper felt curiously dry for something so well-handled. Vampires, after all, didn't sweat. Carefully, I unfolded the papers and looked. One closely typewritten page with a law firm letterhead—clearly some kind of legal document.

"What is—"

"Just read it from the top!" he shouted. The words echoed for several seconds after he fell silent. I shrugged and began.

"Hereby begins the Last Will and Testament of RINALDO SAN-GUINETTI of the area known as Little Italy in Manhattan, well-known businessman. I revoke all wills and testamentary writings by me at any time heretofore made and declare this to be my Last Will and Testament. I appoint my business partner Dore, no surname, Executor of this will. I give and bequeath control of my business holdings and interests to the aforesaid Dore, to maintain and expand our areas of operation at his full discretion, until such time that Giudo, my son, reaches his majority at eighteen years. I hereby consign Giudo into the care of his mother, Katerina, until this time. He is to receive an allowance of two thousand dollars per annum toward his rearing and education. Katerina is to receive one thousand dollars per annum, until her death, provided she refrains from carnal contact with other men and remains faithful to my memory.

"Pending Dore's approval of the following as regards specific, unforeseen circumstances, I hereby divide management of my business holdings as follows—"

Nicholas jumped to his feet and smashed his hand against the cave wall. Stone shattered and fell in a puff of dust. He'd cut his hand, but the ragged edges of skin didn't bleed at all.

"I knew it!" he yelled.

I held myself very still and made sure my face betrayed no emotion. Nicholas was unstable in the best of circumstances, but now I was afraid that he was angry enough to hurt me without even realizing it.

"Giudo!" he said, his voice tangled with an unvoiced sob. "Giudo.

Does it mention me, Zephyr? You can read it to yourself, right? Does it mention me?"

I was aware of a tight pain in my chest, the source of which I could hardly credit. Could Nicholas's father care for him so little? Nicholas was a monster—I couldn't forget that, or I'd never be able to live with what Daddy and Troy were about to do to him—but beneath it he was still a thirteen-year-old boy, locked in a dark room while vampire poison ravaged his brain. I looked away from his needy, open face and back at the letter. For several paragraphs Rinaldo detailed which streets and contacts would go to various members of his gang. Finally, I saw Nicholas's name mentioned at the bottom of the page.

"To my son Nicholas," I read, "I bequeath my musical collection, comprising of recordings, playback devices and instruments. Nicholas may also, should he so choose, retain control of his division of my business, though I encourage him to pursue his talents elsewhere."

I kept my eyes on my lap. "That's it," I said. "The rest is just legal jargon. Nicholas . . . how did you get this?"

He walked so close to me that I could see the scuffed leather of his expensive boy's shoes, but I couldn't look up. "Lawyer came and found me after Dore got popped. Said Papa had to change the will, so I Swayed him and took it. Wanted to see how much the *bastardo* really loves me, after all. I'm going," he said, plucking the paper from my stiff fingers. "Go back to your charity, Zephyr Hollis."

I sat in the empty cave for at least a minute after he left. Was Daddy really going to kill him? This boy whose father could only bother to leave him a few sheets of music in his will? I stood up, and then froze at the abrupt, sudden sound of an aborted scream deep in the tunnels. A rat?

"*Bastardo! Putanna!*"

An Italian rat. He'd told me he was leaving.

Or maybe he was going to see his father.

Overcome with this new idea, I grabbed the lamp he had left for me and turned it down until it was barely a flicker in the darkness. I crept to the opening of the cave and looked up and down the tunnel. Nicholas, being a vampire, wouldn't need a light to see, but the noises seemed to be coming from the left-hand side. I crept forward, hiding the dim lamp beneath my coat. From about fifteen feet away, I could make out his pale shape as a slow-moving hump in the dark. He was definitely heading deeper into the tunnels. I'd had no idea New Yorkers had honeycombed the city to this extent with our demands for transportation. And what a waste to abandon them like this. He made several unhesitating turns at forks in the tunnel: left, right, right. I repeated the sequence under my breath so I could find my way out again. I had no particular desire to starve to death a few yards beneath the city. Nicholas turned right again, abruptly. I waited behind, breathing shallowly for several long seconds, before rounding the corner. This way, the faint light from my lamp wouldn't alert him to my presence.

He wasn't there. I ran forward—had he made another turn? But I didn't hear any noise down either of the two branches up ahead. Even at vampire speed, he shouldn't have been able to vanish so completely. I cursed, very quietly, and dared to turn the light up a little. Empty. I turned in a slow circle. Totally alone.

A sharp, small scuffle behind me. I didn't even have time to shriek before Nicholas knocked me to the wall. My breath expelled in a dramatic whoosh and I struggled, red-faced, to suck air into my lungs. Nicholas's hands were barely large enough to wrap around my throat, but given his strength, it was more than enough. I choked and wondered if now would be a good time to get that knife from beneath my skirt. Nicholas twisted his face into an utterly inhuman snarl. His eyes pulsed with light, but too erratically to Sway me even if I hadn't been immune.

"What are you, who are you working for?"

His mouth was a mere inch from my own. I struggled to breathe. "I'm not . . . you know who I am. I just work . . . for you." *Please believe me, please believe me.*

But his hand now threatened to crush my windpipe. I grew lightheaded. "You were following me. Why, Charity? And you better tell me the truth, 'cause help is pretty far away."

I closed my eyes. "Can't . . . breathe," I croaked. One agonizing second, and he abruptly relaxed his grip. I dropped to my knees, gulping air past my burning throat. "Okay," I said. And damn me if this didn't work, because Nicholas was precisely right: we were too far away from help if I'd misjudged him. I looked up into his eyes, which had returned to relative quiescence. Oh, I knew he was insane. But I had to bet my life on his rationality.

"I want to find Rinaldo. I want to kill him, and you're the only person who knows where he is."

He jerked, as though I'd hit him. But his expression remained strangely inscrutable. He stared at the wall above me. His lips moved, but no sound came from them. I wondered if my revelation, of all things, had finally pushed him over the edge, but eventually he seemed to arrive at a decision. All the coiled, tense violence of the last several minutes left him. I relaxed.

"I can't help you," he said. His voice was very quiet. "I owe Papa that much. I won't stop you, though. If you think you can do it. But I don't think you can. I think you'll probably die." He cocked his head at me and giggled. "You know that makes me sad? I don't want Charity Dogood to die."

I coughed, and it turned, inexplicably, to a laugh. "That makes two of us."

Nicholas led me from the tunnels and made sure I was firmly aboveground before vanishing. I couldn't have followed him even if I was stupid enough to try again. I caught myself shivering in latent shock, but it was more convenient to blame it on the cold. I didn't have time to fall apart over every little threat. My throat was just a little bruised, after all—another to add to my collection. I needed to see Amir and tell him about the party last night and Rinaldo's will, but since I was so close to the subway station I thought I'd check in on our malodorous informant first. Perhaps he had news of Judah's mother. I retrieved my bicycle from a lamppost across the street from the construction site and made my labored way down to Whitehall Street. I'd decided to take it this morning since I had given all of my remaining cab fare to Giuseppe and my bruises seemed to ache marginally less. By the time I made it to Whitehall Street, I'd given up the effort to maneuver the traffic on my bicycle. If the ground weren't so icy, or if I weren't so sore, it might have even been fun, but at the moment I could only think longingly of my bed. Or perhaps something less lumpy. Like Amir's. And warmer, like . . .

I shook my head firmly and jogged down the stairs into the station. The platform itself wasn't nearly as crowded as the streets above: the rush of morning traffic had ended hours ago. So I was surprised to find that the indigent seemed to have vanished. His state of advanced inebriation had led me to believe that he probably spent much of his time down here. I walked over to his corner, and saw that he had left behind a worn burlap blanket that smelled even worse than I remembered and a frayed sack filled with half-eaten candy and two bottles of soda pop. Perhaps he relied on the smell to keep thieves away, but why would someone with so little leave what he had behind? Had something happened to him?

I walked to the station master's booth. The man seated inside was portly and florid—a reassuring sight after so many days surrounded by dangerous, rail-thin and ghost-pale vampires flushed in all the wrong places. He was reading a copy of the *Daily News* with a front-page story about the sudden dry-run of Faust, and speculation that Jimmy Walker's secret narcotics agents had routed out the source. I snorted, which alerted the stationmaster to my presence. He peered at me through the grille.

"Can I help you, miss?" he said.

"Do you know what happened to that indigent who used to sit over there?" I pointed. "I had hoped to bring him some food and fortifying reading from our local charity group."

He squinted, then released his pince-nez and looked again. "Oh, you're that girl, ain't you? The one who beat up that pack of suckers yesterday! I wouldn't've believed it, if I hadn't seen the picture. My ma says a girl has no business getting mixed up with those types, but I don't mind telling you I think it's the berries."

I scowled. "I bet your ma doesn't approve of slang, either."

"'Fraid not, miss. So you want old Rick? He's no sucker, if that's what you mean."

"No, no, I'm just here on an errand of charity." Did he imagine I spent my days tossing errant vampires over my shoulder like sacks of flour?

He nodded, his eyebrows drawn together. "Well, I can't really help you there. Nice of you to do a charitable mission for his type, but a pig came 'round here six this morning and took him off. Didn't even give him time to get his stuff, as you can see. Seemed like Rick got himself mixed up in some nasty business the last couple'a weeks. I wouldn't be surprised if he didn't come back."

Arrested? I recalled the yellowing tracks of hypodermic needles in his arm. Much as I hated it, spirits *were* illegal, and addicts like him were the easiest target of corrupt narcotics agents. The *Daily News* thought Jimmy Walker had the slightest interest in stemming the flow of Faust into the city? While he's at swanky parties on the Upper East Side, carousing with a glass of illegally imported champagne in one hand and a showgirl on the other? But this wasn't good news for Judah.

"Have you ever seen a woman in the station with a young boy? In her thirties, brown hair? The boy has freckles. Not poor, but maybe not obviously wealthy."

As soon as I gave this description, I realized how hopeless it was. As expected, the station manager frowned and shook his head. "A lot of people go through the station, miss. Unless they live down here and smell as bad as old Rick, I don't really notice 'em. Sorry."

I thanked him and walked back up the stairs. A blast of frigid air blew in from the river and my throat spluttered like a clogged exhaust pipe. I coughed, violently, and leaned against the wrought-iron fence of the tiny park for support. A few people looked up at me in momentary concern, but no one stopped. The wind subsided and I managed to breathe again, but I stayed where I was, shivering. I didn't know how much longer I could stand this, truly I didn't. The threats, the fights, the bruises, the relentless recognition, the gnawing worry about Amir's safety. And perhaps the only bright spot was the strange, delicate, tentative attraction Amir and I seemed to have for each other. But I didn't trust or understand him enough to know how much it meant to him or how it could resolve.

"At the risk of pointing out the obvious, Zephyr," I muttered, "he's a djinn. A three-hundred-year-old djinn whose idea of a social movement is crop rotation." And even after we found Rinaldo and hopefully stopped whatever it was that caused Amir's attacks, what then? He'd be my boyfriend? Take me on dates around town? I had to laugh, which my throat regretted. Why did that make me so sad? We ain't the same kind, as Daddy would say. I'd yell at him and insist it didn't matter. But did it?

I knew I looked a mess when I walked into Amir's place, but there was no help for it. I'd at least wiped what I thought were the last traces of errant tears on my cheeks. Maybe I needed a vacation. A trip to a lovely beach house on the Jersey shore. Mornings spent reading trashy novels on the porch, and evenings dancing at the community hall. And at least twelve hours of sleep a night.

He was sitting on his couch, chatting and laughing with another woman whose back was turned to me. I'm not a jealous type, really, but I felt sad and confused and a little vindicated in my pessimism about our relationship.

I almost cleared my throat, then thought better of it. "Should I come back later?" I said, wishing that my voice didn't sound quite so desperate and scratchy.

Amir turned toward me, along with his mysterious guest.

"Zephyr!" my mother exclaimed. "You look terrible!"

I grimaced and wished my blushes were not quite so florid. "Mama, what are you doing here?"

"I came to visit Amir," she said, as though we were back in Yarrow and Amir lived down the street. "To thank him for his lovely present."

"Yes, nothing like a deadly weapon as a gesture of friendship."

"No need to be sarcastic, Zephyr," Mama said.

I sighed and collapsed into the couch opposite them. Amir's expression was one of patented inscrutability. I could see him take in the new bruises on my neck, the cave dust on Lily's clothes, my shuddering tension. I felt like a glass about to crack, and he could see every fissure. His hands fluttered, as though they would reach for me, but he instead combed them through his hair.

"Sweetie, what happened to you?" Mama asked. "How did you get those bruises?"

I glanced nervously at Amir, who seemed entirely too interested in the answer to this question. I knew he was worried about my association with Nicholas, and he'd think this proved his point.

"Well, I . . . I fell."

Mama raised her eyebrows. "Zephyr."

"Someone just . . ." I coughed and then winced. "I mean . . . Nicholas tried to strangle me, that's all."

She threw up her hands. "That's one of those Turn Boys, isn't it? The ones your Daddy's going to kill. Well, good riddance—"

"You won't have to deal with him again," Amir said, neatly cutting off Mama. "I found Rinaldo."

We both turned to stare at him. He looked perfectly blasé, as though he'd announced something of no more import than the score of the latest Yankees game. And it was the first thing he had said since I arrived.

"You . . . you did? How? Was it marked on the maps?"

He nodded. "Quite obvious once I knew what to look for."

I beamed. "That's great! Oh, that's wonderful, Amir. Where is he? We'll have to plan our assault soon. Maybe even let Daddy and Troy in on it. Much as I hate to admit, they know what they're doing about this sort of thing."

Amir frowned. "Zephyr—"

"Well, Troy *is* a pain," I said, laughing nervously. "We don't have—"

"You can't help me."

"What?"

He laced his hands behind his head and shrugged. "You heard me."

I found myself standing up, like a medieval knight dealt a blow to his honor. I was furious, and Amir looked so damnably placid. "We've been through this," I bit out.

"I don't mean I don't want you to. I mean you *can't*. This was never your problem, Zephyr. I just paid you to help."

I could only imagine how I looked: like a child just told her pet dog has died, and never really loved her anyway. Mama looked between me and Amir and stood.

"I'll just go check on little Judah," she said.

"Judah? What's he doing here?" I directed it to Mama, but she'd already ducked into the hallway.

"I thought I'd take him to South Ferry again. See if his memory is better in the daylight."

I couldn't bear to look at him. He knew what he was doing to me—he had to—but he looked so businesslike and coolly attractive that I found myself wondering if I had imagined what had happened between us for the last few days.

"You just paid me to help?" I whispered furiously. "You expect me to believe this was all some bleeding business transaction? I got this"—I pointed to my throat—"for a business transaction? I know what this means to you, even if you refuse to admit it. And you still need my help."

Amir raised his eyebrows, but remained seated. "Has anyone told you you're remarkably needy for someone who spends their days giving to others?" I opened my mouth. He waved his hand. "And don't flatter yourself, dear. I'm a djinn. You're just a human. My business with Rinaldo is my own, and much better accomplished without you getting in the way."

I would not cry. I would not. But I couldn't seem to stand and hold them back at the same time. I bit my tongue until I tasted blood and sat on the edge of his couch.

"I'm afraid I misunderstood," I said, wishing I could keep my voice as cold as his.

"Zephyr, I . . ." Something seemed to have cracked his façade. I could see traces of the confusion and worry and tenderness I'd hoped were still there.

"This didn't mean anything to you?" I whispered.

He leaned forward, so his scent tickled my nose. Comforting, like a hearth fire when you come in from the cold. "I can't answer that. I've behaved . . ." He shook his head. "Wait a week, Zeph. If you can, ask me then."

His eyes were determined and sad, without a hint of seduction. And so I leaned forward to kiss him.

"Amir uncle, Winnie says you want to take me on a trip."

We moved slowly apart, like the heat I felt from him had turned to sticky taffy. I sighed. But he was already smiling and walking toward Judah.

"Yes, she's right," Amir said, letting the boy hold his hand.

If you can, ask me then.

I started to shiver.

I didn't have to, but insisted on coming along with the three of them. Mama thought of it like a tour of the city, and since she seemed to like both Amir and Judah, I couldn't really begrudge her enthusiasm. "He looks so much like Harry at that age," she'd said wistfully as we climbed into the cab. I wondered how much Amir had told her about Judah, but sitting in the back of a carriage with the two of them didn't seem like the ideal time to ask. We insisted the driver pull back the cover, so we could view the city in all its frigid, smelly glory. I had to make do with my worn tweed winter coat, but Mama wore a fox fur stole with a matching muff and hat that wouldn't have looked out of place in a boutique window on Madison Avenue.

"Daddy must be doing well," I said as we headed down Broadway.

She noticed the direction of my gaze and beamed. "Just a little something he got me for our anniversary, sweetie. Lovely, isn't it?"

I scowled. "Sure. Nothing like the satisfaction of knowing that at least a dozen animals sacrificed their lives for your greater comfort."

"Zephyr!"

"I think it's lovely, Mrs. Hollis." Amir glared at me. I ignored him.

"Zephyr is very sad," Judah said. We'd bundled him up carefully—as such a young vampire, he didn't have to worry much about the sun, but it was better to be safe.

"You know," I said under my breath, "I think I liked you better when you didn't speak."

Judah looked up at Mama, his eyes wide and heartbreakingly confused. "I'm sorry," he said. "Should I stop talking, Winnie?"

"Of course not, honey," Mama said. "You can say anything you like to me." She drew him conspicuously into the voluminous folds of her coat. "Apologize, Zephyr."

"I'm very sorry, Judah," I said wearily. "I'm a miserable excuse for a human being."

Amir gave me a sharp glance. Of course we were sitting next to each other, which was bad for my emotional stability, but gave me an excuse not to meet his gaze. "I think Zephyr is hungry, isn't she, Judah?"

Judah looked between Amir and me, and I wanted to squirm beneath that calm, illusion-stripping penetration. "Yes. She is also hungry, Amir uncle."

He smiled a little at that, and told the driver to stop the carriage. He left for a minute, and returned with a box full of hot dogs, loaded with relish and mustard.

"Of course," I said. He handed me a pretzel and roasted nuts. I was hungry, but found myself distracted by Amir's meticulous appreciation of his frankfurter. He'd actually closed his eyes, emitting involuntary vocal exclamations more appropriate to certain other activities.

"Do you know what hot dogs are made of?" I said, because my current mood longed for sour company.

He licked the last of the mustard off his fingers and grinned at me.

"I'm immune to your lectures, Zephyr Hollis. You'll have to harangue your fellows at the suffragette meeting."

Mama laughed. "Yes, honey, don't be such a wet blanket."

Slang? What was next, a feathered turban? I closed my eyes and settled into the corner of the carriage. In my current foul mood, I was clearly not fit for company. Amir and Mama and Judah chatted while I relaxed. I felt curiously warm, given the weather. Amir seemed to have discreetly increased his heat production for my benefit. As Judah talked, I realized how much he'd improved since I first found him. It seemed clear that the turning had damaged him, but in a different way than it had Nicholas. Judah didn't seem particularly violent. His memory had been wiped almost clean, aside from that one episode we'd witnessed. And beneath his uncanny stillness, he was so disturbingly observant. I'm snapping at everyone like a box turtle and he tells Amir that I'm *sad*?

"I hope we're doing to right thing. Giving him back to his parents," I said, quietly enough so that only Amir could hear me. I didn't open my eyes, but felt his heat shift and settle upon me like a blanket.

"I don't think we have another choice," he said, just as softly. "But you're right. This isn't the same little boy they lost."

We drove past what seemed to be every single warehouse and residential building south of Fulton, paying particular attention to the ones closest to Whitehall Street, but Judah stared at each one with precisely the same placid nonrecognition. The sun was sinking, and we fetched up, finally, at Battery Park to witness the weak winter sun descending over the water. We all stepped out of the carriage while Amir paid the driver. I shuddered to think how much our hours of traipsing through the city must have cost, but I was beginning to suspect that Amir literally conjured his money out of thin air. Judah stopped on the threshold of the park and looked around.

"I know this place," he told me.

"Do you?" I said. "Did your papa take you here?"

"I told you, my papa is gone. I remember I like it because I can see the sun."

"Why don't you go with Amir and see if you remember anything more," Mama said, when Amir caught up with us. Judah happily took his hand and they walked off along the barren gravel paths.

"I do like him, Zephyr," Mama said, when we were alone. I realized too late why she'd encouraged Amir to go with Judah. "He's kind, and that's important. Lord knows I'd feel better if he were a human, but . . . well, I think your father will turn around. Don't worry." She patted my hand and I smiled weakly. If only Daddy's bad opinion was the worst of my problems.

"I'm glad, Mama," I managed.

"But you know I don't approve of this modern 'dating' business. If you love a man, he should marry you. You need some stability, Zephyr. Living the way you do is fine when you're young, but . . ."

"I'm twenty-four! Hardly Methuselah. And have you ever heard of a human marrying a djinn?"

She sighed. "Oh, Zephyr. That's what I worry about. You're obviously very fond of him . . ."

I could not believe I was having this conversation. Marriage? Stability? For all I knew, Amir just thought of me as an amusing diversion before he could go back to Shadukiam and his endless privileges of wealth and power. Thankfully, Judah came bounding back up the garden path, providing a blessed distraction.

"Winnie and Zephyr," he said, addressing each of us in turn like a king acknowledging his courtiers, "Amir uncle has become very sick."

I felt as though a horse had kicked me in the stomach. I stared at Judah, momentarily incapable of a response.

"Take us, dear." That was Mama. I was apparently useless for everything except tagging along behind. Another one of Amir's attacks? But he had looked so well, earlier. I remembered his bizarrely childish joy while eating his hot dog. Usually the attacks had warning signs.

He had collapsed by the water. I smelled the sweet, charred scent of burning grass before I noticed the slowly smoldering embers beneath his prone body. His eyes were closed and his face slack. If this was an attack, it was of an order of magnitude worse than the others. Had he been hiding it from me all these hours?

I dropped to my knees, but knew enough not to touch him. "Amir," I said, attempting to sound calm, and failing. "Can you hear me?"

But he didn't move at all. How did djinn's die? Did they burn themselves up, like a phoenix? Did they fade into smoke? Did they pop like vampires? And could I do anything to stop it from happening?

I remembered Amir's strange instructions the night before. Had he known that something like this would happen to him? "We need to find a street conjurer," I told Mama. "Someone who can summon the djinn Kardal, his brother. The summoning won't work, but Kardal will know we need help."

Mama nodded. "You wait here with Judah."

But Judah was suddenly standing before her, blocking her way. Vampire speed.

"I can call Kardal uncle," he said quietly. "He taught me how."

Judah raised his arms and his eyes began to glow as though he were Swaying someone. "I summon the djinn Kardal to my circle," he said, his child voice eerie with intensity and authority. He lowered his arms and then sat down to wait. "He will be here soon," Judah said, as though to reassure us.

I looked away from that disturbing image and back to Amir. I wanted to touch him, but even the twelve inches that separated us felt uncomfortably hot.

Kardal appeared a moment later, a barely differentiated cloud of belching black smoke that enveloped Amir.

"This will be rough," he said, in that gravelly voice that had scared me so much the first time I heard it. And he was right—with so many people in tow, the crossing to his palace was disorienting enough to make me stumble to my knees and gag in the thorny brambles of his rosebushes.

Kardal had taken Mama, Judah and I to one of his courtyard gardens, but he and Amir had vanished. I started to call out to them, but held myself back. *You can't help.* Isn't that what Amir had told me? Too many awful things in this world were indifferent to my help. And no matter how much the sight of Amir collapsed and insensible in the park scared me, I could do nothing about it. I could only wait, and hope that Kardal had gotten to him in time.

I sat in the fragrant mulch and buried my head between my knees. I'm not sure when my uncontrollable shivering gave way to sobs, but Judah sat beside me and laid his head on my thighs in silent comfort. Mama and I sat back-to-back and she ran her cool, lavender-scented fingers through my tangled curls.

"Have you thought of putting olive oil in your hair, sweetie? I hear it works wonders."

I had to smile. Trust Mama to focus on the essentials. "Better than egg whites," I said, sniffling.

"Egg whites? Lordy."

I don't know how long the three of us waited there, in that gentle silence. A fountain delicately gurgled and splashed in the distance. Fat beetles buzzed around the roses and gaudily colored flowers. My tears wet the earth beneath me, but the lazy warmth of Shadukiam's sun seemed to mute the sound of my sobs. I was profoundly aware of how inappropriate my presence in this garden was. I belonged on dirty New York streets, struggling with my bicycle and hiking up ten flights of creaky tenement steps. And Amir belonged here.

"He'll be okay," Mama said. "You'll see." I rarely cried like this. I could tell she didn't know what to make of it. Neither did I, for that matter.

"I . . . hurt all over, and Kardal is a pillar of smoke, and Nicholas has the worst daddy in the world, he didn't deserve what happened to him, though how can I think that, when he's hurt so many other people? But here I am killing suckers again and Amir is three hundred years old, three hundred, Mama, and he can have all the houris and hot dogs that he wants and I don't understand anything, anything, *anything* because he just won't tell me and so I have to watch as this thing eats him alive and nothing I do can help!"

Mama hugged me tightly. And for all that I'm an inch taller, I felt like a little girl again, protected in that embrace. "It'll be all right," she said, her voice rough. "It'll be all right."

And both she and I knew she couldn't promise that—no one could—but the words felt like a balm between us.

I had recovered myself enough to duck my head in the fountain before Kardal came back. He was less bilious than when he rescued Amir, but even the most casual observer couldn't mistake him for human.

"Is he okay?" I asked, before he could say anything.

Kardal's smoky head seemed to duck in a nod. "For now. Zephyr, I need to speak with you."

I looked back at Mama and Judah. "Alone?"

Again, that vague shift of displaced air. "This is Amir's tale, but I think you have a right to hear it. My brother is in no position to hide it from you any longer."

I felt curiously empty as he led me through an arcaded passageway into another room. This was closed to the elements and filled with various arrangements of divans and large pillows for reclining. I didn't quite know how a pillar of smoke benefited from well-made cushions, but I sat down willingly enough. I was sure I wouldn't like what Kardal was about to tell me, and yet instead of dread I mostly felt relief. At least now I would know.

"What has Amir told you about that vampire mobster? Rinaldo?"

"Just that he wanted my help finding him. And maybe to kill him. He wouldn't tell me why."

Kardal sank to the floor, and I could suddenly make out discrete facial features in the smoke. "Amir is the youngest of the djinn. And he was raised . . . differently. Your world was always more a part of him than any of our brothers. So much has changed since Kashkash's time . . . even since mine. It's hard for Amir to relate to the old ones. And yet, he's also never truly complete in your world. He loves humans, but not in the way you do. To him, you're like a rosebush. Something to enjoy, but not to take seriously. He takes human lovers, he plays in human politics, but he can always come back here where it never truly mattered. Except now."

"Now?"

"Three months ago, to be precise. He found a toy, he made a business proposition, and the one thing he had never anticipated happened: he was bound."

I struggled to piece this together with what I knew of djinn and their rules. "He's someone else's djinn? A human bound him?"

"Not a human. A vampire."

And there it was. Amir wanted to kill Rinaldo because . . . "But I thought djinn couldn't kill their masters?"

I could hardly read any expression on Kardal's malleable face, but he visibly bristled at the term *master*. "We can't kill anyone who becomes the vessel to our power, no. They have to die naturally. But it grows more complicated than this. Because Rinaldo, the mobster with whom Amir thought so foolishly to deal, wanted something quite specific from him. Not a djinn's power, but a djinn's blood."

Blood? I thought of Amir's flaming eyes and Kardal's sulfurous smoke. "But how could djinns have—"

"Think of it as an essence, Zephyr, not a liquid. That's what vampires feed on, and each source contributes something different to their power. They're the bottom-feeders, the parasites of our universe. A scourge, as Amir has too late found out." A lecture about the need for mutual understanding and the perils of prejudice lodged like a gumball in the back of my throat, but I restrained myself.

"But why did Rinaldo want Amir's . . . blood? Why wouldn't he want a djinn's power if he could have it?"

Kardal laughed, a sound like ancient rocks beating against each other. "He's too ignorant to know his own good fortune. I doubt Rinaldo has any idea that he's become Amir's vessel. The first of his kind to control a djinn in over a millennia. He wanted Amir's blood because he wanted to cure himself."

I felt like he was tossing me puzzle pieces, but not only did I not understand how they fit together, they didn't even seem to belong to the same puzzle. "Cure himself. Of being a vampire? Is that possible?"

"Not in an absolute sense. But it's possible for a certain kind of vampire to become another kind. That's what Rinaldo wanted, and a misreading of an ancient book led him to believe that a djinn's blood could change him."

There were different kinds of vampires? "What kind is Rinaldo?"

"An unusual one. Most vampires—the kind you spend your days helping, Zephyr—are what you might call type A. They spread their powers like a disease. As they age, many natural things can damage them: sunlight, vegetables that grow in the earth, running water. But these problems come on gradually. And most vampires, to be honest, will never grow old enough for this to worry them. In exchange for their relative invulnerability, they lack certain powers: shape-changing, infernal strength, an impervious Sway. Type B vampires have almost always *chosen* their dark path. I'm sure humans don't need any excuse to behave unjustly, but these vampires might be the root of your historical enmity."

I shook my head, overcome with the implications of what he was saying. It had never even occurred to me to wonder if there might be something more to those ubiquitous "evil vampire" stories. Had Dracula really existed? "And Rinaldo is a type B?"

Kardal shook his head, and some of his smoke floated to the sides. "Not precisely. He was cursed, twenty years ago, by a very powerful *sahir*. And the curse she chose was very close to a type B vampire. Though Rinaldo is a young vampire, the slightest touch of sunlight will burn his skin. And he lacks all the powers. He can change his shape, but not fully. His strength is only half as much as a normal vampire. Stuck between the two forms, with the worst of each, he decided to change himself."

"Into which type?"

"Amir never found out. Rinaldo just had a taste of Amir's blood before my brother escaped. But it was too late. Regular vampire venom would never have hurt a djinn. But Rinaldo, you recall, had some extra benefits. And one was the particular virulence of his bite. Most creatures he bites are killed too quickly to turn."

I felt vomit creeping up my throat, burning me. I knew what Kardal was saying. I knew because I'd heard this story a hundred times, but I'd never expected Amir . . . "That's what his attacks are? He's turning?"

"No, Zephyr. He's a djinn. It's impossible for us to turn. Our essence isn't so malleable as yours."

"But I thought you said that the venom—"

"It's much too strong. He can't defeat it. But a djinn will die before he turns."

I suppose that some part of me had guessed that long ago. But it shocked me to hear Kardal say it out loud. Amir had known he was dying all this time. "But what good will finding Rinaldo do? If he's dying . . ." I couldn't continue.

"It's a strange thing, the essence parasitism of vampires. It can flow both ways. If Amir can drink Rinaldo's blood, the venom itself will stop the turn from ravaging his body."

I thought of Amir's slack face, the burning grass. "But it's almost too late."

"No more than a day or two. Perhaps sooner, if Rinaldo realizes he's become Amir's vessel. The moment a djinn is bound, the store of power in Shadukiam leaks into your world. The longer the vessel waits before making a wish, the more powerful that wish eventually becomes. And Rinaldo has waited several months."

I shook my head. "And Amir doesn't know where Rinaldo lives? After all this?"

Kardal laughed, but the sound was bleak as a bone pit. "I told you, my brother is young. When they first met, he didn't bother to follow him. When Rinaldo summoned him, the vampire was quite careful not to reveal his location."

A day or two. I'd suspected his time was short, but not that short. Amir had told me he'd discovered Rinaldo's location, but after hearing Kardal's story, I realized that must have been a lie. Given his desperate situation, if he'd truly found Rinaldo he would have hunted him down immediately, not gone on a tour of the city with me and my mother. He'd known he was about to die. And so he tried to make sure that at least Judah's story would have a happy ending.

I succeeded, with stomach-clenching effort, to hold back another rush of tears. "Can I see him?" I asked.

"Be gentle, Zephyr," Kardal said, but he showed me the way.

Amir was sitting on a dirt floor deep under Kardal's palace. The only light came from a single lamp in the center of the room, so that half of Amir's face was hidden in deep, wavering shadow. At least he was awake.

"What's he doing down here?" I whispered.

"Kardal prefers I don't singe his carpets, that's all," Amir said. He turned to me, a strained smile on his gaunt face. His irises were dull and dark as two charred lumps of coal. A haze of smoke seemed to hover over his shoulders and hair, giving him an eerie resemblance to his brother. I walked closer to him.

"That's a fascinating concern for a creature made out of smoke," I said.

His eyes searched my face. "My brother is a peculiar fellow." He hesitated. "And why are you here? Come to rescue me from the dungeon?"

I knelt so my face was level with his. I remembered the first of his attacks that I'd witnessed. Then, he had been struggling against the vampire venom that was slowly devouring him from the inside. But now it was as though I could see him fading. And perhaps I could.

"Kardal told me everything," I said.

His eyes widened.

"She deserved to know, Amir," Kardal said, his voice clipped.

"You have no idea what . . ." He shook his head and looked back at me, almost shyly. "Dare I ask what you're still doing here, then?"

I had to smile. "I just wish you'd told me the truth."

"You'll forgive me for thinking I had a greater chance of securing your help with a few well-placed omissions."

"Well, knowing that the most ruthless mob boss in the city has access to your rapidly burgeoning powers is hardly comforting, but it would have only made me work harder to find him."

Amir briefly touched my hand, the bare tips of his fingers singeing like stray sparks from a fire. "Any harder and you'd be dead now, dear."

It took me a moment to catch my breath. "Did you find anything in those papers, Amir?"

He shrugged. "Sure, if you'd like to know where he delivers his cocaine shipments, or which of his officers control the city blocks. I imagine your friend Lily would love it. For our purposes, however . . ."

"You're giving up."

"Are you aware of any other options?"

His smile was incredulous, not a little patronizing. I slapped him. I could feel the burn on my open palm, but the sensation was perversely fortifying. My voice filled with quiet fury. "You will not do this. I won't allow you to. This attack will pass, and you will get your lazy, spoiled, careless bottom off the ground and *help me save your life*. Do you understand? We will find Rinaldo. I don't care what I have to do."

I don't know how long we stared at each other. My throat rebelled; I coughed, and it seemed to echo deep in my chest and throughout that bare room. Amir grimaced and forced himself up from the floor. It hurt me to watch. He moved like an old man whose joints were nearly frozen with rheumatism, and he had to keep his back against the wall just to stay upright.

"You only met me two weeks ago," he said, his voice soft but very far from mild. "There are hundreds of things you won't do to find Rinaldo. This too shall pass, Zephyr. If I don't mind, you shouldn't, either."

"You can't—"

"Again, you seem to be under the impression that I have some choice in the matter. It's not a tragedy. I've lived quite a long time by your standards."

Which was true. But he didn't look aged or infirm or in need of release from this mortal coil. He looked like a man I'd kissed just yesterday. He looked like a man for whom yawning chasms opened up inside of me when I thought of what we had not yet done. But now there wouldn't be a "yet."

"What should I do?" I hadn't meant to say it aloud. My voice wavered like a vaudeville actress's.

He closed his eyes. In pain, I thought. "Find Judah's mother. Tell Winnie it was a pleasure to meet her. Get some sleep."

"I'm not doing this," I said abruptly. "I'm not." I turned around, but not soon enough to avoid catching a glimpse of Amir's expression: stunned and bleak. I heard him sink back to the floor behind me. Kardal had been standing quietly by the door this whole time. I paused before him.

"For fuck's sake," I said, my voice low though I knew Amir could hear me, "let him burn your carpets. Give him some hot dogs."

Kardal billowed in surprise. "Djinni don't benefit from animal sacrifice."

Amir's laugh seemed to warm the room. "A snack, brother. A strange human snack, that might involve actual dogs but everyone hopes doesn't."

My hands started to shake but I kept walking.

"There was music, Zephyr," he called. "When Rinaldo summoned me. I couldn't see a thing, but there was music on a phonograph. I don't know enough about your music to be sure, but it sounded new. Like what you sang at the speakeasy."

I took that in the spirit in which it was offered, as an apology and a parting gift, and held it to my chest when I left him behind.

CHAPTER EIGHT

Kardal took me and Mama back to the city, near the Whitehall Street station. I gathered that he wasn't terribly familiar with New York, and so had a limited repertoire of places to which he could teleport. The streets were dark, but the pedestrians didn't seem quite as wary as they had for the last few nights. Faust hadn't made a significant reappearance, then.

"I think he'd like to see you," Kardal said, "when—"

"No," I said, shaking my head firmly. "I'll find Rinaldo."

It was getting easier for me to read his amorphous expressions. The clues weren't so much in his face as the general quality of his smoke. Now, he settled into something like a human shrouded in fog—a literal depression. "And if you don't?" he asked.

My ears began to hurt; I relaxed my jaw. *You've only known him for two weeks.* Why did that seem entirely beside the point? "Kardal . . . would you let me . . . be your vessel? If I had your powers, we could find Rinaldo. We could save—"

But he was already shaking his head. "The vessel of a djinn can only be someone capable of overpowering us."

Not me, then. "But couldn't we find someone . . ."

"You do not want anyone capable of subduing me in control of my powers. No one becomes that powerful by being kind."

"I'm sorry."

He put his hand on my shoulder. It was heavier than I expected, and very stiff, as though he had only read about comforting human contact without ever actually practicing it. "You are a remarkable human," he said. "It is not your fault you couldn't save him."

I wasn't crying when he faded, but Mama hugged me anyway, pulling my head onto her shoulder and whispering the sort of platitudes you expect mothers to say.

"I have to go to class," I said, when I finally pulled away. It felt strange to even say it. After all that had happened, I had to go back to Chrystie Elementary for something as routine and mundane as night school? But it was too late to cancel, and the sad truth was that, as bad as things got, I still had to eat. Amir could last a few more days, Kardal had said. I'd start canvassing the entire damn city later tonight.

Mama nodded. "Call us if you need anything, dear. I'll do what I can to get your father and Troy to hold off, but . . . I heard the client plans to pay Troy the last of the money tomorrow morning. They'll probably strike tomorrow night."

It was too soon. I felt like begging my mother to make them wait, but she knew the stakes as well as I, and she knew the futility of stopping Daddy or Troy when they set their minds on something. Especially something involving significant monetary remuneration. So I just clenched my fists a little tighter and told her that I'd call. She hailed a taxi, but I waited for the train, since my bicycle was still locked up near Amir's. Old Rick hadn't yet returned to his corner. Someone would have to actually touch his belongings if the police didn't return soon.

As I waited, I wondered what business transaction Amir could have arranged with Rinaldo. Knowing Amir, he probably wanted to rob someone else of a priceless antique. He really did treat our world like a sandbox. Beside me, a vampire staggered against a pillar, so inebriated he seemed in danger of plunging onto the tracks. I had started to move discreetly away when a bottle fell from his hands and shattered on the concrete of the platform. He cursed, but the rest of the humans in the station covered their noses. The stench from even a small bottle of Faust was overpowering this close. I realized that I'd smelled it before—faintly, on Giuseppe's breath, and earlier, in Amir's apartment when we'd encountered the revenant tomcat.

I huddled in the corner of the train once it arrived, wishing that the pieces didn't fit together quite neatly. Why would Rinaldo have wasted Faust to threaten Amir? I very much doubted he'd meant the stench to strike a special terror. Amir and Faust . . . no. There had to be a better explanation.

I had to stop by the boardinghouse to pick up some materials before class, but I didn't even make it up the stairs. Lily, of all people, was lounging in one of the worn chintz armchairs and watching with apparent delight an argument unfolding between Aileen and Mrs. Brodsky. All three looked up when I walked in.

"Zephyr!" said Mrs. Brodsky, her voice rising above the rest like a great ship buoyed on waves. "You will tell your wayward roommate to drink. She is sick. She is not herself."

Mrs. Brodsky held a tall glass of a strange amber liquid, thick enough to cling to the sides. I swallowed, hard, and gave Aileen a sympathetic look. She was seated on the couch, draped in what looked like four different knitted comforters of violently clashing hues. Hot water bladders covered her feet. And from beneath all this, she gazed at me with forlorn hope.

"I had no idea you lived with such fascinating people, Zephyr," quipped Lily. "Though I'm not entirely sure this is safe for us. I think your friend must be dying of consumption."

Aileen's skin *had* taken on an unhealthy pallor. "What is that sludge?" I asked Mrs. Brodsky.

"Traditional Moscow cure for storms of the mind," she said.

A morbid curiosity made me take a sniff. I gagged. It looked, if anything, better than it smelled. "Resist the Bolshevik tyranny," I said, which provoked Aileen and Lily to fits of laughter and Mrs. Brodsky to a voluble stream of Russian.

"What happened?" I said, sitting on the couch beside Aileen.

She sighed. "I was reading on the street and one of the visions just knocked me out cold. I don't even remember it now."

I put my arm around her. "Mrs. Brodsky," I said, as firmly as I could. "Aileen will be fine, I promise. But a hangover cure isn't going to help her."

Mrs. Brodsky glared at the two of us and then finally shrugged in the manner of an infinitely-put-upon mother. "Fine. See if I try to help you ungrateful girls again." She cupped her hand over her face. "Katya! The kitchen will need cleaning!"

Lily cautiously approached us once Mrs. Brodsky was safely out of the parlor. "What are you doing here, anyway?" I asked.

She put a manila envelope down on the floor beside two large Macy's boxes and gave me a curiously tentative glance. "Yes, well . . . well, I was invited to some election fund-raiser of Beau Jimmy's at the Waldorf and I thought, why not invite Zephyr!"

"You did?"

"Well, I'd been out all day . . . reporting things, you know, and anyway had no time at all to go back to my place so I had to dash into Macy's, though you know I just abhor department stores, and found the only two decent things on the rack and brought them here. You can have the one I don't like as much."

Aileen and I glanced at each other. "That's . . . nice," I said, unsure what to make of this side of Lily.

"You look like you want something," said Aileen, politic as always.

Lily raised her eyebrows and gave a speaking look at the tatty knitted shawls draped over her shoulders. "I don't believe we've met," she said.

I sighed. "Lily, Aileen. Fortune-telling roommate, meet deb journalist."

"I thought you must be that one. So, what's in the envelope, Lily?" Aileen said.

Lily smiled thinly. "What do you care? Do you *sense* something?"

Aileen blushed, but her glare could have staked a vampire. "Mock me all you like, but I doubt you'd have the balls for a real fortune-telling."

"I don't have the *balls* for anything." Lily did her best to look down her regal nose at Aileen, though it didn't seem to be working. She seemed a little too curious for it, in fact. "You mean to tell me you actually have some power? I have to tell you, I'm not gullible enough to think it comes with the accent."

"See for yourself, if you can stomach it."

"Oh, go ahead, please. I'm dreadfully curious."

I didn't like the sound of this at all, but both Aileen and Lily looked identically mule-headed. Nothing I could do would make either one back down. But I worried about Aileen—Lily didn't know any better, but I saw how much these visions cost her, and how they could overwhelm her if they came on too strongly. At least on the street she didn't invoke them deliberately, but with Lily she'd be sure to use as much of her fledgling seer power as she could command. I moved over so Lily could sit beside Aileen, who took Lily's hands, palms up. She drew a deep breath and closed her eyes. After a moment, Lily laughed nervously.

"Well? Should I clear my mind? Envision a field of daisies?"

"Try closing your mouth."

I turned my giggle into a cough. *Oh, Aileen, I love you.* After a minute of strained silence, Lily shifted, but Aileen's grip on her hands was stronger than it looked. Lily gave me a panicked glance, but I just shrugged my shoulders and leaned back. She'd asked for this, after all. Only thing we could do was watch the show.

"You don't like it, but you learn to get used to it," Aileen said, her voice breathy and deep. Lily looked positively nonplussed. "Your kind are more forgiving than you believe. Less forgiving than mine. You crave success, but you won't achieve it unless you stop caring so much what they think." And then, in sudden panic, "Zephyr! You have to let him!"

Aileen slumped, tumbling onto Lily's chest and shivering like she'd just come in from the cold.

"Are you serious?" Lily said. "What kind of a fortune was that? It didn't mean anything!" I could tell that she was struggling to affect her nonchalance, and mostly failing. Even I felt a bit disconcerted. She looked down at Aileen, still shivering, and tentatively put an arm around her back.

"Well, there there. It's over now. Whatever that was."

The parlor grandfather clock started to chime unsteadily, startling the three of us. I stood up and cursed. "Sorry, Lily, can't go to the party, I'm already late for Locution and Personal Finance." Her face actually fell, which would have made me as suspicious as Aileen if I'd had any time for it. I dashed upstairs to get the course materials, but when I came back down, Lily was still there. She was holding the manila envelope.

"You should see these, Zephyr."

Her voice was so uncharacteristically solemn that despite everything I paused and took it from her. I was going to be late, anyway. And I didn't at all like her anxious, worried expression. There were photographs in the envelope. Recently developed, I could tell from the chemical smell. They were of some dimly lit room in a warehouse.

"Crates of boxes, crates of boxes, crates of . . . Harold Weisskopf and Sons Frankfurters?" I looked up. "You want me to see photos of a hot dog warehouse?"

She shook her head. "Just keep going."

So I did. There were the hot dog crates. The next one, someone had cracked it open. And then inside. Those tall bottles definitely weren't frankfurters. Illegal hooch? Likely. Next photo, the bottle was broken open. The liquid was dark and thick . . . *almost* indistinguishable from red wine in the photograph, but not quite. I looked up at her. "Faust?" I said, my voice shaking for no reason I could name.

She nodded. I didn't need her encouragement to keep looking. The photographer had broken open a few more crates of the frankfurters. All of them held bottles of Faust. I looked back at the initial photo of the room: this warehouse must hold hundreds of thousands of bottles.

"The Negro supplier," I whispered.

Now Lily actually looked away, and I found myself drawn to the last remaining photographs. There were two. The elevator shot looked familiar, but then, Otis service elevators ought to be remarkably similar. The final shot rendered the series unmistakable. The front of a warehouse on East Twenty-sixth Street. A broken padlock on the door. Perhaps even my footprints in the snow?

I sat down abruptly at the foot of the steps and forced myself to breathe. A business transaction, indeed. He'd found Faust and arranged for it to be purchased by one of the most vicious crime lords in the city and now he was culpable for the deaths and destruction it had caused.

"How could he?" I said, realizing I was close to tears. "How could he do this and ask for my help and just pretend that he had nothing—" I choked to cut myself off.

Aileen had stood and was looking through the photographs I'd dropped. Lily seemed torn between trying to comfort me and running away.

"I'm sorry, Zephyr. I'd started to suspect, but I didn't want to tell you until I knew for sure. I snuck into the warehouse today on a hunch and took those pictures. They were on the fifth floor, plain sight."

I had to laugh. "Well, no one's going to question why some frankfurter boxes smell a little funny. He loves hot dogs. What kind of a person loves hot dogs and Ming vases and just decides to supply a whole city with a dangerous drug . . . like it's some sort of joke?"

Lily bit her lip and put a hand on my shoulder. "But he's not a person, Zephyr. He's an Other."

And for the first time in my life, I didn't argue.

I arrived fifteen minutes late to class, and staggered through my lessons with the verve of a dying tortoise. Aileen had decided to wear the extra dress and go to the Jimmy Walker fund-raiser with Lily. I didn't begrudge them the night out. I could hardly think. Or, rather, I could

think all too well. At least class distracted me. Giuseppe, to my surprise, played truant, though he usually attended Locution. And apparently, I wasn't the only one hoping to catch him. Several of the other
students came up to me after class and requested that I tell Giuseppe
to contact them if I saw him. And why? Because it seemed that he owed
them all money.

"He's had terrible luck, recently," I explained, wondering why they
were transferring onto me their hostility at not having been paid back.
"His whole family's in danger. His son . . ."

Marta, a Jewish vampire originally from Germany, frowned. "Yes,
we heard that. And that terrible mobster. And his dying mother. And
his evil landlord. Oy, the luck this man has, I'm afraid to touch him."

Mother? Landlord? I'd thought Giuseppe had his own rain cloud,
but it seemed closer to a tropical depression. I assured Marta that I was
in the same situation, and that she should at least wait until February,
when the tunnel workers get their paychecks. I wouldn't mind some
replenished funds myself, but Giuseppe should probably placate the
rest of the mob first.

After they left, I nearly staggered back home, too overwhelmed to
think of much other than my bed. And in fact, I didn't even make it
that far. Aileen's discarded shawls still covered the couch and I found
myself lying down with them as covers, mind whirring despite my exhaustion. Amir might die if I didn't help him. He was Rinaldo's dealer.
He might die . . . I fell asleep without realizing it, and had a glorious
vision of myself dazzling the stuffy guests at some exclusive party. And
there was someone in particular I wanted to impress . . . where had he
gone? Oh, of course, he was up on the stage, plucking masterfully at a
bass while Nicholas crooned with his beautiful voice. They both
stopped when they saw me, their mouths in perfect O's of admiration
and surprise. Amir looked so beautiful in his tailored suit and steel-
gray tie. All the strain had left his eyes, replaced with something closer
to smoldering desire. The kind of tenderness I felt when he touched
my cheek, and called me—

"Zephyr, *habibti*," Amir said, in front of the whole party. "You'll remember me when I'm gone?"

A djinn? The assembled whispered in horrified tones. How gauche.

Nicholas hissed. "You betrayed me! You *putanna*! All this time, with that wog!"

"He's not a—"

"Zephyr! Zephyr!"

The voice jolted me out of my sleep so harshly that I fell onto the carpet. I rolled on my back and looked up at Lily. She was dressed in a green gown similar to the confection that had graced my recent dream. But she didn't look at all like the composed, faintly supercilious reporter I knew. And she was alone.

I sat up. "Where's Aileen?"

Lily shook her head and sat down on the couch. She raised her hand to her mouth and I could see tears in the corner of her eyes. "God. Oh, God, Zephyr, she's gone. They took her and I couldn't do a damn thing about it and Zephyr, I don't know what to do."

Deep breath. Don't curse. Someone took Aileen. Fuck fuck fuck. Well, that's better. "What happened?" I said, as calmly as I could.

"Suckers," she said. "A whole posse of them. And not the Turn Boys, before you ask. Older. They found us after we left the party. I think a few of them might have been guests, Zephyr. I didn't *really* think that suckers came to our parties. Sucker mobsters! No one else was on the street. They said they wanted Aileen in revenge for Dore. You know, that gin-runner of Rinaldo's you told me was killed. They said something about Rinaldo wanting the killer, and a bounty on her head. She tried to get away, but one of them just Swayed her and picked her up."

"Did you see which way they went?"

"We were near Gramercy Park. They went south, but it was too fast to really tell. What should we do? I'd call the police, but . . ."

"It's Rinaldo. They might arrest *us*." I stood up and started pacing the room to clear my thoughts. "Tell me exactly what they said, Lily. Why did they single out Aileen and leave you alone?"

She shook her head. "They thought she'd killed that gin-runner! She swore she hadn't, but they didn't listen. They didn't even care about me. They said they wanted the reward. 'Can't believe Dore got himself popped by a girl,' they said. That's it. They were sure."

"Sure of *what*? Aileen barely knows how to pop a balloon, let alone a sucker. Hell, the first time she even saw one exsanguinate was last Friday . . ." I paused midstep. Was it possible?

"Lily," I said, very carefully, "what was Aileen wearing tonight?"

"I lent her a dress. A revision of Balenciaga from 'twenty-four. Black—"

"No, no, I mean, was she wearing any jewelry? Cuff links? Diamonds?"

Lily shook her head. "Why on earth would she be wearing cuff links, Zephyr? I'm not that forward a dresser. She had a nice pair of diamond earrings, though. She said they were a gift from you."

"A gift." My laugh was giddy, the kind of laugh that generally preceded a full-on fit of the vapors. I sat next to Lily, and she looked at me as though I had finally lost my mind.

"They aren't earrings. I took those cuff links off of a vampire I popped last Friday," I said quietly. "He had Aileen under his Sway and was about to take a snack. He was old, good at hiding, wealthy enough to wear diamond cuff links. Wealthy enough to be someone important. I never even considered the possibility."

She gripped my wrist. "Are you saying . . ."

"I killed Dore. And now Rinaldo's going to kill Aileen for it."

I convinced Lily to go back to the newspaper and file what she had in time for the morning edition. It didn't take much convincing, to be honest—she had been unnerved by the casual power and ruthlessness of Rinaldo's gang, and the thought of confronting them directly apparently scared her as much as it scared me. The only difference between us was a certain level of personal stupidity and the certain knowledge that someone I loved would die if I didn't find Rinaldo tonight and stake him. And Amir? Well, I just couldn't think about him.

For the first time in nearly two years, I was hunting with intent to kill. I might regret it later, but I didn't have time now. I borrowed money from Lily and hailed a cab to the Gramercy Park Hotel. It seemed especially awful that Aileen had been kidnapped so close to help, if only Daddy or Troy had seen her. But they'd have their chance to help her now. I barreled past the concierge and into an open elevator.

"Penthouse," I told the operator, and he took one look at my face and closed the doors.

I'd expected to see preparations for the strike tomorrow, but when I entered the penthouse I was nearly overwhelmed by the sheer amount of weapons and armor and the volume of quickly shouted instructions. They even wore the practical black jean and canvas clothes that served as the de facto Defender uniform. Were they having a dress rehearsal? I counted eight men total, including Daddy and Troy. I recognized a few of them from my Defender days, but they didn't pay any attention to me. Mama was sitting by the couch, shouting into the telephone. Daddy wasn't making it any easier for her to hear, since by far the loudest noise in the din was his deep bass chanting one of his favorite warped mining songs. I think he liked to imagine himself as a soldier preparing for war, and of course every soldier needs a marching song. This song had started life as "The Avondale Mining Disaster," but was now the story of one of Daddy's and Troy's more colorful vampire hunts near Helena.

I rolled my eyes. A poet my daddy was not. "Daddy!" I shouted, cupping my hands over my mouth to cut through the din. "We need to talk!"

He was sitting near the window, strapping on his weapons, and called my name in near unison with Mama when they saw me.

"Don't start that do-gooder crusade of yours again, you hear? Your mama said she couldn't find you anyway." He twisted his lips. "Don't know what's gotten into you women lately. I told your mama I'd send her back to Yarrow if she kept on about it."

I rounded on her. "Mama! You told me I had until tomorrow night!"

She shook her head, and I realized that these preparations must be last-minute. Short of hog-tying them, she couldn't stop the Defenders from fulfilling a contract any more than I could. "I'm sorry, sweetie. I tried to call you."

But I had been asleep. I felt a wave of terror powerful enough to make my knees shake. I rested against the edge of the couch, closer to Daddy. "What happened?" I asked.

He shrugged. "Funds came through. Ask your boy over there, Zeph. I don't bother with the details."

Troy shrugged. "The client paid us this afternoon. I was told that plans had changed, and it was imperative for us to move against the Turn Boys immediately." He grinned. "And the Defenders never disappoint our clients, as you well know."

Christ, but I wish I didn't. "Who is this client, Troy?"

"You know I can't tell you that."

"This is not any time to mess with me! My best friend has just been kidnapped by Rinaldo's men, you're about to kill the Turn Boys and I need to know what in sucker-bleeding hell is going on!"

The room had suddenly gone silent. "Zephyr!" Mama whispered. I could never understand how she managed to live with Daddy and still be sensitive to "unladylike" language.

Troy even seemed taken aback. "Giudo. That's all I know. We meet on different street corners around Little Italy. Thick accent, but he wears a cowl like a monk and I can't see a bit of his face. He hands me the money, gives me his instructions, I leave. Considering who he wants us to kill, I never questioned his secrecy."

Giudo? Wasn't that the name of Rinaldo's other son? "How old?"

He shrugged. "Judging by his voice, at least over thirty, but it's hard to tell in situations like these."

I thought back to Rinaldo's will. He'd explicitly stated that Giudo was to be in his mother's care until he came of age. So unless the will was very old, it seemed unlikely that a deep-voiced man Troy thought was over thirty could be the same person. Still, how common of a name was Giudo, anyway? Why would this one want to kill Nicholas? It couldn't just be a coincidence, could it?

I shook my head. "And you're doing this right now? Rinaldo has my friend. The second he finds out what you're doing, he might kill her."

"Yes, Troy," said Mama, "can't you do something?"

Troy shook his head. "It's too late to go back on this. Giudo was quite emphatic that we needed to do this tonight."

"And you won't ruin your precious reputation for some paltry thing like another woman's life."

Troy looked hurt that I'd impugn his honor. "And when we kill the Turn Boys, we'll save hundreds of lives."

Like Judah's, I thought. I sighed. "Then promise me, *promise me* that when you get to the Turn Boys, you will find out where Rinaldo is before you kill them. Nicholas knows. Make him tell you. And afterward, you guys will help me kill Rinaldo."

Daddy stood up and hollered, "Now, that's my girl! You want to take on the meanest sucker in the city? Count me in."

Troy, on the other hand, did not look nearly so enthused. "Well, John," he said, turning to Daddy, "that isn't actually in our contract. We're only paid for—"

"Who gives a rat's ass what we're paid for? Don't worry, we'll finish the job, Troy. But then let's have some fun afterward."

I ran and hugged Daddy so tightly that my feet cleared the ground. His muscles were hard as ever as he lifted me, and I felt myself suddenly, immensely grateful that he was still a match for the vampires he hunted.

"Hey, Zeph," he said, ruffling my hair, "it'll be okay, you'll see." He set me down. I looked up at him, then Mama.

"Well, wish me luck," I said. "I'm going to go after him myself, in case you fellas are too late."

"You're gonna hunt in that getup?" Daddy said. I looked at my clothes, and admitted that it seemed a little impractical. I was still running through Lily's discards, and the current offering featured a scalloped blue silk skirt with a matching tunic top tied low on my hips. The shoes were my practical boots with one-inch heels, but none of it exactly screamed "Defender on a mission." Well, I wasn't a Defender anymore, now was I? No, I was Zephyr Hollis, Vampire Suffragette, and she knew how to dress.

I grinned. "What else?"

I scanned the weapons table and picked up a leftover short sword in a scabbard (knowing Daddy, they'd all be sharp enough to slice a hair lengthwise). I jammed it through the tie of my tunic and then hefted the last remaining pistol. It was a bit older and heavier than I knew the other boys liked, but it would suit my purposes.

"It isn't loaded," Troy said, his voice oddly quiet.

"Well, you know damn well I can't shoot anyway." I gave the empty barrel a meditative twirl and then dropped it into the deep pockets in the tunic. Lily would not have approved.

I walked to the door, still feeling surprisingly jaunty, all things considered, and waved. "See you folks later. I hope."

"Zephyr, wait!" Mama wore a familiar expression: the abject terror she always attempted to mask when Daddy or I (or one of my brothers) went out on a mission.

"I'll be—"

She shook her head. "No, take this." She handed me a short sword. I'd seen so many weapons in the room it took me a moment to place its plain scabbard and wrapped leather pommel. The pagan-blessed blade Amir bought off of Troy. I took it, though sudden dread made my fingertips prickle with cold.

She hugged me. "I think he'd like you to have it, sweetie," she whispered, so softly I knew only I could hear her.

The Beast's Rum was rowdier than it had been the last several times I'd stopped by—packed with loud humans and vampires, almost all conspicuously male and smelling like it, too. I spied Nicholas near the bar, holding up a glass of dark liquid and proposing a toast.

"Let those bleeders shake in their houses!" he yelled. "I'd say it's time we had a little fun. And no damn nigger is going to stop us, am I right?"

A loud chorus of ayes greeted this rhetorical question. I looked around a little more carefully. Yes, these vampires were in an advanced state of inebriation. And since none of them were bleeding onto the floor, I could only assume that Rinaldo had found some way around his recalcitrant distributor. At the very least, Amir had come to regret his involvement with Faust. I remembered his chagrin at Ysabel's, when he was first confronted with its effects. Thinking about that, and what had happened after, my chest ached.

"Zephyr!" Charlie yelled, pushing his way through the crowd to reach me. "Oh, fancy seeing you here. You're looking lovely."

I smiled in what I hoped was a beguiling, charming way and thanked him. "What's all this? I thought you told me your dealer cut off the Faust shipments."

Charlie smiled, apparently happy to be the first person to tell me the news. "Oh, turns out the Boss found a runaround this morning. Not as high quality as the nigger, but good enough."

Oh, Amir had chosen such charming business partners. Well, nothing else for it. Nicholas had spotted me and gave me a regal nod. I hated to admit it, but there were many things I liked about the head Turn Boy. And as for the rest, knowing his history, I felt more pity for him than hatred. I wouldn't stop Daddy from killing him, if it came to that, but I had to try to save Aileen first. And that meant using a certain type of persuasion.

"Hey, take me to Nicholas," I shouted in Charlie's ear. "I need to speak to him about something."

Charlie nodded and grabbed my hand. Some bodyguard he was. He didn't even comment on the conspicuous blades in my belt.

"What's so important, Charity?" Nicholas asked, when Charlie pushed us to the bar. He was clearly a little intoxicated, but thank God not too addled for my purposes. In fact, his inebriation might work out to the good.

"I have a favor to ask," I said, reaching into my pocket.

He raised his eyebrows. "A favor? Don't you know I'm a Turn Boy?"

I smiled. "Ah, but see, I have this sneaking suspicion that you like me."

"Do I?"

"Which is why I hope you won't be too mad at me for doing this." I hefted the pistol and put the barrel smoothly to Nicholas's chest. Charlie and several nearby patrons yelled. Nicholas didn't even flinch. In fact, he leaned forward

"I don't think I have to tell you, but the bullets are silver," I lied.

He cocked his head. "What do you want?"

"Get everyone who isn't a Turn Boy out of here, for starters."

"You heard the girl! Get your sorry asses out of here! Charlie, deal with it." Charlie's parting glance at me was so hurt that I almost winced.

"Hey, Nick, let me get her," one of the Turn Boys shouted when the other patrons had left the bar. "She's just a bleeder, no match for one of us."

"You wanna bet his life on it?" I said. "All I have to do is twitch a finger."

"Leave it, Tomaso," Nicholas snapped. "Well, Zephyr Hollis, I think I like you even more, now. What's this all about?"

"Your dad has a friend of mine and I really want her back. And see, it happens that you're the only person in this damn town who knows where he is, so I have a simple proposition for you: help me get her back, and I'll give you boys a head start on a pack of Defenders that have a contract to kill you."

Nicholas narrowed his eyes at me, then wobbled. "Bruno!" he said. "Give me a Virgin Mary."

Bruno, looking as calm as ever behind the bar, poured a glass of clean blood and slid it across to Nicholas.

"Mind?" he said, gesturing to the glass. I shook my head, and he picked it up and drained it quickly. I could see how it revived him. His eyes grew brighter, his movements quicker. He could probably disarm me before I could pull the trigger, and he might even know it. "So, I know my papa says I'm slow, but let's see if I got this. The Boss has a friend of yours, and for some reason you don't think he's sucked her dry already?"

I gulped. I had no real reason to think that, except that the prospect of revenge might make him stretch out his pleasure. "The fellas who took her thought that she killed Dore. They were after the bounty."

"But she didn't kill Dore?"

"No. I did that."

Nicholas laughed, and I wished he didn't. He sounded so young in his pleasure I had to remind myself that I wasn't actually pointing a gun at a thirteen-year-old boy. "I owe you a drink, Charity. If I'm still alive after these mighty Defenders get to us." He looked appreciatively at the eight other vampires in the room and they laughed at the thought.

"You think a bunch of two-bit vampire slayers can touch us?" Charlie shouted.

"When one of them is John Hollis? Yes, I do. And I don't think you want to mess with Troy Kavanagh, Nicholas. Someone's paid him a lot of money for you boys, and he won't stop until the job is done."

The other Boys still hooted and mocked, but Nicholas at least seemed to realize the threat they were under. The Turn Boys weren't invincible, they just profited from a combination of random terror and weak targets. Against a group of hardened men who knew precisely where to point a stake? The odds had just evened out.

"Why are you telling me this if your papa is the one doing the killing?"

"I told you, I want my friend back. And you are going to take me to her and help me save her. And once you do, I suggest you and your Boys make yourselves scarce for the next year or so, or my daddy will find you and I won't mind telling him where to look."

"I could just kill you now."

I adjusted my grip on the pistol with teasing deliberateness. "I'd kill you first."

Nicholas locked eyes with me for nearly a minute, but to his credit he didn't even attempt to Sway. My advantage wasn't nearly as great as I was pretending (even if the gun *were* loaded), but I saw him consider

his options, and then nod. "We'll do it. You read his damn will. It's time
Papa learned a lesson. What do you say, Boys? Should we take a trip to
see the Boss?"

The answering roar was deafening. I think they were so drunk
they'd agree to anything. Or maybe just so in love with Nicholas.

I gestured with the gun. "Let's go."

Nicholas led us through the streets, and I followed with the gun to his
back. The speed with which every other living creature took pains to
get out of our way was more than slightly unnerving. Especially when
he led us, of all places, into the subway station at Canal Street. The
entire platform cleared of people so quickly you'd have thought a giant
hand swept them away.

"What we need to take the subway for, Nick?" Charlie asked, but
Nicholas didn't even seem to have heard. He was staring into the dark
of the tunnel, and I knew enough not to disturb him. God, but I hoped
he didn't have one of his flashbacks now. I needed him (relatively)
sane. The train came five minutes later, and the one sleeping bum inside took one look at us and practically sprinted into another car.

I can't say I was terribly surprised when we got off again at Whitehall Street. Too much about Nicholas seemed to center in this area. Of
course it had something to do with Rinaldo. Rick was back, I saw, but
when I lifted my hand to wave, he just raised his fetid blanket over his
head as though that would prevent us from seeing him. Oh, well. I
could understand why he might not want to acknowledge me in present company.

Instead of walking up the stairs, Nicholas led us all to the very end
of the tracks. He looked back and forth through the tunnels and then
hopped into the pit. We all stared at him.

"Come on, Boys, you don't wanna get popped by a train, do ya?"

This got them moving. I eyed the muck on the tracks and the gray streaks of innumerable squeaking rats and thought, improbably, of what Lily would say if she could see what I was doing to her clothes. I laughed to myself and let Charlie help me down. We headed deep into the tunnels, with the light from the station behind us fading into black. Soon I had to keep hold of Charlie's hand just so I could stay with them. Without night vision, I was in danger of falling flat on my face. This proved too awkward with the gun, and they all seemed to have forgotten about it anyway, so I dropped it discreetly back in my pocket. We heard an approaching train long before we saw it, an echoing, sustained screech of metal wheels on metal tracks.

"It's on the other side," Nicholas called, before we could panic. And then, under his breath, I heard him say, "A flat."

A flat. The exact pitch of train wheels as they squeal around a particular turn in a subway tunnel.

"I'm a bleeding moron," I muttered. Of course Rinaldo lived underground. Hadn't he turned Nicholas in the nearby storm drains? Hadn't he locked him up down here, for Lord knows how long? Now I was sure that Nicholas was taking us to the right place.

We could hear the next train roaring behind us when Nicholas finally opened a small iron door set into the concrete tunnel walls and led us through. The ground shook as it rumbled past, three seconds to spare. Nicholas struck a match and lit an oil lamp that was waiting by the door. He handed it to me. "Almost there," he said, his eyes distant. He seemed like a man about to be marched to the gallows, abstractly terrified and concretely relieved.

"Do you think the bleeder's still alive, Nick?" a Turn Boy asked.

Nicholas shrugged. "Papa's angry enough. It isn't just a snack to him. He'll probably toy with her a bit. I'd say we've got some time."

The idea of Rinaldo toying with Aileen made me want to vomit, but at least it meant she was still alive. *Please let her still be alive.*

The tunnels were narrower now, though obviously man-made. Similar to the strange labyrinth Nicholas had led me through the other day, but finished. I wondered who would have put a lamp by the door, though. That indicated a human presence in these tunnels. But how could a human live so close to the trains, so far below the city? Even worse, with Rinaldo?

We ran across the answer to my question soon enough. A woman in a neat blue day-frock with a raised hemline and wide-brimmed hat was hurrying toward us. Her hair was longer than I was used to seeing in New York these days, and given the bizarre surroundings, I was momentarily convinced that we had stumbled upon a ghost. But a ghost wouldn't be carrying her own lamp.

"Nicholas! What are you doing here? With all of them?" She shook her head. "He'll be furious."

Nicholas spat. "Let him. I don't care anymore. About him, about you, or your stupid little Giudo."

She went very still, in the way people do when the other option might simply be a mindless wail. I peered at her more closely: she seemed haggard and exhausted, despite her impeccable attire. I suspected that she must be the mysterious Kathryn who had come into the Beast's Rum the other day looking for some man. Rinaldo's *puttana*, as I recalled. And then I thought of the will, of Rinaldo's son Giudo . . . and his mother, Katerina.

"So I was right," she said, her voice wavering. "It was you. He was just a little boy, Nicholas! He'd never have harmed you—"

Katerina sounded very much like Kathryn, if Italian is your first language. Much like Giudo sounded like . . .

Nicholas rocked back and forth on his feet. I could almost taste his coiled tension. "He hated me."

"You terrified him! And now, what, you just killed him? I looked in all the morgues, asked after any little boys they might have brought in and staked. So what did you do to him? Tell me which gutter, Nicholas, so at least I can bury my son!"

Asked after any little boys they might have brought in and staked. They would have, I wanted to say, if I hadn't interfered. The name he'd remembered was the name his mother had given him. Judah, Rinaldo's son. Judah, who had admired boats with his mother and was turned by Nicholas in the storm drain.

"An alley near Lafayette," Nicholas said, taunting her. "But we turned him good, Katerina. So if the pols haven't picked up any little suckers lately, maybe it's 'cause he's still alive."

Kathryn looked like she was going to choke. "You're not alive," she managed.

Nicholas hit her, blindingly quick and hard enough to knock her against the wall of the tunnel. Her mouth was bleeding and her cheek looked puffy. She started to cry.

"Then you're sleeping with a dead man, *puttana*."

I desperately wanted to stay behind and help her, but the specter of Aileen being tortured compelled my silence and pushed me forward. I'd rescued Rinaldo's other son. The mortal enemy of the one I now followed into his father's lair. What a mess. And if Giudo was really Judah, then who in hell was Troy's client? *Could* it just be a coincidence?

"How common a name is Giudo?" I asked Charlie, in a low whisper. "You know a bunch?"

He shook his head, eyes wide. "Only that one. And good thing, 'cause Nick can get a little *pazzo* about that kid."

I nearly hit him myself. That kid you helped him puncture like a pincushion? That kid who'd lost nearly all of his memories thanks to being turned so young? But then, hey, the same thing had happened to Charlie. We were all of us damaged, and I'd lost the knack of pinning blame.

At least now I knew: someone was playing Troy. The client had used that name deliberately, but it was a reference Troy couldn't possibly have known. So he was connected to the Turn Boys, but probably not as a member of the gang. Hell, for all I knew maybe Rinaldo himself had gotten wind of who had killed Judah and had taken the hit out on them himself.

"Well, that's going to make this family reunion a little awkward," I muttered.

Charlie looked back at me and then froze. "Uh . . . Nick," he called.

"What now, *idiota?*"

"I think there's something—"

Which is all he had time to get out before the Defenders came upon us like rats from the dark of the tunnel.

Shots echoed off the walls, ricocheting dangerously. Nicholas cursed. "Around me, Boys!" he yelled, as Daddy and Troy and half a dozen other men wielded their swords like extensions of their arms. I was lost in a moment of inappropriate admiration. Then I realized how they must have found us.

"You bloody scoundrels!" I shouted to Troy, as he grappled with a Turn Boy going for his neck. "I can't believe you followed me!"

"Giudo told us to," he said, gasping. "Listen, could this wait—"

I unsheathed Daddy's sword with one hand and hauled the unsuspecting vampire off of Troy with the other. The Turn Boy was strong and would have gotten away to do some damage, but I held the blade against his neck and pressed gently.

"So, you were saying?"

Troy stared at me, and wiped beaded sweat from his forehead. "Christ, Zephyr. Giudo found me when we were about to leave, and said to follow you. He said you knew the Turn Boys, and could get them off guard."

"Giudo" knew that about me? This was getting a little frightening. "Is he with you?"

Troy shook his head. "He came as far as the tunnel, but someone he knew was there. You were getting away, so I didn't ask."

I cursed and tossed the vampire on the ground at his feet. "Carry on."

Troy smiled suddenly and saluted me. So he was stuffy and pompous and utterly backward and generally impossible to take in large doses. But sometimes I still sort of liked him. Someone hit me hard in the back between my shoulder blades. I coughed and spun around, holding my scabbard before me like a shield. It was another of the Turn Boys, teeth bared and snarling. He was one of the biggest of the group—nearly an inch taller than me, and strong. He hit me again and I slashed at his arm.

"Hey, I'm not a Defender!" I shouted, even while I realized how this must look. "Nicholas, call him off!"

But when I glanced at Nicholas, I could see that he wasn't in much of a position to do so. Daddy had, predictably, gone for the biggest kill, and Nicholas looked like he was barely able to dodge the twin force of Daddy's long swords.

"How'd they find us, then?" the Turn Boy yelled, swiping my legs out from under me.

I controlled the fall. "I didn't know they were following!"

Obviously, logic wasn't going to get through to him. He lunged for my neck. I didn't stop him, just scooted a crucial few inches to the right, so he face-planted into the cold rock. I scrambled up and tossed myself on top of his back—no time now for anything fancy. He grunted. I placed the heel of my impractical boots on his neck and raised my sword. I didn't want to pop him, but he needed to be incapacitated. I settled on nicking his jugular with the blade. The blood that spilled wouldn't kill him, but he wouldn't be able to do more than crawl for days. As he gurgled, I clambered off and looked again for Nicholas. Troy's stupid plan meant an even greater delay getting to Aileen. I had to grab Nicholas and go. Daddy hadn't killed him yet, thankfully. But while Daddy's eyes were filled with the demented energy that had made him the most famous demon hunter in Montana, Nicholas seemed like he was flagging. The Faust, I realized. It slowed his reflexes and sapped his energy, even with his recent infusion of fresh blood.

Time to save the big boss vampire from my daddy.

I sprinted through the milling, bloody fight, nearly tripping over some sucker's popped skin. *Please don't let that be Charlie.* But I didn't have time to look. Nicholas had fallen down, his back propped against the tunnel wall. Daddy raised his blades high above his head. I was just in time. I dove beneath Daddy and raised my own blade to block his. The force of his blows smashed me against Nicholas and the stone. I barely felt it.

"What the devil?" Daddy looked as though he could barely restrain himself from hitting me, but I didn't feel any danger.

"I've got to borrow him for a moment, Daddy," I said, "since your clever Defender stunt is about to kill my best friend. Find us after you've worked your way through these guys."

To his credit, Daddy shrugged his shoulders and turned back to the fight at hand. I pushed Nicholas forward. "We have to get to Rinaldo now," I hissed.

He looked back at his gang, and for a moment I thought he would refuse to abandon them. But then he nodded and started jogging down the tunnel.

The sounds of battle faded behind us to distorted grunts and clashes. If I didn't know better, I'd think that Nicholas had been possessed. Something in the way he so determinedly marched toward a place he obviously did not want to go was eerie.

When we turned a corner the shift from tunnel to house could not have been more obvious. The floor was inlaid with mosaic marble, and the walls were wood with a dark veneer. We clicked along the entranceway until it opened into a foyer. Several other tunnels and doors branched out like spokes from a wheel. Nicholas didn't hesitate. He turned to a large oak door on the right and turned the handle. Locked.

"Stand back." His voice was quiet. I scrambled away like he'd shouted. With no further warning he launched himself at the door. The force of the blow echoed like an earthquake over the marble, but the wood was only dented. He launched himself again. Handle smashed, the door glided open gently on its hinges. I unsheathed my sword, took out the useless pistol, and followed Nicholas inside.

It was a study of some kind, with a bare wooden floor and instruments and books lining the walls. I saw Aileen first, blessedly alive. She was trussed up and seated on the floor in the middle of a circle drawn with chalk. The sides of her neck were bloody, and I realized after a moment that Rinaldo must have ripped the cuff links from her ears. She leaned forward when she saw me and shouted against her gag. I gave her a smile I hoped was reassuring and scuffed the chalk with my shoe. Slowly, I turned my gaze to the other person in the room. He was standing in front of a larger, but empty, chalk circle, reading from what looked like a grimoire. Something about him seemed familiar to me, but I couldn't place where I'd seen him before. He finished whatever he was reading and laid a sprig of an herb in the circle.

"There," he said, turning to us. "He should be here any moment now." He smiled, and suddenly I realized where I'd seen him before. He was a taller, paler, slightly doughier version of the white piano player at Horace's and that party I'd gone to with Lily. Modern music, Amir had told me. And poor Nicholas with his beautiful arrested voice. Rinaldo's accent now was faintly Italian, but he'd be able to mask it easily enough.

"Nice to see you again," I said, with affected casualness. "You look different."

He shrugged. "Just a little ability I have. I see you've found my son."

"That's funny. Which one?"

That surprised him. "I only see Nicholas," he said carefully.

"And only I know where the other one is. If you want him back, I suggest you give me my friend."

"You have little Giudo?" he asked. I winced. If I was going to have to kill this sucker, I wished he didn't have to sound so much like a distraught father. But I nodded.

"And you want this girl for him? But she murdered my good friend, Miss Hollis."

I suspected that now was not the time to tell him who had actually done the foul deed, so I just shrugged. "What's worth more? Your son, or revenge?"

The air in the empty circle began to shimmer. Some of the instruments rattled on their shelves. "I'm afraid the choice isn't quite so simple," he said.

What was happening? I turned to Nicholas, but he was still as a statue. His eyes flicked around the room, but so quickly I suspected he was deep in the throes of a flashback. Anything I did to pull him out would only put me in danger.

The room stopped trembling. Inside the circle, the shimmering gradually resolved itself into a figure.

It was one of the Djinni, but not quite so dark or billowy as Kardal. He was very tall—almost eight feet—and the deep smoke swirling around his body and flashing eyes seemed to glow with an internal flame. I'd never seen this djinn before, and yet something about the obvious theatrics smacked of a certain sense of the absurd I almost recognized . . .

"O fiery one," Rinaldo said, "I offer you a sacrifice of a virgin pure, so your strength can grow and in turn feed mine."

"Good lord," said the great djinn. He shook his head, and the swirling smoke blew away while the figure inside shrank to a more familiar size. I blinked. I hadn't known he could do that.

Amir was dressed in knickers and a cashmere sweater, and so sick that despite even this effort he looked as though he needed to lie down. I cursed myself for caring. He could damn well take care of himself this time. I washed my hands of him, the Faust-selling lout. Rinaldo seemed surprised at what his summoning had wrought, though he'd done this at least once before.

Amir looked disdainfully at Rinaldo and then at Aileen. "You again?" he said to her. "Well, this hasn't exactly been the best week for either of us, has it?"

Rinaldo seemed confused. "Ah, you are Amir, the great and youngest djinn of Shadukiam—"

"Sorry to disappoint. I just don't have the energy right now to look large and billowing."

Amir had noticed me, of course, but apart from a split-second surprised glance, he kept his attention trained on Rinaldo. I edged forward. I thought about attacking Rinaldo, but Aileen was closer and I wanted to make sure she was safe. Hopefully Daddy and Troy and the other Defenders would be along soon. I knelt to slice through the tight knots binding her ankles and wrists.

"And I hope you've realized by now my blood can't do a thing to change you. That *sahir* curse was of the permanent variety." Amir was rambling, but deliberately saying things to provoke Rinaldo.

"I felt its power," Rinaldo said.

"You would. It doesn't mean it can change you."

"It can. And if it doesn't, I'll still be the most powerful vampire in the world, with your blood."

I untied Aileen's gag. She took a deep breath, but thankfully Rinaldo didn't notice.

"Get up very carefully," I whispered. "Run through that door. Hide in a corner and don't come out until you hear me, Troy or Daddy tell you it's okay."

Aileen looked at me. "Be careful," she whispered. "I'm getting this feeling . . ."

I nodded. She shook out her wrists, stood up and sprinted for the door. As expected, Rinaldo could hardly fail to notice his bait running away, but by that time I was already sprinting at him with my sword raised in one hand and the pistol in the other. He knocked the pistol to the floor, but disregarded the sword. I swung it hard, and felt it bite into his rib cage. He grunted when I yanked it out, but there was none of the characteristic sizzle of a silver blessed blade hitting vampire skin. Another spell? He pulled a long sword from one of the shelves and unsheathed it. I swallowed. Blessings didn't matter one way or another to me, but sharp steel certainly did.

"Well," he said, "one virgin is as good as another."

"Why do vampires insist on thinking that everyone behaves like them?" Amir said from the prison of his chalk circle. "I don't get power from the blood of virgins, you fool. And as you can see, at the present moment I'm not likely to give you much power anyway. So why don't you just let us all go home?"

"And if you want to see your son again," I said, ducking under his blade and nicking his thigh with a quick thrust, "I suggest you don't kill me."

He paused, our blades inches from each other. "Why should I believe you? I thought Giuseppe stole him. And Katerina thought it was my boy Nicholas. I didn't even know who you were a week ago."

Giuseppe? He had something to do with this? My head hurt. "I found him on the street. Someone had turned him. But he reminded me of my brother . . . so I took him home."

Rinaldo seemed incredulous. "You took him home? Do you live in a fortress? Don't you know how long it takes to acclimatize—"

I shook my head. "I'm learning. But I guess you're the expert. Turning your own son at thirteen and all."

Rinaldo looked between me and Nicholas, who was twitchy, but apparently more aware of his surroundings. "Is this *your* doing, Nicholas? Was Katerina right all this time? Did you turn your own brother?"

"The *bastardo* wasn't my brother, Papa. He was your whore's son, and you gave him everything. You think I wouldn't hear how you changed your will? I'm learning how to read. I read about how little you care about me. Besides, I just did to him what you did to me."

Rinaldo let his sword arm fall. Then, with as much sudden fury as a beserker pilot, he hurtled toward Nicholas, ejecting a stream of Italian expletives. Nicholas struggled beneath the onslaught. I looked back at Amir. He had sunk to the ground, but he smiled at me. I crawled over. "It's a little terrifying to watch you work," he whispered.

"Lucky that you have nothing to do with it," I said, with such obvious fury that for a moment he seemed afraid. "I should let you rot."

"You should?"

"A *business transaction*?" My tone could have withered grapes on a vine. How sick was he? How much time did he have left? I hated that I still cared.

Amir looked as though I'd hit him. "Oh, *habibti*," he whispered. "You didn't . . . I thought Kardal told you."

So that's why he'd been so surprised when I was still willing to help him. "Not enough," I said. I closed my eyes.

Something heavy as a boulder smashed into me, knocking me flat against the ground. It hurt. I thought I might have heard a rib crack. Amir shouted my name. The thing rolled off of me. Oh, not a thing— Rinaldo had tossed Nicholas across the room to stop me from breaking Amir's circle.

I stood up with a wince. Put the pain away, deal with it later. I'd been good at that in the old days. "If you hurt Amir," I heard myself saying, "you'll never see your son again."

He laughed. "That's just the thing, *bella*. If I hurt Amir, I'll be strong enough to force you to tell me."

The fight between Nicholas and Rinaldo had masked the sounds of the approaching Defenders, but when they finally burst through the door I could have mistaken them for descending angels. Daddy and Troy led the pack, but in the crowd that tumbled in behind them I counted eight men. Four vampires and four Defenders. It looked like the battle back in the tunnels had turned deadly. Rinaldo tightened his grip on his sword and backed very close to Amir's circle.

"Charity, watch out!" Nicholas called. I turned just in time to see some kind of stringed instrument flying at my head. I ducked. The Turn Boys were getting creative with their weapons, and I didn't have any time to hash this out with Amir. The thought of what he had done made me physically ill, but no matter how despicable his actions, stopping Rinaldo from controlling his power had to be my first priority. Daddy found me and hauled me upright. His shirt was soaked with sweat, but he still looked as though he could happily fight for another hour.

"Zeph, hey," he gasped, "try and be a little more careful! Your mama'll kill me if anything happens to you."

I nodded, but then we were both distracted by another commotion by the door.

"Stop, please stop!" Kathryn was yelling, tugging on the long dark sleeves of someone in a cowl. I immediately recognized him as the same man who'd threatened me the other night in Little Italy. He shook her off, and in the process his hood fell back.

"Giudo?" Troy said.

But no, it was Giuseppe. He didn't even glance at Troy—his stare was riveted on Nicholas, who glared back. The hatred between them spoke volumes; a fraught past I hadn't even been aware existed.

"You killed my son," Giuseppe said, inexplicably.

Nicholas laughed, high-pitched and giddy. "Hear that, Papa? The *bastardo* isn't even your own son! Did you forget that?"

Of course, how could a child as young as Judah be the son of Rinaldo, who'd been turned long before Judah was born? Vampires were sterile. I stared at Giuseppe. His son. He'd borrowed all that money for a reason, but not any of the ones he'd given me. The three of them—Giuseppe, Rinaldo and Nicholas—came at each other at the same time; the dull smack of bodies colliding at inhuman speed echoed throughout the room.

"Giuseppe!" Kathryn shrieked from the doorway. "Rinaldo, let him be!"

Rinaldo's *puttana*, but she was something else entirely to Giuseppe. The mother of his children. His lost wife.

With Rinaldo otherwise engaged, I had a chance to free Amir. Maybe I *should* have left him to rot, but I couldn't. Later, I would sort it all out. I just needed to make it to "later" alive. I tried to wipe the chalk away with my boot, but the second I touched the edge of the circle, a force like an electrical current roared up my body and I collapsed onto the floor, twitching and gasping. What the hell was that?

"Zephyr! Are you okay?" Amir was kneeling as close to me as he could. I struggled up on one shaky elbow. Rinaldo had noticed my interference. With a roar, he tore himself away from Nicholas and Giuseppe and sprinted toward me, sword raised.

"Enough!" he said. "You're too much trouble."

I tried to roll out of his way, but the effects of the circle's protective force had made me as uncoordinated as a baby. I reached for my short sword; he stepped on my hand. Something snapped. I screamed. But at least the pain seemed to have galvanized the rest of me. I wrenched my throbbing hand out from under him and rolled over. His sword bit deep into the wood.

"Get your filthy sucker hands off my little girl!"

Daddy probably shouldn't have announced his presence, since the blade that would have otherwise gone straight through Rinaldo's back and into his sternum was deflected into a less harmful blow to his right arm.

I grit my teeth and forced myself to my knees. At least Rinaldo had stepped on my left hand. I could still fight. But I needed the blade. I saw it, an inch away from Amir's circle. His eyes locked with mine when I knelt to get it. He looked how I felt: stricken, in pain, longing.

"Get away," he whispered. "Please. Just get away."

I grabbed the knife and stood. My head spun, but I steadied myself with fury. "*Shut up*, Amir."

Focus. Find Rinaldo. Force him to release Amir. I didn't know how I'd manage that, but I knew I would. Or die trying. But Rinaldo had his hands full; Daddy was laughing like a madman, using his double blades to badger his target into submission. Blood was dripping down Daddy's temple and something had sliced his chest, but I don't think he even noticed he was hurt. The other Defenders were still occupied with the Turn Boys. If I could sneak up behind him, Rinaldo wouldn't have a chance. I stumbled forward, willing the weakness from my muscles.

"Amir!" Rinaldo screamed suddenly. "I command you to give me more power! Do you hear that? I summoned you, so give it to me!"

Amir didn't even have a chance to resist. His eyes rolled into the back of his head; he slumped into a boneless heap on the floor. For a moment, all the air seemed to rush from the room, like the tide going out before a great wave. And then we heard it: a crescendo of noise like a plane swooping overhead. My skin tingled with its effects, but Rinaldo seemed to glow. His hair stood on end. His clothes rippled in the absence of any breeze. He laughed, and it reminded me—though I wish it didn't—of Nicholas.

"Try me now, Defender," he said.

Daddy wouldn't have survived. I couldn't have made it in time. And the thing that saved him had nothing to do with steel or silver.

"Papa," Nicholas said, his voice strangled. "Papa, he's gonna kill me."

We all turned to look. Giuseppe had found my discarded, unloaded gun and had placed the barrel on Nicholas's chest. No one but me, Daddy and Troy knew it wasn't loaded.

"You killed my son," Giuseppe said.

None of us saw Rinaldo move. One second he was standing over Daddy, and the next he had moved in front of Giuseppe, knocking the gun from his hand. Giuseppe whimpered. Rinaldo snarled and pushed his fist straight through Giuseppe's chest, like he was no more substantial than a cardboard diorama at a fair.

"He's not your son," Rinaldo bit out, as what was left of his rival seeped onto the floor. Kathryn screamed from the doorway and ran to him, heedless of the vampires and Defenders in her way. She knelt beside the slick exsanguination. She wept. So that's what it's like to watch someone you love get killed, I thought.

Rinaldo laughed again; a child with a new toy. "And I didn't even have to bleed you!" he said. Had he *still* failed to understand the power he held over Amir? Then it wasn't too late. We still had time to kill him. He strolled back to Daddy. When Troy attempted to get in his way, Rinaldo threw him into a bookcase. Troy groaned. I looked at Daddy: a little unsteady now, but gamely holding his ground. As for Amir, he had roused himself from the effort of granting that wish, but he'd given up. If I'd handed him my knife then, I suspect he might have used it on himself. I needed to subdue Rinaldo for Amir's sake, but at this point anything less than death would risk all of our lives. He was too powerful, and Amir couldn't take back the wish.

Rinaldo was playing with Daddy, taking his time. I had one chance. If I didn't take him out now, he would be unstoppable. If I took him out before Amir had a chance to drink his blood, Amir would die. Amir, who had been responsible for at least a dozen deaths across the city over a drug he'd probably thought was a joke. Amir, who called me *habibti*, who had tried to stop the imports once he realized what he'd done, who burned when he touched me.

And my daddy, who was about to die.

Don't think. Blade in hand. Take off the damn shoes so you don't make noise over the floor. No one is paying any attention to you. Keep it that way. *Oh fuck, my hand hurts.* Ignore it, you're not using it anyway. Breathe, but not too deeply. One, two . . .

The strike was textbook-perfect, through the back and under the sternum. I felt the sweet spot, that mushy vampire heart that, when ruptured, turned the rest of their bodies to fetid paste.

But it didn't rupture. I wiggled the blade. Nothing.

Rinaldo roared like a wounded bull. He twisted around so hard the blade shattered in his body. I dropped the useless pommel to the floor and scrambled to get away.

"You again?" he said, gasping. My textbook strike had at least weakened him, but he was still stronger than any other vampire in that room. How the hell had he survived? Any vampire should pop when a blessed blade hit that sweet spot.

"You kill me, and you'll never find your son," I said, stalling. What could I do? My other blessed blade was hidden under my skirt and he'd snap me in half before I had time to reach it. And it looked like it would take a blessed two-by-four to kill this sucker anyway.

"I kill you, and I can call your ghost to tell me where he is," he said, but he hesitated. Good. I saw Daddy stalking him behind me. But would his blades do any better than mine? We needed something different, something unexpected. Rinaldo was a strange vampire, right? So maybe he needed a strange method of killing.

You're using the wrong blade.

Aileen's brogue came back to me so strongly that for a moment I thought she'd walked into the room. That had been her first vision, the morning after Dore nearly killed her in the alley. I'd dismissed it as nonsense, then. But now . . .

"Daddy!" I shouted.

Rinaldo glanced away. Daddy jumped back. I took the short sword, the one passed from Troy to Amir to Mama and then me, the pagan-blessed blade that wouldn't hurt a normal vampire any more than a butter knife, and jammed it home. The angle was sloppy, sideways through his ribs and then down through the heart. I felt it knock against the lodged silver blade, just barely pricking his sweet spot.

It was enough.

His skin seemed to rot into a paper-thin membrane, like a withered onion. Then the blood and rendered fat splashed over my socks and dress. We all stared, silent. Then Nicholas suddenly scrambled up and ran for the door. The three remaining Turn Boys—Charlie, to my relief, and two others I didn't recognize—followed him out. I didn't stop them. Neither did Troy.

Amir stumbled out of the circle. A few trembling steps, and he was beside me and what was left of the body. His eyes were bleak as he looked at his death sentence, but I didn't see any reproach for what I'd done.

"Zephyr." His voice was rough, that of a dying man.

"I'm so sorry—"

He put his hand on mine. It was cold as stone. He said something in that other language, a long string of words I couldn't parse, but made me tremble.

"Kardal," he said. "It's time."

Amir collapsed. I caught him, painfully, and lowered him to the floor. His warm brown skin had taken on more than a hint of gray. Kardal came through a moment later, in a form as solid as any I'd seen.

"Come soon," he said, as he took his brother from me. I nodded. They vanished.

Daddy's hand on my shoulder jolted me. I looked up, and wondered why it was so hard to focus on him. He handed me a handkerchief. Surprised, I wiped my tears away.

"Come on, little girl," he said roughly. "Let's get you back to your mama."

CHAPTER NINE

The emergency room at the New York Infirmary had seen some odd sights in the past few days, but surely the arrival early Wednesday morning of seven Defenders and three women covered in vampire gore constituted one of their stranger visits. Troy had been forced to stake one of his men in the tunnels—he'd been about to turn and that sort of useless gesture was a point of honor among people like Daddy and Troy. Derek was pretty badly hurt—Troy carried him in, but the nurses carted him away almost immediately on a gurney when they saw the gashes around his neck and stomach. Which left nine of us, stuffed into the back of the waiting room so the other afflicted didn't have to deal with the stench. I hardly noticed it. Really, I hardly noticed anything, even my throbbing hand. I kept going back to those last moments when I'd killed Rinaldo. Amir's face when he lost all hope. I'd done that to him. I'd picked my daddy over him. My daddy and all the other people Rinaldo might kill if he wasn't stopped. And he'd said . . . whatever it was he said to me. That beautiful language.

Daddy handed me a fresh handkerchief. Aileen put her arm around me. Kathryn had stopped crying, but she seemed even more dazed than I. We hadn't wanted to leave her in the tunnels after everything that had happened. She'd come along willingly enough.

"Kathryn," I said, since I hardly knew what to do with myself and my thoughts were about to drive me mad, "could you tell us . . . I mean, was Giuseppe your husband? Is Judah your son?"

She rocked back and forth. "Yes," she said, her voice filled with the tears that had ceased pouring down her face. "Yes. We were happy for a while, you know. We had four children. He did some jobs for Rinaldo, but nothing much. Then Rinaldo met me. He . . ." She shrugged. "Rinaldo had . . . violent passions. He loved like an Italian, they say. He loved me. But I was Giuseppe's. I didn't want to leave him. Rinaldo wouldn't let go. He threatened us. He made Giuseppe lose his job. It was hard, but then that boy of his, that Nicholas turned Giuseppe. Rinaldo said my children would be next. So I took Judah—he was too little, then, he still needed me—and I ran away. I left my husband so he'd be safe. I lived with Rinaldo. He was . . . he wasn't cruel, really. He loved me. He loved Judah. I got used to it."

"But then Judah disappeared?" I said.

She nodded. "Rinaldo was . . . furious. Distraught. He was sure Giuseppe had kidnapped him back. I knew it was Nicholas, though. Rinaldo changed his will to take care of little Judah, and Nicholas . . . he was jealous. Rinaldo loved Nicholas, you have to understand, but in his son he saw something different than a little boy. He saw an instrument, a perfect instrument. You've heard his voice? Rinaldo wanted to preserve it. An eternal instrument of perfection, he said. But Nicholas never got over it. It's such a horrible thing to do to a boy . . . and now he's done it to my boy, too."

She buried her face in her hands, and we waited while she wept. "So I knew," she said. "I knew that it was Nicholas, but Rinaldo wouldn't hear a thing against him. He threatened poor Giuseppe, told him he'd kill our children if he didn't give Judah back. Giuseppe just . . . snapped, I suppose. He couldn't stand the pressure. He found all this money God knows where and hired you to kill Nicholas and the others. He thought that even if he couldn't get to Rinaldo, that would send a message. It would finally make him leave us alone." She paused. "But you, Zephyr, started tutoring those boys. Giuseppe knew what was going to happen to them. He liked you. Didn't want you to get hurt. So he tried to threaten you, but pretended it was Rinaldo. You were too stubborn, I guess. They all were."

"At least your boy is still alive," Aileen said, into the bleak silence.

Kathryn started crying again. "My boy was too young. It . . . changes them. He'll be like Nicholas. Not my little Judah. No more roses . . ."

He still loves roses. I'd fulfilled Amir's last wish. I'd found Judah's mother. But it turned out she didn't want him.

A nurse with a pinched expression that might have been disdain, or merely offense at our smell, approached us with a clipboard.

"It looks like that other one will be okay. Lord knows we need every pint of blood in this city, but we got him some in time. Which of you is next?"

Daddy went with me to the treatment room. Another nurse took one look at the two of us and insisted we remove all of our clothes and change into hospital gowns. We waited another fifteen minutes or so for the doctor, who then proceeded to prod me for thirty seconds before declaring that I'd cracked a rib and broken my thumb at the base and he'd call for some plaster. Daddy looked uncharacteristically abstracted while the nurse who'd taped my ribs wrapped my hand. He patted my knee, but I wasn't sure who he was reassuring.

"You just let that rest for a few minutes, dear," she said, when she'd finished. The wet plaster was puffy, and made my wrist and hand look like they'd been suspended in a cloud. "You can leave when it's dry. And you, sir, should come with me—"

Daddy shook his head. "I want to speak with my daughter for a minute, if you don't mind."

The nurse shrugged and walked out, pulling the curtain behind her. An illusion of privacy, at least.

"Zephyr, sweetie . . . did your mama ever tell you how you came to be immune?"

I shook my head. I used to ask when I was younger, but both of them always refused to discuss it. I'd never seemed very different, otherwise, from my siblings and the other kids. Eventually, it just didn't seem that important.

He cleared his throat. "See, well . . . when your mother was pregnant with you, and we were so happy to be having a baby, an heir, you see, to me and my demon hunting, and I thought about what would make the greatest demon hunter in the world, right? Immunity. A sort of . . . anti-Other power."

I frowned. "But, Daddy . . . I don't have any power. I can't even summon an ant."

He shook his head earnestly. "That's just the thing, sweetie. That's your power. That master vampire back there, the one with the fire blood? His bite is strong enough to kill a genie. But you? A horsefly would bother you more."

I'd known that. But it took Daddy saying it out loud for me to realize how astonishing and scary the implications were. My very *existence* was anti-Other?

"How did you and Mama do it? Why doesn't everyone?"

He shook his head. "Never mind that. The point is, Zeph, you can still save that . . . that genie of yours, if you want. I saw you . . . I mean, hell, sweetie, I don't ever want to see you hurt that bad. You know I don't approve of his type, but if you want to, then you can save him."

My senses dilated: the sudden, intense throbbing of my hand; Daddy's averted gaze; my labored breathing.

"How?"

"Let him drink your blood. It's blood that did this to him, it's blood that will get him out."

"That's it?"

He bit the inside of his cheek. "It's not nothing. I think it might bind him to you, in that genie way. You'd have his powers. You saw what happened back there, with just that little wish? Their power sort of twists things over here. The longer you wait to wish, the worse it gets. Their powers are . . . strange."

"I wouldn't anti-Other them?"

He frowned. "Well, they're his, ain't they? You'd only be taking them out on loan."

I swallowed. "For the rest of my life."

"I told you it wasn't nothing," he said.

But he had given it to me anyway. He thought I'd be throwing away my life on Amir, but he'd let it be my decision. I sat up. The wet plaster was heavy, but I didn't want to wait for it to dry.

Daddy shook his head. "You sure about this, Zeph?" he asked.

"No," I said. But I would do it anyway.

Kardal didn't comment on either the hospital gown or my plastered hand. He seemed abstracted with grief, and for a horrible moment I thought I had come too late. Daddy had, reluctantly, cast the summoning spell for me.

"He's in the garden," Kardal said, when we arrived. Let him burn your carpets, I'd said. I remembered the unhealthy chill of Amir's skin before he fainted. No danger of that now. Amir lay unconscious on the grass. Kardal had dressed him in the older clothes that he favored—a long silk tunic and embroidered over-jacket, tied with a burgundy sash. For once, Amir looked like a prince. But in some ways, he had always looked like that. It was better, I supposed, that he wasn't awake to make excuses for himself. I'd made my decision, but I didn't want any false reassurances about his intrinsic goodness.

Amir had, in full possession of the facts about the drug, released Faust upon an unsuspecting marketplace via the most unscrupulous mob boss in the city. Yes, he tried to salvage the situation, but it was already too late. At least without Amir's direct pipeline to the purest goods, the effects would probably be more manageable. But Faust was here to stay. And why had he done it? Fun. Kardal had told me that

Amir loved our world, but like a boy loves a toy set. Maybe he'd never thought of us as real people with real lives to ruin. After all, he lived on such a radically different time scale. If he became emotionally attached to humans, he'd have to grieve every time they died. He'd have to wonder at the injustice of his long, easy life and the short, nasty and brutish nature of ours. So he collected our artifacts, which lasted longer, and our poetry and our stories and occasionally, when he came across something interesting, he dropped it in our world like a playful god, just to see what happened.

"And now look what's happened, Amir," I whispered. But he had gone too far away to hear me.

"Kardal," I said, "Amir said something in that other language, just before . . . it sounded like, I don't know, a confession. But rhythmic, like a poem. Jabinya min sakam something."

"*Ta' jabiyna min saqami / sihhati hiya l-'ajabu / kulama 'intafa sababun / minki, ja'ani sababu,*" he said. The words, even in his rumbling bass, sounded gentle.

"Yes, that's it!"

Kardal smiled and touched his brother's hand. "Abu Nuwas. A great poet from several centuries ago. I was young when he wrote that."

"What does it mean?"

"*You wondered at my ills / But my health was the wonder / Each time a bond broke / Through you a new bond came.*" He paused. "The rest of it is nice, too."

He hadn't ever asked for my forgiveness, had he? Even at the last, he had hid the meaning of his confession from me.

I still had one blade left. Strapped to that inconvenient spot on the inside of my thigh, it had been spared any contact with vampires this past night. It felt like an old friend in my hand. Kardal looked at me, but didn't say anything. I think he could hardly bear to speak.

I cut my left arm a few inches above the plaster. Deep, since I didn't know how much blood this would take. I somehow doubted that anyone had ever done this before. I pushed his mouth open and let the blood dribble down. For a horrible moment, it filled his mouth use-lessly, spilling over the sides. And then he started to drink. It only took a few gulps, in the end, to bring him back. He stirred and then opened his eyes. I brought my arm down and staunched the cut against the edge of my hospital gown. He looked first at Kardal, whose form had loosened with shock, and then at me.

"I hope I'm not dead," he said, "because I've gone through a lot of trouble to make sure you two didn't come with me."

Kardal gripped his brother's hands. "You are . . . Zephyr did . . . Something in her essence saved you."

Amir regarded me. "Is that your blood in my mouth, then?"

"Yes."

This seemed to upset him, but he just nodded. "Do you feel it, brother? The presence of a new vessel."

"She saved your life!"

"Against her better judgment." He struggled upright and brushed the fingers of my left hand with his own. They were warm again. Suddenly my chest felt as though it might burst.

"Welcome to the rest of your life, *habibti*. You look terrible."

It was so good to hear his voice that for a moment I didn't care what he'd done.

For a moment.

I coughed, an unconvincing cover for a sob. "I have to go," I said, getting unsteadily to my feet. "We'll . . . figure something out, Amir. I won't let you be shackled like this for the rest of my life. There has to be some way."

"Yes, I'm sure." His voice was dull; his eyes pierced me like a lover's sword. "Take her home, brother. Let her dream she never met me."

"We should let Judah see his mother," I said, when Kardal gave me some clean clothes to wear—a set of loose silk pants and a tunic I might have appreciated in another century.

He considered this. "Yes. I'll get the boy."

Kardal vanished and reappeared with Judah an instant later. The boy didn't seem in the least disconcerted, however. He must have teleported a lot in the past few days. When Kardal vanished again, I knelt in front of Judah.

"We've found your mother," I told him.

I expected him to be happy, but instead he seemed as pensive and worried as I. "I wonder what she looks like," he said, finally. "But I think she will like Kardal's garden."

Kardal reappeared at that moment, Kathryn in tow. She looked around at the courtyard, her expression bleak and distant. Then she saw Judah.

"Oh . . ." She took a few steps toward him and then stopped short. "Judah? Judah, do you remember me?"

He pursed his lips together, as though considering. "You're very pretty," he said. "I knew that."

Kathryn began to cry. "I kept your toy horse Tanto. You remember him?"

Judah considered and shook his head.

"And Mr. Farinelli at the bakery and that hat you love with the peacock feather and the shiny rocks you collect from the park—do you remember any of it?"

Judah seemed very sad, maybe baffled by her tears. "No, Mother," he said. "But I do remember the roses."

And so mother and son, at last, embraced.

Sleep. Eighteen hours of blissful sleep. Lily stopped by, I think, but the sounds of her and Aileen's voices blended into my dreams and I didn't wake. Mama was there when I awoke, groggy and aching but feeling better than I had for a week. She handed me a glass of water and then got me another.

"I brought you your sword," she said, pointing to the foot of my bed.

"The hospital burned your clothes." I smiled. Somehow I doubted even Lily could fault them for that.

"Your daddy and I are leaving in a few hours," she said. "We're going to take Judah with us."

I blinked. "Daddy's letting a sucker in his house?"

Mama drew herself up. "It's my house, too. I put my foot down. And anyway, I think he's starting to like Judah."

"What about Kathryn?"

"She's afraid of him, sweetie. After what that boy Nicholas did to her family, well, I can't blame her. And now she has to take Giuseppe's place with the other kids. It would be too much to deal with an adolescent vampire. She just doesn't understand them the way we do."

"Even though she was fucking one for eight years."

"Zephyr!"

"Sorry."

She sighed. "Your daddy told me about Amir, and what you did to save him. I would have told you myself, dear, but I don't know as much about your . . . immunity as your daddy does. I didn't know it could do that."

And what else did Daddy know, I wondered. How did he give me this gift that I've never heard of before?

"I just wanted to tell you that I think you did the right thing, and I hope you and Amir can be happy together. Even though he is a djinn."

My stomach twisted. Oh, we'd be together, but I didn't know if we'd ever manage happy. "Thank you, Mama," I said, forcing a smile. "I'm just glad this is all over."

She hugged me. "Oh me too, sweetie, me too. You'll come and visit us soon, right? Harry keeps asking for you. I think they'll all be happy to have a new little brother, don't you?"

"I'm sure they will, Mama. I'll come as soon as I can. In the summer." No need to willingly subject myself to a Montana winter. Even worse than New York.

"Good." She dabbed at her eyes with a handkerchief. "Your daddy will be glad. He was so happy to see you, Zephyr. You just don't know how much you mean to him. Well, I guess I should go. Don't get up, dear. John would never forgive me if you went outside in this weather. You should rest."

I went to the window after she left, and saw what she meant. The falling snow was so thick I could see my mother's cab for only a few seconds before it disappeared into the swirling white. Already the ground was covered a foot deep. A strong gust blew, and suddenly I noticed a tall, dark figure looking up at the building from the bottom of the stoop.

I gasped and pressed my nose against the glass. Happy. Could we be happy? Could I forgive him for the Faust? Could he forgive me for becoming his vessel? Could we get back to the way we had been on the balcony in his brother's palace, full of warm, laughing sarcasm and sweet lips?

"Each time a bond broke . . ."

But the snow eased for a moment, and I saw it was just Troy, probably bracing himself before venturing inside such a low-class establishment. I sighed and crawled back under my covers.

So I would talk to Troy and hopefully sleep a little more and then, when the sun went down and all the respectable humans scurried indoors to their beds or fabulous parties, I would find the last of Lily's discarded daywear and tramp through this weather, without the benefit of my bicycle and against the sound advice of my mother, back to the corner of Chrystie and Rivington, where all this had first started.

And why, you might ask?

I had to teach night school.

ACKNOWLEDGMENTS

There are dozens of people who have helped me in the conception and writing of Zephyr's story. Amanda Hollander, for being Amir's first (and probably still biggest) fan. Lauren, my sister, for listening to me ramble for hours about thorny story problems. Andrea Robinson, Tamar Bihari, Diane Patterson, Cristina and Mariel Fernandez, Tatiana Galitzin, and Abby Pritchard, for being the best first readers anyone could ask for. Justine Larbalestier, for research tips. Kris Dikeman, for her beautiful map. My editor, Karyn Marcus, for believing in this book and helping me make it better. My literary manager, Ken Atchity, for his unflagging support of my career and the varied directions I want to take it. And Scott, for always being there.

You are all the bat's pajamas.